ALICE'S ADVENTURES IN WONDERLAND

AND

THROUGH THE LOOKING-GLASS

LEWIS CARROLL was the pseudonym of the Revd Charles Lutwidge Dodgson, born 27 January 1832 at Daresbury, Cheshire. He went to Christ Church, Oxford, in 1851, where he became a Senior Student, and lived there for the rest of his life. He was Mathematical Lecturer (1855–81) and was admitted to deacon's orders in 1861, although he did not proceed to priest's orders. He was a noted photographer, especially of children, a prolific diarist, letter-writer and pamphleteer; although in some ways reclusive, he had a wide range of acquaintances in literary and theatrical circles. His many mathematical publications include *Euclid and his Modern Rivals* (1879) and *Symbolic Logic* (1896). His two most famous books, *Alice's Adventures in Wonderland* (1865) and *Through the Looking-Glass and What Alice Found There* (1872), were initially inspired by his friendship with Alice Liddell, the daughter of the Dean of Christ Church. He also published a facsimile of the original manuscript of *Alice's Adventures in Wonderland, Alice's Adventures under Ground* (1886), and an adaptation for young children, *The Nursery Alice* (1890). *The Hunting of the Snark* (1876) is widely regarded as a surreal masterpiece, but his other works of fiction, *Sylvie and Bruno* (1889) and *Sylvie and Bruno Concluded* (1893), were not successful. He died at Guildford on 14 January 1898, and is buried there.

PETER HUNT is Professor Emeritus in Children's Literature at Cardiff University. He has written or edited fifteen books on the subject, including *An Introduction to Children's Literature* (OUP, 1994) and the *International Companion Encyclopedia of Children's Literature* (2004). He has also written novels for children, including *Backtrack* (1986).

OXFORD WORLD'S CLASSICS

*For over 100 years Oxford World's Classics have brought
readers closer to the world's great literature. Now with over 700
titles—from the 4,000-year-old myths of Mesopotamia to the
twentieth century's greatest novels—the series makes available
lesser-known as well as celebrated writing.*

*The pocket-sized hardbacks of the early years contained
introductions by Virginia Woolf, T. S. Eliot, Graham Greene,
and other literary figures which enriched the experience of reading.
Today the series is recognized for its fine scholarship and
reliability in texts that span world literature, drama and poetry,
religion, philosophy and politics. Each edition includes perceptive
commentary and essential background information to meet the
changing needs of readers.*

OXFORD WORLD'S CLASSICS

═══

LEWIS CARROLL

Alice's Adventures in Wonderland
and
Through the Looking-Glass

AND WHAT ALICE FOUND THERE

═══

Edited with an Introduction and Notes by
PETER HUNT

With illustrations by
JOHN TENNIEL

OXFORD
UNIVERSITY PRESS

OXFORD
UNIVERSITY PRESS

Great Clarendon Street, Oxford OX2 6DP

Oxford University Press is a department of the University of Oxford.
It furthers the University's objective of excellence in research, scholarship,
and education by publishing worldwide in

Oxford New York

Auckland Cape Town Dar es Salaam Hong Kong Karachi
Kuala Lumpur Madrid Melbourne Mexico City Nairobi
New Delhi Shanghai Taipei Toronto

With offices in

Argentina Austria Brazil Chile Czech Republic France Greece
Guatemala Hungary Italy Japan Poland Portugal Singapore
South Korea Switzerland Thailand Turkey Ukraine Vietnam

Oxford is a registered trade mark of Oxford University Press
in the UK and in certain other countries

Published in the United States
by Oxford University Press Inc., New York

Editorial material © Peter Hunt 2009

The moral rights of the author have been asserted
Database right Oxford University Press (maker)

First published as a World's Classics paperback 1982
Reissued as an Oxford World's Classics paperback 1998
This edition published 2009

British Library Cataloguing in Publication Data

Data available

Library of Congress Cataloging in Publication Data

Data available

Typeset in Ehrhardt
by RefineCatch Limited, Bungay, Suffolk
Printed in Great Britain
on acid-free paper by
Clays Ltd, Elcograf S.p.A.

ISBN 978-0-19-955829-2

16

CONTENTS

INTRODUCTION

Alice's Adventures in Wonderland (1865) and *Through the Looking-Glass and What Alice Found There* (1871, dated 1872) are two of the most famous, most translated, and most quoted books in the world. They have some claim to be the most influential children's books ever, which is to say, possibly the most influential works of literature ever—as children's books often have a more profound and lasting influence on their audiences than adults' books.

Alice (or Alis, Alisa, Alenka, Elsje, and many other variations) has had her adventures im Wunderland, du pays des merveilles, and I eventyrland, and in almost every country from Iceland to Australia—where the native peoples who live around Uluru, or Ayer's Rock, and whose language is Pitjantjatjara, can read about *Alitjinja ngura tjukurtjarangka* (*Alitji in the Dreamtime*). The book was translated into Russian by Vladimir Nabokov (as V. Sirin), a link that has not escaped critics: an Italian edition in 1962, *La meravigliosa Alice*, was subtitled *Una lucida invenzione, la creazione poetica di una 'lolita' vittoriana.*[1] Like other great pieces of popular culture, the books are highly adaptable: Alice has been everywhere from Blufferland to Debitland, and she has been borrowed by feminists (Maeve Kelly's *Alice in Thunderland*, 1993), satirists (Latham R. Reid's *Frankie in Wonderland: With Apologies to Lewis Carroll, the Originator and Pre-Historian of the New Deal*, 1934), and propagandists (James Dyrenforth's *Adolf in Blunderland*, 1940).

Several words that first appeared in the books, such as 'chortled', have entered the language, and phrases have become axioms: 'The rule is, jam to-morrow and jam yesterday—but

[1] See Pompeo Vagliani (ed.), *Quando Alice incontrò Pinocchio: Le edizioni italiane de Alice tra testo e contesto* (Torino: Trauben Edizioni, per Libreria Stampatori, 1998); Beverly Lyon Clark, *Reflections of Fantasy: The Mirror-Worlds of Carroll, Nabokov and Pynchon* (New York: Peter Lang, 1986), 43–52.

never jam *to-day*'. The words 'Alice' and 'Wonderland' appear in everyday media relating to economics, politics, literary theory, sociology, and a hundred other topics thought worthy of scorn. Interestingly, 'Wonderland' is not used to equal 'stupid' or 'idiotic': as in the books, Wonderland is the place where everyone *else* is mad, blindly playing absurd, solipsistic games; *we* are invited to identify with the outsider, the sane and clear-eyed Alice, and to regard the others (as she does) with astonishment or pity. And *Alice's Adventures in Wonderland* has even become a yardstick for other books: Flann O'Brien's surreal masterpiece, *The Third Policeman* (1967), was described by the *Observer* as 'comparable only to *Alice in Wonderland* as an allegory of the absurd'. And, one might add, as funny, and as chilling.

The author is almost as famous as the books: there have been at least fifteen biographies in English alone of Charles Lutwidge Dodgson, who wrote a small number of his books under the name of Lewis Carroll. It seems that all the minutiae of his life have been examined: quite apart from the twelve volumes of his diaries and two volumes of his letters, recent works have included *Lewis Carroll in His Own Account: The Complete Bank Account of the Rev. C. L. Dodgson*, and 'The Illnesses of Lewis Carroll'.[2] Even Alice Liddell, the little girl who initially inspired the books, has been the subject of *two* biographies.[3] Parts of the story of Dodgson and Alice Liddell have been fictionalized in Katie Riophe's novel *Still She Haunts Me* (2001), and Donald Thomas's crime novel *Belladonna: A Lewis Carroll Nightmare* (1983). Dodgson's life and its intricate connections have been explored exhaustively in the graphic 'entertainment' *Alice in Sunderland* (2007) by Bryan Talbot.

In short, Dodgson, 'Lewis Carroll', and the 'Alice' books are international phenomena, and British national institutions.

[2] Jenny Woolf, *Lewis Carroll in His Own Account: The Complete Bank Account of the Rev. C. L. Dodgson* (London: Jabberwock Press, 2005); Selwyn H. Goodacre, *The Practitioner* (August 1972), 209, 230–9.

[3] Anne Clark, *The Real Alice: Lewis Carroll's Dream Child* (London: Michael Joseph, 1981); Colin Gordon, *Beyond the Looking Glass: Reflections of Alice and Her Family* (London: Hodder and Stoughton, 1982).

There are *Alice in Wonderland* rides at Disneyland in Paris and California, a White Rabbit Statue (unveiled by Lloyd George in 1933) at Llandudno (where Dodgson never actually visited); 2,525 items on Dodgson-Carroll are held at the University of Texas at Austin, and James Joyce's ultimate experiment in fiction, *Finnegans Wake* (1939), is suffused with Carrollian allusions.

But what exactly *are* the 'Alice' books? What gives them their global, perennial fascination? Are they harmless, innocent children's stories, simple fantasies with eccentric characters and nonsense verses? Or are they studies of Victorian female repression, stories that take place in nightmare worlds of aggression and godlessness, allegories of Victorian and Oxford society, intricate textures of mathematical, philosophical, and semantic puzzles, or symbolic explorations of 'some of the deepest existential problems in a light-hearted way'?[4] Or gifts of love (or possibly lust) from a frustrated academic to a young girl?

Much of this confusion stems from the fact that they are, or at least *were*, books for children—and because they are perhaps now more accessible to, and interesting for, adults. They pivot on the clash between the idealized view of what a children's book should be and what childhood should be, and the often uncomfortable fact that the relationships between adults, child-hood, and stories are rarely pure and never simple. As a result of these deep-seated attitudes to children's books, questions are asked of the 'Alice' books that would not be considered par-ticularly interesting if they were 'adult' books: are they 'suitable' for their audience, do children enjoy them, can children see what adults see—and, especially, was Dodgson the kind of man that should have been *allowed* to write for children? The need to protect an idea of innocence comes up against the difficult realities of the books.

Of course, the 'Alice' books were popular with children when they were first published: they were not only witty and inventive,

[4] David Holbrook, *Nonsense Against Sorrow: A Phenomenological Study of Lewis Carroll's 'Alice' Books* (London: Open Gate Press, 2001), viii.

but they were subversive, parodying pious nursery verses, and, almost for the first time, having a narrative voice that is soundly on the side of the child. In one of the most-quoted remarks on the books, F. J. Harvey Darton described *Alice's Adventures in Wonderland* as 'the spiritual volcano of children's books . . . the first unapologetic . . . appearance in print, for readers who sorely needed it, of liberty of thought in children's books . . . Henceforth . . . there was to be in hours of pleasure no more dread about the moral value . . . of the pleasure itself.'[5] This has usually been taken to mean that the 'Alice' books are free of the moralizing that had marked the majority of children's books since their beginnings in the mid-eighteenth century, and that is true enough. But what Dodgson replaced it with was not, as so many critics have assumed, some kind of light-hearted freedom: the books are actually concerned with discipline, logic, life and death, passion, and a ruthless critique of the adult world. And that does *not* mean that they are therefore *not* for children. For, unlike the vast majority of both his predecessors and successors, Dodgson had no doubts as to what children could and should be capable of dealing with. The most important, most neglected, fact about 'Wonderland' is that it is not a 'land of wonders', but rather 'a land where one wonders'.

When *Alice's Adventures in Wonderland* was first published, Dodgson noted in his Diary nineteen reviews, which used words such as 'glorious', 'original', 'charming', and 'graceful'. The *Athenaeum*, however, demurred: 'We fancy that any child might be more puzzled than enchanted by this stiff, overwrought story' (16 December 1865)[6] and it has not been alone. A Canadian critic, Michelle Landsberg, omitted it from her compendious guide, *The World of Children's Books* (1989), on the grounds that it 'terrified me so much as a child (particularly those sinister, surrealistic Tenniel drawings) that it is the only book that I have ever defaced; the nightmare of shrinking and stretching held a

[5] F. J. Harvey Darton, *Children's Books in England: Five Centuries of Social Life*, rev. Brian Alderson (3rd edn., Cambridge: Cambridge University Press, 1982), 260.
[6] Quoted in Morton N. Cohen, *Lewis Carroll: A Biography* (London and Basingstoke: Macmillan, 1995), 131.

fevered horror for me'.[7] Peter Coveney thought that it had 'the claustrophobic atmosphere of a children's Kafka'.[8]

Readers have often found themselves tempted into complex analyses of the books—and with good reason, for, as we shall see, Dodgson's literary method was to embed intricate allusions into his texts, and to play with both the language and his readers. However, some of the interpretations of the books may seem more probable than others: Richard Wallace, for example, 'proves' that Dodgson was Jack the Ripper, and that 'these crimes began as a caper, fuelled by rage, boredom, anti-establishment feelings, and emboldened by years of successfully hiding Victorian smut in his children's works'.[9] At the other extreme is Virginia Woolf, no less, who wrote (perhaps a little unguardedly) in 1939: 'Only Lewis Carroll has shown us the world upside down as a child sees it, and has made us laugh as children laugh, irresponsibly. Down the groves of pure nonsense we whirl laughing, laughing—'.[10] However, with that comment, she was perpetuating a myth that had been carefully developed by Dodgson, who described his books as 'innocent and healthy amusement . . . for the children I love so well'. And yet there is actually very little 'nonsense' in the books—but plenty of satire and parody, and, as Walter de la Mare wrote, 'all satire and most parody in themselves are mortal enemies of true Nonsense, which is concerned with the joys of a new world not with the follies and excesses of an old'.[11] The 'Alice' books are never quite what they seem, and they relate in a complex way to the complex personality of their author, and to a rapidly changing world. Juliet Dusinberre notes that 'cultural change was both reflected and pioneered in the books which children read. Radical experiments in the arts in the early modern period began

---

[7] Michelle Landsberg, *The World of Children's Books* (New York: Simon and Schuster, 1989), 5.

[8] Peter Coveney, *The Image of Childhood* (Harmondsworth: Penguin, 1967), 246.

[9] Richard Wallace, *Jack the Ripper, 'Light-hearted Friend'* (Melrose, Mass.: Gemini Press, 1996), 262.

[10] Virginia Woolf, 'Lewis Carroll', *Collected Essays* (London: Hogarth Press, 1966), 2. 255.

[11] Walter de la Mare, *Lewis Carroll* (London: Faber and Faber, 1932), 13–14.

in the books which Lewis Carroll and his successors wrote for children.'[12] Similarly, Humphrey Carpenter notes that *Alice's Adventures in Wonderland* 'was published just as the two great religious spearheads of the nineteenth century, the Evangelicals and the Oxford Movement, were losing their original force, and in its anti-religious sentiments it heralded the coming of an era of scepticism'.[13]

And yet the idea of the innocence of the book persists, and it is rooted in another myth, of how the book was written. On 4 July 1862, an idyllic 'golden afternoon', a shy, stuttering Oxford mathematician-clergyman, Charles Dodgson, and his friend the Revd (later Canon) Robinson Duckworth, took three little girls, the daughters of the Dean of their college, for a picnic on the River Thames or Isis. As they rowed, Dodgson made up an impromptu story about one of the girls, Alice, and at the end of the day, she begged him to write it down. He wrote it out and illustrated the story, *Alice's Adventures under Ground*, and gave it to her on 26 November 1864, later expanding it as *Alice's Adventures in Wonderland*. It is an attractive story, perhaps none the worse for the fact that it is only partially true; but, like other myths about books supposedly written for specific children—Kenneth Grahame's *The Wind in the Willows* or A. A. Milne's *Winnie-the-Pooh*—it is culturally important that it *should* be true.

The Life

Dodgson has been described as 'One of the great Victorian eccentrics'[14] but his background was more than respectable. His great-grandfather Charles Dodgson (1722?–1795 or 1796)—who was grandfather of both his parents—was bishop of Elphin, in Ireland (part of United Diocese of Kilmore, Elphin and

[12] Juliet Dusinberre, *Alice to the Lighthouse: Children's Books and Radical Experiments in Art* (London: Macmillan Press, 1987), 5.

[13] Humphrey Carpenter, *Secret Gardens* (1985; London: Unwin, 1987), 68–9.

[14] Derek Hudson, *Lewis Carroll: An Illustrated Biography* (1954; rev. edn., London: Constable, 1976), 25.

Ardagh, since 1841). His grandfather Captain Charles Dodgson (1769?–1803) was killed in an ambush by Irish rebels near Phillipstown in Ireland. His father, the Revd Charles Dodgson (1800–68), took a double first in classics and mathematics at Christ Church, Oxford, and married his cousin, Frances Jane Lutwidge (1803–51) in 1827, thus failing to comply with the requirement for Christ Church scholars to remain single. He was granted the curacy at Daresbury, an isolated village in Cheshire in 1827; in 1843, he moved to St Peter's church, Croft, and later became a canon of Ripon cathedral, and archdeacon of Richmond. Although a witty man, his 'reverence for sacred things was so great that he was never known to relate a story which included a jest upon words from the Bible'.[15]

Charles Lutwidge was born 27 January 1832 at the parsonage at Daresbury; he was the third child and eldest son of a family of eleven (seven girls and four boys) all of whom lived to old age—two of the boys, Skeffington and Wilfred, and one of the girls, Mary, married. His brother Edwin became a missionary on Tristan da Cunha and later on the Cape Verde Islands.

Given that almost all biographies of Charles Lutwidge Dodgson contain an element of hagiography, it does seem that he was brought up in a pious, loving family atmosphere. When he was 12 he was sent to Richmond Grammar School for two terms, and then in January 1846 to Rugby School—of which he wrote in his Diary in 1855: 'I cannot say that I look back upon my life at a Public School with any sensations of pleasure, or that any earthly considerations would induce me to go through my three years again.' (There is a school book, dated 13 November 1846, with Dodgson's name in it followed by the words, in a different hand, 'is a muff'.) But he was academically successful, and a survivor.

He and his siblings produced a series of family magazines, beginning with *Useful and Instructive Poetry* in 1845, followed by *The Rectory Magazine* (while he was at Rugby), *The Rectory*

[15] Stuart Dodgson Collingwood, *The Life and Letters of Lewis Carroll* (London: T. Fisher Unwin, 1899), 8.

Umbrella (all his own work), and *Mischmasch*, and Dodgson shows a taste for lively comedy, reminiscent of Edward Lear, and a talent for parody.

His life at Christ Church, Oxford, began sadly: two days after he arrived on 24 January 1851, his mother died. The following year he was nominated to a Studentship (Fellowship) which allowed him to live at Christ Church for the rest of his life, on condition that he did not marry, and that he proceed to Holy Orders. He took a first class in mathematics, and in 1855 was appointed mathematical lecturer (a post that he held, giving, by his own account, uninspiring lectures which his students sometimes openly mocked, until 1881). Although a deeply religious and pious man, he felt himself unsuited to work in a parish (possibly because of his speech impediment); he was admitted to deacon's orders on 22 December 1861, 'as a sort of experiment', as he wrote in his Diary, and regarded himself 'as *practically* a layman'. He did not proceed to priest's orders, although he did occasionally preach long 'plain, evangelical sermon(s) of the old-fashioned kind'.[16]

He took his responsibilities as head of his family seriously, after his father died in 1868, and took a lease on 'The Chestnuts', Guildford, for his unmarried siblings. He continued to support them throughout his life—his recently published bank-accounts suggest that this may have put a great strain on his finances (although he makes no mention of this in his Diary). He often spent time with his cousins in the Sunderland area, and was involved in nursing his godson at Guildford in 1874; from 1877, he spent his summers at Eastbourne.

For a man in such an apparently sheltered situation, Dodgson led an obsessively hard-working and varied life. He produced several works on mathematics, notably on Euclid, which have been highly regarded. And he wrote endlessly. In 1853 he began his Diary; his Register of letters sent and received, maintained for thirty-seven years, recorded 98,721 items, not counting his extensive correspondence from 1882 to 1892 when he was

---

[16] Cohen, *Biography*, 294.

curator of Christ Church common room. (This appears to have been a particularly lively period, producing a flood of letters, pamphlets, and notices.) In 1856 he bought his first camera; this used collodiol wet-plate techniques (invented in 1855) which tended to stain the hands—hence Dodgson's habit of wearing gloves when in society. He was a pioneer photographer, especially of children, and was noted for the naturalness of his compositions: 'Very few amateurs from Dodgson's period constantly photographed for so many years. [He was] a polymath of remarkable talent.'[17] It was a hobby that brought him into contact with many distinguished contemporaries, notably the Tennysons and the MacDonalds; Dodgson and MacDonald were both members of the Society for Psychical Research, and shared interests in homeopathy and anti-vivisection.

Dodgson was an avid theatregoer, making the acquaintance of Ellen Terry and her family, and took a vocal interest in national issues. For example, he had some influence in bringing about the Net Book Agreement (1900–97) which regulated the prices at which booksellers could sell books. W. T. Stead's campaign against child prostitution in the *Pall Mall Gazette* in the 1880s, which led in 1885 to the raising of the age of consent to 16, provoked Dodgson into a passionate response: he wanted Stead to be prosecuted for obscene libel for the graphic way in which he presented his findings.

In Oxford, he settled down to a life of local controversy, publishing dozens of privately printed pamphlets generally on the conservative side of arguments, and often in conflict with Henry George Liddell who became Dean of Christ Church in 1855. He also used the talent for versification which he had shown in his 'domestic' writings, and in 1855 he contributed pieces to the *Comic Times* and its successor, *The Train*. Its editor, Edmund Yates, asked him for a pseudonym, and Dodgson noted in his Diary for 11 February, 1856: 'Wrote to Mr Yates sending him a choice of names: 1. *Edgar Cuthwellis*

---

[17] Roger Taylor and Edward Wakeling, *Lewis Carroll, Photographer* (Princeton: Princeton University Press, 2002), 110, 111.

(made by transposition out of "Charles Lutwidge"). 2. *Edgar U. C. Westhill* (ditto). 3. *Louis Carroll* (derived from Lutwidge . . Ludovic . . Louis, and Charles). *Lewis Carroll* (ditto).' On 1 March, he added the note: ' "*Lewis Carroll*" was chosen'.

As 'Lewis Carroll', apart from the two highly successful 'Alice' books, he published verse: *Phantasmagoria and Other Poems* (1869), his surreal nonsense masterpiece, *The Hunting of the Snark* (1876), and *Rhyme? And Reason?* (1883). His other sizeable attempts at fiction for children, *Sylvie and Bruno* (1889) and *Sylvie and Bruno Concluded* (1893), are, as his biographer Morton Cohen puts it, 'overburdened by seriousness, calculated messages, ponderous cogitations, and fulminations that reflect the map of Charles's aging mind and broken heart. They are at one and the same time his *apologia pro vita mea* and his *consolatio philosophiae*.'[18] They resemble another solipsistic epic, Charles Kingsley's *The Water Babies* (1863)—which at least had a rather stronger narrative to support its many digressions and eccentricities—and their religiosity is quite alien to the world of Alice. In 1892, Dodgson wrote to the Revd C. A. Goodhart, Rector of Lambourne, Essex: 'In "Sylvie and Bruno" I took courage to introduce what I had entirely avoided in the two "Alice" books—some reference to subjects which are, after all, the *only* subjects of real interest in life, subjects which are so intimately bound up with every topic of human interest that it needs more effort to avoid them than to touch on them; and I felt that such a book was more suitable to a clerical writer than one of mere fun.'[19] His final collection, of 'serious' poems, *Three Sunsets and Other Poems*, was published in February 1898.

He died, still working hard on his sermons and on Euclid, on 14 January 1898 at 'The Chestnuts' in his sixty-sixth year; he is buried at the Mount cemetery in Guildford. In his will (his effects were sold for £729. 2s. 6d. at Holywell Music Room, Oxford, on 10 and 11 May 1898) he divided his estate between his siblings, and requested a plain funeral: 'simple and inexpensive, avoiding all things that are merely done for show, and

---

[18] Cohen, *Biography*, 455.   [19] Collingwood, *Life*, 308–9.

retaining only what is . . . requisite for its decent and reverent performance'.

After his death, it was suggested, following the example of a project run by *Aunt Judy's Magazine* from 1868, that a subscription be got up to endow a cot at Great Ormond Street Hospital in his name. Subscribers included not only the 'original' Alice, Alice Pleasance (Liddell) Hargreaves, Canon Duckworth, and Sir John Tenniel, but a galaxy of eminent Victorians, including George Meredith, George MacDonald, Jerome K. Jerome, Dante Gabriel Rossetti, Anthony Hope Hawkins, R. D. Blackmore, Holman Hunt, Walter Crane, Sir Henry Irving, Sir Walter Besant, Alice Meynall, and the Princess Alice.

And what was the man who led this life of detail like? The American writer Mark Twain, who met him at the MacDonalds' in July 1879, described him as 'the stillest and shyest full-grown man' he had ever met.[20] The Revd W. Tuckwell in his *Reminiscences of Oxford* (1900) regarded him as 'austere, shy, precise, absorbed in mathematical reverie, watchfully tenacious of his dignity, stiffly conservative in political, theological, social theory, his life mapped out in squares like Alice's landscape, he struck discords in the frank harmonious *camaraderie* of College life'.[21] John Goldthwaite has an even less flattering view:

His own piety made him a public nuisance. His illustrators were forbidden to illustrate on Sundays. Upon discovering that a stage production of *The Water Babies* contained a burlesque of a Salvation Army Hymn, he campaigned to have the theatre's licence revoked. The infamous Bowdler edition of Shakespeare was a scandal to the prudish don . . . He doted on maudlin songs, the pathetic in drama . . . Unembarrassed by his own bad taste, he was a snob and a lion hunter, chasing after celebrities with his camera.[22]

Certainly he tried to keep the lives of Charles Dodgson and Lewis Carroll separate—although he denied that there was any

[20] Cohen, *Biography*, 295.

[21] Hudson, *Illustrated Biography*, 175.

[22] John Goldthwaite, *The Natural History of Make-Believe* (New York: Oxford University Press, 1996), 80.

truth in the story that when Queen Victoria wrote to him, having read *Alice's Adventures in Wonderland*, asking for his next book, he sent her *An Elementary Treatise on Determinants*.[23]

But one aspect of his character has tended to overshadow everything else—Dodgson was devoted to 'child-friends', little girls for preference, whom he liked to entertain, photograph, and sketch. For several of these, his friendship extended into adulthood, and there is no record of any of them having anything but praise for his care and kindness. Rather, he was remembered with much affection—and certainly there was no hint of any impropriety. However, some of the parents of these children did have their objections, and it seems that there was some gossip in Oxford, which may well have been the reason that he gave up photography in 1880. In a letter of 7 June 1894 to the actress Ellen Terry, he wrote: 'Now that I have entered on the stage of being a "lean and slippered pantaloon", and no longer dread the frown of Mrs Grundy [a byword for propriety] I have taken to giving tête-à-tête dinner-parties—the guest being, in most cases, a lady of age varying from 12 to 67.'

But many modern readers have found it difficult to accept that the photographs that Dodgson took of undressed or partly dressed young girls are not salacious, or that his letters to parents negotiating in detail whether the girls could or could not wear drawers while he photographed them are anything less than excruciatingly embarrassing. The famous, or notorious, picture of Alice Liddell posing as a beggar-girl, in carefully revealing rags, has seemed to make the case against Dodgson as a latent paedophile incontestable. The question is, whether this is actually relevant to the reading of his books? (Roger Taylor points out that the 'beggar-girl' portrait is almost always judged out of context: it is one of a contrasting pair, the other showing Alice 'in her best outfit'.)[24]

It is, however, as well to remember that times change: for example, until 1885 the age of consent was 12, and at the end of

[23] Robin Wilson, *Lewis Carroll in Numberland* (London: Allen Lane, 2008), 101.
[24] Taylor and Wakeling, *Carroll, Photographer*, 64.

the century the average age of menarche was about 16. As
Kimberley Reynolds points out, 'it was not uncommon in the
nineteenth century for grown men to be attracted to young
girls—girls too young to be sexually demanding or threatening'
and she cites the examples of Swinburne, Ruskin, Mayne Reid,
'E. W. Benson (who became Archbishop of Canterbury) [who]
fell in love with an eleven-year-old to whom he proposed when
she was twelve'—and Queen Victoria's daughter, Beatrice, who
was engaged at 13.[25]

Equally, as Anne Higonnet observed, attitudes to certain
images differed, too: 'To [Dodgson's] contemporaries . . .
Alice's beggar portrait did not look prurient at all . . . In their
time [such pictures] were . . . seen as . . . images of natural
innocence and therefore naturally innocent themselves . . . Carroll was absolutely convinced that the innocence of the child was
a natural quality.'[26] James Kincaid's pioneering *Child-Loving:
The Erotic Child and Victorian Culture* also places the Victorian
fascination with the child in its context, suggesting, of the 'Alice'
books, that they are characteristic of 'a paradigm of play [that] is
not seeking fulfilment, wants not even to construct a seduction
drama but to stand on the threshold of such a drama. It is an
erotics of temptation and flirtation . . . because, in the catching,
the world would collapse and desire would end.'[27]

Nevertheless, it seems unlikely that an unbiased observer in
the twenty-first century could read the following account of
Dodgson without, at the very least, a raised eyebrow. Written
by the founding editor of Puffin Books, Eleanor Graham, it is
aimed at children, and appeared in the 1946 Puffin edition
of the 'Alice' books, under the title 'How the Story Was Told'.
The Revd Dodgson, Graham wrote, without any perceptible
irony, was

[25] Kimberley Reynolds, *Radical Children's Literature* (Basingstoke: Palgrave, 2007),
52.
[26] Anne Higonnet, *Pictures of Innocence* (London: Thames and Hudson, 1998), 125,
110.
[27] James R. Kincaid, *Child-Loving: The Erotic Child and Victorian Culture* (New
York and London: Routledge, 1992), 196.

very fond of children and had many child friends, though often he did not keep them long. He took great pains for their entertainment and invited them, sometimes to tea or lunch in his rooms, sometimes to go to London with him for the day, to a theatre or to the zoo. Even when he set out alone on a journey by train, he took with him a supply of puzzles, games, and small toys in case he found a child in his compartment. Moreover, when he went to the seaside he kept a bunch of large safety pins in his pocket for the convenience of little girls who might want their frocks pinned up so that they could paddle more comfortably.[28]

Or, perhaps, we might read that with a feeling of regret for a lost, innocent age—that age being the 1940s as much as the 1860s. In 1937, Edward Ardizzone's picture-book *Lucy Brown and Mr Grimes* portrayed a small girl befriending an old man in a park: because of what Ardizzone described as 'silly women librarians' the story was modified for its reissue in 1970, so that Mr Grimes became an old family friend.

But even the most sympathetic of Dodgson's biographers, Morton Cohen, finds it necessary to face this particular problem directly (given that his index contains the item, 'Dodgson, nude female form, attachment to') and makes what has become a common connection:

We cannot know to what extent sexual urges lay behind Charles's preference for drawing and photographing children in the nude. He contended that the preference was entirely aesthetic . . . but . . . he probably felt more than he dared acknowledge, even to himself . . . For posterity, however, there were compensations. If Charles Dodgson's suppressed and diverted sexual energies caused him unspeakable torments, and they did, they were in all probability the source of those exceptional flashes of genius that gave the world his remarkable creative works.[29]

This aspect of Dodgson's character has led to a library of analytical works, which were prophesied by J. B. Priestley in

---

[28] Eleanor Graham, 'How the Story Was Told', in Lewis Carroll, *Alice's Adventures in Wonderland* and *Through the Looking-Glass* (Harmondsworth: Puffin (Penguin), 1946), 12.

[29] Cohen, *Biography*, 228, 231.

1921 (apropos of *Alice's Adventures in Wonderland* being translated into German):

A cloud of commentators will gather, and . . . sit down to write huge
volumes of comment and criticism; they will contrast and compare the
characters (there will even be a short chapter on Bill the Lizard), and
will offer numerous conflicting interpretations of the jokes. After that,
Freud and Jung and their followers will inevitably arrive upon the
scene, and they will give us appalling volumes on the 'Sexualtheorie' of
Alice in Wonderland . . . We shall understand, for the first time, the
particularly revolting symbolism of the Mad Hatter's Tea-Party.[30]

Consequently, there is a good deal of irony in the fact that the
first 'Freudian' study, '*Alice in Wonderland* Psycho-Analysed'
(*The New Oxford Outlook*, 1933), by an Oxford undergraduate,
A. M. E. (Tony) Goldschmidt, was almost certainly intended as
satire. He began: 'no critic upon whom the Freudian theory has
made even the slightest impression can refrain from recognising
sexual symbolism . . . when it is very clearly manifested', and he
then explores Alice falling down a deep hole ('perhaps the best-
known symbol of coitus'), pursuing the White Rabbit ('trying to
make up disparity in ages'), and the symbolism of locks, keys,
doors, changing sizes, neck length, and little houses. 'Had
[Dodgson] lived today,' Goldschmidt concludes (blandly),
'he might have undergone analysis, discovered the cause of his
neurosis, and lived a more contented life.'[31]

What followed, however, was rather more serious, or was
taken more seriously. Dodgson's psyche, and his relationship
with the real Alice, became happy hunting grounds for psycholo-
gists and psychological critics, notably Paul Schilder in *The
Journal of Nervous and Mental Disease* (1938), Florence Becker
Lennon in *Victoria Through the Looking Glass: The Life of Lewis
Carroll* (1945), and Phyllis Greenacre in *Swift and Carroll: A*

---

[30] J. B. Priestley, 'A Note on Humpty Dumpty', *I For One* (London: John Lane The
Bodley Head, 1923), 191–2.

[31] Robert Phillips (ed.), *Aspects of Alice: Lewis Carroll's Dreamchild as Seen Through
the Critics' Looking-Glasses 1865–1971* (London: Gollancz, 1972; Harmondsworth;
Penguin, 1974), 329, 332.

Psychoanalytical Study of Two Lives (1955).[32] More recent critics have been more pragmatic; as Martin Gardner noted, 'the point here is not that Carroll was not neurotic (we all know that he was), but that books of nonsense fantasy for children are not such fruitful sources of psychoanalytic insight as one might suppose them to be. They are much too rich in symbols. The symbols have too many explanations.'[33]

Specifically, Dodgson's muse was Alice Pleasance Liddell, second daughter of Dean Liddell of Christ Church. Alexander L. Taylor was convinced that Dodgson was in love with her: 'She and she alone was his lost love . . . the little ghost that was to come crying in the night to the windows of his bachelor room in Tom Quad.'[34] Dodgson became a friend of the family, and especially the children—Harry and the three (later five) daughters— whom he photographed and took for excursions, including river trips. The friendship continued until June 1863, when there was a sudden estrangement; Dodgson was no longer welcome at the Deanery, and Mrs Liddell tore up his letters to Alice. (In 1932, Alice wrote: 'I cannot remember what any of them were like, but it is an awful thought to contemplate what may have perished in the Deanery waste-paper basket.')[35] From that time, Dodgson saw the girls only occasionally. There has been a great deal of speculation on what happened, especially as key pages have been cut from Dodgson's Diary, probably by his niece, Menella. (Four of the thirteen volumes of his diaries have been lost, and pages were removed from the others by members of Dodgson's family.) The most common speculation has been that Mrs Liddell felt that Dodgson was becoming too fond of Alice and the girls, and felt that with their aristocratic connections, her daughters could aim higher. Others were that he proposed to

[32] See e.g. ibid. 333–43, 99–113, 369–86.

[33] *The Annotated Alice: The Definitive Edition*, ed. Martin Gardner (New York: Norton, 2000), xv.

[34] Alexander L. Taylor, *The White Knight* (Edinburgh: Oliver and Boyd, 1952), 32–3.

[35] 'Alice's Recollections of Carrollian Days, as Told to Her Son', *Cornhill Magazine* 73 (July 1932), in Morton N. Cohen (ed.), *Lewis Carroll: Interviews and Recollections* (London: Palgrave Macmillan, 1989), 85.

Alice, or to Lorina (who was 14), that he displeased Mrs Liddell
by disapproving of a party proposed by an eligible undergraduate, Lord Newry—or, as in Katie Roiphe's novel, *Still
She Haunts Me*, that Dodgson overstepped the photographic
mark. It has also been suggested that there was no rift, but that
Mrs Liddell and Dodgson mutually agreed to reduce his
involvement with the family to end rumours about his intentions
towards Lorina and/or Miss Prickett, the governess. Karoline
Leach has argued (controversially) in *In the Shadow of the
Dreamchild: A New Understanding of Lewis Carroll* that the
generally accepted views of Dodgson's life and character
are based on unsubstantiated psychological readings, and on
the biography by Dodgson's nephew, Stuart Dodgson Collingwood (1899), which she describes as 'absurd and ultimately
deceitful'.[36]

Dodgson transferred his affections to a long succession of
other 'child-friends', but there can be little doubt that Alice was
very important to him (he took his last photograph of her in
1870). While there may be something in Humphrey Carpenter's
suggestion that all of this complex story 'hardly matters, for
Alice's Adventures in Wonderland is not about Alice Liddell at
all'[37] she was certainly its inspiration.

The Books

As we have seen, Friday, 4 July 1862 has acquired mythological
status as the day upon which Dodgson began *Alice's Adventures
in Wonderland*, and as the prefatory poem has it: 'All in the
golden afternoon | Full leisurely we glide ... Beneath such
dreamy weather'. (And, as Walter de la Mare observed, in his
short book on Dodgson: 'afternoons in July, if fair and cloudless,
are apt to be narcotic. The rhythm of sculling quiets the mind
and sets the workaday wits drowsing.'[38]) In 1887, in an article

[36] Karoline Leach, *In the Shadow of the Dreamchild: A New Understanding of Lewis Carroll* (London: Peter Owen, 1999), 258.
[37] Carpenter, *Secret Gardens*, 55.
[38] Walter de la Mare, *Lewis Carroll*, 47.

for *The Theatre*, ' "Alice" on the Stage', Dodgson recalled, in
romantic tones, that

Many a day had we rowed together on that quiet stream . . . and many a
fairy tale had been extemporised for their benefit . . . yet none of these
many tales got written down: they lived and died, like summer midges,
each in its golden afternoon . . . Full many a year has slipped away, since
that 'golden afternoon' that gave thee birth, but I can call it up almost as
clearly as if it were yesterday—the cloudless blue above, the watery
mirror below.[39]

As to the date, Dodgson had taken the Liddell sisters on
several river trips—a trip downriver to Nuneham Park on 3 July
1862 was cancelled because of rain. On the following day,
Dodgson made this entry in his Diary:

Duckworth and I made an expedition *up* the river to Godstow with the
3 Liddells: we had tea on the bank there, and did not reach Christ
Church again until ½ past 8, when we took them on to my rooms to
see my collection of micro-photographs, and restored them to the
Deanery, just before 9.

So far, so good. But, curiously, that entry does not mention
the birth of the book: it was not until six months *later*, on 10
February 1863, that Dodgson added, on a blank page opposite
the 4 July entry: 'On which occasion I told them the fairy-tale of
Alice's Adventures under Ground which I undertook to write out
for Alice, and which is now finished.' His first mention of the
book in his Diary is on 6 August 1862 when, on another trip to
Godstow he noted, 'had to go on with my interminable fairy-tale
of *Alice's Adventures*'. Even more curiously, 4 July wasn't a
'golden afternoon': the records of the Meteorological Office in
London show that the weather near Oxford was 'cool and rather
wet'. The records at the Radcliffe Observatory, Oxford, give
'rain after 2 p.m., and cloud cover 10/10; temperature 67.9°F.'.
And then there is the letter from Alice (now Mrs Hargreaves),

---

[39] Stuart Dodgson Collingwood (ed.), *The Lewis Carroll Picture Book* (London:
T. Fisher Unwin, 1899), 165, 168.

printed in 1899 by Stuart Collingwood, which supports the good
weather, but not the destination:

I believe the beginning of 'Alice' was told one summer afternoon when
the sun was so burning that we had landed in the meadows down the
river [which suggests that they had gone to Nuneham Park], deserting
the boat to take refuge in the only bit of shade that was to be found,
which was under a new-made hayrick.[40]

As an old lady, Alice altered this story to fit the accepted
version: 'that blazing summer afternoon with the heat haze
shimmering over the meadows . . . near Godstow'.[41] Nor is
Canon Duckworth, the other passenger, any help: his account, in
1899, although it has joined the much-quoted folklore, does not
mention either the date or the weather:

I rowed *stroke* and he rowed *bow* in the famous Long Vacation voyage to
Godstow, when the three Miss Liddells were our passengers, and the
story was actually composed and spoken *over my shoulder* for the benefit
of Alice Liddell, who was acting as 'cox' of our gig. I remember turning
round and saying, 'Dodgson, is this an extempore romance of yours?'
And he replied, 'Yes I'm inventing as we go along.'[42]

When subscribing to the Lewis Carroll Memorial Cot in 1898,
Duckworth maintained the story: 'on that beautiful summer
afternoon in the Long Vacation which is described in the introductory verses to the story'.[43]

And so, sad to say, the only actual evidence that the story was
begun on 4 July, seems to be an afterthought. But the myth of a
happy, innocent, sunny, and spontaneous story was established,
and Dodgson, according to Duckworth, 'sat up nearly the whole
night' writing the story down.

What happened then seems to be that Dodgson produced a
draft version (now lost), sometime before 10 February 1863, and
sent it to George MacDonald's son, Henry. The family endorsed
it, and encouraged by Duckworth, Dodgson began to expand
the book. Meanwhile, he also hand-lettered and illustrated a

[40] Collingwood, *Life*, 96.   [41] Cohen (ed.), *Interviews*, 86.
[42] Collingwood (ed.), *Picture Book*, 359–60.
[43] Hudson, *Illustrated Biography*, 22.

version as a gift for Alice Liddell, a green leather booklet called
Alice's Adventures under Ground which he presented to her as a
Christmas gift in 1864. Interestingly, Dodgson seems to have
made no attempt to depict Alice Liddell in his pictures, except in
a cameo on the final page, which he then covered with a small
photograph of her. Henry Kingsley (brother of Charles) saw
Alice's Adventures under Ground at the Deanery and suggested
that Dodgson be encouraged to publish it. As Humphrey
Carpenter points out, it seems that Alice Liddell was one of the
few people *not* consulted over the publication.[44]

Alice's Adventures under Ground is just over half as long as
Alice's Adventures in Wonderland. In producing the full text,
Dodgson made many small revisions—for example, he
smoothed out the oddity that the Red Queen is also the 'Marchioness of Mock Turtles'—and made several major additions.
There were two completely new chapters—Chapter VI, 'Pig and
Pepper', and Chapter VII, 'The Mad Tea Party'—and he
expanded the chapters on the Queen's croquet ground, and the
lobster quadrille; the trial scene was expanded from one page to
two chapters. He also made the book less personal. The Caucus
race, led by the Dodo, replaced the thinly disguised true-to-life
account of a picnic that had taken place on Tuesday, 17 June
1862. He recorded in his Diary an expedition downriver to
Nuneham; the party included his sisters, Frances and Elizabeth,
his aunt, Lucy Lutwidge, Duckworth, the three Liddell sisters,
and (almost certainly) their governess, Miss Prickett. (Some of
them appear in the story: the sulky Lory is Alice's eldest sister
Lorinda, the mouse is probably Miss Prickett—who reads from
the lesson-book that she had been using with the children,
Dodo is Dodgson, and the Duck, Duckworth.) When it rained,
Dodgson took the children to a house that he knew nearby to dry
themselves. In *Alice's Adventures under Ground*, the story is very
much the same: the Dodo walks on 'with Alice, the Lory, and the
Eaglet, and soon brought them to a little cottage, and there they
sat snugly by the fire, wrapped up in blankets, until the rest of

---

[44] Carpenter, *Secret Gardens*, 57.

the party had arrived, and they were all dry again'. The version in *Alice's Adventures in Wonderland* removes these real-life references: ' "What I was going to say," said the Dodo in an offended tone, "was, that the best thing to get us dry would be a Caucus-race" ' (p. 26) which, as several critics have pointed out, seems to have rather wider political and satirical implications.

Through an acquaintance, Dodgson met Alexander Macmillan, whose firm had published Charles Kingsley's *The Water Babies*, and he began to look for an illustrator: partly at Duckworth's suggestion, he recruited John Tenniel, one of the political cartoonists for *Punch*—which some critics have seen as demonstrating Dodgson's satirical intent.

From then on, the history of the 'Alice' books says a great deal about their author's character—meticulous to the point of fussiness, and perfectionist to the point of pettiness. His relationship with Macmillan was sometimes fractious: Charles Morgan, the historian of the company, observed that 'There never was an author more elaborately careful than Lewis Carroll for the details of production, or one that can have more sorely tried the patience of his publisher . . . [He] never allowed himself to be far absent from the minds of publisher, printer, or binder . . . Books, ingenuities and trouble poured from him.'[45] John Pudney notes that 'not even the packers escaped his attention. He sent in a diagram, showing how parcels were to be stringed and how the knots were to be tied. This hung for years in the Macmillan post-room.'[46]

The first problem with the printing of *Alice's Adventures in Wonderland*, however, was not Dodgson's fault. In June 1865, 2,000 copies were printed (at Dodgson's expense) by the Clarendon Press in Oxford, to be published on 4 July—three years after the ostensible date of the boat ride. Tenniel, however, objected to the quality of the printing—it had been set up from 'improperly sorted' type, the layout was erratic, and a poor

[45] Quoted by John Pudney, *Lewis Carroll and His World* (London: Thames and Hudson, 1976), 77–8.
[46] Ibid. 78.

mixture of ink had led to pigment seeping through the pages[47]—and Dodgson wrote in his Diary (2 August): 'Finally decided on the re-print of *Alice*, and that the first 2000 shall be sold as waste paper.' He had the book reprinted (by Richard Clay) at a cost to himself of £600, and calculated that he would have to sell 4,000 copies merely to break even. The unbound sheets were not, in the end, sold as waste paper, but were bound and sold to the American publisher D. Appleton. Forty-eight copies had already been given away, of which twenty-three—which have become bibliophiles' treasures—are known to survive. Dodgson did not make a loss—in fact, the book had sold 12,000 copies by 1868.

Through the Looking-Glass had a less dramatic birth, although Tenniel at first refused to illustrate it. Dodgson invited (among others) Kingsley's illustrator, Sir Joseph Noel Paton—a painter in the lush Pre-Raphaelite style—which some critics have seen as further evidence of Dodgson's lack of taste or idea of appropriateness. Noel Paton refused, on the grounds of illness, and Tenniel was, after two and a half years, finally persuaded. Early in 1871, Dodgson consulted some mothers of young children over whether the picture of the Jabberwock should be the frontispiece, on the grounds that it was 'too terrible a monster, and likely to alarm nervous and imaginative children', and it was replaced by a picture of the White Knight. The book was published for Christmas 1871, the 9,000 copies printed proving inadequate to the demand. When Macmillan wanted to print another 6,000 copies 'as fast as possible', Dodgson objected: 'My decision is, we must have *no more hurry* . . . You will think me a lunatic for thus wishing to send away money from the doors. . . . I wish I could put into words how entirely such arguments go for nothing with me. As to how many copies we sell I care absolutely nothing: the one thing I *do* care is, that all copies that *are* sold shall be artistically first-rate.'[48]

---

[47] Justin G. Schiller, *Alice's Adventures in Wonderland. An 1865 printing re-described* . . . ([Kingston, NY]: privately printed for *The Jabberwock*, 1990).
[48] Hudson, *Illustrated Biography*, 155.

The book was in galley proof, when there was another inter-
vention from Tenniel. Just after Alice's meeting with the White
Knight, and before she crosses the last brook to become a queen,
Dodgson had included another episode, 'The Wasp in a Wig'. In
a letter to Dodgson on 1 June 1870, Tenniel wrote: 'Don't think
me brutal, but I am bound to say that the "wasp" chapter doesn't
interest me in the least, & ~~that~~ I can't see my way to a picture.
If you want to shorten the book, I can't help thinking—with
all submission—that <u>there</u> is your opportunity.' Collingwood,
who published the letter in *Life and Letters*, added: 'Apart
from the difficulties of illustration, the "wasp" chapter was not
considered to be up to the rest of the book, and this was probably
the principal reason of its being left out.'[49]

Through the Looking-Glass was enthusiastically reviewed,
and sold 25,000 copies within the year. At Dodgson's death,
it had sold over 100,000, compared with *Alice's Adventures
in Wonderland*'s 150,000. (Comparing it to *Alice's Adventures in
Wonderland*, in 1898, the *Academy* observed that 'we now and
then hear the pump at work'.)

The next 'Alice' venture was the facsimile edition of *Alice's
Adventures under Ground*, published in 1886. On 1 March 1885
Dodgson wrote to Alice Hargreaves, to ask her to lend him the
original hand-lettered copy. If there is any doubt that Dodgson
retained strong feelings for her (as a child) one might consider
the perhaps inadvertent passion of the opening of the letter:

My dear Mrs Hargreaves,

I fancy this will come to you almost like a voice from the dead, after so
many years of silence [although he had sent her an inscribed copy of his
Rhyme? and Reason? in 1883]—and yet those years have made no
difference, that I can perceive, in my clearness of memory of the days
when we did correspond . . . my mental picture is as vivid as ever, of one
who was, through so many years, my ideal child-friend. I have had scores
of child-friends since your time: but they have been quite a different
thing.

[49] Collingwood, *Life*, 146, and see note to p. 223. 'The Wasp in a Wig' episode can be
found in the Appendix, pp. 251–5.

However, I did not begin this letter to say all that. What I want to ask is . . .

In 1928, Alice Hargreaves, in some need of money, sold the manuscript at Sotheby's in London; it was bought by Dr A. S. W. Rosenbach for £15,400, who sold it on 'for nearly double that sum' to Eldridge R. Johnson of New York. It returned to England in 1948 as a gift from Rosenbach (who had bought it again after Johnson's death in 1944) and other benefactors (who raised £12,500) as an expression of thanks to the British, 'a noble people', for their war effort. Dr Luther Evans of the Library of Congress brought it across the Atlantic (keeping it under his pillow) and it was received by the Archbishop of Canterbury. (It is now in the British Library and can be read online.)

The final version of *Alice's Adventures in Wonderland* prepared by Dodgson, *The Nursery Alice* (1890), is the most curious of all: all that remains of the sharpness of the original book is Tenniel's illustrations. Dodgson adopts a totally different tone of voice, which can be demonstrated from the 'Preface (addressed to any mother)':

And my ambition *now* is (is it a vain one?) to be read by Children aged from Nought to Five. To be read? Nay, not so! Say rather to be thumbed, to be cooed over, to be dogs'-eared, to be rumpled, to be kissed by the illiterate, ungrammatical, dimpled Darlings, that fill your Nursery with merry uproar, and your inmost heart of hearts with a restful gladness!

Such, for instance, as a child I once knew, who—having been carefully instructed that *one* of any earthly thing was enough for any little girl; and that to ask for *two* buns, *two* oranges, *two* of anything, would certainly bring upon her the awful charge of being 'greedy'—was found one morning sitting up in bed, solemnly regarding her *two* little naked feet, and murmuring to herself, softly and penitently, 'deedy!'

Predictably enough, Dodgson condemned the first printing, of 10,000, in 1889 as 'far too bright and gaudy': 4,000 copies were sold to America and 500 to Australia and many more given away to hospitals.

Several critics, notably Humphrey Carpenter, have suggested that *Alice's Adventures in Wonderland* and *Through the Looking-Glass* represented Dodgson's glimpse into the abyss of a godless world, in which adults are mad, and children selfish. *The Nursery Alice*, together with the sentimental verses, and the pious pamphlets that appeared in later editions of *Alice's Adventures in Wonderland* and *Through the Looking-Glass* were ways of 'unwriting' these frightening and radical texts.[50] Certainly there is a profound paradox in the man who parodied religious verses and who created what can be seen as nihilistic and emotionally questionable texts, and yet who changed the passion flower in Alice's garden to a tiger lily when it was pointed out to him that the passion in passion flower referred to Christ's passion.

'Alice' in the History of Children's Literature

From the beginnings of modern children's literature in the mid-eighteenth century, delight had been harnessed to instruction, particularly religious and moral instruction. Perhaps the most famous and characteristic of such books was Mary Martha Sherwood's best-selling *The Fairchild Family* (1818—third volume 1847) (which Dodgson read as a child) whose cautionary tales each ended with a hymn and a prayer. Good actions were rewarded (in heaven, at least), bad ones graphically punished—often by gruesome deaths; the families were loving, although perhaps rather stern by today's standards, and there was a rigid hierarchy from the father (standing in place of God) to the mother and the children.

But from around the 1830s, the evangelical grip on children's education and books was gradually eroded. One of the key books was Catherine Sinclair's *Holiday House* (1839): Sinclair noted in the 'Preface' that 'the minds of young people are now manufactured like webs of linen, all alike, and nothing left to Nature. From the hour when children can speak . . . they are carefully prompted what to say, and what to think, and how to look, and

---

[50] Carpenter, *Secret Gardens*, 68.

how to feel; while in most school-rooms Nature has been turned
out of doors with obloquy, and Art has entirely supplanted her.'
Building her book 'on the solid foundation of Christian faith and
sound morality', she wished to show 'that species of noisy,
frolicsome, mischievous children [which is] now almost extinct',
and she did so by distinguishing between wickedness and
thoughtlessness. An equally influential proponent of a more
balanced view of childhood was Heinrich Hoffman, a German
doctor who, despairing of the diet of moralistic tales, produced
his own best-selling satire on them, *Strewwelpeter* (English
translation 1848). Edward Lear, another writer with a penchant
for entertaining children (and thus camouflaging his own
feelings), produced his first collection of eccentric limericks,
A Book of Nonsense, in 1846 (revised 1861).

Dodgson, then, was not alone: he was writing at a time of
radical cultural change, which was reflected in changes in attitudes to childhood and children's books. Louisa May Alcott's
Little Women (1868), with its latent feminism, marks a turning
point in attitudes to girls and to religion; Richard Jefferies's
Bevis, the Story of a Boy (1882) and Robert Louis Stevenson's
Treasure Island (1883) both rethought the adventure story,
and brought moral ambiguity and amorality into a world of
polarized certainties. Of course, the older attitudes persisted in
best-sellers such as Mary Louisa Charlesworth's *Ministering
Children* (1854), Martha Finlay's *Elsie Dinsmore* (1867), or Susan
Coolidge's *What Katy Did* (1872).

But because Dodgson was so close to the minds of his first
readers (or listeners), and because he respected their intelligence
and their situation, he was able to voice their silent rebellion.
Thus he parodied the oldest of the moralists—Isaac Watts—
whose often savage *Divine Songs Attempted in Easy Language for
the Use of Children* (1715) was still current. The 'little busy bee'
in Watts's song 'Against Idleness and Mischief' becomes a 'little
crocodile', and Robert Southey's 'The Old Man's Comforts and
How He Gained Them' ('You are old, Father William') and
Mary Howitt's 'The Spider and the Fly' ('Will you walk a little
faster . . .') are put to the parodic sword. And when Alice comes

upon the bottle labelled 'DRINK ME', she pauses because 'she had read several nice little stories about children who had got burnt, and eaten up by wild beasts, and other unpleasant things, all because they *would* not remember the simple rules their friends had taught them' (p. 13).

This leads us to Dodgson's major contribution to children's literature, which was to find a narrative voice that closed, or gave the impression of closing, the gap between writer and reader. By doing so he shifted the balance of power within the texts, removing the adult's controlling voice and allowing children to think for themselves. Previous to that, the adult narrators were in firm control—take Thomas Hughes in *Tom Brown's Schooldays* (1857), who interrupts his narrative for a brief homily: 'So it is, and must be always, my dear boys . . . You only want to have your heads set straight to take the right side: so bear in mind that majorities, especially respectable ones are nine times out of ten in the wrong.' Or, notoriously, the narrator's voice in Charles Kingsley's *The Water Babies*—a book commonly held to be the first book in the first 'golden age' of children's books. It begins: 'Once upon a time there was a little chimney-sweep, and his name was Tom. That is a short name, and you have heard it before, so you will not have much trouble in remembering it.' It is not difficult to see why Goldthwaite feels that 'much of *Alice* is a running argument with Kingsley over how one goes about telling a children's story'.[51]

Dodgson's focus on a real child, Alice Liddell, in *Alice's Adventures in Wonderland* (and his nostalgic memory of her in *Through the Looking-Glass*) may have been the catalyst for this change. As Barbara Wall notes, it meant that the narrator-Dodgson

could share with ten-year-old narratee-Alice delight in the adventures of seven-year-old character-Alice . . . Alice's became the first child-mind, in the history of children's fiction, to occupy the centre. No narrator of a story for children had stood so close to a child protagonist, observing nothing except that child, describing, never criticising,

---

[51] Goldthwaite, *Make-Believe*, 98.

showing only what that child saw . . . he never, until she has woken from her dream, looks away from her.[52]

Consequently, unlike in books by Kingsley, or many of Dodgson's imitators, the jokes do not go over the child-character's head, aimed at the knowing adult. For example, the first (of several) death-jokes—' "Why, I wouldn't say anything about it, even if I fell off the top of the house!" (Which was very likely true)'—is there to be understood and appreciated and pondered on by the child reader. (Not all critics concur: Zohar Shavit argues, for example, that Dodgson left the parodies out of *The Nursery Alice* precisely because he had previously been aiming for two audiences.)[53]

In *Through the Looking-Glass*, not surprisingly, as he was now six years away from his close contact with Alice Liddell, Dodgson's touch is slightly less sure. He provides a frame of reference by repeating phrases such as, 'as she described it afterwards' (p. 137), and indulges in romantic musings that break the narrator-narratee contract: 'And here I wish I could tell you half the things Alice used to say' (p. 126), or '(here came the favourite little toss of the head)' (p. 148). At its most extreme, there is the overladen scene when Alice and the sheep encounter the scented rushes: 'And then the little sleeves were carefully rolled up, and the little arms were plunged in elbow-deep [and] she caught at one bunch after another of the darling scented rushes' (p. 181).

This sentimental attitude, which is anathema to the general tough-mindedness that gives the 'Alice' books their place in history, lurks around edges of the books, because, when it came to the crunch, Dodgson was no revolutionary. He repudiates the fictional Alice's moments of power by making them dreams, and then hedges them round with ultra-conventional sentimental-religious verse. As in A. A. Milne's *Winnie-the-Pooh* and *The House at Pooh Corner*, these discordant frames suggest that

[52] Barbara Wall, *The Narrator's Voice* (Basingstoke: Macmillan, 1991), 100, 97–8.
[53] Zohar Shavit, *Poetics of Children's Literature* (Athens, Ga.: University of Georgia Press, 1986), 72.

the author is not keeping faith with his ostensible audience, and is now aiming over their heads, and constructing, or falling in with, an audience that sees childhood quite differently. The Dodgson of *The Nursery Alice* is relating to the *fin de siècle* 'beautiful-child' cult which was such a feature of late nineteenth-century British society. It was a modification of the Romantics' attitude to children, and survived into the 1920s when Richmal Crompton administered an effective antidote with her 'William' books.

There were many direct imitations of *Alice's Adventures in Wonderland* and *Through the Looking-Glass* (indeed, Dodgson began to collect 'books of the *Alice* type') but the influence of the 'Alice' books has been more important over the long term than the short term. This is because, for all their ingenuity, the imitations generally tried to reproduce the comic surface-elements of the books, rather than the subtle undercurrents or the radical, child-centred voice. Carolyn Sigler estimates that between 1869 and 1930 there were 'almost two hundred literary imitations, revisions, and parodies'.[54] Perhaps the most famous was G. E. Farrow's *The Wallypug of Why* (1895 and two sequels), which has a female hero called, ominously, 'Girlie', and which in its attempts at verbal wit, often talks over the heads of its supposed audience:

'What is the microscope for?' asked Girlie in a whisper.
    'To see the jokes with,' replied the Penguin. 'Some of them cannot be seen at all without it.'

Others, such as Alice Corkran's *Down the Snow Stairs* (1887) or Christina Rossetti's *Speaking Likenesses* (1870), use 'Alice'-like devices to reinvent the didactic tale. Later, as Sigler suggests, the post-1930 imitations 'tend simply to make reference to the *Alice* mythos, while commenting upon issues and concerns far from Alice's world'.[55]

---

[54] Carolyn Sigler, *Alternative Alices: Visions and Revisions of Lewis Carroll's* Alice *Books* (Lexington, Ky.: The University Press of Kentucky, 1997), xi.
[55] Ibid.

Thus the true (and profound) legacy of Dodgson can be found in those writers who followed his lead in respecting the intelligence of the child-readers, and who developed a narrative voice that treated them as equals. Some of these attempts were faltering—as with Edith Nesbit—but with Rudyard Kipling, the later Frances Hodgson Burnett, John Masefield's fantasies, Arthur Ransome, and Noel Streatfeild, a tradition was established for writing genuinely *for* children, that has survived through to J. K. Rowling.

Reading the 'Alice' Books

In 1887, Dodgson described the composition of *Alice's Adventures in Wonderland*: having first told the story while rowing on the river,

to please a child I loved (I don't remember any other motive), I printed in manuscript . . . the book which I have just had published in facsimile. In writing it out, I added many fresh ideas, which seemed to grow themselves upon the original stock; and many more added themselves when . . . I wrote it all over again for publication . . . 'Alice' and the 'Looking-Glass' are made up almost wholly of bits and scraps, single ideas that came of themselves.[56]

Perhaps as a result of this process, the books are intricately layered. There is the conscious, personal level, using incidents, characters, and places familiar to Alice Liddell and Dodgson's immediate circle. Next there is the matrix of philosophy, mathematics, and linguistics—serious games for both child and adult readers. Then there is a wider world of references to Oxford and national personalities and politics—both the pre-occupations of a singular mind, and the natural furniture of the mind of a well-educated Victorian scholar and gentleman. Finally, and more contentiously, there are passages which seem (notably in *Through the Looking-Glass*) to be very personal—conscious or unconscious manifestations of Dodgson's psyche. As Derek Hudson put it, 'the "Alice" books were in some degree

[56] Collingwood (ed.), *Picture Book*, 106–7.

an autobiographical miscellany, woven together with extraordinary skill: an Odyssey of the subconscious'.[57] All of this
suggests that whatever the books may be, they are scarcely
'nonsense', if nonsense is defined as occurring when the mind is
unable to make an association: as Elizabeth Sewell pointed out,
'nonsense . . . requires as few relations . . . as possible'.[58]

Dodgson's conscious use of his personal circle can be seen
during the Mad Tea-Party, in *Alice's Adventures in Wonderland*.
The Dormouse begins a story:

'Once upon a time there were three little sisters . . . and their names
were Elsie, Lacie, and Tillie: and they lived at the bottom of a well—'
    'What did they live on?' said Alice, who always took a great interest in
questions of eating and drinking.
    'They lived on treacle,' said the Dormouse, after thinking a minute
or two. (p. 65)

There is a lot going on here. Leaving aside speculations on
who the Dormouse is supposed to be (candidates include the
Christian Socialist theologian F. D. Maurice, and Dante Gabriel
Rossetti's pet wombat), it is clear that it is the three little/
Liddell sisters in the well. Elsie is a pun on Lorinda Charlotte's
initials, 'Lacie' is an anagram of Alice, and Tillie is an abbreviation of Matilda, Edith's nickname. And the treacle well is not
nonsense. Medicinal springs in Oxfordshire were known as
'treacle wells'—treacle being an obsolete word for 'balm' (the
'Treacle Bibles' of 1568 are those where the word 'balm' is
rendered as 'treacle', as at Jeremiah 8: 22—'Is there not treacle in
Gilead?'). There is a treacle well in the grounds of St Margaret's
church at Binsey, near Oxford, dedicated to, and said to have
appeared as the answer to the prayers of, the Saxon St
Frideswide, patron saint of Oxford. Dodgson's college, Christ
Church, founded in 1564, took over the site of St Frideswide's
Abbey. St Frideswide's window in Christ Church Cathedral, by
Edward Burne-Jones (1858), has a panel depicting pilgrims
going to the well.

[57] Hudson, *Illustrated Biography*, 73.
[58] Elizabeth Sewell, *The Field of Nonsense* (Chatto and Windus, 1952), 143.

All of this would almost certainly have been within the grasp of the real Alice, as would (at least in Dodgson's expectations) the mathematical and logical puzzles scattered through the text, on as it were 'the next level'. Dodgson, after all, is the man who wrote *A Tangled Tale*, for Charlotte Yonge's *The Monthly Packet* (the full title of which was *The Monthly Packet of Evening Readings for Younger Members of the English Church*). His series, beginning in April 1880, consisted of twelve 'knots', and the idea was, in Dodgson's words, 'to embody in each Knot (like the medicine so dexterously, but ineffectively, concealed in the jam of our early childhood) one or more mathematical questions—in Arithmetic, Algebra, or Geometry, as the case may be—for the amusement, and possible edification, of the fair readers of that magazine'. The word 'amusement' is important here, for Dodgson would certainly not have recognized the critic David Holbrook's description of him as 'a man who led a more or less dull life, often producing dull mathematical and logical texts . . . but also producing the "Alice" books'.[59] To Dodgson, there was nothing dull about mathematics.

And so, when the puzzled Alice is trying over lessons she used to know:

'Let me see: four times five is twelve, and four times six is thirteen, and four times seven is—oh dear! I shall never get to twenty at that rate!' (p. 19)

Dodgson is having a good deal of fun with dullness (or, perhaps, dull readers). As Martin Gardner points out, this mathematical progression is *not* nonsense.

The multiplication table traditionally stops with the twelves, so if you continue this nonsense progression—4 times 5 is 12, 4 times 6 is 13, 4 times 7 is 14, and so on—you end with 4 times 12 (the highest she can go) is 19—just one short of 20.[60]

If this seems to a modern reader to take the books outside the range of children (that is, of what we suppose to be the

[59] Holbrook, *Nonsense Against Sorrow*, viii.
[60] Gardner, *Annotated Alice*, 23.

capabilities of twenty-first-century children), Dodgson would probably have disagreed. Thus he doesn't evade themes generally considered to be taboo for children's books: when Alice encounters the sleeping Red King in *Through the Looking-Glass*, she finds herself in a discussion with Tweedledum and Tweedledee of what is in effect Bishop Berkeley's view that we are all nothing but ideas in the mind of God. Alice, the pragmatist, dismisses the idea ('If I wasn't real . . . I shouldn't be able to cry', p. 168) but the question of who dreams who, and how dreams relate to death runs darkly through both books.

As in many fantasies, the worlds which Alice enters are not places of freedom or escape, but are full of other people's rules. Dodgson's fascination with the discipline inherent in games is clear throughout the books, and especially in *Through the Looking-Glass*. Although perhaps initially derived from real-life chess games with Alice Liddell and her siblings, Dodgson's version plays with the logic and validity of moves and turns. And Alice may say enthusiastically, 'It's a great huge game of chess that's being played—all over the world' (p. 144), but the story dwells rather more on the predetermination of moves, the lack of communication, and arbitrary fate.

Perhaps the most critical ink has been expended on the layer (alleged or actual) of social and political reference in the books. Early in *Alice's Adventures in Wonderland*, she encounters a huge, playful (or threatening) puppy. In Tenniel's drawing not only is the puppy an English Beagle (a heavier dog in the nineteenth century than now), but its face clearly resembles that of the young Charles Darwin. Alice, to avoid being trampled, 'dodges behind a great thistle'—and it so happens that there was a notable biologist at Christ Church—a non-Darwinian—with the singular name of William Turner Thistleton Dyer. The 'dodging' Dodgson was not a Darwinian, although he had nineteen volumes by Darwin and his critics in his library; in 1872, he read Darwin's *The Expression of Emotion in Man and Animals* and sent him one of his photographs, possibly offering to supply more, if needed. Had Dodgson, on another level from his pleasure in telling a story to a favourite child, also found in the

children's book (like many writers after him) a medium for
satire and criticism? For all his apparently circumscribed life,
Dodgson, as we have seen, was a polymath, and his wide interests
saturate the two 'Alice' books: as companions to Victorian
culture, from melodramatic novels to sentimental ditties, and
from matters of faith and doubt to matters of snobbery and
tyranny, they have few rivals. And had he also found a way of
discussing his own needs and obsessions? Victor Watson takes a
charitable view of this.

[Dodgson] . . . established new possibilities for children's books. He
showed how they could be made into an imaginative space for writing
about the dynamics that exist when adults and children engage with
one another—dynamics that might be complex, loving, intimate or
problematical, but were no longer just authoritarian. He demonstrated
how a children's story could become a celebratory utterance of
greeting, farewell, or longing. Since that time, many of the greatest
children's books have had about them a touch of the valedictory.[61]

Critics are generally agreed that Dodgson wrote himself into the
books—usually as misunderstood or sympathetic characters—
the Dodo, the Knave of Hearts, the Gnat, the Gryphon, the
excised ancient Wasp, and perhaps the sardonic Cheshire Cat.
But his private-public farewell to his 'dreamchild' is taken most
vividly in the scenes with the White Knight in *Through the
Looking-Glass*, who says to Alice: ' "I'll see you safe to the end of
the wood—and then I must go back, you know. That's the end
of my move." ' (p. 211). The Knight is easily seen as an ironic
self-portrait of a harmless, simple-minded man who invents
eccentric and unsuccessful things, who delivers a lecture on the
logic of language, sings a nonsense song to a sentimental tune,
and, of course, keeps on falling off his horse, 'generally . . . on
the side on which Alice was walking' (p. 214). The image that
Dodgson then creates, the image that Alice 'always remembered
most clearly', is a romantic, Pre-Raphaelite picture, and there is

[61] Victor Watson, 'The Possibilities of Children's Fiction', in Morag Styles, Eve
Bearne, and Victor Watson (eds.), *After Alice* (London: Cassell, 1992), 18.

a sharp and sad acknowledgement of the inevitability of loss. The Knight says, turning back,

'You'll wait and wave your handkerchief when I get to that turn in the road! I think it'll encourage me, you see.'

'Of course I'll wait,' said Alice: 'and thank you very much for coming so far—and for the song—I liked it very much.'

'I hope so,' the Knight said doubtfully: 'but you didn't cry as much as I thought you would.' (p. 222)

As J. M. Barrie wrote at the end of *Peter and Wendy* (1911) 'and thus it will go on, so long as children are gay and innocent and heartless'—but what is going on, although it may be steeped in an unfashionably Victorian sentimentality, is a complex statement of desire and loss.

The 'Alice' books, then, can be profitably read as proto-feminist, as modernist or postmodernist, as hugely experimental and eclectic, or as deeply conservative and egotistical. They crystallize the dilemmas of adult readers confronted with texts designed for childhood (whether or not that childhood is still recognizable), and they challenge assumptions about the nature of fantasy, and perhaps even the nature of fiction.

And where do they now stand in a century in which literary criticism has become an industry? As Dodgson's biographer Donald Thomas has pointed out:

The works of the Reverend Dodgson seem particularly hazardous to critics, whether the psychoanalytical school, so piteously hoaxed in the 1930s, or the later schools of critical theory and practice. Such diligent hunters of the seminar room, waddling along with nets and traps in the wake of the Cheshire Cat and its companions, are apt to take a picture which uncannily deconstructs itself, leaving only a grin for their contemplation.[62]

The books have certainly proved to be fruitful for more advanced theorists such as Karen Coats in *Looking Glasses and Neverlands:*

---

[62] Donald Thomas, *Lewis Carroll: A Portrait with Background* (London: John Murray, 1996), xi.

Lacan, Desire, and Subjectivity in Children's Literature,[63] or Alan Lopez, who, in an article 'Deleuze with Carroll: Schizophrenia and Simulacrum and the Philosophy of Lewis Carroll's Nonsense', suggests that 'a more productive examination of the question of a critical subject in Alice would occur in the context of the complex negotiations between the madness of nonsense and the epistemic and ontological doubt grounded in the simulacrum'.[64]

Increasingly, the 'Alice' books are taken in their historical context, from John Docherty's argument that Dodgson's books form a complex dialogue with George MacDonald's,[65] to Fred Inglis's view that 'the theory of education and childhood development which the Romantics put into circulation has Alice as its first, best triumph'.[66] Perhaps a little more arcanely, there has been research into where the books fit into 'the oral-literary continuum'—and it has been suggested that, if *Alice's Adventures in Wonderland* is tested against Antti Aarne and Stith Thompson's classic *The Types of the Folk-tale* (1961), then, morphologically, it has the sequence

$$\alpha\beta aBC\!\uparrow\!D\S E\S F\S G^{\clubsuit}\!\clubsuit D\S E\S F\S G^{\clubsuit}\!\clubsuit HIK\!\downarrow\!oMNQExTUW$$

and thus 'fulfils the criteria of one specific folktale, namely type AT 480 . . . Probably the best-known exponent of the type is "Mother Holle". . . in the second selection of *German Popular Stories* (1826).'[67] This is, one can't help feeling, the kind of research that would have delighted Charles Dodgson.

It has been said that children do not find the 'Alice' books as extraordinary as adults do, because they present an all-too-

[63] Karen Coats, *Looking Glasses and Neverlands: Lacan, Desire, and Subjectivity in Children's Literature* (Iowa City: University of Iowa Press, 2004).

[64] *Angelaki. Journal of the Theoretical Humanities*, 9/9 (Dec. 2004), 101–20, at 102.

[65] John Docherty, *The Literary Products of the Lewis Carroll–George MacDonald Friendship* (Lewiston: Mellen), 1995.

[66] Fred Inglis, *The Promise of Happiness* (Cambridge: Cambridge University Press, 1981), 108.

[67] Björn Sundmark, *Alice in the Oral-Literary Continuum* (Lund: Lund University Press, 1999), 58, 66.

familiar world to a child—a world of rude, aggressive adults, all playing complex, bewildering games. And even if Alice does, for a while, hold her own against them, in the end, it's only a dream. For adults, the books provide some uncomfortable images and pose uncomfortable questions—and challenge many accepted ideas about themselves and their children. That the books *were* for children—in a way that books had seldom been before—is unquestionable, and very important, because it means that adult readers are, as it were, listening in to a conversation not intended for them. Whether the books are *still* for children is a question really only of interest to those who mediate books for children. But all adult readers can do well to ponder W. H. Auden's observation: 'In assessing their value, there are two questions one can ask: first, what insight do they provide as to how the world appears to a child?; and the second, to what extent is the world really like that?'[68]

[68] W. H. Auden, 'Today's "Wonder-World" Needs Alice', in Phillips (ed.), *Aspects of Alice*, 37.

NOTE ON THE TEXT

DODGSON had made numerous small revisions, largely to the punctuation, of the text of *Alice's Adventures in Wonderland* in its various printings; *Through the Looking-Glass* was printed from electrotypes from the outset, and so the main text was not altered.

This text is printed from the revised editions of 1897, which contain Dodgson's final corrections and additions. He made these in copies of the 1882 edition of *Alice's Adventures in Wonderland* and the 1880 edition of *Through the Looking-Glass*, bound in one volume, which he borrowed from May Barber (later Mrs H. T. Stretton), one of his child-friends, whom he had first met at Eastbourne. (He had previously made many revisions to the 1887 'People's Edition.')

Details of the changes can be found in Selwyn H. Goodacre, 'The Textual Alterations for the 1897 6s Edition of *Alice's Adventures in Wonderland*', *Jabberwocky*, 51 (11/3) (Summer 1982), and Stanley Godman, 'Lewis Carroll's Final Corrections to "Alice"', *TLS*, 2 May 1958. Dodgson made more than four hundred changes, including standardizing contractions such as 'ca'n't'. At least two of these changes were not picked up by the printer, but have been made in this edition: p. 136.5 '*And hast*' becomes '*And, hast*'; p. 230.5 '*smooth*' becomes '*smoothe*'.

The page references for the chess game were wrong in the 1897 edition, which had been set up from the 1887 'People's Edition'.

The list of *Dramatis Personæ* was omitted from the 1897 and subsequent editions, but retained in reprints of the 'People's Edition'.

Advertisement [60th thousand]: this was a loose sheet inserted in the first edition of *Sylvie and Bruno Concluded* (1893).

This edition also includes:

'Christmas-Greetings [From a Fairy to a Child]', first published in *Phantasmagoria* (1869), reprinted separately 1884, and included in *Alice's Adventures under Ground* (1886), and in *Alice's Adventures in Wonderland* and *Through the Looking-Glass* from 1887.

'To All Child-Readers of "Alice's Adventures in Wonderland"', printed separately as a miniature pamphlet of four pages (4³/₁₆ × 2³/₄ in) in December 1871; it was inserted in the first edition of *Through the Looking-Glass*, and the 1872 edition of *Alice's Adventures in Wonderland*.

'An Easter Greeting to Every Child who Loves "Alice"' which had a similar format and was printed for Easter 1876 and inserted in copies of *The Hunting of the Snark*. It was reprinted in the People's Edition of *Through the Looking-Glass* in 1887 and the People's Edition of *Alice's Adventures in Wonderland*, *Alice's Adventures under Ground* (1886), and in *The Nursery Alice* (1890).

'The Wasp in a Wig', an episode cut from the galley-proofs of *Through the Looking-Glass*, and reproduced by permission of A. P. Watt Ltd on behalf of The Trustees of the C. L. Dodgson Estate.

SELECT BIBLIOGRAPHY

A GREAT deal of material is available on various 'Lewis Carroll' websites. A selection of the key print materials is given here. Authoritative articles on every aspect of Dodgson's work can be found in the journal of The Lewis Carroll Society, *Jabberwocky* (1969–97), renamed *The Carrollian* (1998–).

Works by Charles Dodgson/Lewis Carroll

Lewis Carroll, *The Annotated Alice: The Definitive Edition*, ed. Martin Gardner (New York: Norton, 2000; London: Penguin, 2001) [includes 'The Wasp in a Wig' episode].
—— *Alice's Adventures in Wonderland* and *Through the Looking-Glass*, ed. Hugh Haughton (London: Penguin, 1998) [includes *Alice's Adventures under Ground*].
—— *Alice in Wonderland*, ed. Donald J. Gray (1971; 2nd edn., New York: Norton, 1992) [includes *The Hunting of the Snark*].
—— *Alice's Adventures in Wonderland*, ed. Richard Kelly (Peterborough, Ontario: Broadview Press, 2000) [includes *Alice's Adventures under Ground, The Nursery Alice, Symbolic Logic*].
—— *Alice's Adventures under Ground* (facsimile), introd. Martin Gardner (New York: Dover, 1965); introd. Mary Jean St Clair (London: Pavilion/British Library, 1995).
—— *The Nursery Alice* (facsimile) (London: Macmillan, 1970); introd. Martin Gardner (New York: Dover, 1966).
—— *The Complete Illustrated Lewis Carroll* (New York: Nonesuch Press, 1939; London: Penguin, 1988; Ware: Wordsworth Classics, 1996).
—— *The Annotated Hunting of the Snark*, ed. Martin Gardner (Centenary edn.: New York: Norton, 2006).
Stuart Dodgson Collingwood (ed.), *The Lewis Carroll Picture Book* (London: T. Fisher Unwin, 1899; reissued as *Diversions and Digressions of Lewis Carroll*, New York: Dover, 1961; and as *The Unknown Lewis Carroll*, New York: Dover, n.d. [1961]).
C. L. Dodgson, *The Oxford Pamphlets, Leaflets and Circulars of Charles Lutwidge Dodgson*, ed. Edward Wakeling, The Pamphlets of Lewis

Carroll, vol. i (Charlottesville, Va.: University Press of Virginia for
the Lewis Carroll Society of North America, 1993).

—— *The Political Pamphlets and Letters of Lewis Carroll and Related
Pieces. A Mathematical Approach*, ed. Francine F. Abeles, The
Pamphlets of Lewis Carroll, vol. iii (Charlottesville, Va.: University
Press of Virginia for the Lewis Carroll Society of North America,
2002).

—— *The Rectory Umbrella* and *Mischmasch* (facsimile) (London:
Cassell, 1932; New York: Dover, 1971).

*Lewis Carroll's Diaries: The Private Journals of Charles Lutwidge
Dodgson*, ed. Edward Wakeling, 10 vols. (Luton: The Lewis Carroll
Society, 1993–2008).

The Letters of Lewis Carroll, ed. Morton N. Cohen with the assistance
of Roger Lancelyn Green, 2 vols. (London: Macmillan, 1979).

The Selected Letters of Lewis Carroll, ed. Morton N. Cohen (London
and Basingstoke: Macmillan, 1989/1996).

Biography

Michael Bakewell, *Lewis Carroll: A Biography* (London: Heinemann,
1996).

Morton N. Cohen, *Lewis Carroll: A Biography* (London and Basingstoke: Macmillan, 1995).

—— (ed.), *Lewis Carroll: Interviews and Recollections* (London:
Palgrave Macmillan; Iowa City: Iowa State University Press,
1989).

—— and Anita Gandolfo, *Lewis Carroll and the House of Macmillan*
(Cambridge: Cambridge University Press, 1987).

—— and Edward Wakeling, *Lewis Carroll and His Illustrators:
Collaborations and Correspondence, 1865–1898* (New York: Cornell
University Press; London: Macmillan, 2003).

Stuart Dodgson Collingwood, *The Life and Letters of Lewis Carroll
(Rev. C. L. Dodgson)* (London: T. Fisher Unwin, 1899).

Derek Hudson, *Lewis Carroll: An Illustrated Biography* (1954; rev.
edn., London: Constable, 1976).

Karoline Leach, *In the Shadow of the Dreamchild: A New Understanding
of Lewis Carroll* (London: Peter Owen, 1999; 2nd edn. as *In the
Shadow of the Dreamchild: The Myth and Reality of Lewis Carroll*,
2008).

Roger Taylor and Edward Wakeling, *Lewis Carroll, Photographer*
(Princeton: Princeton University Press, 2002).

Donald Thomas, *Lewis Carroll: A Portrait with Background* (London: John Murray, 1996).

Robin Wilson, *Lewis Carroll in Numberland: His Fantastical Mathematical Logical Life* (London: Allen Lane, 2008).

Jenny Woolf, *Lewis Carroll in His Own Account: The Complete Bank Account of the Rev. C. L. Dodgson* (London, Jabberwock Press, 2005).

Contexts

Mavis Batey, *The World of Alice* (Norwich: Pitkin, 1998).

Will Brooker, *Alice's Adventures: Lewis Carroll in Popular Culture* (New York: Continuum, 2004).

Michael Hancher, *The Tenniel Illustrations to the 'Alice' Books* (Columbus, Ohio: Ohio State University Press, 1986).

Jo Elwyn Jones and J. Francis Gladstone, *The Alice Companion* (Basingstoke: Macmillan, 1998).

————— *The Red King's Dream or Lewis Carroll in Wonderland* (London: Cape, 1995).

Charlie Lovett, *Lewis Carroll's England* (London: White Stone Publishing/The Lewis Carroll Society, 1998).

Carolyn Sigler (ed.), *Alternative Alices: Visions and Revisions of Lewis Carroll's Alice Books* (Lexington, Ky.: The University Press of Kentucky, 1997).

Stephanie Lovett Stoffel, *Lewis Carroll and Alice* (London: Thames and Hudson, 1997).

Bryan Talbot, *Alice in Sunderland* (London: Cape, 2007).

Bibliography

Rachel Fordyce, *Lewis Carroll: A Reference Guide* (Boston: G. K. Hall, 1988).

Edward Guiliano, *Lewis Carroll: An Annotated International Bibliography, 1960–1977* (Charlottesville, Va.: University Press of Virginia, 1980; Brighton: Harvester, 1981).

Charles C. Lovett, *Lewis Carroll and the Press: An Annotated Bibliography of Charles Dodgson's Contributions to Periodicals* (New Castle, Dela.: Oak Knoll Press; London: British Library, 1999).

S. H. Williams, Falconer Madan, Roger Lancelyn Green, and Denis Crutch, *The Lewis Carroll Handbook* (1931; 4th edn., Folkstone: Dawson Archon Books, 1979).

Criticism

Rachel Fordyce (ed.), *Semiotics and Linguistics in Alice's Worlds* (Berlin: de Gruyter, 1994).

Edward Guiliano (ed.), *Lewis Carroll: A Celebration* (New York: Clarkson N. Potter, 1981).

Robert Phillips (ed.), *Aspects of Alice: Lewis Carroll's Dreamchild as Seen Through the Critics' Looking-Glasses 1865–1971* (London: Gollancz, 1972; Harmondsworth: Penguin, 1974).

Donald Rackin, *Alice's Adventures in Wonderland* and *Through the Looking-Glass: Nonsense, Sense and Meaning* (New York: Twayne, 1991).

Ronald Reichertz, *The Making of the Alice Books: Lewis Carroll's Uses of Earlier Children's Literature* (Montreal: McGill-Queen's University Press, 1997).

Chapters on Dodgson and the 'Alice' Books

Gillian Avery and Julia Briggs (eds.), *Children and Their Books* (Oxford: Clarendon Press, 1989).

Humphrey Carpenter, *Secret Gardens* (1985; London: Unwin, 1987).

Karen Coats, *Looking Glasses and Neverlands: Lacan, Desire, and Subjectivity in Children's Literature* (Iowa City: University of Iowa Press, 2004).

Juliet Dusinberre, *Alice to the Lighthouse: Children's Books and Radical Experiments in Art* (London: Macmillan Press, 1987).

John Goldthwaite, *The Natural History of Make-Believe* (New York: Oxford University Press, 1996).

Roderick McGillis, *The Nimble Reader* (New York: Twayne, 1996).

Elizabeth Sewell, *The Field of Nonsense* (London: Chatto and Windus, 1952).

Deborah Cogan Thacker and Jean Webb, *Introducing Children's Literature: From Romanticism to Postmodernism* (London: Routledge, 2002).

Articles

Jennifer Geer, ' "All Sorts of Pitfalls and Surprises": Competing Views of Idealized Girlhood in Lewis Carroll's *Alice* Books', *Children's Literature*, 31 (2003), 1–24.

Cecily Raysor Hancock, 'Musical Notes to *The Annotated Alice*', *Children's Literature*, 16 (1988), 1–30.

Michael Holquist, 'What is a Boojum? Nonsense and Modernism', *Yale French Studies*, 43 (1969), 145–64.

U. C. Knoepflmacher, 'Avenging Alice: Christina Rossetti and Lewis Carroll', *Nineteenth Century Literature*, 41/1 (1986), 299–328.

Carolyn Sigler, 'Authorizing Alice: Professional Authority, the Literary Marketplace, and Victorian Women's Re-Visions of the *Alice* Books', *The Lion and the Unicorn*, 22 (1998), 351–63.

A CHRONOLOGY OF
C. L. DODGSON/'LEWIS CARROLL'

1827   The Revd Charles Dodgson marries Frances Jane Lutwidge, and is presented to the living of Daresbury, Cheshire.

1832   (27 Jan.) Charles Lutwidge Dodgson, third child and first son, born at Daresbury Parsonage.

1839   Catherine Sinclair, *Holiday House*.

1843   Family moves to Croft, near Richmond, Yorkshire; father becomes Rector.

1844–5 Attends Richmond School.

1845   Composes first 'family magazine', *Useful and Instructive Poetry* (published 1954).

1846   Edward Lear, *A Book of Nonsense*.

1846   Attends Rugby School.

1848   Heinrich Hoffman, *The English Struwwelpeter*.

1849   Returns to Croft to prepare for Oxford; has mumps, which leave him permanently deaf in his right ear; writes *The Rectory Umbrella* (to 1850).

1851   (24 Jan.) Comes into Residence at Christ Church, Oxford; death of his mother. John Ruskin, *King of the Golden River*

1852   1st Class in Mathematical and 2nd in Classical Moderations; nominated by Dr Pusey to a studentship.

1854   1st Class in Mathematics (Final Schools); spends summer being coached by Bartholomew Price at Whitby for his mathematics examination; first publications, in *The Whitby Gazette*; BA; epidemic of cholera at Oxford.

1855   (1 Jan.) Begins diary; (8 Sept.) 'She's All My Fancy Painted Him' (first version of poem in *Alice's Adventures in Wonderland*, chapter 12) published in *Comic Times*; made 'A Master of the House' and Senior Student; 'Stanza of Anglo-Saxon Poetry' (first stanza of 'Jabberwocky') written in family

magazine, *Mischmasch*; Henry George Liddell appointed
Dean of Christ Church. W. M. Thackeray, *The Rose and the
Ring*.

1855–7 Sub-librarian at Christ Church (salary £35).

1855–81 Lecturer in Mathematics at Christ Church.

1856 (Mar.) First uses pseudonym 'Lewis Carroll' to poem
'Solitude' in *The Train* (i. 154–5); (18 Mar.) buys first camera,
made by Thomas Ottewill for £15 (delivered 1 May); (25 Apr.)
meets Lorina, Alice, and Edith Liddell.

1857 Takes MA; (May) meets Thackeray; (June) meets Holman
Hunt; (Sept.) meets Tennyson; (Oct.) meets Ruskin; (Dec.)
'Hiawatha's Photographing' published in *The Train*.

1858 Publication of his first book: *The Fifth Book of Euclid treated
Algebraically*, 'By a College Tutor'. George MacDonald's
Phantastes.

1859 Begins therapy for his 'stammer' with Dr James Hunt at
Hastings; meets George MacDonald.

1860 Publication of his first acknowledged book, *A Syllabus of
Plane Algebraical Geometry*, 'by Charles Lutwidge Dodgson';
publishes 'A Photographer's Day Out' in the *South Shields
Amateur Magazine*.

1861 (22 Dec.) Admitted to Deacon's Orders ('regard myself . . . as
practically a layman') by Samuel Wilberforce, Bishop of
Oxford.

1862 River trips with Liddell sisters: genesis of *Alice's Adventures in
Wonderland*; (13 Nov.) begins writing. Christina Rossetti,
Goblin Market.

1863 (10 Feb.) Completes *Alice's Adventures under Ground*; (May)
sends MS of *Alice's Adventures in Wonderland* to the Mac-
Donalds; (June) estrangement from Liddell family; (Sept.)
first visits Dante Gabriel Rossetti at Cheyne Walk, Chelsea;
(Oct.) meets Alexander Macmillan; John Tenniel agrees to
illustrate the book. Charles Kingsley's *The Water Babies*.

1864 (26 Nov.) Sends hand-lettered copy of *Alice's Adventures
under Ground* to Alice Liddell.

1865 (27 June) Receives first copies of *Alice's Adventures in Wonderland*; (14 July) photographs Ellen Terry; (2 Aug.) orders
reprint of *Alice*; (14 Dec.) sends copy to Alice Liddell.

1866   (June) Meets Charlotte M. Yonge.

1867   (12 July–14 Sept.) Travels with Henry Parry Litton to Moscow (his only trip abroad); (Dec.) publishes 'Bruno's Revenge' in *Aunt Judy's Magazine*, iv; Electoral Reform Act. 'Hesba Stretton', *Jessica's First Prayer*.

1868   (21 June) Death of his father: 'the greatest blow that has ever fallen on my life'; moves into rooms on Tom quad, which he occupies for the rest of his life; leases 'The Chestnuts', Guildford; begins *Through the Looking-Glass*. Louisa May Alcott, *Little Women*.

1869   (Jan.) Publication of *Phantasmagoria, and Other Poems*; (12 Jan.) 'Finished and sent to Macmillan the first chapter of *Behind the Looking-Glass, and What Alice Saw There*'; first German and French translations of *Alice's Adventures in Wonderland*. Jean Ingelow, *Mopsa the Fairy*.

1870   (4 Jan.) 'Finished the MS of *Through the Looking-Glass*'.

1871   (Dec.) *Through the Looking-Glass* published (9,000 copies, dated 1872).

1872   First Italian translation of *Alice's Adventures in Wonderland*; *The New Belfry of Christ Church, Oxford*.

1874   First Dutch translation of *Alice's Adventures in Wonderland*; publication of *Notes by an Oxford Chiel*. Christina Rossetti, *Speaking Likenesses*.

1875   (June) 'Some Popular Fallacies about Vivisection', *Fortnightly Review*. Tom Hood, *From Nowhere to the North Pole*.

1876   (29 Mar.) Publication of *The Hunting of the Snark*.

1877   (31 July) Takes rooms at 27 Lushington Road, Eastbourne, for the summer; he returns to them each summer for the rest of his life.

1878   45th thousand of *Through the Looking-Glass*.

1879   (Mar.) Publication of *Euclid and his Modern Rivals*; *Doublets, a Word Puzzle*.

1880   (July) Gives up photography; marriage of Alice Liddell to Reginald Hargreaves; begins *A Tangled Tale* in *The Monthly Packet*.

1882–92 Curator of Christ Church Common Room.

1882   Richard Jefferies, *Bevis*.

1883   (6 Dec.) Publication of *Rhyme? and Reason?* Robert Louis Stevenson, *Treasure Island*.

1884   (Nov.) *The Principles of Parliamentary Representation*.

1885   Criminal Law Amendment Act raises age of consent to 16; (22 Dec.) publication of *A Tangled Tale*.

1886   (22 Dec.) Publication of *Alice's Adventures under Ground*; (23 Dec.) first night of Henry Savile Clarke's 'Dream Play', *Alice in Wonderland* (Prince of Wales Theatre; the play was published in early 1887—dated 1886). Frances Hodgson Burnett, *Little Lord Fauntleroy*.

1887   (21 Feb.) Publication of *The Game of Logic* (an edition printed in 1886 was cancelled and sold to America).

1888   *Curiosa Mathematica: A New Theory of Parallels*.

1889   (12 Dec.) Publication of *Sylvie and Bruno*. Andrew Lang, *The Blue Fairy Book*.

1890   Publication of *The Nursery Alice, Eight or Nine Wise Words about Letter-Writing*, and (July) the *Wonderland Stamp Case*.

1893   (29 Dec.) Publication of *Sylvie and Bruno Concluded*; *Pillow Problems (Curiosa Mathematica II)*.

1894   Rudyard Kipling, *The Jungle Book*.

1895   G. E. Farrow, *The Wallypug of Why*; Kenneth Grahame, *The Golden Age*.

1896   (21 Feb.) Publication of *Symbolic Logic, Part 1*.

1898   (14 Jan.) Dies at 'The Chestnuts', Guildford; (Feb.) publication of *Three Sunsets and Other Poems*; (Dec.) *The Life and Letters of Lewis Carroll* (dated 1899).

ALICE'S ADVENTURES
IN WONDERLAND

All in the golden afternoon
    Full leisurely we glide;
For both our oars, with little skill,
    By little arms are plied,
While little hands make vain pretence
    Our wanderings to guide.

Ah, cruel Three! In such an hour,
    Beneath such dreamy weather,
To beg a tale of breath too weak
    To stir the tiniest feather!
Yet what can one poor voice avail
    Against three tongues together?

Imperious Prima flashes forth
    Her edict 'to begin it':
In gentler tones Secunda hopes
    'There will be nonsense in it!'
While Tertia* interrupts the tale
    Not *more* than once a minute.

Anon, to sudden silence won,
    In fancy they pursue
The dream-child moving through a land
    Of wonders wild and new,
In friendly chat with bird or beast—
    And half believe it true.

And ever, as the story drained
    The wells of fancy dry,
And faintly strove that weary one
    To put the subject by,
'The rest next time—' 'It *is* next time!'
    The happy voices cry.

Thus grew the tale of Wonderland:
　　Thus slowly, one by one,
Its quaint events were hammered out—
　　And now the tale is done,
And home we steer, a merry crew,
　　Beneath the setting sun.

Alice! A childish story take,
　　And, with a gentle hand,
Lay it where Childhood's dreams are twined
　　In Memory's mystic band,
Like pilgrim's wither'd wreath of flowers
　　Pluck'd in a far-off land.

PREFACE TO THE
SEVENTY-NINTH THOUSAND

As Alice is about to appear on the Stage,* and as the lines beginning: ' 'Tis the voice of the Lobster' were found to be too fragmentary for dramatic purposes four lines have been added to the first stanza and six to the second, while the Oyster has been developed into a Panther.

Christmas, 1886

PREFACE TO THE
EIGHTY-SIXTH THOUSAND
OF THE 6/- EDITION

ENQUIRIES have been so often addressed to me, as to whether any answer to the Hatter's Riddle (see p. 60) can be imagined, that I may as well put on record here what seems to me to be a fairly appropriate answer, viz. 'Because it can produce a few notes, though they are *very* flat; and it is never put with the wrong end in front!' This, however, is merely an afterthought: the Riddle, as originally invented, had no answer at all.

For this eighty-sixth thousand, fresh electrotypes have been taken from the wood-blocks (which, never having been used for printing from, are in as good condition as when first cut in 1865), and the whole book has been set up afresh with new type. If the artistic qualities of this re-issue fall short, in any particular, of those possessed by the original issue, it will not be for want of painstaking on the part of author, publisher, or printer.

I take this opportunity of announcing that the Nursery 'Alice,'* hitherto priced at four shillings, net, is now to be had on the same terms as the ordinary shilling picture-books—although I feel sure that it is, in every quality (except the *text* itself, on which I am not qualified to pronounce), greatly superior to them. Four shillings was a perfectly reasonable price to charge, considering the very heavy initial outlay I had incurred: still, as the Public have practically said 'We will *not* give more than a shilling for a picture-book, however artistically got-up', I am content to reckon my outlay on the book as so much dead loss, and, rather than let the little ones, for whom it was written, go without it, I am selling it at a price which is, to me, much the same thing as *giving* it away.

Christmas, 1896

CONTENTS

Exposes the sheer chaos
of the Victorian mind and
literature at times

✳ fixation on child's perspective
and consciousness especially
in its teaching of lessons

Victorian Child
- extremely orderly
- pure soul from heaven
  and God as put into
  body at birth
- corrupted by society
  and the world which
  clouds soul from the
  divine

Destabilizing heirarchy of
Victorian order via interaction
of humans and animals

Caroll frames the story
in a unthreatening way ⟩ via growing up
for children/readers
through Alice's composure
and calmness in these
situations

CHAPTER I

DOWN THE RABBIT-HOLE

Amazing interplay of words & images

Notes how integral this is

ALICE was beginning to get very tired of sitting by her sister on the bank, and of having nothing to do: once or twice she had peeped into the book her sister was reading, but it had no pictures or conversations in it, 'and what is the use of a book,' thought Alice, 'without pictures or conversations?'

So she was considering, in her own mind (as well as she could, for the hot day made her feel very sleepy and stupid), whether the pleasure of making a daisy-chain would be worth the trouble of getting up and picking the daisies, when suddenly a White Rabbit* with pink eyes ran close by her.

All of this chaos emerging from within Alice.

There was nothing so *very* remarkable in that; nor did Alice think it so *very* much out of the way to hear the Rabbit say to itself 'Oh dear! Oh dear! I shall be too late!' (when she thought it over afterwards, it occurred to her that she ought to have wondered at this, but at the time it all seemed quite natural); but, when the Rabbit actually *took a watch out of its waistcoat-pocket*, and looked at it, and then hurried on, Alice started to her feet, for it flashed across her mind that she had never before seen a rabbit with either a waistcoat-pocket, or a watch to take out of it, and, burning with curiosity, she ran across the field after it, and was just in time to see it pop down a large rabbit-hole under the hedge.

In another moment down went Alice after it, never once considering how in the world she was to get out again.

The rabbit-hole went straight on like a tunnel for some way, and then dipped suddenly down, so suddenly that Alice had not a moment to think about stopping herself before she found herself falling down what seemed to be a very deep well.

Either the well was very deep, or she fell very slowly, for she had plenty of time as she went down to look about her, and to wonder what was going to happen next. First, she tried to look down and make out what she was coming to, but it was too dark to see anything: then she looked at the sides of the well, and noticed that they were filled with cupboards and book-shelves: here and there she saw maps and pictures hung upon pegs. She took down a jar from one of the shelves as she passed: it was labeled 'ORANGE MARMALADE,'* but to her great disappointment it was empty: she did not like to drop the jar, for fear of killing somebody underneath, so managed to put it into one of the cupboards as she fell past it.

'Well!' thought Alice to herself. 'After such a fall as this, I shall think nothing of tumbling down-stairs! How brave they'll all think me at home! Why, I wouldn't say anything about it, even if I fell off the top of the house!'* (Which was very likely true.)

Down, down, down. Would the fall *never* come to an end? 'I wonder how many miles I've fallen by this time?' she said aloud. 'I must be getting somewhere near the centre of the earth. Let me see: that would be four thousand miles down, I think—' (for, you see, Alice had learnt several things of this

sort in her lessons in the school-room, and though this was
not a *very* good opportunity for showing off her knowledge,
as there was no one to listen to her, still it was good practice to
say it over) '—yes, that's about the right distance—but then
I wonder what Latitude or Longitude I've got to?' (Alice had
not the slightest idea what Latitude was, or Longitude either,
but she thought they were nice grand words to say.)

(margin note: focus on education)

Presently she began again. 'I wonder if I shall fall right
through the earth!* How funny it'll seem to come out among the
people that walk with their heads downwards! The antipathies,
I think—' (she was rather glad there *was* no one listening, this
time, as it didn't sound at all the right word) '—but I shall
have to ask them what the name of the country is, you know.
Please, Ma'am, is this New Zealand? Or Australia?' (and she
tried to curtsey as she spoke—fancy, *curtseying* as you're falling through the air! Do you think you could manage it?) 'And
what an ignorant little girl she'll think me for asking! No, it'll
never do to ask: perhaps I shall see it written up somewhere.'

Down, down, down. There was nothing else to do, so Alice
soon began talking again. 'Dinah'll miss me very much to-night,
I should think!' (Dinah* was the cat.) 'I hope they'll remember
her saucer of milk at tea-time. Dinah, my dear! I wish you
were down here with me! There are no mice in the air, I'm
afraid, but you might catch a bat, and that's very like a mouse,
you know. But do cats eat bats, I wonder?' And here Alice
began to get rather sleepy, and went on saying to herself, in
a dreamy sort of way, 'Do cats eat bats? Do cats eat bats?'
and sometimes 'Do bats eat cats?', for, you see, as she couldn't
answer either question, it didn't much matter which way she
put it. She felt that she was dozing off, and had just begun to
dream that she was walking hand in hand with Dinah, and was
saying to her, very earnestly, 'Now, Dinah, tell me the truth:
did you ever eat a bat?', when suddenly, thump! thump!
down she came upon a heap of sticks and dry leaves, and the
fall was over. *(margin note: Interchangeable relationship)*

Alice was not a bit hurt, and she jumped up on to her feet
in a moment: she looked up, but it was all dark overhead:

(left margin note: preoccupation w/ food chains)

before her was another long passage, and the White Rabbit
was still in sight, hurrying down it. There was not a moment
to be lost: away went Alice like the wind, and was just in time
to hear it say, as it turned a corner, 'Oh my ears and whiskers,
how late it's getting!' She was close behind it when she turned
the corner, but the Rabbit was no longer to be seen: she found
herself in a long, low hall, which was lit up by a row of lamps
hanging from the roof.

There were doors all round the hall, but they were all locked;
and when Alice had been all the way down one side and up the
other, trying every door, she walked sadly down the middle,
wondering how she was ever to get out again.

Suddenly she came upon a little three-legged table, all made
of solid glass: there was nothing on it but a tiny golden key,*
and Alice's first idea was that this might belong to one of the
doors of the hall; but, alas! either the locks were too large, or
the key was too small, but at any rate it would not open any of
them. However, on the second time round, she came upon
a low curtain she had not noticed before, and behind it was
a little door about fifteen inches high: she tried the little
golden key in the lock, and to her great delight it fitted!

Alice opened the door and found that it led into a small passage, not much larger than a rat-hole: she knelt down and looked along the passage into the loveliest garden you ever saw. How she longed to get out of that dark hall, and wander about among those beds of bright flowers and those cool fountains, but she could not even get her head through the doorway;* 'and even if my head *would* go through,' thought poor Alice, 'it would be of very little use without my shoulders. Oh, how I wish I could shut up like a telescope! I think I could, if I only knew how to begin.' For, you see, so many out-of-the-way things had happened lately, that Alice had begun to think that very few things indeed were really impossible.

There seemed to be no use in waiting by the little door, so she went back to the table, half hoping she might find another key on it, or at any rate a book of rules for shutting people up like telescopes: this time she found a little bottle on it ('which certainly was not here before,' said Alice), and tied round the neck of the bottle was a paper label, with the words 'DRINK ME' beautifully printed on it in large letters.

It was all very well to say 'Drink me,' but the wise little Alice was not going to do *that* in a hurry. 'No, I'll look first,' she said, 'and see whether it's marked "*poison*" or not'; for she had read several nice little stories about children who had got burnt, and eaten up by wild beasts, and other unpleasant things, all because they *would* not remember the simple rules their friends had taught them: such as, that a red-hot poker will burn you if you hold it too long; and that, if you cut your finger *very* deeply with a knife, it usually bleeds; and she had never forgotten that, if you drink much from a bottle marked 'poison,' it is almost certain to disagree with you, sooner or later.

However, this bottle was *not* marked 'poison,' so Alice ventured to taste it, and, finding it very nice (it had, in fact, a sort of mixed flavour of cherry-tart, custard, pine-apple, roast turkey, toffy, and hot buttered toast), she very soon finished it off.

*   *   *   *

*   *   *

*   *   *   *

'What a curious feeling!' said Alice. 'I must be shutting up like a telescope!'

And so it was indeed: she was now only ten inches high, and her face brightened up at the thought that she was now the right size for going through the little door into that lovely garden. First, however, she waited for a few minutes to see if she was going to shrink any further: she felt a little nervous about this; 'for it might end, you know,' said Alice to herself, 'in my going out altogether, like a candle. I wonder what I should be like then?' And she tried to fancy what the flame of a candle looks like after the candle is blown out, for she could not remember ever having seen such a thing.

After a while, finding that nothing more happened, she decided on going into the garden at once; but, alas for poor Alice! when she got to the door, she found she had forgotten the little golden key, and when she went back to the table for it, she found she could not possibly reach it: she could see it quite plainly through the glass, and she tried her best to climb up one of the legs of the table, but it was too slippery; and when she had tired herself out with trying, the poor little thing sat down and cried.

'Come, there's no use in crying like that!' said Alice to herself rather sharply. 'I advise you to leave off this minute!' She generally gave herself very good advice (though she very seldom followed it), and sometimes she scolded herself so severely as to bring tears into her eyes; and once she remembered trying to box her own ears for having cheated herself in a game of croquet she was playing against herself, for this curious child was very fond of pretending to be two people. 'But it's no use now,' thought poor Alice, 'to pretend to be two people! Why, there's hardly enough of me left to make *one* respectable person.'

Soon her eye fell on a little glass box that was lying under the table: she opened it, and found in it a very small cake, on which the words 'EAT ME'* were beautifully marked in currants. 'Well, I'll eat it,' said Alice, 'and if it makes me grow larger, I can reach the key; and if it makes me grow smaller, I can creep under the door: so either way I'll get into the garden, and I don't care which happens!'

She ate a little bit, and said anxiously to herself 'Which way? Which way?', holding her hand on the top of her head to feel which way it was growing; and she was quite surprised to find that she remained the same size. To be sure, this is what generally happens when one eats cake; but Alice had got so much into the way of expecting nothing but out-of-the-way things to happen, that it seemed quite dull and stupid for life to go on in the common way.

So she set to work, and very soon finished off the cake.

    *   *   *   *

        *   *   *

    *   *   *   *

CHAPTER II

THE POOL OF TEARS

'CURIOUSER and curiouser!' cried Alice (she was so much surprised, that for the moment she quite forgot how to speak good English). 'Now I'm opening out like the largest telescope that ever was! Good-bye, feet!' (for when she looked down at her feet, they seemed to be almost out of sight, they were getting so far off). 'Oh, my poor little feet, I wonder who will put on your shoes and stockings for you now, dears? I'm sure *I* sha'n't be able! I shall be a great deal too far off to trouble myself about you: you must manage the best way you can—but I must be kind to them,' thought Alice, 'or perhaps they wo'n't walk the way I want to go! Let me see. I'll give them a new pair of boots every Christmas.'

And she went on planning to herself how she would manage it. 'They must go by the carrier,' she thought; 'and how funny it'll seem, sending presents to one's own feet! And how odd the directions will look!

Alice's Right Foot, Esq.
Hearthrug,
near the Fender,
(with Alice's love).

Oh dear, what nonsense I'm talking!'

Just at this moment her head struck against the roof of the hall: in fact she was now rather more than nine feet high, and she at once took up the little golden key and hurried off to the garden door.

Poor Alice! It was as much as she could do, lying down on one side, to look through into the garden with one eye; but to get through was more hopeless than ever: she sat down and began to cry again.

'You ought to be ashamed of yourself,' said Alice, 'a great girl like you,' (she might well say this), 'to go on crying in this way! Stop this moment, I tell you!' But she went on all the same, shedding gallons of tears, until there was a large pool all round her, about four inches deep, and reaching half down the hall.

After a time she heard a little pattering of feet in the distance, and she hastily dried her eyes to see what was coming. It was the White Rabbit returning, splendidly dressed, with a pair of white kid-gloves in one hand and a large fan* in the other: he came trotting along in a great hurry, muttering to himself, as he came, 'Oh! The Duchess, the Duchess! Oh! *Wo'n't* she be savage if I've kept her waiting!' Alice felt so desperate that she was ready to ask help of any one: so, when the Rabbit came near her, she began, in a low, timid voice, 'If you please, Sir——' The Rabbit started violently, dropped the white kid-gloves and the fan, and skurried away into the darkness as hard as he could go.

Alice took up the fan and gloves, and, as the hall was very hot, she kept fanning herself all the time she went on talking. 'Dear, dear! How queer everything is to-day! And yesterday

things went on just as usual. I wonder if I've been changed in the night? Let me think: *was* I the same when I got up this morning? I almost think I can remember feeling a little different. But if I'm not the same, the next question is "Who in the world am I?" Ah, *that's* the great puzzle!' And she began thinking over all the children she knew that were of the same age as herself, to see if she could have been changed for any of them.

'I'm sure I'm not Ada,' she said, 'for her hair goes in such long ringlets, and mine doesn't go in ringlets at all; and I'm sure I ca'n't be Mabel,* for I know all sorts of things, and she, oh, she knows such a very little! Besides, *she's* she, and *I'm* I,

and—oh dear, how puzzling it all is! I'll try if I know all the
things I used to know. Let me see: four times five is twelve,
and four times six is thirteen, and four times seven is—oh
dear! I shall never get to twenty at that rate!* However, the
Multiplication-Table doesn't signify: let's try Geography.
London is the capital of Paris, and Paris is the capital of Rome,
and Rome—no, *that's* all wrong, I'm certain! I must have been
changed for Mabel! I'll try and say "*How doth the little—*",'
and she crossed her hands on her lap, as if she were saying
lessons, and began to repeat it, but her voice sounded hoarse
and strange, and the words did not come the same as they
used to do:—

> '*How doth the little crocodile**
> *Improve his shining tail,*
> *And pour the waters of the Nile*
> *On every golden scale!*
>
> '*How cheerfully he seems to grin,*
> *How neatly spreads his claws,*
> *And welcomes little fishes in,*
> *With gently smiling jaws!*'

'I'm sure those are not the right words,' said poor Alice,
and her eyes filled with tears again as she went on, 'I must be
Mabel after all, and I shall have to go and live in that poky
little house, and have next to no toys to play with, and oh,
ever so many lessons to learn! No, I've made up my mind
about it: if I'm Mabel, I'll stay down here! It'll be no use their
putting their heads down and saying "Come up again, dear!"
I shall only look up and say "Who am I, then? Tell me that
first, and then, if I like being that person, I'll come up: if not,
I'll stay down here till I'm somebody else"—but, oh dear!'
cried Alice, with a sudden burst of tears, 'I do wish they
would put their heads down! I am so *very* tired of being all
alone here!'

As she said this she looked down at her hands, and was
surprised to see that she had put on one of the Rabbit's little

white kid-gloves while she was talking. 'How *can* I have done that?' she thought. 'I must be growing small again.' She got up and went to the table to measure herself by it, and found that, as nearly as she could guess, she was now about two feet high, and was going on shrinking rapidly: she soon found out that the cause of this was the fan* she was holding, and she dropped it hastily, just in time to save herself from shrinking away altogether.

'That *was* a narrow escape!' said Alice, a good deal frightened at the sudden change, but very glad to find herself still in existence. 'And now for the garden!' And she ran with all speed back to the little door; but, alas! the little door was shut again, and the little golden key was lying on the glass table as before, 'and things are worse than ever,' thought the poor child, 'for I never was so small as this before, never! And I declare it's too bad, that it is!'

As she said these words her foot slipped, and in another moment, splash! she was up to her chin in salt-water. Her first

idea was that she had somehow fallen into the sea, 'and in that case* I can go back by railway,' she said to herself. (Alice had been to the seaside once in her life,* and had come to the general conclusion that, wherever you go to on the English coast, you find a number of bathing-machines* in the sea, some children digging in the sand with wooden spades, then a row of lodging-houses, and behind them a railway-station.) However, she soon made out that she was in the pool of tears which she had wept when she was nine feet high.

'I wish I hadn't cried so much!' said Alice, as she swam about, trying to find her way out. 'I shall be punished for it now, I suppose, by being drowned in my own tears! That *will* be a queer thing, to be sure! However, everything is queer to-day.'

Just then she heard something splashing about in the pool a little way off, and she swam nearer to make out what it was: at first she thought it must be a walrus or hippopotamus, but then she remembered how small she was now, and she soon made out that it was only a mouse,* that had slipped in like herself.

'Would it be of any use, now,' thought Alice, 'to speak to this mouse? Everything is so out-of-the-way down here, that I should think very likely it can talk: at any rate, there's no harm in trying.' So she began: 'O Mouse, do you know the way out of this pool? I am very tired of swimming about here, O Mouse!' (Alice thought this must be the right way of speaking to a mouse: she had never done such a thing before, but she remembered having seen, in her brother's* Latin Grammar,* 'A mouse—of a mouse—to a mouse—a mouse—O mouse!')* The mouse looked at her rather inquisitively, and seemed to her to wink with one of its little eyes, but it said nothing.

'Perhaps it doesn't understand English,' thought Alice. 'I daresay it's a French mouse, come over with William the Conqueror.' (For, with all her knowledge of history, Alice had no very clear notion how long ago anything had happened.) So she began again: 'Où est ma chatte?', which was the first sentence in her French lesson-book.* The Mouse gave a sudden leap out of the water, and seemed to quiver all over with fright. 'Oh, I beg your pardon!' cried Alice hastily, afraid that she had hurt the poor animal's feelings. 'I quite forgot you didn't like cats.'

'Not like cats!' cried the Mouse in a shrill, passionate voice. 'Would *you* like cats, if you were me?'

'Well, perhaps not,' said Alice in a soothing tone: 'don't be angry about it. And yet I wish I could show you our cat Dinah.* I think you'd take a fancy to cats, if you could only see her. She is such a dear quiet thing,' Alice went on, half to herself, as she swam lazily about in the pool, 'and she sits purring so

nicely by the fire, licking her paws and washing her face—and she is such a nice soft thing to nurse—and she's such a capital one for catching mice——oh, I beg your pardon!' cried Alice again, for this time the Mouse was bristling all over, and she felt certain it must be really offended. 'We wo'n't talk about her any more, if you'd rather not.'

'We, indeed!' cried the Mouse, who was trembling down to the end of its tail. 'As if *I* would talk on such a subject! Our family always *hated* cats: nasty, low, vulgar things! Don't let me hear the name again!'

'I wo'n't indeed!' said Alice, in a great hurry to change the subject of conversation. 'Are you—are you fond—of—of dogs?' The Mouse did not answer, so Alice went on eagerly: 'There is such a nice little dog, near our house, I should like to show you! A little bright-eyed terrier, you know, with oh, such long curly brown hair! And it'll fetch things when you throw them, and it'll sit up and beg for its dinner, and all sorts of things—I ca'n't remember half of them—and it belongs to a farmer, you know, and he says it's so useful, it's worth a hundred pounds! He says it kills all the rats and—oh dear!' cried Alice in a sorrowful tone. 'I'm afraid I've offended it again!' For the Mouse was swimming away from her as hard as it could go, and making quite a commotion in the pool as it went.

So she called softly after it, 'Mouse dear! Do come back again, and we wo'n't talk about cats, or dogs either, if you don't like them!' When the Mouse heard this, it turned round and swam slowly back to her: its face was quite pale (with passion, Alice thought), and it said, in a low trembling voice, 'Let us get to the shore, and then I'll tell you my history, and you'll understand why it is I hate cats and dogs.'

It was high time to go, for the pool was getting quite crowded with the birds and animals that had fallen into it: there was a Duck and a Dodo, a Lory and an Eaglet, and several other curious creatures.* Alice led the way, and the whole party swam to the shore.

Sea of Alices tears become a premordial bringing together / gathering of species

Darwin? + species merging

(Hard to find Alice; not spatially seperated)

CHAPTER III

A CAUCUS-RACE AND A LONG TALE

THEY were indeed a queer-looking party that assembled on the bank—the birds with draggled feathers, the animals with their fur clinging close to them, and all dripping wet, cross, and uncomfortable.

The first question of course was, how to get dry again: they had a consultation about this, and after a few minutes it seemed quite natural to Alice to find herself talking familiarly with them, as if she had known them all her life. Indeed, she had quite a long argument with the Lory, who at last turned sulky, and would only say 'I'm older than you, and must know better.' And this Alice would not allow, without knowing how old it was, and, as the Lory positively refused to tell its age, there was no more to be said.

At last the Mouse, who seemed to be a person of some authority among them, called out 'Sit down, all of you, and listen to me! *I'll* soon make you dry enough!' They all sat

this connection comfort

down at once, in a large ring, with the Mouse in the middle. Alice kept her eyes anxiously fixed on it, for she felt sure she would catch a bad cold if she did not get dry very soon.

'Ahem!' said the Mouse with an important air. 'Are you all ready? This is the driest thing I know. Silence all round, if you please! "William the Conqueror, whose cause was favoured by the pope, was soon submitted to by the English, who wanted leaders, and had been of late much accustomed to usurpation and conquest. Edwin and Morcar, the earls of Mercia and Northumbria——" '

'Ugh!' said the Lory, with a shiver.

'I beg your pardon!' said the Mouse, frowning, but very politely. 'Did you speak?'

'Not I!' said the Lory, hastily.

'I thought you did,' said the Mouse. 'I proceed. "Edwin and Morcar, the earls of Mercia and Northumbria, declared for him; and even Stigand, the patriotic archbishop of Canterbury, found it advisable——" '

'Found *what*?' said the Duck.

'Found *it*,' the Mouse replied rather crossly: 'of course you know what "it" means.'

'I know what "it" means well enough, when *I* find a thing,' said the Duck: 'it's generally a frog, or a worm. The question is, what did the archbishop find?'

The Mouse did not notice this question, but hurriedly went on, ' "—found it advisable to go with Edgar Atheling to meet William and offer him the crown. William's conduct at first was moderate. But the insolence of his Normans——"* How are you getting on now, my dear?' it continued, turning to Alice as it spoke.

'As wet as ever,' said Alice in a melancholy tone: 'it doesn't seem to dry me at all.'

'In that case,' said the Dodo solemnly, rising to its feet, 'I move that the meeting adjourn, for the immediate adoption of more energetic remedies——'

'Speak English!' said the Eaglet. 'I don't know the meaning of half those long words, and what's more, I don't believe you do either!' And the Eaglet bent down its head to hide a smile: some of the other birds tittered audibly.

'What I was going to say,' said the Dodo in an offended
tone, 'was, that the best thing to get us dry would be a Caucus-
race.'*

'What *is* a Caucus-race?' said Alice; not that she much
wanted to know, but the Dodo had paused as if it thought that
somebody ought to speak, and no one else seemed inclined to
say anything.

'Why,' said the Dodo, 'the best way to explain it is to do it.'
(And, as you might like to try the thing yourself, some winter-
day, I will tell you how the Dodo managed it.)

First it marked out a race-course, in a sort of circle, ('the
exact shape doesn't matter,' it said,) and then all the party
were placed along the course, here and there. There was no
'One, two, three, and away!', but they began running when
they liked, and left off when they liked, so that it was not easy
to know when the race was over. However, when they had
been running half an hour or so, and were quite dry again,* the
Dodo suddenly called out 'The race is over!', and they all
crowded round it, panting, and asking 'But who has won?'

This question the Dodo could not answer without a great
deal of thought, and it stood for a long time with one finger
pressed upon its forehead (the position in which you usually
see Shakespeare, in the pictures of him*), while the rest waited
in silence. At last the Dodo said '*Everybody* has won, and *all*
must have prizes.'

'But who is to give the prizes?' quite a chorus of voices
asked.

'Why, *she*, of course,' said the Dodo, pointing to Alice with
one finger; and the whole party at once crowded round her,
calling out, in a confused way, 'Prizes! Prizes!'

Alice had no idea what to do, and in despair she put her
hand in her pocket, and pulled out a box of comfits* (luckily
the salt water had not got into it), and handed them round as
prizes. There was exactly one a-piece, all round.

'But she must have a prize herself, you know,' said the
Mouse.

'Of course,' the Dodo replied very gravely. 'What else have
you got in your pocket?' it went on, turning to Alice.

'Only a thimble,' said Alice sadly.

[handwritten annotations:] Ape included in illustration as connecting this topsy-turvy animal world w/ Darwinian developments

[handwritten annotations:] Darwin

[handwritten annotation:] Human & animal hierarchy

'Hand it over here,' said the Dodo.

Then they all crowded round her once more, while the Dodo solemnly presented the thimble, saying 'We beg your acceptance of this elegant thimble'; and, when it had finished this short speech, they all cheered.

Alice thought the whole thing very absurd, but they all looked so grave that she did not dare to laugh; and, as she could not think of anything to say, she simply bowed, and took the thimble, looking as solemn as she could.

The next thing was to eat the comfits: this caused some noise and confusion, as the large birds complained that they could not taste theirs, and the small ones choked and had to be patted on the back. However, it was over at last, and they sat down again in a ring, and begged the Mouse to tell them something more.

'You promised to tell me your history, you know,' said

Alice, 'and why it is you hate—C and D,' she added in a whisper, half afraid that it would be offended again.

'Mine is a long and a sad tale!' said the Mouse, turning to Alice, and sighing.

'It *is* a long tail, certainly,' said Alice, looking down with wonder at the Mouse's tail; 'but why do you call it sad?' And she kept on puzzling about it while the Mouse was speaking, so that her idea of the tale was something like this:——*

```
              'Fury said to
                a mouse, That
                  he met in the
                    house, "Let
                      us both go
                        to law: I
                          will prose-
                            cute you.—
                              Come, I'll
                            take no de-
                          nial: We
                        must have
                    the trial;
                For really
              this morn-
            ing I've
          nothing
        to do."
      Said the
        mouse to
          the cur,
            "Such a
              trial, dear
                sir, With
                  no jury
                    or judge,
                      would
                        be wast-
                          ing our
                        breath."
                    "I'll be
                  judge,
                I'll be
              jury,"
            said
          cun-
            ning
              old
                Fury:
                  "I'll
                    try
                      the
                        whole
                          cause,
                            and
                              con-
                                demn
                              you to
                            death".'
```

pet as unfairly
condemning
mouse to death
w/no sympathy

'You are not attending!' said the Mouse to Alice, severely. 'What are you thinking of?'

'I beg your pardon,' said Alice very humbly: 'you had got to the fifth bend, I think?'

'I had *not!*' cried the Mouse, sharply and very angrily.

'A knot!' said Alice, always ready to make herself useful, and looking anxiously about her 'Oh, do let me help to undo it!'*

'I shall do nothing of the sort,' said the Mouse, getting up and walking away. 'You insult me by talking such nonsense!'

'I didn't mean it!' pleaded poor Alice. 'But you're so easily offended, you know!'

The Mouse only growled in reply.

'Please come back, and finish your story!' Alice called after it. And the others all joined in chorus 'Yes, please do!' But the Mouse only shook its head impatiently, and walked a little quicker.

'What a pity it wouldn't stay!' sighed the Lory, as soon as it was quite out of sight. And an old Crab took the opportunity of saying to her daughter 'Ah, my dear! Let this be a lesson to you never to lose *your* temper!' 'Hold your tongue, Ma!' said the young Crab, a little snappishly. 'You're enough to try the patience of an oyster!'

'I wish I had our Dinah here, I know I do!' said Alice aloud, addressing nobody in particular. '*She'd* soon fetch it back!'

'And who is Dinah, if I might venture to ask the question?' said the Lory.

Alice replied eagerly, for she was always ready to talk about her pet: 'Dinah's our cat. And she's such a capital one for catching mice, you ca'n't think! And oh, I wish you could see her after the birds! Why, she'll eat a little bird as soon as look at it!'

This speech caused a remarkable sensation among the party. Some of the birds hurried off at once: one old Magpie began wrapping itself up very carefully, remarking 'I really must be getting home: the night-air doesn't suit my throat!' And a Canary called out in a trembling voice, to its children, 'Come away, my dears! It's high time you were all in bed!' On various pretexts they all moved off, and Alice was soon left alone.

'I wish I hadn't mentioned Dinah!' she said to herself in a melancholy tone. 'Nobody seems to like her, down here, and I'm sure she's the best cat in the world! Oh, my dear Dinah! I wonder if I shall ever see you any more!' And here poor Alice began to cry again, for she felt very lonely and low-spirited. In a little while, however, she again heard a little pattering of footsteps in the distance, and she looked up eagerly, half hoping that the Mouse had changed his mind, and was coming back to finish his story.*

CHAPTER IV

THE RABBIT SENDS IN A LITTLE BILL

IT was the White Rabbit, trotting slowly back again, and looking anxiously about as it went, as if it had lost something, and she heard it muttering to itself, 'The Duchess!* The Duchess! Oh my dear paws! Oh my fur and whiskers! She'll get me executed, as sure as ferrets are ferrets! Where *can* I have dropped them, I wonder?' Alice guessed in a moment that it was looking for the fan and the pair of white kid-gloves, and she very good-naturedly began hunting about for them, but they were nowhere to be seen—everything seemed to have changed since her swim in the pool; and the great hall, with the glass table and the little door, had vanished completely.

Very soon the Rabbit noticed Alice, as she went hunting about, and called out to her, in an angry tone, 'Why, Mary Ann,* what *are* you doing out here? Run home this moment, and fetch me a pair of gloves and a fan! Quick, now!' And Alice was so much frightened that she ran off at once in the direction it pointed to, without trying to explain the mistake that it had made.

'He took me for his housemaid,' she said to herself as she ran. 'How surprised he'll be when he finds out who I am! But I'd better take him his fan and gloves—that is, if I can find them.' As she said this, she came upon a neat little house, on the door of which was a bright brass plate with the name 'W. RABBIT' engraved upon it. She went in without knocking, and hurried upstairs, in great fear lest she should meet the real Mary Ann, and be turned out of the house before she had found the fan and gloves.

'How queer it seems,' Alice said to herself, 'to be going messages for a rabbit! I suppose Dinah'll be sending me on messages next!' And she began fancying the sort of thing that would happen: '"Miss Alice! Come here directly, and get ready for your walk!" "Coming in a minute, nurse! But I've got to watch this mouse-hole till Dinah comes back, and see that the mouse doesn't get out." Only I don't think,' Alice went on, 'that they'd let Dinah stop in the house if it began ordering people about like that!'

By this time she had found her way into a tidy little room with a table in the window, and on it (as she had hoped) a fan and two or three pairs of tiny white kid-gloves: she took up the fan and a pair of the gloves, and was just going to leave the room, when her eye fell upon a little bottle that stood near the looking-glass. There was no label this time with the words 'DRINK ME,' but nevertheless she uncorked it and put it to her lips. 'I know *something* interesting is sure to happen,' she said to herself, 'whenever I eat or drink anything: so I'll just see what this bottle does. I do hope it'll make me grow large again, for really I'm quite tired of being such a tiny little thing!'

It did so indeed, and much sooner than she had expected: before she had drunk half the bottle, she found her head pressing against the ceiling, and had to stoop to save her neck from being broken. She hastily put down the bottle, saying to herself 'That's quite enough—I hope I sha'n't grow any more—As it is, I ca'n't get out at the door—I do wish I hadn't drunk quite so much!'

Alas! It was too late to wish that! She went on growing, and growing, and very soon had to kneel down on the floor: in another minute there was not even room for this, and she tried the effect of lying down with one elbow against the door, and the other arm curled round her head. Still she went on growing, and, as a last resource, she put one arm out of the window, and one foot up the chimney, and said to herself 'Now I can do no more, whatever happens. What *will* become of me?'

Luckily for Alice, the little magic bottle had now had its full effect, and she grew no larger: still it was very uncom-

Dinah as only thread from back home and this real-world

fortable, and, as there seemed to be no sort of chance of her ever getting out of the room again, no wonder she felt unhappy.

'It was much pleasanter at home,' thought poor Alice, 'when one wasn't always growing larger and smaller, and being ordered about by mice and rabbits. I almost wish I hadn't gone down that rabbit-hole—and yet—and yet—it's rather curious, you know, this sort of life! I do wonder what *can* have happened to me! When I used to read fairy tales, I fancied that kind of thing never happened, and now here I am in the middle of one! There ought to be a book written about me, that there ought! And when I grow up, I'll write one—but I'm grown up now,' she added in a sorrowful tone: 'at least there's no room to grow up any more *here*.'

'But then,' thought Alice, 'shall I *never* get any older than I am now? That'll be a comfort, one way—never to be an old woman—but then—always to have lessons to learn! Oh, I shouldn't like *that*!'

'Oh, you foolish Alice!' she answered herself. 'How can you learn lessons in here? Why, there's hardly room for *you*, and no room at all for any lesson-books!'

And so she went on, taking first one side and then the other, and making quite a conversation of it altogether; but after a few minutes she heard a voice outside, and stopped to listen.

'Mary Ann! Mary Ann!' said the voice. 'Fetch me my gloves this moment!' Then came a little pattering of feet on the stairs. Alice knew it was the Rabbit coming to look for her, and she trembled till she shook the house, quite forgetting that she was now about a thousand times as large as the Rabbit, and had no reason to be afraid of it.

Presently the Rabbit came up to the door, and tried to open it; but, as the door opened inwards, and Alice's elbow was pressed hard against it, that attempt proved a failure. Alice

heard it say to itself 'Then I'll go round and get in at the window.'

'*That* you wo'n't!' thought Alice, and, after waiting till she fancied she heard the Rabbit just under the window, she suddenly spread out her hand, and made a snatch in the air. She did not get hold of anything, but she heard a little shriek and a fall, and a crash of broken glass, from which she concluded that it was just possible it had fallen into a cucumber-frame, or something of the sort.

Next came an angry voice—the Rabbit's—'Pat! Pat! Where are you?' And then a voice she had never heard before, 'Sure then I'm here! Digging for apples,* yer honour!'

'Digging for apples, indeed!' said the Rabbit angrily. 'Here!

Come and help me out of *this!*' (Sounds of more broken glass.)

'Now tell me, Pat, what's that in the window?'

'Sure, it's an arm, yer honour!' (He pronounced it 'arrum.')

'An arm, you goose! Who ever saw one that size? Why, it fills the whole window!'

'Sure, it does, yer honour: but it's an arm for all that.'

'Well, it's got no business there, at any rate: go and take it away!'

There was a long silence after this, and Alice could only hear whispers now and then; such as 'Sure, I don't like it, yer honour, at all, at all!' 'Do as I tell you, you coward!', and at last she spread out her hand again, and made another snatch in the air. This time there were *two* little shrieks, and more sounds of broken glass. 'What a number of cucumber-frames there must be!' thought Alice. 'I wonder what they'll do next! As for pulling me out of the window, I only wish they *could!* I'm sure *I* don't want to stay in here any longer!'

She waited for some time without hearing anything more: at last came a rumbling of little cart-wheels, and the sound of a good many voices all talking together: she made out the words: 'Where's the other ladder?—Why, I hadn't to bring but one. Bill's got the other—Bill! Fetch it here, lad!—Here, put 'em up at this corner—No, tie 'em together first—they don't reach half high enough yet—Oh, they'll do well enough. Don't be particular—Here, Bill! Catch hold of this rope— Will the roof bear?—Mind that loose slate—Oh, it's coming down! Heads below!' (a loud crash)—'Now, who did that? —It was Bill, I fancy—Who's to go down the chimney?— Nay, *I* sha'n't! *You* do it!—*That* I wo'n't, then!—Bill's got to go down—Here, Bill! The master says you've got to go down the chimney!'

'Oh! So Bill's got to come down the chimney, has he?' said Alice to herself. 'Why, they seem to put everything upon Bill! I wouldn't be in Bill's place for a good deal: this fireplace is narrow, to be sure; but I *think* I can kick a little!'

She drew her foot as far down the chimney as she could, and waited till she heard a little animal (she couldn't guess of what sort it was) scratching and scrambling about in the chimney close above her: then, saying to herself 'This is Bill', she gave one sharp kick, and waited to see what would happen next.

The first thing she heard was a general chorus of 'There goes Bill!' then the Rabbit's voice alone—'Catch him, you by the hedge!' then silence, and then another confusion of voices—'Hold up his head—Brandy now—Don't choke him—How was it, old fellow? What happened to you? Tell us all about it!'

Last came a little feeble, squeaking voice ('That's Bill,' thought Alice), 'Well, I hardly know—No more, thank ye; I'm better now—but I'm a deal too flustered to tell you—all I know is, something comes at me like a Jack-in-the-box, and up I goes like a sky-rocket!'

'So you did, old fellow!' said the others.

'We must burn the house down!' said the Rabbit's voice. And Alice called out, as loud as she could, 'If you do, I'll set Dinah at you!'

There was a dead silence instantly, and Alice thought to herself 'I wonder what they *will* do next! If they had any

sense, they'd take the roof off.' After a minute or two, they
began moving about again, and Alice heard the Rabbit say
'A barrowful will do, to begin with.'

'A barrowful of *what?*' thought Alice. But she had not long
to doubt, for the next moment a shower of little pebbles came
rattling in at the window, and some of them hit her in the face.
'I'll put a stop to this,' she said to herself, and shouted out
'You'd better not do that again!', which produced another
dead silence.

Alice noticed, with some surprise, that the pebbles were all
turning into little cakes as they lay on the floor, and a bright
idea came into her head. 'If I eat one of these cakes,' she
thought, 'it's sure to make *some* change in my size; and, as it
ca'n't possibly make me larger, it must make me smaller,
I suppose.'

So she swallowed one of the cakes, and was delighted to find
that she began shrinking directly. As soon as she was small
enough to get through the door, she ran out of the house, and
found quite a crowd of little animals and birds waiting outside. The poor little Lizard, Bill,* was in the middle, being
held up by two guinea-pigs, who were giving it something
out of a bottle. They all made a rush at Alice the moment she
appeared; but she ran off as hard as she could, and soon found
herself safe in a thick wood.

'The first thing I've got to do,' said Alice to herself, as she
wandered about in the wood, 'is to grow to my right size again;
and the second thing is to find my way into that lovely garden.
I think that will be the best plan.'

It sounded an excellent plan, no doubt, and very neatly
and simply arranged: the only difficulty was, that she had not
the smallest idea how to set about it; and, while she was peer-
ing about anxiously among the trees, a little sharp bark just
over her head made her look up in a great hurry.

An enormous puppy was looking down at her with large
round eyes, and feebly stretching out one paw, trying to
touch her. 'Poor little thing!' said Alice, in a coaxing tone, and
she tried hard to whistle to it; but she was terribly frightened

all the time at the thought that it might be hungry, in which
case it would be very likely to eat her up in spite of all her
coaxing.

Hardly knowing what she did, she picked up a little bit of
stick, and held it out to the puppy: whereupon the puppy
jumped into the air off all its feet at once, with a yelp of delight,
and rushed at the stick, and made believe to worry it: then
Alice dodged behind a great thistle, to keep herself from being
run over; and, the moment she appeared on the other side,
the puppy made another rush at the stick, and tumbled head
over heels in its hurry to get hold of it: then Alice, thinking it

was very like having a game of play with a cart-horse, and expecting every moment to be trampled under its feet, ran round the thistle again: then the puppy began a series of short charges at the stick, running a very little way forwards each time and a long way back, and barking hoarsely all the while, till at last it sat down a good way off, panting, with its tongue hanging out of its mouth, and its great eyes half shut.

This seemed to Alice a good opportunity for making her escape: so she set off at once, and ran till she was quite tired and out of breath, and till the puppy's bark sounded quite faint in the distance.

'And yet what a dear little puppy it was!' said Alice, as she leant against a buttercup to rest herself, and fanned herself with one of the leaves. 'I should have liked teaching it tricks very much, if—if I'd only been the right size to do it! Oh dear! I'd nearly forgotten that I've got to grow up again! Let me see—how *is* it to be managed? I suppose I ought to eat or drink something or other; but the great question is "What?"'

The great question certainly was 'What?' Alice looked all round her at the flowers and the blades of grass, but she could not see anything that looked like the right thing to eat or drink under the circumstances. There was a large mushroom growing near her, about the same height as herself; and, when she had looked under it, and on both sides of it, and behind it, it occurred to her that she might as well look and see what was on the top of it.

She stretched herself up on tiptoe, and peeped over the edge of the mushroom, and her eyes immediately met those of a large blue caterpillar, that was sitting on the top, with its arms folded, quietly smoking a long hookah, and taking not the smallest notice of her or of anything else.

just this
pair of eyes

CHAPTER V

ADVICE FROM A CATERPILLAR

malleable identity

idea of not about how
you're perceived, but
what you are

weird
characterization

THE Caterpillar and Alice looked at each other for some
time in silence: at last the Caterpillar took the hookah
out of its mouth, and addressed her in a languid, sleepy
voice.

'Who are *you?*' said the Caterpillar.

This was not an encouraging opening for a conversation.
Alice replied, rather shyly, 'I—I hardly know, Sir, just at
present—at least I know who I *was* when I got up this morn-

ing, but I think I must have been changed several times since then.'

'What do you mean by that?' said the Caterpillar, sternly. 'Explain yourself!'

'I ca'n't explain *myself*, I'm afraid, Sir,' said Alice, 'because I'm not myself, you see.'

'I don't see,' said the Caterpillar.

'I'm afraid I ca'n't put it more clearly,' Alice replied, very politely, 'for I ca'n't understand it myself, to begin with; and being so many different sizes in a day is very confusing.'

'It isn't,' said the Caterpillar.

'Well, perhaps you haven't found it so yet,' said Alice; 'but when you have to turn into a chrysalis—you will some day, you know—and then after that into a butterfly, I should think you'll feel it a little queer, wo'n't you?'

'Not a bit,' said the Caterpillar.

'Well, perhaps *your* feelings may be different,' said Alice: 'all I know is, it would feel very queer to *me*.'

'You!' said the Caterpillar contemptuously. 'Who are *you?*'

Which brought them back again to the beginning of the conversation. Alice felt a little irritated at the Caterpillar's making such *very* short remarks, and she drew herself up and said, very gravely, 'I think you ought to tell me who *you* are, first.'

'Why?' said the Caterpillar.

Here was another puzzling question; and, as Alice could not think of any good reason, and the Caterpillar seemed to be in a *very* unpleasant state of mind, she turned away.

'Come back!' the Caterpillar called after her. 'I've something important to say!'

This sounded promising, certainly. Alice turned and came back again.

'Keep your temper,' said the Caterpillar.

'Is that all?' said Alice, swallowing down her anger as well as she could.

Novel using girlhood identity for a lens on Darwinian theory and species change

'No,' said the Caterpillar.

Alice thought she might as well wait, as she had nothing else to do, and perhaps after all it might tell her something worth hearing. For some minutes it puffed away without speaking; but at last it unfolded its arms, took the hookah out of its mouth again, and said 'So you think you're changed, do you?'

'I'm afraid I am, Sir,' said Alice. 'I ca'n't remember things as I used—and I don't keep the same size for ten minutes together!'

'Ca'n't remember *what* things?' said the Caterpillar.

'Well, I've tried to say "*How doth the little busy bee*," but it all came different!' Alice replied in a very melancholy voice.

'Repeat "*You are old, Father William*,"* said the Caterpillar.

Alice folded her hands, and began:—

'*You are old, Father William,*' *the young man said,*
   '*And your hair has become very white;*
And yet you incessantly stand on your head—
   Do you think, at your age, it is right?'

'*In my youth,*' *Father William replied to his son,*
   '*I feared it might injure the brain;*
But, now that I'm perfectly sure I have none,
   Why, I do it again and again.'

'*You are old,*' *said the youth,* '*as I mentioned before,*
   And have grown most uncommonly fat;
Yet you turned a back-somersault in at the door—
   Pray, what is the reason of that?'

'*In my youth,*' *said the sage, as he shook his grey locks,*
   '*I kept all my limbs very supple*
By the use of this ointment—one shilling the box—*
   Allow me to sell you a couple?'

(handwritten margin note: Novel as a parable/fable with Alice relaying messages of her own learning)

'You are old,' said the youth, 'and your jaws are too weak
  For anything tougher than suet;
Yet you finished the goose, with the bones and the beak—
  Pray, how did you manage to do it?'

'In my youth,' said his father, 'I took to the law,
  And argued each case with my wife;
And the muscular strength, which it gave to my jaw
  Has lasted the rest of my life.'

'You are old,' said the youth, 'one would hardly suppose
  That your eye was as steady as ever;
Yet you balanced an eel on the end of your nose—
  What made you so awfully clever?'

'I have answered three questions, and that is enough,'
  Said his father. 'Don't give yourself airs!
Do you think I can listen all day to such stuff?
  Be off, or I'll kick you down-stairs!'

'That is not said right,' said the Caterpillar.

'Not *quite* right, I'm afraid,' said Alice, timidly: 'some of the words have got altered.'

'It is wrong from beginning to end,' said the Caterpillar, decidedly; and there was silence for some minutes.

The Caterpillar was the first to speak.

'What size do you want to be?' it asked.

'Oh, I'm not particular as to size,' Alice hastily replied; 'only one doesn't like changing so often, you know.'

'I *don't* know,' said the Caterpillar.

Alice said nothing: she had never been so much contradicted in all her life before, and she felt that she was losing her temper.

'Are you content now?' said the Caterpillar.

'Well, I should like to be a *little* larger, Sir, if you wouldn't mind,' said Alice: 'three inches is such a wretched height to be.'

'It is a very good height indeed!' said the Caterpillar angrily, rearing itself upright as it spoke (it was exactly three inches high).

'But I'm not used to it!' pleaded poor Alice in a piteous tone. And she thought to herself 'I wish the creatures wouldn't be so easily offended!'

'You'll get used to it in time,' said the Caterpillar; and it put the hookah into its mouth, and began smoking again.

This time Alice waited patiently until it chose to speak again. In a minute or two the Caterpillar took the hookah out of its mouth, and yawned once or twice, and shook itself. Then it got down off the mushroom, and crawled away into the grass, merely remarking, as it went, 'One side will make you grow taller, and the other side will make you grow shorter.'*

'One side of *what*? The other side of *what*?' thought Alice to herself.

'Of the mushroom,' said the Caterpillar, just as if she had asked it aloud; and in another moment it was out of sight.

Alice remained looking thoughtfully at the mushroom for a minute, trying to make out which were the two sides of it; and, as it was perfectly round, she found this a very difficult question. However, at last she stretched her arms round it as far as they would go, and broke off a bit of the edge with each hand.

'And now which is which?' she said to herself, and nibbled a little of the right-hand bit to try the effect. The next moment she felt a violent blow underneath her chin: it had struck her foot!

She was a good deal frightened by this very sudden change, but she felt that there was no time to be lost, as she was shrinking rapidly: so she set to work at once to eat some of the other bit. Her chin was pressed so closely against her foot, that there was hardly room to open her mouth; but she did it at last, and managed to swallow a morsel of the left-hand bit.

*   *   *   *   *

   *   *   *   *

*   *   *   *

'Come, my head's free at last!' said Alice in a tone of delight, which changed into alarm in another moment, when she found that her shoulders were nowhere to be found: all she could see, when she looked down, was an immense length of neck, which seemed to rise like a stalk out of a sea of green leaves that lay far below her.

'What *can* all that green stuff be?' said Alice. 'And where *have* my shoulders got to? And oh, my poor hands, how is it I ca'n't see you?' She was moving them about, as she spoke, but no result seemed to follow, except a little shaking among the distant green leaves.

As there seemed to be no chance of getting her hands up to her head, she tried to get her head down to *them*, and was delighted to find that her neck would bend about easily in any direction, like a serpent. She had just succeeded in curving it down into a graceful zigzag, and was going to dive in among the leaves, which she found to be nothing but the tops of the trees under which she had been wandering, when a sharp hiss made her draw back in a hurry: a large pigeon had flown into her face, and was beating her violently with its wings.

'Serpent!'* screamed the Pigeon.

'I'm *not* a serpent!' said Alice indignantly. 'Let me alone!'

'Serpent, I say again!' repeated the Pigeon, but in a more subdued tone, and added, with a kind of sob, 'I've tried every way, but nothing seems to suit them!'

'I haven't the least idea what you're talking about,' said Alice.

'I've tried the roots of trees, and I've tried banks, and I've tried hedges,' the Pigeon went on, without attending to her; 'but those serpents! There's no pleasing them!'

Alice was more and more puzzled, but she thought there was no use in saying anything more till the Pigeon had finished.

'As if it wasn't trouble enough hatching the eggs,' said the Pigeon; 'but I must be on the look-out for serpents, night and day! Why, I haven't had a wink of sleep these three weeks!'

'I'm very sorry you've been annoyed,' said Alice, who was beginning to see its meaning.

'And just as I'd taken the highest tree in the wood,' continued the Pigeon, raising its voice to a shriek, 'and just as I was thinking I should be free of them at last, they must needs come wriggling down from the sky! Ugh, Serpent!'

'But I'm *not* a serpent, I tell you!' said Alice. 'I'm a——I'm a——'

'Well! *What* are you?' said the Pigeon. 'I can see you're trying to invent something!'

'I—I'm a little girl,' said Alice, rather doubtfully, as she remembered the number of changes she had gone through, that day.

'A likely story indeed!' said the Pigeon, in a tone of the deepest contempt. 'I've seen a good many little girls in my time, but never *one* with such a neck as that! No, no! You're a serpent; and there's no use denying it. I suppose you'll be telling me next that you never tasted an egg!'

'I *have* tasted eggs, certainly,' said Alice, who was a very truthful child; 'but little girls eat eggs quite as much as serpents do, you know.'

'I don't believe it,' said the Pigeon; 'but if they do, why, then they're a kind of serpent: that's all I can say.'

This was such a new idea to Alice, that she was quite silent for a minute or two, which gave the Pigeon the opportunity of adding 'You're looking for eggs, I know *that* well enough; and what does it matter to me whether you're a little girl or a serpent?'

'It matters a good deal to *me*,' said Alice hastily; 'but I'm not looking for eggs, as it happens; and, if I was, I shouldn't want *yours*: I don't like them raw.'

'Well, be off, then!' said the Pigeon in a sulky tone, as it settled down again into its nest. Alice crouched down among the trees as well as she could, for her neck kept getting entangled among the branches, and every now and then she had to stop and untwist it. After a while she remembered that she still held the pieces of mushroom in her hands, and she set to work very carefully, nibbling first at one and then at the other, and growing sometimes taller, and sometimes shorter, until she had succeeded in bringing herself down to her usual height.

It was so long since she had been anything near the right size, that it felt quite strange at first; but she got used to it in a few minutes; and began talking to herself, as usual, 'Come, there's half my plan done now! How puzzling all these changes are! I'm never sure what I'm going to be, from one minute to another! However, I've got back to my right size: the next thing is, to get into that beautiful garden—how *is* that to be done, I wonder?' As she said this,* she came suddenly upon an open place, with a little house in it about four feet high. 'Whoever lives there,' thought Alice, 'it'll never do to come upon them *this* size: why, I should frighten them out of their wits!' So she began nibbling at the right-hand bit again, and did not venture to go near the house till she had brought herself down to nine inches high.

CHAPTER VI

PIG AND PEPPER

FOR a minute or two she stood looking at the house, and wondering what to do next, when suddenly a footman in livery came running out of the wood—(she considered him to be a footman because he was in livery: otherwise, judging by his face only, she would have called him a fish)—and rapped loudly at the door with his knuckles. It was opened by another footman in livery, with a round face, and large eyes like a frog; and both footmen, Alice noticed, had powdered hair that curled all over their heads. She felt very curious to know what it was all about, and crept a little way out of the wood to listen.

The Fish-Footman began by producing from under his arm a great letter, nearly as large as himself, and this he handed over to the other, saying, in a solemn tone, 'For the Duchess. An invitation from the Queen to play croquet.' The Frog-Footman repeated, in the same solemn tone, only changing the order of the words a little, 'From the Queen. An invitation for the Duchess to play croquet.'

Then they both bowed low, and their curls got entangled together.

Alice laughed so much at this, that she had to run back into the wood for fear of their hearing her; and, when she next peeped out, the Fish-Footman was gone, and the other was sitting on the ground near the door, staring stupidly up into the sky.

Alice went timidly up to the door, and knocked.

'There's no sort of use in knocking,' said the Footman, 'and that for two reasons. First, because I'm on the same side of the door as you are: secondly, because they're making such a noise inside, no one could possibly hear you.' And certainly there *was* a most extraordinary noise going on within—a constant howling and sneezing, and every now and then a great crash, as if a dish or kettle had been broken to pieces.

'Please, then,' said Alice, 'how am I to get in?'

'There might be some sense in your knocking,' the Footman went on, without attending to her, 'if we had the door between us. For instance, if you were *inside*, you might knock, and I could let you out, you know.' He was looking up into the sky all the time he was speaking, and this Alice thought decidedly uncivil. 'But perhaps he ca'n't help it,' she said to herself; 'his eyes are so *very* nearly at the top of his head. But at any rate he might answer questions.—How am I to get in?' she repeated, aloud.

'I shall sit here,' the Footman remarked, 'till to-morrow——'

At this moment the door of the house opened, and a large plate came skimming out, straight at the Footman's head: it just grazed his nose, and broke to pieces against one of the trees behind him.

'——or next day, maybe,' the Footman continued in the same tone, exactly as if nothing had happened.

'How am I to get in?' asked Alice again, in a louder tone.

'*Are* you to get in at all?' said the Footman. 'That's the first question, you know.'

It was, no doubt: only Alice did not like to be told so. 'It's really dreadful,' she muttered to herself, 'the way all the creatures argue. It's enough to drive one crazy!'

The Footman seemed to think this a good opportunity for repeating his remark, with variations. 'I shall sit here,' he said, 'on and off, for days and days.'

'But what am *I* to do?' said Alice.

'Anything you like,' said the Footman, and began whistling.

'Oh, there's no use in talking to him,' said Alice desperately: 'he's perfectly idiotic!' And she opened the door and went in.

The door led right into a large kitchen,* which was full of smoke from one end to the other: the Duchess* was sitting on a three-legged stool in the middle, nursing a baby: the cook

was leaning over the fire, stirring a large cauldron which seemed to be full of soup.

'There's certainly too much pepper* in that soup!' Alice said to herself, as well as she could for sneezing.

There was certainly too much of it in the *air*. Even the Duchess sneezed occasionally; and as for the baby, it was sneezing and howling alternately without a moment's pause. The only two creatures in the kitchen, that did *not* sneeze, were the cook, and a large cat, which was lying on the hearth and grinning from ear to ear.

'Please would you tell me,' said Alice, a little timidly, for she was not quite sure whether it was good manners for her to speak first, 'why your cat grins like that?'

'It's a Cheshire-Cat,'* said the Duchess, 'and that's why. Pig!'

She said the last word with such sudden violence that Alice quite jumped; but she saw in another moment that it was addressed to the baby, and not to her, so she took courage, and went on again:—

'I didn't know that Cheshire-Cats always grinned; in fact, I didn't know that cats *could* grin.'

'They all can,' said the Duchess; 'and most of 'em do.'

'I don't know of any that do,' Alice said very politely, feeling quite pleased to have got into a conversation.

'You don't know much,' said the Duchess; 'and that's a fact.'

Alice did not at all like the tone of this remark, and thought it would be as well to introduce some other subject of conversation. While she was trying to fix on one, the cook took the cauldron of soup off the fire, and at once set to work throwing everything within her reach at the Duchess and the baby—the fire-irons came first; then followed a shower of saucepans, plates, and dishes. The Duchess took no notice of them even when they hit her; and the baby was howling so much already, that it was quite impossible to say whether the blows hurt it or not.

'Oh, *please* mind what you're doing!' cried Alice, jumping up and down in an agony of terror. 'Oh, there goes his *precious* nose!', as an unusually large saucepan flew close by it, and very nearly carried it off.

'If everybody minded their own business,' the Duchess said, in a hoarse growl, 'the world would go round a deal faster than it does.'

'Which would *not* be an advantage,' said Alice, who felt very glad to get an opportunity of showing off a little of her knowledge. 'Just think what work it would make with the day and night! You see the earth takes twenty-four hours to turn round on its axis——'

'Talking of axes,' said the Duchess, 'chop off her head!'

Alice glanced rather anxiously at the cook, to see if she meant to take the hint; but the cook was busily stirring the soup, and seemed not to be listening, so she went on again: 'Twenty-four hours, I *think*; or is it twelve? I——'

'Oh, don't bother *me!*' said the Duchess. 'I never could abide figures!' And with that she began nursing her child again, singing a sort of lullaby to it as she did so, and giving it a violent shake at the end of every line:—

> '*Speak roughly to your little boy,** *Parody of*
> *And beat him when he sneezes:* *gentle lullaby*
> *Sneezing as* *He only does it to annoy,*
> *a calculated* *Because he knows it teases.'*
> *response*

CHORUS

(in which the cook and the baby joined):—

> '*Wow! wow! wow!*'

While the Duchess sang the second verse of the song, she kept tossing the baby violently up and down, and the poor little thing howled so, that Alice could hardly hear the words:—

> *'I speak severely to my boy,*
> *I beat him when he sneezes;*
> *For he can thoroughly enjoy*
> *The pepper when he pleases!'*

[handwritten: conditioning]

CHORUS

'Wow! wow! wow!'

'Here! You may nurse it a bit, if you like!' the Duchess said to Alice, flinging the baby at her as she spoke. 'I must go and get ready to play croquet with the Queen,' and she hurried out of the room. The cook threw a frying-pan after her as she went, but it just missed her.

Alice caught the baby with some difficulty, as it was a queer-shaped little creature, and held out its arms and legs in all directions, 'just like a star-fish,' thought Alice. The poor little thing was snorting like a steam-engine when she caught it, and kept doubling itself up and straightening itself out again, so that altogether, for the first minute or two, it was as much as she could do to hold it.

As soon as she had made out the proper way of nursing it (which was to twist it up into a sort of knot, and then keep tight hold of its right ear and left foot, so as to prevent its undoing itself) she carried it out into the open air. 'If I don't take this child away with me,' thought Alice, 'they're sure to kill it in a day or two. Wouldn't it be murder to leave it behind?' She said the last words out loud, and the little thing grunted in reply (it had left off sneezing by this time). 'Don't grunt,' said Alice; 'that's not at all a proper way of expressing yourself.'

[handwritten: taking on of new responsibilities]

The baby grunted again, and Alice looked very anxiously into its face to see what was the matter with it. There could be no doubt that it had a *very* turn-up nose, much more like a snout than a real nose: also its eyes were getting extremely small for a baby: altogether Alice did not like the look of the thing at all. 'But perhaps it was only sobbing,' she thought, and looked into its eyes again, to see if there were any tears.

No, there were no tears. 'If you're going to turn into a pig, my dear,' said Alice, seriously, 'I'll have nothing more to do with you. Mind now!' The poor little thing sobbed again (or grunted, it was impossible to say which), and they went on for some while in silence.

Alice was just beginning to think to herself, 'Now, what am I to do with this creature, when I get it home?' when it grunted

again, so violently, that she looked down into its face in some alarm. This time there could be *no* mistake about it: it was neither more nor less than a pig,* and she felt that it would be quite absurd for her to carry it any further.

So she set the little creature down, and felt quite relieved to see it trot away quietly into the wood. 'If it had grown up,' she said to herself, 'it would have made a dreadfully ugly child: but it makes rather a handsome pig, I think.' And she began thinking over other children she knew, who might do very well as pigs, and was just saying to herself 'if one only knew the right way to change them——' when she was a little startled by seeing the Cheshire-Cat sitting on a bough of a tree a few yards off.

The Cat only grinned when it saw Alice. It looked good-natured, she thought: still it had *very* long claws and a great many teeth, so she felt that it ought to be treated with respect.

'Cheshire-Puss,' she began, rather timidly, as she did not at all know whether it would like the name: however, it only

grinned a little wider. 'Come, it's pleased so far,' thought Alice, and she went on. 'Would you tell me, please, which way I ought to go from here?'

'That depends a good deal on where you want to get to,' said the Cat.

'I don't much care where——' said Alice.

'Then it doesn't matter which way you go,' said the Cat.

'——so long as I get *some-where*,' Alice added as an explanation.

'Oh, you're sure to do that,' said the Cat, 'if you only walk long enough.'

Alice felt that this could not be denied, so she tried another question. 'What sort of people live about here?'

'In *that* direction,' the Cat said, waving its right paw round, 'lives a Hatter: and in *that* direction,' waving the other paw, 'lives a March Hare. Visit either you like: they're both mad.'*

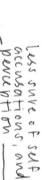

less sure of self accusations, and perception

'But I don't want to go among mad people,' Alice remarked.

'Oh, you ca'n't help that,' said the Cat: 'we're all mad here. I'm mad. You're mad.'

'How do you know I'm mad?' said Alice.

'You must be,' said the Cat, 'or you wouldn't have come here.'

Alice didn't think that proved it at all: however, she went on: 'And how do you know that you're mad?'

'To begin with,' said the Cat, 'a dog's not mad. You grant that?'

'I suppose so,' said Alice.

'Well, then,' the Cat went on, 'you see a dog growls when it's angry, and wags its tail when it's pleased. Now *I* growl when I'm pleased, and wag my tail when I'm angry. Therefore I'm mad.'

'*I* call it purring, not growling,' said Alice.

'Call it what you like,' said the Cat. 'Do you play croquet with the Queen to-day?'

'I should like it very much,' said Alice, 'but I haven't been invited yet.'

'You'll see me there,' said the Cat, and vanished.

Alice was not much surprised at this, she was getting so well used to queer things happening. While she was still looking at the place where it had been, it suddenly appeared again.

'By-the-bye, what became of the baby?' said the Cat. 'I'd nearly forgotten to ask.'

'It turned into a pig,' Alice answered very quietly, just as if the Cat had come back in a natural way.

'I thought it would,' said the Cat, and vanished again.

Alice waited a little, half expecting to see it again, but it did not appear, and after a minute or two she walked on in the direction in which the March Hare was said to live. 'I've seen hatters before,' she said to herself: 'the March Hare will be much the most interesting, and perhaps, as this is May,* it wo'n't be raving mad—at least not so mad as it was in March.'

As she said this, she looked up, and there was the Cat again, sitting on a branch of a tree.

'Did you say "pig", or "fig"?' said the Cat.

'I said "pig",' replied Alice; 'and I wish you wouldn't keep appearing and vanishing so suddenly: you make one quite giddy!'

'All right,' said the Cat; and this time it vanished quite slowly, beginning with the end of the tail, and ending with the grin, which remained some time after the rest of it had gone.

'Well! I've often seen a cat without a grin,' thought Alice; 'but a grin without a cat! It's the most curious thing I ever saw in all my life!'

She had not gone much farther before she came in sight of the house of the March Hare: she thought it must be the right house, because the chimneys were shaped like ears and the roof was thatched with fur. It was so large a house, that she did not like to go nearer till she had nibbled some more of the left-hand bit of mushroom, and raised herself to about two feet high: even then she walked up towards it rather timidly, saying to herself 'Suppose it should be raving mad after all! I almost wish I'd gone to see the Hatter instead!'

CHAPTER VII

A MAD TEA-PARTY

THERE was a table set out under a tree in front of the house, and the March Hare and the Hatter were having tea at it: a Dormouse was sitting between them, fast asleep, and the other two were using it as a cushion, resting their elbows on it, and talking over its head. 'Very uncomfortable for the Dormouse,' thought Alice; 'only as it's asleep, I suppose it doesn't mind.'

The table was a large one, but the three were all crowded together at one corner of it. 'No room! No room!' they cried out when they saw Alice coming. 'There's *plenty* of room!' said Alice indignantly, and she sat down in a large arm-chair at one end of the table.

'Have some wine,' the March Hare said in an encouraging tone.

Alice looked all round the table, but there was nothing on it but tea. 'I don't see any wine,' she remarked.

'There isn't any,' said the March Hare.

'Then it wasn't very civil of you to offer it,' said Alice angrily.

'It wasn't very civil of you to sit down without being invited,' said the March Hare.

'I didn't know it was *your* table,' said Alice: 'it's laid for a great many more than three.'

'Your hair wants cutting,' said the Hatter. He had been looking at Alice for some time with great curiosity, and this was his first speech.

'You should learn not to make personal remarks,' Alice said with some severity: 'it's very rude.'

The Hatter opened his eyes very wide on hearing this; but all he *said* was 'Why is a raven like a writing-desk?'*

'Come, we shall have some fun now!' thought Alice. 'I'm glad they've begun asking riddles—I believe I can guess that,' she added aloud.

'Do you mean that you think you can find out the answer to it?' said the March Hare.

'Exactly so,' said Alice.

'Then you should say what you mean,' the March Hare went on.

'I do,' Alice hastily replied; 'at least—at least I mean what I say—that's the same thing, you know.'

'Not the same thing a bit!' said the Hatter. 'Why, you might just as well say that "I see what I eat" is the same thing as "I eat what I see"!' ✳

'You might just as well say,' added the March Hare, 'that "I like what I get" is the same thing as "I get what I like"!'

'You might just as well say,' added the Dormouse, which seemed to be talking in its sleep, 'that "I breathe when I sleep" is the same thing as "I sleep when I breathe"!'

'It *is* the same thing with you,' said the Hatter, and here the conversation dropped, and the party sat silent for a minute,

Words as more literal in this world

Exclusion and inability to penetrate

✳ *Nonsense doesn't come from a rejection of rules, but rather extreme dramatization from learning rules / conventions*

while Alice thought over all she could remember about ravens
and writing-desks, which wasn't much.

The Hatter was the first to break the silence. 'What day of
the month is it?' he said, turning to Alice: he had taken his
watch out of his pocket, and was looking at it uneasily, shaking
it every now and then, and holding it to his ear.

Alice considered a little, and then said 'The fourth.'

'Two days wrong!'* sighed the Hatter. 'I told you butter
wouldn't suit the works!' he added, looking angrily at the
March Hare.

'It was the *best* butter,' the March Hare meekly replied.

'Yes, but some crumbs must have got in as well,' the Hatter
grumbled: 'you shouldn't have put it in with the bread-
knife.'

The March Hare took the watch and looked at it gloomily:
then he dipped it into his cup of tea, and looked at it again:
but he could think of nothing better to say than his first
remark, 'It was the *best* butter, you know.'

Alice had been looking over his shoulder with some curiosity. 'What a funny watch!' she remarked. 'It tells the day
of the month, and doesn't tell what o'clock it is!'

'Why should it?' muttered the Hatter. 'Does *your* watch
tell you what year it is?'

'Of course not,' Alice replied very readily: 'but that's
because it stays the same year for such a long time together.'

'Which is just the case with *mine*,' said the Hatter.

Alice felt dreadfully puzzled. The Hatter's remark seemed
to her to have no sort of meaning in it, and yet it was certainly
English. 'I don't quite understand you,' she said, as politely
as she could.

'The Dormouse is asleep again,' said the Hatter, and he
poured a little hot tea upon its nose. mistreatment

The Dormouse shook its head impatiently, and said, without opening its eyes, 'Of course, of course: just what I was
going to remark myself.'

'Have you guessed the riddle yet?' the Hatter said, turning
to Alice again.

'No, I give it up,' Alice replied. 'What's the answer?'

'I haven't the slightest idea,' said the Hatter.

'Nor I,' said the March Hare.

Alice sighed wearily. 'I think you might do something better with the time,' she said, 'than wasting it in asking riddles that have no answers.'

'If you knew Time as well as I do,' said the Hatter, 'you wouldn't talk about wasting it. It's him.'

'I don't know what you mean,' said Alice.

'Of course you don't!' the Hatter said, tossing his head contemptuously. 'I dare say you never even spoke to Time!'

'Perhaps not,' Alice cautiously replied; 'but I know I have to beat time when I learn music.'

'Ah! That accounts for it,' said the Hatter. 'He wo'n't stand beating. Now, if you only kept on good terms with him, he'd do almost anything you liked with the clock. For instance, suppose it were nine o'clock in the morning, just time to begin lessons: you'd only have to whisper a hint to Time, and round goes the clock in a twinkling! Half-past one, time for dinner!'

('I only wish it was,' the March Hare said to itself in a whisper.)

'That would be grand, certainly,' said Alice thoughtfully; 'but then—I shouldn't be hungry for it, you know.'

'Not at first, perhaps,' said the Hatter: 'but you could keep it to half-past one as long as you liked.'

'Is that the way *you* manage?' Alice asked.

The Hatter shook his head mournfully. 'Not I!' he replied. 'We quarreled last March——just before *he* went mad, you know——' (pointing with his teaspoon at the March Hare,) '——it was at the great concert given by the Queen of Hearts, and I had to sing

> "*Twinkle, twinkle, little bat!**
> *How I wonder what you're at!*"

You know the song, perhaps?'

'I've heard something like it,' said Alice.

[handwritten in left margin: Word play]

'It goes on, you know,' the Hatter continued, 'in this way:—

> *"Up above the world you fly*
> *Like a tea-tray in the sky.*
> *Twinkle, twinkle——"'*

Here the Dormouse shook itself, and began singing in its sleep '*Twinkle, twinkle, twinkle, twinkle——*' and went on so long that they had to pinch it to make it stop.

'Well, I'd hardly finished the first verse,' said the Hatter, 'when the Queen bawled out "He's murdering the time! Off with his head!"'

'How dreadfully savage!' exclaimed Alice.

'And ever since that,' the Hatter went on in a mournful tone, 'he wo'n't do a thing I ask! It's always six o'clock now.'

A bright idea came into Alice's head. 'Is that the reason so many tea-things are put out here?' she asked.

'Yes, that's it,' said the Hatter with a sigh: 'it's always tea-time, and we've no time to wash the things between whiles.'

'Then you keep moving round, I suppose?' said Alice.

'Exactly so,' said the Hatter: 'as the things get used up.'

'But what happens when you come to the beginning again?' Alice ventured to ask.

'Suppose we change the subject,' the March Hare inter-

Time functioning as a sentient being

rupted, yawning. 'I'm getting tired of this. I vote the young lady tells us a story.'

'I'm afraid I don't know one,' said Alice, rather alarmed at the proposal.

'Then the Dormouse shall!' they both cried. 'Wake up, Dormouse!' And they pinched it on both sides at once.

The Dormouse slowly opened its eyes. 'I wasn't asleep,' it said in a hoarse, feeble voice, 'I heard every word you fellows were saying.'

'Tell us a story!' said the March Hare.

'Yes, please do!' pleaded Alice.

'And be quick about it,' added the Hatter, 'or you'll be asleep again before it's done.'

'Once upon a time there were three little sisters,' the Dormouse began in a great hurry; 'and their names were Elsie, Lacie, and Tillie;* and they lived at the bottom of a well——'

'What did they live on?' said Alice, who always took a great interest in questions of eating and drinking.

'They lived on treacle,' said the Dormouse, after thinking a minute or two.

'They couldn't have done that, you know,' Alice gently remarked. 'They'd have been ill.'

'So they were,' said the Dormouse; '*very* ill.'

Alice tried a little to fancy to herself what such an extraordinary way of living would be like, but it puzzled her too much: so she went on: 'But why did they live at the bottom of a well?'

'Take some more tea,' the March Hare said to Alice, very earnestly.

'I've had nothing yet,' Alice replied in an offended tone: 'so I ca'n't take more.'

'You mean you ca'n't take *less*,' said the Hatter: 'it's very easy to take *more* than nothing.' ✳

'Nobody asked *your* opinion,' said Alice.

'Who's making personal remarks now?' the Hatter asked triumphantly.

Alice did not quite know what to say to this: so she helped

herself to some tea and bread-and-butter, and then turned to the Dormouse, and repeated her question. 'Why did they live at the bottom of a well?'

The Dormouse again took a minute or two to think about it, and then said 'It was a treacle-well.'*

'There's no such thing!' Alice was beginning very angrily, but the Hatter and the March Hare went 'Sh! Sh!' and the Dormouse sulkily remarked 'If you ca'n't be civil, you'd better finish the story for yourself.'

'No, please go on!' Alice said very humbly. 'I wo'n't interrupt you again. I dare say there may be *one*.'

'One, indeed!' said the Dormouse indignantly. However, he consented to go on. 'And so these three little sisters—they were learning to draw, you know——'

'What did they draw?' said Alice, quite forgetting her promise.

'Treacle,' said the Dormouse, without considering at all, this time.

'I want a clean cup,' interrupted the Hatter: 'let's all move one place on.' Most human, top of chain

He moved on as he spoke, and the Dormouse followed him: the March Hare moved into the Dormouse's place, and Alice rather unwillingly took the place of the March Hare. The Hatter was the only one who got any advantage from the change; and Alice was a good deal worse off than before, as the March Hare had just upset the milk-jug into his plate.

Alice did not wish to offend the Dormouse again, so she began very cautiously: 'But I don't understand. Where did they draw the treacle from?'

'You can draw water out of a water-well,' said the Hatter; 'so I should think you could draw treacle out of a treacle-well —eh, stupid?'

'But they were *in* the well,' Alice said to the Dormouse, not choosing to notice this last remark.

'Of course they were,' said the Dormouse: 'well in.'

This answer so confused poor Alice, that she let the Dormouse go on for some time without interrupting it.

'They were learning to draw,' the Dormouse went on,
yawning and rubbing its eyes, for it was getting very sleepy;
'and they drew all manner of things—everything that begins
with an M——'

'Why with an M?' said Alice.

'Why not?' said the March Hare.

Alice was silent.

The Dormouse had closed its eyes by this time, and was
going off into a doze; but, on being pinched by the Hatter, it
woke up again with a little shriek, and went on: '——that
begins with an M, such as mouse-traps, and the moon, and
memory, and muchness—you know you say things are "much
of a muchness"—did you ever see such a thing as a drawing of
a muchness!'

'Really, now you ask me,' said Alice, very much confused,
'I don't think——'

'Then you shouldn't talk,' said the Hatter.

This piece of rudeness was more than Alice could bear: she
got up in great disgust, and walked off: the Dormouse fell
asleep instantly, and neither of the others took the least notice
of her going, though she looked back once or twice, half
hoping that they would call after her: the last time she saw
them, they were trying to put the Dormouse into the teapot.*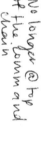

'At any rate I'll never go *there* again!' said Alice, as she picked her way through the wood. 'It's the stupidest tea-party I ever was at in all my life!'

Just as she said this, she noticed that one of the trees had a door leading right into it. 'That's very curious!' she thought. 'But everything's curious to-day. I think I may as well go in at once.' And in she went.

Once more she found herself in the long hall, and close to the little glass table. 'Now, I'll manage better this time,' she said to herself, and began by taking the little golden key, and unlocking the door that led into the garden. Then she set to work nibbling at the mushroom (she had kept a piece of it in her pocket) till she was about a foot high: then she walked down the little passage: and *then*—she found herself at last in the beautiful garden, among the bright flower-beds and the cool fountains.

CHAPTER VIII

THE QUEEN'S CROQUET-GROUND

A LARGE rose-tree stood near the entrance of the garden: the roses growing on it were white, but there were three gardeners at it, busily painting them red. Alice thought this a very curious thing, and she went nearer to watch them, and, just as she came up to them, she heard one of them say 'Look out now, Five! Don't go splashing paint over me like that!'

Nature vs appearances

'I couldn't help it,' said Five, in a sulky tone. 'Seven jogged my elbow.'

On which Seven looked up and said 'That's right, Five! Always lay the blame on others!'

'*You'd* better not talk!' said Five. 'I heard the Queen say only yesterday you deserved to be beheaded.'

'What for?' said the one who had spoken first.

'That's none of *your* business, Two!' said Seven.

'Yes, it *is* his business!' said Five. 'And I'll tell him—it was for bringing the cook tulip-roots instead of onions.'

Seven flung down his brush, and had just begun 'Well, of

all the unjust things—' when his eye chanced to fall upon
Alice, as she stood watching them, and he checked himself
suddenly: the others looked round also, and all of them
bowed low.

'Would you tell me, please,' said Alice, a little timidly, 'why
you are painting those roses?'

Five and Seven said nothing, but looked at Two. Two
began, in a low voice, 'Why, the fact is, you see, Miss, this
here ought to have been a *red* rose-tree, and we put a white one
in by mistake; and, if the Queen was to find it out, we should
all have our heads cut off, you know. So you see, Miss, we're
doing our best, afore she comes, to—' At this moment, Five,
who had been anxiously looking across the garden, called out
'The Queen! The Queen!', and the three gardeners instantly
threw themselves flat upon their faces. There was a sound of
many footsteps, and Alice looked round, eager to see the
Queen.

First came ten soldiers carrying clubs: these were all
shaped like the three gardeners, oblong and flat, with their
hands and feet at the corners: next the ten courtiers: these
were ornamented all over with diamonds, and walked two and
two, as the soldiers did. After these came the royal children:
there were ten of them, and the little dears came jumping
merrily along, hand in hand, in couples: they were all ornamented with hearts. Next came the guests, mostly Kings and
Queens, and among them Alice recognised the White Rabbit:
it was talking in a hurried nervous manner, smiling at everything that was said, and went by without noticing her. Then
followed the Knave of Hearts, carrying the King's crown
on a crimson velvet cushion; and, last of all this grand procession, came THE KING AND THE QUEEN OF
HEARTS.

Alice was rather doubtful* whether she ought not to lie
down on her face like the three gardeners, but she could not
remember ever having heard of such a rule at processions;
'and besides, what would be the use of a procession,' thought
she, 'if people had all to lie down on their faces, so that

they couldn't see it?' So she stood where she was, and waited.

When the procession came opposite to Alice, they all stopped and looked at her, and the Queen said, severely, 'Who is this?' She said it to the Knave of Hearts,* who only bowed and smiled in reply.

'Idiot!' said the Queen, tossing her head impatiently; and, turning to Alice, she went on: 'What's your name, child?'

'My name is Alice, so please your Majesty,' said Alice very

Retained species superiority [handwritten marginalia]

politely; but she added, to herself, 'Why, they're only a pack of cards,* after all. I needn't be afraid of them!'

'And who are *these?*' said the Queen, pointing to the three gardeners who were lying round the rose-tree; for, you see, as they were lying on their faces, and the pattern on their backs was the same as the rest of the pack, she could not tell whether they were gardeners, or soldiers, or courtiers, or three of her own children. *Class not visible* [handwritten marginalia]

'How should *I* know?' said Alice, surprised at her own courage. 'It's no business of *mine*.'

The Queen turned crimson with fury,* and, after glaring at her for a moment like a wild beast, began screaming 'Off with her head! Off with——'

'Nonsense!' said Alice, very loudly and decidedly, and the Queen was silent.

The King laid his hand upon her arm, and timidly said 'Consider, my dear: she is only a child!'

The Queen turned angrily away from him, and said to the Knave 'Turn them over!'

The Knave did so, very carefully, with one foot.

'Get up!' said the Queen in a shrill, loud voice, and the three gardeners instantly jumped up, and began bowing to the King, the Queen, the royal children, and everybody else.

'Leave off that!' screamed the Queen. 'You make me giddy.' And then, turning to the rose-tree, she went on 'What *have* you been doing here?'

'May it please your Majesty,' said Two, in a very humble tone, going down on one knee as he spoke, 'we were trying——'

'*I* see!' said the Queen, who had meanwhile been examining the roses. 'Off with their heads!' and the procession moved on, three of the soldiers remaining behind to execute the unfortunate gardeners, who ran to Alice for protection.

'You sha'n't be beheaded!' said Alice, and she put them into a large flower-pot that stood near. The three soldiers wandered about for a minute or two, looking for them, and then quietly marched off after the others.

'Are their heads off?' shouted the Queen.

'Their heads are gone, if it please your Majesty!' the soldiers shouted in reply.

'That's right!' shouted the Queen. 'Can you play croquet?'*

The soldiers were silent, and looked at Alice, as the question was evidently meant for her.

'Yes!' shouted Alice.

'Come on, then!' roared the Queen, and Alice joined the procession, wondering very much what would happen next.

'It's—it's a very fine day!' said a timid voice at her side. She was walking by the White Rabbit, who was peeping anxiously into her face.

'Very,' said Alice. 'Where's the Duchess?'

'Hush! Hush!' said the Rabbit in a low hurried tone. He looked anxiously over his shoulder as he spoke, and then raised himself upon tiptoe, put his mouth close to her ear, and whispered 'She's under sentence of execution.'

'What for?' said Alice.

'Did you say "What a pity!"?' the Rabbit asked.

'No, I didn't,' said Alice. 'I don't think it's at all a pity. I said "What for?"'

'She boxed the Queen's ears—' the Rabbit began. Alice gave a little scream of laughter. 'Oh, hush!' the Rabbit whispered in a frightened tone. 'The Queen will hear you! You see she came rather late, and the Queen said—'

'Get to your places!' shouted the Queen in a voice of thunder, and people began running about in all directions, tumbling up against each other: however, they got settled down in a minute or two, and the game began.

Alice thought she had never seen such a curious croquet-ground in her life: it was all ridges and furrows: the croquet balls were live hedgehogs, and the mallets live flamingoes,* and the soldiers had to double themselves up and stand on their hands and feet, to make the arches.

The chief difficulty Alice found at first was in managing her flamingo: she succeeded in getting its body tucked away, comfortably enough, under her arm, with its legs hanging down, but generally, just as she had got its neck nicely straightened out, and was going to give the hedgehog a blow

with its head, it *would* twist itself round and look up in her face, with such a puzzled expression that she could not help bursting out laughing; and, when she had got its head down, and was going to begin again, it was very provoking to find that the hedgehog had unrolled itself, and was in the act of crawling away: besides all this, there was generally a ridge or a furrow in the way wherever she wanted to send the hedgehog to, and, as the doubled-up soldiers were always getting up and walking off to other parts of the ground, Alice soon came to the conclusion that it was a very difficult game indeed.

The players all played at once, without waiting for turns, quarreling all the while, and fighting for the hedgehogs; and in a very short time the Queen was in a furious passion, and went stamping about, and shouting 'Off with his head!' or 'Off with her head!' about once in a minute.*

Alice began to feel very uneasy: to be sure, she had not as yet had any dispute with the Queen, but she knew that it might happen any minute, 'and then,' thought she, 'what would become of me? They're dreadfully fond of beheading people here: the great wonder is, that there's any one left alive!'

She was looking about for some way of escape, and wondering whether she could get away without being seen, when she noticed a curious appearance in the air: it puzzled her very much at first, but after watching it a minute or two she made it out to be a grin, and she said to herself 'It's the Cheshire-Cat: now I shall have somebody to talk to.'

'How are you getting on?' said the Cat, as soon as there was mouth enough for it to speak with.

Alice waited till the eyes appeared, and then nodded. 'It's no use speaking to it,' she thought, 'till its ears have come, or at least one of them.' In another minute the whole head appeared, and then Alice put down her flamingo, and began an account of the game, feeling very glad she had some one to listen to her. The Cat seemed to think that there was enough of it now in sight, and no more of it appeared.

'I don't think they play at all fairly,' Alice began, in rather a complaining tone, 'and they all quarrel so dreadfully one ca'n't hear oneself speak—and they don't seem to have any rules in particular: at least, if there are, nobody attends to them—and you've no idea how confusing it is all the things being alive: for instance, there's the arch I've got to go through next walking about at the other end of the ground—and I should have croqueted the Queen's hedgehog* just now, only it ran away when it saw mine coming!'

'How do you like the Queen?' said the Cat in a low voice.

'Not at all,' said Alice: 'she's so extremely—' Just then she noticed that the Queen was close behind her, listening: so she went on '—likely to win, that it's hardly worth while finishing the game.'

The Queen smiled and passed on.

'Who *are* you talking to?' said the King, coming up to Alice, and looking at the Cat's head with great curiosity.

'It's a friend of mine—a Cheshire-Cat,' said Alice: 'allow me to introduce it.'

'I don't like the look of it at all,' said the King: 'however, it may kiss my hand, if it likes.'

'I'd rather not,' the Cat remarked.

'Don't be impertinent,' said the King, 'and don't look at me like that!' He got behind Alice as he spoke.

'A cat may look at a king,'* said Alice. 'I've read that in some book, but I don't remember where.'

'Well, it must be removed,' said the King very decidedly; and he called to the Queen, who was passing at the moment, 'My dear! I wish you would have this cat removed!'

The Queen had only one way of settling all difficulties, great or small. 'Off with his head!' she said without even looking round.

'I'll fetch the executioner myself,' said the King eagerly, and he hurried off.

Alice thought she might as well go back and see how the game was going on, as she heard the Queen's voice in the distance, screaming with passion. She had already heard her sentence three of the players to be executed for having missed their turns, and she did not like the look of things at all, as the game was in such confusion that she never knew whether it was her turn or not. So she went off in search of her hedgehog.

The hedgehog was engaged in a fight with another hedgehog, which seemed to Alice an excellent opportunity for croqueting one of them with the other: the only difficulty was, that her flamingo was gone across to the other side of the garden, where Alice could see it trying in a helpless sort of way to fly up into a tree.

By the time she had caught the flamingo and brought it back, the fight was over, and both the hedgehogs were out of sight: 'but it doesn't matter much,' thought Alice, 'as all the arches are gone from this side of the ground.' So she tucked it away under her arm, that it might not escape again, and went back to have a little more conversation with her friend.

When she got back to the Cheshire-Cat, she was surprised to find quite a large crowd collected round it: there was a dispute going on between the executioner, the King, and the Queen, who were all talking at once, while all the rest were quite silent, and looked very uncomfortable.

The moment Alice appeared, she was appealed to by all

three to settle the question, and they repeated their arguments to her, though, as they all spoke at once, she found it very hard to make out exactly what they said.

The executioner's argument was, that you couldn't cut off a head unless there was a body to cut it off from: that he had never had to do such a thing before, and he wasn't going to begin at *his* time of life.

The King's argument was that anything that had a head could be beheaded, and that you weren't to talk nonsense.

The Queen's argument was that, if something wasn't done about it in less than no time, she'd have everybody executed, all round. (It was this last remark that had made the whole party look so grave and anxious.)

Alice could think of nothing else to say but 'It belongs to the Duchess: you'd better ask *her* about it.'

'She's in prison,' the Queen said to the executioner: 'fetch her here.' And the executioner went off like an arrow.

The Cat's head began fading away the moment he was gone, and, by the time he had come back with the Duchess, it had entirely disappeared: so the King and the executioner ran wildly up and down, looking for it, while the rest of the party went back to the game.

CHAPTER IX

THE MOCK TURTLE'S STORY

'YOU ca'n't think how glad I am to see you again, you dear old thing!' said the Duchess, as she tucked her arm affectionately into Alice's, and they walked off together.

Alice was very glad to find her in such a pleasant temper, and thought to herself that perhaps it was only the pepper that had made her so savage when they met in the kitchen.

'When *I'm* a Duchess,' she said to herself (not in a very hopeful tone, though), 'I wo'n't have any pepper in my kitchen *at all*. Soup does very well without—Maybe it's always pepper that makes people hot-tempered,' she went on, very much pleased at having found out a new kind of rule, 'and vinegar that makes them sour—and camomile* that makes them bitter—and—and barley-sugar and such things that make children sweet-tempered. I only wish people knew *that:* then they wouldn't be so stingy about it, you know——'

She had quite forgotten the Duchess by this time, and was a little startled when she heard her voice close to her ear. 'You're thinking about something, my dear, and that makes you forget to talk. I ca'n't tell you just now what the moral of that is, but I shall remember it in a bit.'

'Perhaps it hasn't one,' Alice ventured to remark.

'Tut, tut, child!' said the Duchess. 'Every thing's got a moral, if only you can find it.'* And she squeezed herself up closer to Alice's side as she spoke.

Alice did not much like her keeping so close to her: first, because the Duchess was *very* ugly; and secondly, because she was exactly the right height to rest her chin on Alice's shoulder, and it was an uncomfortably sharp chin. However, she did not like to be rude: so she bore it as well as she could.

'The game's going on rather better now,' she said, by way of keeping up the conversation a little.

' 'Tis so,' said the Duchess: 'and the moral of that is—"Oh, 'tis love, 'tis love, that makes the world go round!"'*

'Somebody said,' Alice whispered, 'that it's done by everybody minding their own business!'

'Ah, well! It means much the same thing,' said the Duchess, digging her sharp little chin into Alice's shoulder as she added 'and the moral of *that* is—"Take care of the sense, and the sounds will take care of themselves."'*

'How fond she is of finding morals in things!' Alice thought to herself.

'I dare say you're wondering why I don't put my arm round your waist,' the Duchess said, after a pause: 'the reason is, that I'm doubtful about the temper of your flamingo. Shall I try the experiment?'

'He might bite,' Alice cautiously replied, not feeling at all anxious to have the experiment tried.

'Very true,' said the Duchess: 'flamingoes and mustard both bite. And the moral of that is—"Birds of a feather flock together."'

'Only mustard isn't a bird,' Alice remarked.

'Right, as usual,' said the Duchess: 'what a clear way you have of putting things!'

'It's a mineral, I *think*,'* said Alice.

'Of course it is,' said the Duchess, who seemed ready to agree to everything that Alice said: 'there's a large mustard-mine near here. And the moral of that is—"The more there is of mine, the less there is of yours."'

'Oh, I know!' exclaimed Alice, who had not attended to this last remark. 'It's a vegetable. It doesn't look like one, but it is.'

'I quite agree with you,' said the Duchess; 'and the moral of that is—"Be what you would seem to be"—or, if you'd like it put more simply—"Never imagine yourself not to be otherwise than what it might appear to others that what you were or might have been was not otherwise than what you had been would have appeared to them to be otherwise."'

'I think I should understand that better,' Alice said very politely, 'if I had it written down: but I ca'n't quite follow it as you say it.'

'That's nothing to what I could say if I chose,' the Duchess replied, in a pleased tone.

'Pray don't trouble yourself to say it any longer than that,' said Alice.

'Oh, don't talk about trouble!' said the Duchess. 'I make you a present of everything I've said as yet.'

'A cheap sort of present!' thought Alice. 'I'm glad people don't give birthday-presents like that!' But she did not venture to say it out loud.

'Thinking again?' the Duchess asked, with another dig of her sharp little chin.

'I've a right to think,' said Alice sharply, for she was beginning to feel a little worried.

'Just about as much right,' said the Duchess, 'as pigs have to fly;* and the m——'

But here, to Alice's great surprise, the Duchess's voice died away, even in the middle of her favourite word 'moral,' and the arm that was linked into hers began to tremble. Alice looked up, and there stood the Queen in front of them, with her arms folded, frowning like a thunderstorm.

'A fine day, your Majesty!' the Duchess began in a low, weak voice.

'Now, I give you fair warning,' shouted the Queen, stamping on the ground as she spoke; 'either you or your head must be off, and that in about half no time! Take your choice!'

The Duchess took her choice, and was gone in a moment.

'Let's go on with the game,' the Queen said to Alice; and Alice was too much frightened to say a word, but slowly followed her back to the croquet-ground.

The other guests had taken advantage of the Queen's absence, and were resting in the shade: however, the moment they saw her, they hurried back to the game, the Queen merely remarking that a moment's delay would cost them their lives.

All the time they were playing the Queen never left off quarreling with the other players, and shouting 'Off with his head!' or 'Off with her head!' Those whom she sentenced were taken into custody by the soldiers, who of course had to leave off being arches to do this, so that, by the end of half an hour or so, there were no arches left, and all the players, except the King, the Queen, and Alice, were in custody and under sentence of execution.

Then the Queen left off, quite out of breath, and said to Alice 'Have you seen the Mock Turtle yet?'

'No,' said Alice. 'I don't even know what a Mock Turtle is.'

'It's the thing Mock Turtle Soup* is made from,' said the Queen.

'I never saw one, or heard of one,' said Alice.

'Come on, then,' said the Queen, 'and he shall tell you his history.'

As they walked off together, Alice heard the King say in a low voice, to the company generally, 'You are all pardoned.' 'Come, *that's* a good thing!' she said to herself, for she had felt quite unhappy at the number of executions the Queen had ordered.

They very soon came upon a Gryphon,* lying fast asleep in the sun. (If you don't know what a Gryphon is, look at the picture.) 'Up, lazy thing!' said the Queen, 'and take this young lady to see the Mock Turtle, and to hear his history. I must go back and see after some executions I have ordered;' and she walked off, leaving Alice alone with the Gryphon. Alice did not quite like the look of the creature, but on the whole she thought it would be quite as safe to stay with it as to go after that savage Queen: so she waited.

Animals as safer than humans now

The Gryphon sat up and rubbed its eyes: then it watched the Queen till she was out of sight: then it chuckled. 'What fun!' said the Gryphon, half to itself, half to Alice.

'What *is* the fun?' said Alice.

'Why, *she*,' said the Gryphon. 'It's all her fancy, that: they never executes nobody, you know. Come on!'

'Everybody says "come on!" here,' thought Alice, as she went slowly after it: 'I never was so ordered about before, in all my life, never!' *power shift*

They had not gone far before they saw the Mock Turtle in the distance; sitting sad and lonely on a little ledge of rock, and, as they came nearer, Alice could hear him sighing as if his heart would break. She pitied him deeply. 'What is his sorrow?' she asked the Gryphon. And the Gryphon answered, very nearly in the same words as before, 'It's all his fancy, that: he hasn't got no sorrow, you know. Come on!'

So they went up to the Mock Turtle, who looked at them with large eyes full of tears, but said nothing.

'This here young lady,' said the Gryphon, 'she wants for to know your history, she do.'

'I'll tell it her,' said the Mock Turtle in a deep, hollow tone. 'Sit down, both of you, and don't speak a word till I've finished.'

So they sat down, and nobody spoke for some minutes. Alice thought to herself 'I don't see how he can *ever* finish, if he doesn't begin.' But she waited patiently.

'Once,' said the Mock Turtle at last, with a deep sigh, 'I was a real Turtle.'

These words were followed by a very long silence, broken only by an occasional exclamation of 'Hjckrrh!'* from the Gryphon, and the constant heavy sobbing of the Mock Turtle. Alice was very nearly getting up and saying 'Thank you, Sir, for your interesting story,' but she could not help thinking there *must* be more to come, so she sat still and said nothing.

'When we were little,' the Mock Turtle went on at last, more calmly, though still sobbing a little now and then, 'we went to school in the sea. The master was an old Turtle—we used to call him Tortoise——'

'Why did you call him Tortoise, if he wasn't one?' Alice asked.

'We called him Tortoise because he taught us,' said the Mock Turtle angrily. 'Really you are very dull!'

'You ought to be ashamed of yourself for asking such a simple question,' added the Gryphon; and then they both sat silent and looked at poor Alice, who felt ready to sink into the earth. At last the Gryphon said to the Mock Turtle 'Drive on, old fellow! Don't be all day about it!', and he went on in these words:—

'Yes, we went to school in the sea,* though you mayn't believe it——'

'I never said I didn't!' interrupted Alice.

'You did,' said the Mock Turtle.

'Hold your tongue!' added the Gryphon, before Alice could speak again. The Mock Turtle went on.

'We had the best of educations—in fact, we went to school every day——'

'*I've* been to a day-school, too,' said Alice. 'You needn't be so proud as all that.'

'With extras?' asked the Mock Turtle, a little anxiously.

'Yes,' said Alice: 'we learned French and music.'

'And washing?' said the Mock Turtle.

'Certainly not!' said Alice indignantly.

'Ah! Then yours wasn't a really good school,' said the Mock Turtle in a tone of great relief. 'Now, at *ours*, they had, at the end of the bill, "French, music, *and washing*—extra".'

'You couldn't have wanted it much,' said Alice; 'living at the bottom of the sea.'

'I couldn't afford to learn it,' said the Mock Turtle, with a sigh. 'I only took the regular course.'

'What was that?' inquired Alice.

'Reeling and Writhing, of course, to begin with,' the Mock Turtle replied; 'and then the different branches of Arithmetic—Ambition, Distraction, Uglification, and Derision.'

'I never heard of "Uglification,"' Alice ventured to say. 'What is it?'

The Gryphon lifted up both its paws in surprise. 'Never heard of uglifying!' it exclaimed. 'You know what to beautify is, I suppose?'

'Yes,' said Alice doubtfully: 'it means—to—make—anything—prettier.'

'Well, then,' the Gryphon went on, 'if you don't know what to uglify is, you *are* a simpleton.'

Alice did not feel encouraged to ask any more questions about it: so she turned to the Mock Turtle, and said 'What else had you to learn?'

'Well, there was Mystery,' the Mock Turtle replied, counting off the subjects on his flappers,—'Mystery, ancient and modern, with Seaography: then Drawling—the Drawling-master* was an old conger-eel, that used to come once a week: *he* taught us Drawling, Stretching, and Fainting in Coils.'

'What was *that* like?' said Alice.

'Well, I ca'n't show it you, myself,' the Mock Turtle said: 'I'm too stiff. And the Gryphon never learnt it.'

'Hadn't time,' said the Gryphon: 'I went to the Classical master, though. He was an old crab, *he* was.'

'I never went to him,' the Mock Turtle said with a sigh. 'He taught Laughing and Grief,* they used to say.'

'So he did, so he did,' said the Gryphon, sighing in his turn; and both creatures hid their faces in their paws.

'And how many hours a day did you do lessons?' said Alice, in a hurry to change the subject.

'Ten hours the first day,' said the Mock Turtle: 'nine the next, and so on.'

'What a curious plan!' exclaimed Alice.

'That's the reason they're called lessons,' the Gryphon remarked: 'because they lessen from day to day.'

This was quite a new idea to Alice, and she thought it over a little before she made her next remark. 'Then the eleventh day must have been a holiday?'

'Of course it was,' said the Mock Turtle.

'And how did you manage on the twelfth?' Alice went on eagerly.

'That's enough about lessons,' the Gryphon interrupted in a very decided tone. 'Tell her something about the games now.'

reached a logical dead end

Challenges of 'making sense'
·Bizarre accusations

CHAPTER X

THE LOBSTER-QUADRILLE

THE Mock Turtle sighed deeply, and drew the back of one flapper across his eyes. He looked at Alice and tried to speak, but, for a minute or two, sobs choked his voice. 'Same as if he had a bone in his throat,' said the Gryphon; and it set to work shaking him and punching him in the back. At last the Mock Turtle recovered his voice, and, with tears running down his cheeks, he went on again:—

'You may not have lived much under the sea—' ('I haven't,' said Alice)—'and perhaps you were never even introduced to a lobster—' (Alice began to say 'I once tasted——' but checked herself hastily, and said 'No, never') '——so you can have no idea what a delightful thing a Lobster-Quadrille* is!'

'No, indeed,' said Alice. 'What sort of a dance is it?'

'Why,' said the Gryphon, 'you first form into a line along the sea-shore——'

'Two lines!' cried the Mock Turtle. 'Seals, turtles, salmon, and so on: then, when you've cleared all the jelly-fish out of the way——'

'*That* generally takes some time,' interrupted the Gryphon.

'—you advance twice——'

'Each with a lobster as a partner!' cried the Gryphon.

'Of course,' the Mock Turtle said: 'advance twice, set to partners——'

'—change lobsters, and retire in same order,' continued the Gryphon.

'Then, you know,' the Mock Turtle went on, 'you throw the——'

'The lobsters!' shouted the Gryphon, with a bound into the air.

'—as far out to sea as you can——'

'Swim after them!' screamed the Gryphon.

'Turn a somersault in the sea!' cried the Mock Turtle, capering wildly about.

'Change lobsters again!' yelled the Gryphon at the top of its voice.

'Back to land again, and—that's all the first figure,' said the Mock Turtle, suddenly dropping his voice; and the two creatures, who had been jumping about like mad things all this time, sat down again very sadly and quietly, and looked at Alice.

'It must be a very pretty dance,' said Alice timidly.

'Would you like to see a little of it?' said the Mock Turtle.

'Very much indeed,' said Alice.

'Come, let's try the first figure!' said the Mock Turtle to the Gryphon. 'We can do it without lobsters, you know. Which shall sing?'

'Oh, *you* sing,' said the Gryphon. 'I've forgotten the words.'

So they began solemnly dancing round and round Alice, every now and then treading on her toes when they passed too close, and waving their fore-paws to mark the time, while the Mock Turtle sang this, very slowly and sadly:—*

'Will you walk a little faster?* said a whiting to a snail,
'There's a porpoise close behind us, and he's treading on my tail.
See how eagerly the lobsters and the turtles all advance!
They are waiting on the shingle—will you come and join the
        dance?
    Will you, wo'n't you, will you, wo'n't you, will you join the
        dance?
    Will you, wo'n't you, will you, wo'n't you, wo'n't you join the
        dance?

'You can really have no notion how delightful it will be
When they take us up and throw us, with the lobsters, out to sea!'
But the snail replied 'Too far, too far!', and gave a look
        askance—
Said he thanked the whiting kindly, but he would not join the
        dance.
    Would not, could not, would not, could not, would not join the
        dance.
    Would not, could not, would not, could not, could not join the
        dance.

'What matters it how far we go?' his scaly friend replied.
'There is another shore, you know, upon the other side.
The further off from England the nearer is to France—
Then turn not pale, beloved snail, but come and join the dance.
    Will you, wo'n't you, will you, wo'n't you, will you join the
        dance?
    Will you, wo'n't you, will you, wo'n't you, wo'n't you join the
        dance?'

'Thank you, it's a very interesting dance to watch,' said Alice, feeling very glad that it was over at last: 'and I do so like that curious song about the whiting!'

'Oh, as to the whiting,' said the Mock Turtle, 'they—you've seen them, of course?'

'Yes,' said Alice, 'I've often seen them at dinn——' she checked herself hastily.

'I don't know where Dinn may be,' said the Mock Turtle; 'but, if you've seen them so often, of course you know what they're like?'

'I believe so,' Alice replied thoughtfully. 'They have their tails in their mouths*—and they're all over crumbs.'

'You're wrong about the crumbs,' said the Mock Turtle: 'crumbs would all wash off in the sea. But they *have* their tails in their mouths; and the reason is—' here the Mock Turtle yawned and shut his eyes. 'Tell her about the reason and all that,' he said to the Gryphon.

'The reason is,' said the Gryphon, 'that they *would* go with the lobsters to the dance. So they got thrown out to sea. So they had to fall a long way. So they got their tails fast in their mouths. So they couldn't get them out again. That's all.'

'Thank you,' said Alice, 'it's very interesting. I never knew so much about a whiting before.'

'I can tell you more than that, if you like,' said the Gryphon. 'Do you know why it's called a whiting?'

'I never thought about it,' said Alice. 'Why?'

'*It does the boots and shoes,*' the Gryphon replied very solemnly.

Alice was thoroughly puzzled. 'Does the boots and shoes!' she repeated in a wondering tone.

'Why, what are *your* shoes done with?' said the Gryphon. 'I mean, what makes them so shiny?'

Alice looked down at them, and considered a little before she gave her answer. 'They're done with blacking,* I believe.'

'Boots and shoes under the sea,' the Gryphon went on in a deep voice, 'are done with whiting. Now you know.'

'And what are they made of?' Alice asked in a tone of great curiosity.

'Soles and eels, of course,' the Gryphon replied, rather impatiently: 'any shrimp could have told you that.'

'If I'd been the whiting,' said Alice, whose thoughts were still running on the song, 'I'd have said to the porpoise "Keep back, please! We don't want *you* with us!"'

'They were obliged to have him with them,' the Mock Turtle said. 'No wise fish would go anywhere without a porpoise.'

'Wouldn't it, really?' said Alice, in a tone of great surprise.

'Of course not,' said the Mock Turtle. 'Why, if a fish came to *me*, and told me he was going a journey, I should say "With what porpoise?"'

'Don't you mean "purpose"?'* said Alice.

'I mean what I say,' the Mock Turtle replied, in an offended tone. And the Gryphon added 'Come, let's hear some of *your* adventures.'

'I could tell you my adventures—beginning from this morning,' said Alice a little timidly; 'but it's no use going back to yesterday, because I was a different person then.'

'Explain all that,' said the Mock Turtle.

'No, no! The adventures first,' said the Gryphon in an impatient tone: 'explanations take such a dreadful time.'

So Alice began telling them her adventures from the time when she first saw the White Rabbit. She was a little nervous about it, just at first, the two creatures got so close to her, one on each side, and opened their eyes and mouths so *very* wide; but she gained courage as she went on. Her listeners were perfectly quiet till she got to the part about her repeating '*You are old, Father William,*' to the Caterpillar, and the words all coming different, and then the Mock Turtle drew a long breath, and said 'That's very curious!'

'It's all about as curious as it can be,' said the Gryphon.

'It all came different!' the Mock Turtle repeated thoughtfully. 'I should like to hear her try and repeat something now.

Tell her to begin.' He looked at the Gryphon as if he thought it had some kind of authority over Alice.

'Stand up and repeat " *'Tis the voice of the sluggard*," ' said the Gryphon.

'How the creatures order one about, and make one repeat lessons!' thought Alice. 'I might just as well be at school at once.' However, she got up, and began to repeat it, but her head was so full of the Lobster-Quadrille, that she hardly knew what she was saying; and the words came very queer indeed:—

awesome ↗

' *'Tis the voice of the Lobster:* * I heard him declare
"*You have baked me too brown, I must sugar my hair.*"
*As a duck with its eyelids, so he with his nose
Trims his belt and his buttons, and turns out his toes.
When the sands are all dry, he is gay as a lark,
And will talk in contemptuous tones of the Shark:
But, when the tide rises and sharks are around,
His voice has a timid and tremulous sound.*'

'That's different from what *I* used to say when I was a child,' said the Gryphon.

'Well, *I* never heard it before,' said the Mock Turtle; 'but it sounds uncommon nonsense.'

Alice said nothing: she had sat down with her face in her

hands, wondering if anything <u>would *ever* happen</u> in a natural
<u>way again.</u> Disruption of nature

'I should like to have it explained,' said the Mock
Turtle.

'She ca'n't explain it,' said the Gryphon hastily. 'Go on
with the next verse.'

'But about his toes?' the Mock Turtle persisted. 'How
could he turn them out with his nose, you know?'

'It's the first position in dancing,'* Alice said; but she was
dreadfully puzzled by the whole thing, and longed to change
the subject.

'Go on with the next verse,' the Gryphon repeated: 'it
begins "*I passed by his garden.*"'

Alice did not dare to disobey, though she felt sure it would
all come wrong, and she went on in a trembling voice:—

> '*I passed by his garden,* and marked, with one eye,
> How the Owl and the Panther were sharing a pie:
> The Panther took pie-crust, and gravy, and meat,
> While the Owl had the dish as its share of the treat.
> When the pie was all finished, the Owl, as a boon,
> Was kindly permitted to pocket the spoon:
> While the Panther received knife and fork with a growl,
> And concluded the banquet by——'

'What *is* the use of repeating all that stuff?' the Mock
Turtle interrupted, 'if you don't explain it as you go on? It's
by far the most confusing thing *I* ever heard!'

'Yes, I think you'd better leave off,' said the Gryphon, and
Alice was only too glad to do so.

'Shall we try another figure of the Lobster-Quadrille?' the
Gryphon went on. 'Or would you like the Mock Turtle to sing
you another song?'

'Oh, a song, please, if the Mock Turtle would be so kind,'
Alice replied, so eagerly that the Gryphon said, in a rather
offended tone, 'Hm! No accounting for tastes! Sing her
"*Turtle Soup,*" will you, old fellow?'

The Mock Turtle sighed deeply, and began, in a voice choked with sobs, to sing this:—

> '*Beautiful Soup, so rich and green,**
> *Waiting in a hot tureen!*
> *Who for such dainties would not stoop?*
> *Soup of the evening, beautiful Soup!*
> *Soup of the evening, beautiful Soup!*
>   *Beau—ootiful Soo—oop!*
>   *Beau—ootiful Soo—oop!*
> *Soo—oop of the e—e—evening,*
>   *Beautiful, beautiful Soup!*

> '*Beautiful Soup! Who cares for fish,*
> *Game, or any other dish?*
> *Who would not give all else for two p*
> *ennyworth only of beautiful Soup?*
> *Pennyworth only of beautiful soup?*
>   *Beau—ootiful Soo—oop!*
>   *Beau—ootiful Soo—oop!*
> *Soo—oop of the e—e—evening,*
>   *Beautiful, beauti—FUL SOUP!*'

'Chorus again!' cried the Gryphon, and the Mock Turtle had just begun to repeat it, when a cry of 'The trial's beginning!' was heard in the distance.

'Come on!' cried the Gryphon, and, taking Alice by the hand, it hurried off, without waiting for the end of the song.

'What trial is it?' Alice panted as she ran; but the Gryphon only answered 'Come on!' and ran the faster, while more and more faintly came, carried on the breeze that followed them, the melancholy words:—

> '*Soo—oop of the e—e—evening,*
>   *Beautiful, beautiful Soup!*'

CHAPTER XI

WHO STOLE THE TARTS?*

THE King and Queen of Hearts were seated on their throne when they arrived,* with a great crowd assembled about them —all sorts of little birds and beasts, as well as the whole pack of cards: the Knave was standing before them, in chains, with a soldier on each side to guard him; and near the King was the White Rabbit, with a trumpet in one hand, and a scroll of parchment in the other. In the very middle of the court was a table, with a large dish of tarts upon it: they looked so good, that it made Alice quite hungry to look at them—'I wish they'd get the trial done,' she thought, 'and hand round the refreshments!' But there seemed to be no chance of this; so she began looking at everything about her to pass away the time.

Alice had never been in a court of justice before, but she had read about them in books, and she was quite pleased to find that she knew the name of nearly everything there. 'That's the judge,' she said to herself, 'because of his great wig.'

The judge, by the way, was the King; and, as he wore his crown over the wig (look at the frontispiece if you want to see how he did it), he did not look at all comfortable, and it was certainly not becoming.

'And that's the jury-box,' thought Alice; 'and those twelve creatures,' (she was obliged to say 'creatures,' you see, because some of them were animals, and some were birds,) 'I suppose they are the jurors.' She said this last word two or three times over to herself, being rather proud of it: for she thought, and rightly too, that very few little girls of her age knew the meaning of it at all. However, 'jurymen' would have done just as well. *learning life values*

The twelve jurors were all writing very busily on slates. 'What are they doing?' Alice whispered to the Gryphon.

'They ca'n't have anything to put down yet, before the trial's begun.'

'They're putting down their names,' the Gryphon whispered in reply, 'for fear they should forget them before the end of the trial.'

'Stupid things!' Alice began in a loud indignant voice; but she stopped herself hastily, for the White Rabbit cried out 'Silence in the court!', and the King put on his spectacles and looked anxiously round, to make out who was talking.

Alice could see, as well as if she were looking over their shoulders, that all the jurors were writing down 'Stupid things!' on their slates, and she could even make out that one of them didn't know how to spell 'stupid,' and that he had to ask his neighbour to tell him. 'A nice muddle their slates'll be in, before the trial's over!' thought Alice.

One of the jurors had a pencil that squeaked. This, of course, Alice could *not* stand, and she went round the court and got behind him, and very soon found an opportunity of taking it away. She did it so quickly that the poor little juror (it was Bill, the Lizard) could not make out at all what had become of it; so, after hunting all about for it, he was obliged to write with one finger for the rest of the day; and this was of very little use, as it left no mark on the slate.

'Herald, read the accusation!' said the King.

On this the White Rabbit blew three blasts on the trumpet,

and then unrolled the parchment-scroll, and read as follows:—

> '*The Queen of Hearts, she made some tarts,* *
> *All on a summer day:*
> *The Knave of Hearts, he stole those tarts*
> *And took them quite away!*'

'Consider your verdict,' the King said to the jury.

'Not yet, not yet!' the Rabbit hastily interrupted. 'There's a great deal to come before that!'

'Call the first witness,' said the King; and the White Rabbit blew three blasts on the trumpet, and called out 'First witness!'

The first witness was the Hatter. He came in with a teacup in one hand and a piece of bread-and-butter in the other. 'I beg pardon, your Majesty,' he began, 'for bringing these in; but I hadn't quite finished my tea when I was sent for.'

'You ought to have finished,' said the King. 'When did you begin?'

The Hatter looked at the March Hare, who had followed him into the court, arm-in-arm with the Dormouse. 'Fourteenth of March, I *think* it was,' he said.

'Fifteenth,' said the March Hare.

'Sixteenth,' said the Dormouse.

'Write that down,' the King said to the jury; and the jury eagerly wrote down all three dates on their slates, and then added them up, and reduced the answer to shillings and pence.

'Take off your hat,' the King said to the Hatter.

'It isn't mine,' said the Hatter.

'*Stolen!*' the King exclaimed, turning to the jury, who instantly made a memorandum of the fact.

'I keep them to sell,' the Hatter added as an explanation. 'I've none of my own. I'm a hatter.'

Here the Queen put on her spectacles, and began staring hard at the Hatter, who turned pale and fidgeted.

'Give your evidence,' said the King; 'and don't be nervous, or I'll have you executed on the spot.'

This did not seem to encourage the witness at all: he kept shifting from one foot to the other, looking uneasily at the Queen, and in his confusion he bit a large piece out of his teacup instead of the bread-and-butter.

Just at this moment Alice felt a very curious sensation, which puzzled her a good deal until she made out what it was: she was beginning to grow larger again, and she thought at first she would get up and leave the court; but on second thoughts she decided to remain where she was as long as there was room for her.

'I wish you wouldn't squeeze so,' said the Dormouse, who was sitting next to her. 'I can hardly breathe.'

'I ca'n't help it,' said Alice very meekly: 'I'm growing.'

'You've no right to grow *here*,' said the Dormouse.

'Don't talk nonsense,' said Alice more boldly: 'you know you're growing too.'

'Yes, but *I* grow at a reasonable pace,' said the Dormouse: 'not in that ridiculous fashion.' And he got up very sulkily and crossed over to the other side of the court.

All this time the Queen had never left off staring at the Hatter, and, just as the Dormouse crossed the court, she said, to one of the officers of the court, 'Bring me the list of the singers in the last concert!' on which the wretched Hatter trembled so, that he shook off both his shoes.

'Give your evidence,' the King repeated angrily, 'or I'll have you executed, whether you're nervous or not.'

'I'm a poor man, your Majesty,' the Hatter began, in a trembling voice, 'and I hadn't begun my tea—not above a week or so—and what with the bread-and-butter getting so thin—and the twinkling of the tea——'

'The twinkling of *what?*' said the King.

'It *began* with the tea,' the Hatter replied.

'Of course twinkling *begins* with a T!' said the King sharply. 'Do you take me for a dunce? Go on!'

'I'm a poor man,' the Hatter went on, 'and most things twinkled after that—only the March Hare said——'

'I didn't!' the March Hare interrupted in a great hurry.

'You did!' said the Hatter.

'I deny it!' said the March Hare.

'He denies it,' said the King: 'leave out that part.'

'Well, at any rate, the Dormouse said——' the Hatter went on, looking anxiously round to see if he would deny it too; but the Dormouse denied nothing, being fast asleep.

'After that,' continued the Hatter, 'I cut some more bread-and-butter——'

'But what did the Dormouse say?' one of the jury asked.

'That I ca'n't remember,' said the Hatter.

'You *must* remember,' remarked the King, 'or I'll have you executed.'

The miserable Hatter dropped his teacup and bread-and-butter, and went down on one knee. 'I'm a poor man, your Majesty,' he began.

'You're a *very* poor *speaker*,' said the King.

Here one of the guinea-pigs cheered, and was immediately suppressed by the officers of the court. (As that is rather a hard word, I will just explain to you how it was done. They had a large canvas bag, which tied up at the mouth with strings: into this they slipped the guinea-pig, head first, and then sat upon it.)

'I'm glad I've seen that done,' thought Alice. 'I've so often read in the newspapers, at the end of trials, "There was some attempt at applause, which was immediately suppressed by

understanding nonsense as a complete departure from meaning

the officers of the court," and I never understood what it meant till now.'

'If that's all you know about it, you may stand down,' continued the King.

'I ca'n't go no lower,' said the Hatter: 'I'm on the floor, as it is.'

'Then you may *sit* down,' the King replied.

Here the other guinea-pig cheered, and was suppressed.

'Come, that finishes the guinea-pigs!' thought Alice. 'Now we shall get on better.'

'I'd rather finish my tea,' said the Hatter, with an anxious look at the Queen, who was reading the list of singers.

'You may go,' said the King, and the Hatter hurriedly left the court, without even waiting to put his shoes on.

'——and just take his head off outside,' the Queen added to one of the officers; but the Hatter was out of sight before the officer could get to the door.

'Call the next witness!' said the King.

The next witness was the Duchess's cook. She carried the pepper-box in her hand, and Alice guessed who it was, even before she got into the court, by the way the people near the door began sneezing all at once.

'Give your evidence,' said the King.

'Sha'n't,' said the cook.

The King looked anxiously at the White Rabbit, who said, in a low voice, 'Your Majesty must cross-examine *this* witness.'

'Well, if I must, I must,' the King said with a melancholy air, and, after folding his arms and frowning at the cook till his eyes were nearly out of sight, he said, in a deep voice, 'What are tarts made of?'

'Pepper, mostly,' said the cook.

'Treacle,' said a sleepy voice behind her.

'Collar that Dormouse!' the Queen shrieked out. 'Behead that Dormouse! Turn that Dormouse out of court! Suppress him! Pinch him! Off with his whiskers!'

For some minutes the whole court was in confusion, getting the Dormouse turned out, and, by the time they had settled down again, the cook had disappeared.

'Never mind!' said the King, with an air of great relief. 'Call the next witness.' And, he added, in an under-tone to the Queen, 'Really, my dear, *you* must cross-examine the next witness. It quite makes my forehead ache!'

Alice watched the White Rabbit as he fumbled over the list, feeling very curious to see what the next witness would be like, '—for they haven't got much evidence *yet*,' she said to herself. Imagine her surprise, when the White Rabbit read out, at the top of his shrill little voice, the name 'Alice!'

Chaotic childish nonsense
that rejects Victorian
standards of adulthood

CHAPTER XII

ALICE'S EVIDENCE*

'HERE!' cried Alice, quite forgetting in the flurry of the
moment how large she had grown in the last few minutes, and
she jumped up in such a hurry that she tipped over the jury-
box with the edge of her skirt,* upsetting all the jurymen on
to the heads of the crowd below, and there they lay sprawling
about, reminding her very much of a globe of gold-fish she
had accidentally upset the week before.

'Oh, I *beg* your pardon!' she exclaimed in a tone of great dismay, and began picking them up again as quickly as she could, for the accident of the gold-fish kept running in her head, and she had a vague sort of idea that they must be collected at once and put back into the jury-box, or they would die.

'The trial cannot proceed,' said the King, in a very grave voice, 'until all the jurymen are back in their proper places— *all*,' he repeated with great emphasis, looking hard at Alice as he said so.

Alice looked at the jury-box, and saw that, in her haste, she had put the Lizard in head downwards, and the poor little thing was waving its tail about in a melancholy way, being quite unable to move. She soon got it out again, and put it right; 'not that it signifies much,' she said to herself; 'I should think it would be *quite* as much use in the trial one way up as the other.'

As soon as the jury had a little recovered from the shock of being upset, and their slates and pencils had been found and handed back to them, they set to work very diligently to write out a history of the accident, all except the Lizard, who seemed too much overcome to do anything but sit with its mouth open, gazing up into the roof of the court.

'What do you know about this business?' the King said to Alice.

'Nothing,' said Alice.

'Nothing *whatever?*' persisted the King.

'Nothing whatever,' said Alice.

'That's very important,' the King said, turning to the jury. They were just beginning to write this down on their slates, when the White Rabbit interrupted: '*Un*important, your Majesty means, of course,' he said, in a very respectful tone, but frowning and making faces at him as he spoke.

'*Un*important, of course, I meant,' the King hastily said, and went on to himself in an undertone, 'important— unimportant—unimportant—important——' as if he were trying which word sounded best.

Some of the jury wrote it down 'important,' and some

'unimportant.' Alice could see this, as she was near enough to look over their slates; 'but it doesn't matter a bit,' she thought to herself.

At this moment the King, who had been for some time busily writing in his note-book, called out 'Silence!', and read out from his book, 'Rule Forty-two.* *All persons more than a mile high to leave the court.*'

Everybody looked at Alice.

'*I'm* not a mile high,' said Alice.

'You are,' said the King.

'Nearly two miles high,' added the Queen.

'Well, I sha'n't go, at any rate,' said Alice: 'besides, that's not a regular rule: you invented it just now.'

'It's the oldest rule in the book,' said the King.

'Then it ought to be Number One,' said Alice.

The King turned pale, and shut his note-book hastily. 'Consider your verdict,' he said to the jury, in a low trembling voice.

'There's more evidence to come yet, please your Majesty,' said the White Rabbit, jumping up in a great hurry: 'this paper has just been picked up.'

'What's in it?' said the Queen.

'I haven't opened it yet,' said the White Rabbit; 'but it seems to be a letter, written by the prisoner to—to somebody.'

'It must have been that,' said the King, 'unless it was written to nobody, which isn't usual, you know.'

'Who is it directed to?' said one of the jurymen.

'It isn't directed at all,' said the White Rabbit: 'in fact, there's nothing written on the *outside*.' He unfolded the paper as he spoke, and added 'It isn't a letter, after all: it's a set of verses.'

'Are they in the prisoner's handwriting?' asked another of the jurymen.

'No, they're not,' said the White Rabbit, 'and that's the queerest thing about it.' (The jury all looked puzzled.)

'He must have imitated somebody else's hand,' said the King. (The jury all brightened up again.)

'Please your Majesty,' said the Knave, 'I didn't write it, and they ca'n't prove that I did: there's no name signed at the end.'

'If you didn't sign it,' said the King, 'that only makes the matter worse. You *must* have meant some mischief, or else you'd have signed your name like an honest man.'

There was a general clapping of hands at this: it was the first really clever thing the King had said that day.

'That *proves* his guilt, of course,' said the Queen: 'so, off with——.'

'It doesn't prove anything of the sort!' said Alice. 'Why, you don't even know what they're about!'

'Read them,' said the King.

The White Rabbit put on his spectacles. 'Where shall I begin, please your Majesty?' he asked.

'Begin at the beginning,' the King said, very gravely, 'and go on till you come to the end: then stop.'

There was dead silence in the court, whilst the White Rabbit read out these verses:—

> *'They told me you had been to her,**
> *And mentioned me to him:*
> *She gave me a good character,*
> *But said I could not swim.*
>
> *He sent them word I had not gone*
> *(We know it to be true):*
> *If she should push the matter on,*
> *What would become of you?*
>
> *I gave her one, they gave him two,*
> *You gave us three or more;*
> *They all returned from him to you,*
> *Though they were mine before.*
>
> *If I or she should chance to be*
> *Involved in this affair,*
> *He trusts to you to set them free,*
> *Exactly as we were.*

My notion was that you had been
(Before she had this fit)
An obstacle that came between
Him, and ourselves, and it.

Don't let him know she liked them best,
For this must ever be
A secret, kept from all the rest,
Between yourself and me.'

'That's the most important piece of evidence we've heard yet,' said the King, rubbing his hands; 'so now let the jury——'

'If any one of them can explain it,' said Alice, (she had grown so large in the last few minutes that she wasn't a bit afraid of interrupting him,) 'I'll give him sixpence. *I* don't believe there's an atom of meaning in it.'

The jury all wrote down, on their slates, '*She* doesn't believe there's an atom of meaning in it,' but none of them attempted to explain the paper.

'If there's no meaning in it,' said the King, 'that saves a world of trouble, you know, as we needn't try to find any. And yet I don't know,' he went on, spreading out the verses on his knee, and looking at them with one eye; 'I seem to see some meaning in them, after all. "*—said I could not swim—*" you ca'n't swim, can you?' he added, turning to the Knave.

The Knave shook his head sadly. 'Do I look like it?' he said. (Which he certainly did *not*, being made entirely of cardboard.)

'All right, so far,' said the King; and he went on muttering over the verses to himself: ' "*We know it to be true*"— that's the jury, of course—"*If she should push the matter on*" —that must be the Queen—"*What would become of you?*"— What, indeed!—"*I gave her one, they gave him two*"—why, that must be what he did with the tarts, you know——'

'But it goes on "*they all returned from him to you*,"' said Alice.

'Why, there they are?' said the King triumphantly, pointing to the tarts on the table. 'Nothing can be clearer than *that*. Then again—"*before she had this fit*"—you never had *fits*, my dear, I think?' he said to the Queen.

'Never!' said the Queen, furiously, throwing an inkstand at the Lizard as she spoke. (The unfortunate little Bill had left off writing on his slate with one finger, as he found it made no mark; but he now hastily began again, using the ink, that was trickling down his face, as long as it lasted.)

'Then the words don't *fit* you,' said the King, looking round the court with a smile. There was a dead silence.

'It's a pun!' the King added in an angry tone, and everybody laughed. 'Let the jury consider their verdict,' the King said, for about the twentieth time that day.

'No, no!' said the Queen. 'Sentence first—verdict afterwards.'

'Stuff and nonsense!' said Alice loudly. 'The idea of having the sentence first!'

'Hold your tongue!' said the Queen, turning purple.

'I wo'n't!' said Alice.

'Off with her head!' the Queen shouted at the top of her voice. Nobody moved.

'Who cares for *you*?' said Alice (she had grown to her full size by this time). 'You're nothing but a pack of cards!'

At this the whole pack rose up into the air, and came flying down upon her; she gave a little scream, half of fright and half of anger, and tried to beat them off, and found herself lying

Not a facile, makeshift solution
but rather a growth (physically)

on the bank, with her head in the lap of her sister, who was gently brushing away some dead leaves that had fluttered down from the trees upon her face.

'Wake up, Alice dear!' said her sister. 'Why, what a long sleep you've had!'

'Oh, I've had such a curious dream!'* said Alice. And she told her sister, as well as she could remember them, all these strange Adventures of hers that you have just been reading about; and, when she had finished, her sister kissed her, and said 'It *was* a curious dream, dear, certainly; but now run in to your tea: it's getting late.' So Alice got up and ran off, thinking while she ran, as well she might, what a wonderful dream it had been.

But her sister sat still just as she left her, leaning her head on her hand, watching the setting sun, and thinking of little Alice and all her wonderful Adventures, till she too began dreaming after a fashion, and this was her dream:—*

First, she dreamed about little Alice herself: once again the tiny hands were clasped upon her knee, and the bright eager eyes were looking up into hers—she could hear the very tones of her voice, and see that queer little toss of her head to keep back the wandering hair that *would* always get into her eyes— and still as she listened, or seemed to listen, the whole place around her became alive with the strange creatures of her little sister's dream.

The long grass rustled at her feet as the White Rabbit hurried by—the frightened Mouse splashed his way through the neighbouring pool—she could hear the rattle of the tea-cups as the March Hare and his friends shared their never-ending meal, and the shrill voice of the Queen ordering off her unfortunate guests to execution—once more the pig-baby was sneezing on the Duchess' knee, while plates and dishes crashed around it—once more the shriek of the Gryphon, the squeaking of the Lizard's slate-pencil, and the choking of the

Ends w/ her becoming a woman

suppressed guinea-pigs, filled the air, mixed up with the distant sob of the miserable Mock Turtle.

So she sat on, with closed eyes, and half believed herself in Wonderland, though she knew she had but to open them again, and all would change to dull reality—the grass would be only rustling in the wind, and the pool rippling to the waving of the reeds—the rattling teacups would change to tinkling sheep-bells, and the Queen's shrill cries to the voice of the shepherd-boy—and the sneeze of the baby, the shriek of the Gryphon, and all the other queer noises, would change (she knew) to the confused clamour of the busy farm-yard—while the lowing of the cattle in the distance would take the place of the Mock Turtle's heavy sobs. *Acceptance*

Lastly, she pictured to herself how this same little sister of hers would, in the after-time, be herself a grown woman; and how she would keep, through all her riper years, the simple and loving heart of her childhood; and how she would gather about her other little children, and make *their* eyes bright and eager with many a strange tale, perhaps even with the dream of Wonderland of long ago; and how she would feel with all their simple sorrows, and find a pleasure in all their simple joys, remembering her own child-life, and the happy summer days.

Always can access this

Connection to Southey poem and this growing older

Passing on (inheritance)

reliving own through children

Harmonious world of innocence

something that enriches childhood but needs to be left behind (passed on)

THE END

Question of what is the relationship between Wonderland and the real world?
— escape
— mirror

* her journey as anything but simple

Novel leaves us with a dissonant idea of this harmonious childhood minus the chaos + disorder of Wonderland

THROUGH THE
LOOKING-GLASS
AND WHAT ALICE
FOUND THERE

Grounded in game

114

R E D.

W H I T E.

White Pawn (Alice) to play, and win in eleven moves

DRAMATIS PERSONÆ*

(As arranged before commencement of game.)

	WHITE.			RED.
PIECES.	PAWNS.	PAWNS.		PIECES.
Tweedledee	Daisy.	Daisy		Humpty Dumpty.
Unicorn	Haigha.	Messenger		Carpenter.
Sheep	Oyster.	Oyster		Walrus.
W. Queen	'Lily'.	Tiger-lily		R. Queen.
W. King	Fawn.	Rose		R. King.
Aged man	Oyster.	Oyster		Crow.
W. Knight	Hatta.	Frog		R. Knight.
Tweedledum	Daisy.	Daisy		Lion.

CHILD of the pure unclouded brow
   And dreaming eyes of wonder!
Though time be fleet, and I and thou
   Are half a life asunder,
Thy loving smile will surely hail
The love-gift of a fairy-tale.

I have not seen thy sunny face,
   Nor heard thy silver laughter:
No thought of me shall find a place
   In thy young life's hereafter—
Enough that now thou wilt not fail
To listen to my fairy-tale.

A tale begun in other days,
   When summer suns were glowing—
A simple chime, that served to time
   The rhythm of our rowing—
Whose echoes live in memory yet,
Though envious years would say 'forget.'

Come, hearken then, ere voice of dread,
   With bitter tidings laden,
Shall summon to unwelcome bed
   A melancholy maiden!
We are but older children, dear,
Who fret to find our bedtime near.

Without, the frost, the blinding snow,
   The storm-wind's moody madness—
Within, the firelight's ruddy glow,
   And childhood's nest of gladness.
The magic words shall hold thee fast:
Thou shalt not heed the raving blast.

And, though the shadow of a sigh
   May tremble through the story,
For 'happy summer days' gone by,
   And vanish'd summer glory—
It shall not touch, with breath of bale,
The pleasance* of our fairy-tale.

ADVERTISEMENT

FOR over 25 years, I have made it my chief object, with regard to my books, that they should be of the best workmanship attainable for the price. And I am deeply annoyed to find that the last issue of 'Through the Looking-Glass,' consisting of the Sixtieth Thousand, has been put on sale without its being noticed that most of the pictures have failed so much, in the printing, as to make the book not worth buying.* I request all holders of copies to send them to Messrs. Macmillan & Co., 29 Bedford Street, Covent Garden, with their names and addresses; and copies of the next issue shall be sent them in exchange.

Instead, however, of destroying the unsold copies, I propose to utilise them by giving them away, to Mechanics' Institutes, Village Reading-Rooms, and similar institutions, where the means for purchasing such books are scanty. Accordingly I invite applications for such gifts, addressed to me, 'care of Messrs. Macmillan.' Every such application should be signed by some responsible person, and should state how far they are able to buy books for themselves, and what is the average number of readers.

I take this opportunity of announcing that, if at any future time I should wish to communicate anything to my Readers, I will do so by advertising, in the 'Agony' Column of some of the Daily Papers, *on the first Tuesday in the month*.

LEWIS CARROLL

Christmas, 1893

As the chess-problem,* given on a previous page, has puzzled some of my readers, it may be well to explain that it is correctly worked out, so far as the *moves* are concerned. The *alternation* of Red and White is perhaps not so strictly observed as it might be, and the 'castling' of the three Queens is merely a way of saying that they entered the palace: but the 'check' of the White King at move 6, the capture of the Red Knight at move 7, and the final 'checkmate' of the Red King, will be found, by any one who will take the trouble to set the pieces and play the moves as directed, to be strictly in accordance with the laws of the game.

The new words, in the poem 'Jabberwocky' (see p. 134), have given rise to some differences of opinion as to their pronunciation: so it may be well to give instructions on *that* point also. Pronounce 'slithy' as if it were the two words 'sly, the': make the 'g' *hard* in 'gyre' and 'gimble': and pronounce 'rath' to rhyme with 'bath.'

For this sixty-first thousand, fresh electrotypes have been taken from the wood-blocks (which, never having been used for printing from, are in as good condition as when first cut in 1871), and the whole book has been set up afresh with new type. If the artistic qualities of this re-issue fall short, in any particular, of those possessed by the original issue, it will not be for want of painstaking on the part of author, publisher, or printer.

I take this opportunity of announcing that the Nursery 'Alice,' hitherto priced at four shillings, net, is now to be had on the same terms as the ordinary shilling picture-books—although I feel sure that it is, in every quality (except the *text* itself, on which I am not qualified to pronounce), greatly superior to them. Four shillings was a perfectly reasonable price to charge, considering the very heavy initial outlay I had incurred: still, as the Public have practically said 'We will *not* give more than a shilling for a picture-book, however artistically got-up,' I am content to reckon my outlay on the book as so much dead loss, and, rather than let the little ones, for whom it was written, go without it, I am selling it at a price which is, to me, much the same thing as *giving* it away.

Christmas, 1896

CONTENTS

CONTENTS

CHAPTER I

LOOKING-GLASS HOUSE

ONE thing was certain, that the *white* kitten had had nothing to do with it*—it was the black kitten's fault entirely. For the white kitten had been having its face washed by the old cat for the last quarter of an hour (and bearing it pretty well, considering): so you see that it *couldn't* have had any hand in the mischief.

The way Dinah washed her children's faces was this: first she held the poor thing down by its ear with one paw, and then with the other paw she rubbed its face all over, the wrong way, beginning at the nose: and just now, as I said, she was hard at work on the white kitten, which was lying quite still and trying to purr—no doubt feeling that it was all meant for its good.

But the black kitten had been finished with earlier in the afternoon, and so, while Alice was sitting curled up in a corner of the great arm-chair, half talking to herself and half asleep, the kitten had been having a grand game of romps with the ball of worsted* Alice had been trying to wind up, and had been rolling it up and down till it had all come undone again; and there it was, spread over the hearth-rug, all knots and tangles, with the kitten running after its own tail in the middle.

'Oh, you wicked wicked little thing!' cried Alice, catching up the kitten, and giving it a little kiss to make it understand that it was in disgrace. 'Really, Dinah ought to have taught you better manners! You *ought*, Dinah, you know you ought!' she added, looking reproachfully at the old cat, and speaking in as cross a voice as she could manage—and then she scrambled back into the arm-chair, taking the kitten and the worsted with her, and began winding up the ball again. But she didn't get on very fast, as she was talking all the time, sometimes to the kitten, and sometimes to herself. Kitty sat very demurely on her knee, pretending to watch the progress of the winding, and now and then putting out one paw

and gently touching the ball, as if it would be glad to help if
it might.

'Do you know what to-morrow is,* Kitty?' Alice began.
'You'd have guessed if you'd been up in the window with me
—only Dinah was making you tidy, so you couldn't. I was
watching the boys getting in sticks for the bonfire—and it
wants plenty of sticks, Kitty! Only it got so cold, and it snowed
so, they had to leave off. Never mind, Kitty, we'll go and see
the bonfire to-morrow.' Here Alice wound two or three turns
of the worsted round the kitten's neck, just to see how it
would look: this led to a scramble, in which the ball rolled
down upon the floor, and yards and yards of it got unwound
again.

'Do you know, I was so angry, Kitty,' Alice went on, as
soon as they were comfortably settled again, 'when I saw all
the mischief you had been doing, I was very nearly opening
the window, and putting you out into the snow! And you'd
have deserved it, you little mischievous darling! What have
you got to say for yourself? Now don't interrupt me!' she
went on, holding up one finger. 'I'm going to tell you all your
faults. Number one: you squeaked twice while Dinah was
washing your face this morning. Now you ca'n't deny it,
Kitty: I heard you! What's that you say?' (pretending that
the kitten was speaking). 'Her paw went into your eye? Well,
that's *your* fault, for keeping your eyes open—if you'd shut
them tight up, it wouldn't have happened. Now don't make
any more excuses, but listen! Number two: you pulled Snowdrop* away by the tail just as I had put down the saucer of
milk before her! What, you were thirsty, were you? How
do you know she wasn't thirsty too? Now for number three:
you unwound every bit of the worsted while I wasn't
looking!

'That's three faults, Kitty, and you've not been punished
for any of them yet. You know I'm saving up all your punishments for Wednesday week—Suppose they had saved up all
my punishments?' she went on, talking more to herself than
the kitten. 'What *would* they do at the end of a year? I should

be sent to prison, I suppose, when the day came. Or—let me see—suppose each punishment was to be going without a dinner: then, when the miserable day came, I should have to go without fifty dinners at once! Well, I shouldn't mind *that* much! I'd far rather go without them than eat them!

'Do you hear the snow against the window-panes, Kitty? How nice and soft it sounds! Just as if some one was kissing the window all over outside. I wonder if the snow *loves* the trees and fields, that it kisses them so gently? And then it covers them up snug, you know, with a white quilt; and perhaps it says "Go to sleep, darlings, till the summer comes again." And when they wake up in the summer, Kitty, they dress themselves all in green, and dance about—whenever the wind blows—oh, that's very pretty!' cried Alice, dropping the ball of worsted to clap her hands. 'And I do so *wish* it was true! I'm sure the woods look sleepy in the autumn, when the leaves are getting brown.

'Kitty, can you play chess? Now, don't smile, my dear, I'm asking it seriously. Because, when we were playing just now, you watched just as if you understood it: and when I said "Check!" you purred! Well, it *was* a nice check, Kitty, and really I might have won, if it hadn't been for that nasty Knight, that came wriggling down among my pieces. Kitty, dear, let's pretend——' And here I wish I could tell you half the things Alice used to say, beginning with her favourite phrase 'Let's pretend.' She had had quite a long argument with her sister only the day before—all because Alice had begun with 'Let's pretend we're kings and queens;' and her sister, who liked being very exact, had argued that they couldn't, because there were only two of them, and Alice had been reduced at last to say 'Well, *you* can be one of them, then, and *I'll* be all the rest.' And once she had really frightened her old nurse by shouting suddenly in her ear, 'Nurse! Do let's pretend that I'm a hungry hyæna, and you're a bone!'

But this is taking us away from Alice's speech to the kitten.

'Let's pretend that you're the Red Queen,* Kitty! Do you know, I think if you sat up and folded your arms, you'd look exactly like her. Now do try, there's a dear!' And Alice got the Red Queen off the table, and set it up before the kitten as a model for it to imitate: however, the thing didn't succeed, principally, Alice said, because the kitten wouldn't fold its arms properly. So, to punish it, she held it up to the Looking-glass, that it might see how sulky it was, '—and if you're not good directly,' she added, 'I'll put you through into Looking-glass House. How would you like *that?*

'Now, if you'll only attend, Kitty, and not talk so much, I'll tell you all my ideas about Looking-glass House. First, there's the room you can see through the glass—that's just the same as our drawing-room, only the things go the other way. I can see all of it when I get upon a chair—all but the bit just behind the fireplace. Oh! I do so wish I could see *that* bit! I want so much to know whether they've a fire in the winter: you never *can* tell, you know, unless our fire smokes, and then smoke comes up in that room too—but that may be only pretence, just to make it look as if they had a fire. Well then, the books are something like our books, only the words go the wrong way: I know *that*, because I've held up one of our books to the glass, and then they hold up one in the other room.

'How would you like to live in Looking-glass House, Kitty? I wonder if they'd give you milk in there? Perhaps Looking-glass milk isn't good to drink—but oh, Kitty! now we come to the passage. You can just see a little *peep* of the passage in Looking-glass House, if you leave the door of our drawing-room wide open: and it's very like our passage as far as you can see, only you know it may be quite different on beyond. Oh, Kitty, how nice it would be if we could only get through into Looking-glass House! I'm sure it's got, oh! such beautiful things in it! Let's pretend there's a way of getting through into it, somehow, Kitty. Let's pretend the glass has got all soft like gauze, so that we can get through. Why, it's turning into a sort of mist now, I declare! It'll be easy enough to get

through——' She was up on the chimney-piece while she said this, though she hardly knew how she had got there. And certainly the glass *was* beginning to melt away, just like a bright silvery mist.

In another moment Alice was through the glass, and had jumped lightly down into the Looking-glass room. The very first thing she did was to look whether there was a fire in the fireplace, and she was quite pleased to find that there was a real one, blazing away as brightly as the one she had left behind. 'So I shall be as warm here as I was in the old room,' thought Alice: 'warmer, in fact, because there'll be no one

here to scold me away from the fire. Oh, what fun it'll be, when they see me through the glass in here, and ca'n't get at me!'

Then she began looking about, and noticed that what could be seen from the old room was quite common and uninteresting, but that all the rest was as different as possible. For instance, the pictures on the wall next the fire seemed to be all alive, and the very clock on the chimney-piece (you know you can only see the back of it in the Looking-glass) had got the face of a little old man, and grinned at her.

'They don't keep this room so tidy as the other,' Alice thought to herself, as she noticed several of the chessmen down in the hearth among the cinders; but in another moment, with a little 'Oh!' of surprise, she was down on her hands and knees watching them. The chessmen were walking about, two and two!

'Here are the Red King and the Red Queen,' Alice said (in a whisper, for fear of frightening them), 'and there are the White King and the White Queen* sitting on the edge of the shovel—and here are two Castles walking arm in arm—I don't think they can hear me,' she went on, as she put her head closer down, 'and I'm nearly sure they ca'n't see me. I feel somehow as if I was getting invisible——'

Here something began squeaking on the table behind Alice, and made her turn her head just in time to see one of the White Pawns roll over and begin kicking: she watched it with great curiosity to see what would happen next.

'It is the voice of my child!' the White Queen cried out, as she rushed past the King, so violently that she knocked him over among the cinders. 'My precious Lily! My imperial kitten!'* and she began scrambling wildly up the side of the fender.

'Imperial fiddlestick!' said the King, rubbing his nose, which had been hurt by the fall. He had a right to be a *little* annoyed with the Queen, for he was covered with ashes from head to foot.

Alice was very anxious to be of use, and, as the poor little Lily was nearly screaming herself into a fit, she hastily picked up the Queen and set her on the table by the side of her noisy little daughter.

The Queen gasped, and sat down: the rapid journey through the air had quite taken away her breath, and for a minute or two she could do nothing but hug the little Lily in silence. As soon as she had recovered her breath a little, she called out to the White King, who was sitting sulkily among the ashes, 'Mind the volcano!'

'What volcano?' said the King, looking up anxiously into the fire, as if he thought that was the most likely place to find one.

'Blew—me—up,' panted the Queen, who was still a little out of breath. 'Mind you come up—the regular way—don't get blown up!'

Alice watched the White King as he slowly struggled up from bar to bar, till at last she said 'Why, you'll be hours and hours getting to the table, at that rate. I'd far better help you, hadn't I?' But the King took no notice of the question: it was quite clear that he could neither hear her nor see her.

So Alice picked him up very gently, and lifted him across more slowly than she had lifted the Queen, that she mightn't take his breath away; but, before she put him on the table, she thought she might as well dust him a little, he was so covered with ashes.

She said afterwards that she had never seen in all her life

such a face as the King made, when he found himself held in the air by an invisible hand, and being dusted: he was far too much astonished to cry out, but his eyes and his mouth went on getting larger and larger, and rounder and rounder, till her hand shook so with laughing that she nearly let him drop upon the floor.

'Oh! *please* don't make such faces, my dear!' she cried out, quite forgetting that the King couldn't hear her. 'You make me laugh so that I can hardly hold you! And don't keep your mouth so wide open! All the ashes will get into it—there, now I think you're tidy enough!' she added, as she smoothed his hair, and set him upon the table near the Queen.

The King immediately fell flat on his back, and lay perfectly still; and Alice was a little alarmed at what she had done, and went round the room to see if she could find any water to throw over him. However, she could find nothing but a bottle of ink, and when she got back with it she found he had recovered, and he and the Queen were talking together in a frightened whisper—so low, that Alice could hardly hear what they said.

The King was saying 'I assure you, my dear, I turned cold to the very ends of my whiskers!'

To which the Queen replied 'You haven't got any whiskers.'

'The horror of that moment,' the King went on, 'I shall never, *never* forget!'

'You will, though,' the Queen said, 'if you don't make a memorandum of it.'

Alice looked on with great interest as the King took an enormous memorandum-book out of his pocket, and began writing. A sudden thought struck her, and she took hold of the end of the pencil, which came some way over his shoulder, and began writing for him.

The poor King looked puzzled and unhappy, and struggled with the pencil for some time without saying anything; but Alice was too strong for him, and at last he panted out 'My

dear! I really *must* get a thinner pencil. I ca'n't manage this one a bit: it writes all manner of things that I don't intend——'

'What manner of things?' said the Queen, looking over the book (in which Alice had put '*The White Knight is sliding down the poker. He balances very badly*'). 'That's not a memorandum of *your* feelings!'

There was a book lying near Alice on the table, and while she sat watching the White King (for she was still a little anxious about him, and had the ink all ready to throw over him, in case he fainted again), she turned over the leaves, to find some part that she could read, '—for it's all in some language I don't know,' she said to herself.

It was like this.

*JABBERWOCKY.

'Twas brillig, and the slithy toves
Did gyre and gimble in the wabe:
All mimsy were the borogoves,
And the mome raths outgrabe.

She puzzled over this for some time, but at last a bright
thought struck her. 'Why, it's a Looking-glass book, of
course! And, if I hold it up to a glass, the words will all go
the right way again.'

This was the poem that Alice read.'

JABBERWOCKY.

> 'Twas brillig, and the slithy toves
>   Did gyre and gimble in the wabe:
> All mimsy were the borogoves,
>   And the mome raths outgrabe.

> 'Beware the Jabberwock, my son!
>   The jaws that bite, the claws that catch!
> Beware the Jubjub bird, and shun
>   The frumious Bandersnatch!'

> He took his vorpal sword in hand:
>   Long time the manxome foe he sought—
> So rested he by the Tumtum tree,
>   And stood awhile in thought.

> And, as in uffish thought he stood,
>   The Jabberwock, with eyes of flame,
> Came whiffling through the tulgey wood,
>   And burbled as it came!

One, two! One, two! And through and through
The vorpal blade went snicker-snack!
He left it dead, and with its head
He went galumphing back.

'*And, hast thou slain the Jabberwock?*
Come to my arms, my beamish boy!
O frabjous day! Callooh! Callay!'
He chortled in his joy.

'*Twas brillig, and the slithy toves*
Did gyre and gimble in the wabe:
All mimsy were the borogoves,
And the mome raths outgrabe.

'It seems very pretty,' she said when she had finished it, 'but it's *rather* hard to understand!' (You see she didn't like to confess, even to herself, that she couldn't make it out at all.) 'Somehow it seems to fill my head with ideas—only I don't exactly know what they are! However, *somebody* killed *something*: that's clear, at any rate——'

'But oh!' thought Alice, suddenly jumping up, 'if I don't make haste, I shall have to go back through the Looking-glass, before I've seen what the rest of the house is like! Let's have a look at the garden first!' She was out of the room in a moment, and ran down stairs—or, at least, it wasn't exactly running, but a new invention for getting down stairs quickly and easily, as Alice said to herself. She just kept the tips of her fingers on the hand-rail, and floated gently down without even touching the stairs with her feet: then she floated on through the hall, and would have gone straight out at the door in the same way, if she hadn't caught hold of the door-post. She was getting a little giddy with so much floating in the air, and was rather glad to find herself walking again in the natural way.

CHAPTER II

THE GARDEN OF LIVE FLOWERS*

'I SHOULD see the garden far better,' said Alice to herself, 'if I could get to the top of that hill: and here's a path that leads straight to it—at least, no, it doesn't do *that*——' (after going a few yards along the path, and turning several sharp corners), 'but I suppose it will at last. But how curiously it twists! It's more like a corkscrew than a path! Well, *this* turn goes to the hill, I suppose—no, it doesn't! This goes straight back to the house! Well then, I'll try it the other way.'

And so she did: wandering up and down, and trying turn after turn, but always coming back to the house, do what she would. Indeed, once, when she turned a corner rather more quickly than usual, she ran against it before she could stop herself.

'It's no use talking about it,' Alice said, looking up at the house and pretending it was arguing with her. 'I'm *not* going in again yet. I know I should have to get through the Looking-glass again—back into the old room—and there'd be an end of all my adventures!'

So, resolutely turning her back upon the house, she set out once more down the path, determined to keep straight on till she got to the hill. For a few minutes all went on well, and she was just saying 'I really *shall* do it this time——' when the path gave a sudden twist and shook itself (as she described it afterwards), and the next moment she found herself actually walking in at the door.

'Oh, it's too bad!' she cried. 'I never saw such a house for getting in the way! Never!'

However, there was the hill full in sight, so there was nothing to be done but start again. This time she came upon

a large flower-bed, with a border of daisies, and a willow-tree growing in the middle.

'O Tiger-lily!'* said Alice, addressing herself to one that was waving gracefully about in the wind, 'I *wish* you could talk!'

'We *can* talk,' said the Tiger-lily, 'when there's anybody worth talking to.'

Alice was so astonished that she couldn't speak for a minute: it quite seemed to take her breath away. At length, as the Tiger-lily only went on waving about, she spoke again, in a timid voice—almost in a whisper. 'And can *all* the flowers talk?'

'As well as *you* can,' said the Tiger-lily. 'And a great deal louder.'

'It isn't manners for us to begin, you know,' said the Rose,* 'and I really was wondering when you'd speak! Said I to myself, "Her face has got *some* sense in it, though it's not a clever one!" Still, you're the right colour, and that goes a long way.'

'I don't care about the colour,' the Tiger-lily remarked. 'If only her petals curled up a little more, she'd be all right.'

Alice didn't like being criticized, so she began asking questions. 'Aren't you sometimes frightened at being planted out here, with nobody to take care of you?'

'There's the tree in the middle,' said the Rose. 'What else is it good for?'

'But what could it do, if any danger came?' Alice asked.

'It could bark,' said the Rose.

'It says "Bough-wough!"' cried a Daisy. 'That's why its branches are called boughs!'

'Didn't you know *that?*' cried another Daisy. And here they all began shouting together, till the air seemed quite full of little shrill voices. 'Silence, every one of you!' cried the Tiger-lily, waving itself passionately from side to side, and trembling with excitement. 'They know I ca'n't get at them!' it panted, bending its quivering head towards Alice, 'or they wouldn't dare to do it!'

'Never mind!' Alice said in a soothing tone, and, stooping down to the daisies, who were just beginning again, she whispered 'If you don't hold your tongues, I'll pick you!'

There was silence in a moment, and several of the pink daisies turned white.

'That's right!' said the Tiger-lily. 'The daisies are worst of all. When one speaks, they all begin together, and it's enough to make one wither to hear the way they go on!'

'How is it you can all talk so nicely?' Alice said, hoping to get it into a better temper by a compliment. 'I've been in many gardens before, but none of the flowers could talk.'

'Put your hand down, and feel the ground,' said the Tiger-lily. 'Then you'll know why.'

Alice did so. 'It's very hard,' she said; 'but I don't see what that has to do with it.'

'In most gardens,' the Tiger-lily said, 'they make the beds too soft—so that the flowers are always asleep.'

This sounded a very good reason, and Alice was quite pleased to know it. 'I never thought of that before!' she said.

'It's *my* opinion that you never think *at all*,' the Rose said, in a rather severe tone.

'I never saw anybody that looked stupider,' a Violet* said, so suddenly, that Alice quite jumped; for it hadn't spoken before.

'Hold *your* tongue!' cried the Tiger-lily. 'As if *you* ever saw anybody! You keep your head under the leaves, and snore away there, till you know no more what's going on in the world, than if you were a bud!'

'Are there any more people in the garden besides me?' Alice said, not choosing to notice the Rose's last remark.

'There's one other flower in the garden that can move about like you,' said the Rose. 'I wonder how you do it——' ('You're always wondering,' said the Tiger-lily), 'but she's more bushy than you are.'

'Is she like me?' Alice asked eagerly, for the thought crossed her mind, 'There's another little girl in the garden, somewhere!'

'Well, she has the same awkward shape as you,' the Rose said: 'but she's redder—and her petals are shorter, I think.'

'They're done up close, like a dahlia,' said the Tiger-lily: 'not tumbled about, like yours.'

'But that's not *your* fault,' the Rose added kindly. 'You're beginning to fade, you know—and then one ca'n't help one's petals getting a little untidy.'

Alice didn't like this idea at all: so, to change the subject, she asked 'Does she ever come out here?'

'I daresay you'll see her soon,' said the Rose. 'She's one of the kind that has nine spikes,* you know.'

'Where does she wear them?' Alice asked with some curiosity.

'Why, all round her head, of course,' the Rose replied. 'I was wondering *you* hadn't got some too. I thought it was the regular rule.'

'She's coming!' cried the Larkspur. 'I hear her footstep, thump, thump, along the gravel-walk!'*

Alice looked round eagerly and found that it was the Red Queen. 'She's grown a good deal!' was her first remark. She had indeed: when Alice first found her in the ashes, she had been only three inches high—and here she was, half a head taller than Alice herself!

'It's the fresh air that does it,' said the Rose: 'wonderfully fine air it is, out here.'

'I think I'll go and meet her,' said Alice, for, though the flowers were interesting enough, she felt that it would be far grander to have a talk with a real Queen.

'You ca'n't possibly do that,' said the Rose: '*I* should advise you to walk the other way.'

This sounded nonsense to Alice, so she said nothing, but set off at once towards the Red Queen. To her surprise she lost sight of her in a moment, and found herself walking in at the front-door again.

A little provoked, she drew back, and, after looking everywhere for the Queen (whom she spied out at last, a long way off), she thought she would try the plan, this time, of walking in the opposite direction.

It succeeded beautifully. She had not been walking a minute

before she found herself face to face with the Red Queen,* and full in sight of the hill she had been so long aiming at.

'Where do you come from?' said the Red Queen. 'And where are you going? Look up, speak nicely, and don't twiddle your fingers all the time.'

Alice attended to all these directions, and explained, as well as she could, that she had lost her way.

'I don't know what you mean by *your* way,' said the Queen: 'all the ways about here belong to *me*—but why did you come out here at all?' she added in a kinder tone. 'Curtsey while you're thinking what to say. It saves time.'

Alice wondered a little at this, but she was too much in awe of the Queen to disbelieve it. 'I'll try it when I go home,' she thought to herself, 'the next time I'm a little late for dinner.'

'It's time for you to answer now,' the Queen said, looking at her watch: 'open your mouth a *little* wider when you speak, and always say "your Majesty."'

'I only wanted to see what the garden was like, your Majesty——'

'That's right,' said the Queen, patting her on the head, which Alice didn't like at all: 'though, when you say "garden" —*I've* seen gardens, compared with which this would be a wilderness.'

Alice didn't dare to argue the point, but went on: '—and I thought I'd try and find my way to the top of that hill——'

'When you say "hill,"' the Queen interrupted, '*I* could show you hills, in comparison with which you'd call that a valley.'

'No, I shouldn't,' said Alice, surprised into contradicting her at last: 'a hill *ca'n't* be a valley, you know. That would be nonsense——'

The Red Queen shook her head. 'You may call it "nonsense" if you like,' she said, 'but *I've* heard nonsense, compared with which that would be as sensible as a dictionary!'

Alice curtseyed again, as she was afraid from the Queen's tone that she was a *little* offended: and they walked on in silence till they got to the top of the little hill.*

For some minutes Alice stood without speaking, looking out in all directions over the country—and a most curious country it was. There were a number of tiny little brooks running straight across it from side to side, and the ground between was divided up into squares by a

number of little green hedges, that reached from brook to brook.

'I declare it's marked out just like a large chess-board!' Alice said at last. 'There ought to be some men moving about somewhere—and so there are!' she added in a tone of delight, and her heart began to beat quick with excitement as she went on. 'It's a great huge game of chess that's being played—all over the world—if this *is* the world at all, you know. Oh, what fun it is! How I *wish* I was one of them! I wouldn't mind being a Pawn, if only I might join—though of course I should *like* to be a Queen, best.'

She glanced rather shyly at the real Queen as she said this, but her companion only smiled pleasantly, and said 'That's easily managed. You can be the White Queen's Pawn, if you like, as Lily's too young to play; and you're in the Second Square to begin with: when you get to the Eighth Square you'll be a Queen——' Just at this moment, somehow or other, they began to run.

Alice never could quite make out, in thinking it over afterwards, how it was that they began: all she remembers is, that they were running hand in hand, and the Queen went so fast that it was all she could do to keep up with her: and still the Queen kept crying 'Faster! Faster!', but Alice felt she *could not* go faster, though she had no breath left to say so.

The most curious part of the thing was, that the trees and the other things round them never changed their places at all: however fast they went, they never seemed to pass anything. 'I wonder if all the things move along with us?' thought poor puzzled Alice. And the Queen seemed to guess her thoughts, for she cried 'Faster! Don't try to talk!'

Not that Alice had any idea of doing *that*. She felt as if she would never be able to talk again, she was getting so much out of breath: and still the Queen cried 'Faster! Faster!', and dragged her along. 'Are we nearly there?' Alice managed to pant out at last.

'Nearly there!' the Queen repeated. 'Why, we passed it ten minutes ago! Faster!' And they ran on for a time in silence, with the wind whistling in Alice's ears, and almost blowing her hair off her head, she fancied.

'Now! Now!' cried the Queen. 'Faster! Faster!' And they went so fast that at last they seemed to skim through the air, hardly touching the ground with their feet, till suddenly, just as Alice was getting quite exhausted, they stopped, and she found herself sitting on the ground, breathless and giddy.

The Queen propped her up against a tree, and said kindly, 'You may rest a little, now.'

Alice looked round her in great surprise. 'Why, I do believe we've been under this tree the whole time! Everything's just as it was!'

'Of course it is,' said the Queen. 'What would you have it?'

'Well, in *our* country,' said Alice, still panting a little, 'you'd generally get to somewhere else—if you ran very fast for a long time as we've been doing.'

'A slow sort of country!' said the Queen. 'Now, *here*, you see, it takes all the running *you* can do, to keep in the same place. If you want to get somewhere else, you must run at least twice as fast as that!'

'I'd rather not try, please!' said Alice. 'I'm quite content to stay here—only I *am* so hot and thirsty!'

'I know what *you'd* like!' the Queen said good-naturedly, taking a little box out of her pocket. 'Have a biscuit?'

Alice thought it would not be civil to say 'No,' though it wasn't at all what she wanted. So she took it, and ate it as well as she could: and it was *very* dry: and she thought she had never been so nearly choked in all her life.

'While you're refreshing yourself,' said the Queen, 'I'll just take the measurements.' And she took a ribbon out of her pocket, marked in inches, and began measuring the ground, and sticking little pegs in here and there.

'At the end of two yards,' she said, putting in a peg to mark the distance, 'I shall give you your directions—have another biscuit?'

'No, thank you,' said Alice: 'one's *quite* enough!'

'Thirst quenched, I hope?' said the Queen.

Alice did not know what to say to this, but luckily the Queen did not wait for an answer, but went on. 'At the end of *three* yards I shall repeat them—for fear of your forgetting them. At the end of *four*, I shall say good-bye. And at the end of *five*, I shall go!'

She had got all the pegs put in by this time, and Alice looked on with great interest as she returned to the tree, and then began slowly walking down the row.

At the two-yard peg she faced round, and said 'A pawn goes two squares in its first move, you know. So you'll go *very* quickly through the Third Square—by railway, I should think—and you'll find yourself in the Fourth Square in no time. Well, *that* square belongs to Tweedledum and Tweedledee—the Fifth is mostly water—the Sixth belongs to Humpty Dumpty—But you make no remark?'

'I—I didn't know I had to make one—just then,' Alice faltered out.

'You *should* have said,' the Queen went on in a tone of grave reproof, ' "It's extremely kind of you to tell me all this"—however, we'll suppose it said—the Seventh Square is all forest—however, one of the Knights will show you the way—and in the Eighth Square we shall be Queens together, and it's all feasting and fun!' Alice got up and curtseyed, and sat down again.

At the next peg the Queen turned again, and this time she said 'Speak in French when you ca'n't think of the English for a thing—turn out your toes as you walk—and remember who you are!' She did not wait for Alice to curtsey, this time, but walked on quickly to the next peg, where she turned for a moment to say 'Good-bye,' and then hurried on to the last.

How it happened, Alice never knew, but exactly as she came to the last peg, she was gone.* Whether she vanished into the air, or whether she ran quickly into the wood ('and she *can* run very fast!' thought Alice), there was no way of guessing, but she was gone, and Alice began to remember that she was a Pawn, and that it would soon be time for her to move.

CHAPTER III

LOOKING-GLASS INSECTS

OF course the first thing to do was to make a grand survey of the country she was going to travel through. 'It's something very like learning geography,' thought Alice, as she stood on tiptoe in hopes of being able to see a little further. 'Principal rivers—there *are* none. Principal mountains—I'm on the only one, but I don't think it's got any name. Principal towns —why, what *are* those creatures, making honey down there? They ca'n't be bees—nobody ever saw bees a mile off, you know——' and for some time she stood silent, watching one of them that was bustling about among the flowers, poking its proboscis into them, 'just as if it was a regular bee,' thought Alice.

However, this was anything but a regular bee: in fact, it was an elephant—as Alice soon found out, though the idea quite took her breath away at first. 'And what enormous flowers they must be!' was her next idea. 'Something like cottages with the roofs taken off, and stalks put to them—and what quantities of honey they must make! I think I'll go down and—no, I wo'n't go *just* yet,' she went on, checking herself just as she was beginning to run down the hill, and trying to find some excuse for turning shy so suddenly. 'It'll never do to go down among them without a good long branch to brush them away—and what fun it'll be when they ask me how I liked my walk. I shall say "Oh, I liked it well enough——" (here came the favourite little toss of the head), "only it *was* so dusty and hot, and the elephants *did* tease so!"

'I think I'll go down the other way,' she said after a pause; 'and perhaps I may visit the elephants later on. Besides, I *do* so want to get into the Third Square!'

So, with this excuse, she ran down the hill, and jumped over the first of the six little brooks.*

```
*        *        *        *        *
     *        *        *        *
*        *        *        *        *
```

'Tickets, please!' said the Guard, putting his head in at the window. In a moment everybody was holding out a ticket: they were about the same size as the people, and quite seemed to fill the carriage.

'Now then! Show your ticket, child!' the Guard went on, looking angrily at Alice. And a great many voices all said together ('like the chorus of a song,' thought Alice) 'Don't keep him waiting, child! Why, his time is worth a thousand pounds a minute!'*

'I'm afraid I haven't got one,' Alice said in a frightened tone: 'there wasn't a ticket-office where I came from.' And again the chorus of voices went on. 'There wasn't room for one where she came from. The land there is worth a thousand pounds an inch!'

'Don't make excuses,' said the Guard: 'you should have bought one from the engine-driver.' And once more the chorus of voices went on with 'The man that drives the engine. Why, the smoke alone is worth a thousand pounds a puff!'

Alice thought to herself 'Then there's no use in speaking.' The voices didn't join in, *this* time, as she hadn't spoken, but, to her great surprise, they all *thought* in chorus (I hope you understand what *thinking in chorus* means—for I must confess that *I* don't), 'Better say nothing at all. Language is worth a thousand pounds a word!'

'I shall dream about a thousand pounds to-night, I know I shall!' thought Alice.

All this time the Guard was looking at her, first through a telescope, then through a microscope, and then through an

opera-glass. At last he said 'You're traveling the wrong way,' and shut up the window, and went away.

'So young a child,' said the gentleman sitting opposite to her,* (he was dressed in white paper,) 'ought to know which way she's going, even if she doesn't know her own name!'

A Goat, that was sitting next to the gentleman in white, shut his eyes and said in a loud voice, 'She ought to know her way to the ticket-office, even if she doesn't know her alphabet!'

There was a Beetle sitting next the Goat (it was a very queer carriage-full of passengers altogether), and, as the rule seemed to be that they should all speak in turn, *he* went on with 'She'll have to go back from here as luggage!'

Alice couldn't see who was sitting beyond the Beetle, but a hoarse voice spoke next. 'Change engines——' it said, and there it choked and was obliged to leave off.

'It sounds like a horse,' Alice thought to herself. And an extremely small voice, close to her ear, said 'You might make a joke on that—something about "horse" and "hoarse," you know.'

Then a very gentle voice in the distance said, 'She must be labeled "Lass, with care," you know——'

And after that other voices went on ('What a number of people there are in the carriage!' thought Alice), saying 'She must go by post, as she's got a head on her——'* 'She must be sent as a message by the telegraph——' 'She must draw the train herself the rest of the way——,' and so on.

But the gentleman dressed in white paper leaned forwards and whispered in her ear, 'Never mind what they all say, my dear, but take a return-ticket every time the train stops.'

'Indeed I sha'n't!' Alice said rather impatiently. 'I don't belong to this railway journey at all—I was in a wood just now—and I wish I could get back there!'

'You might make a joke on *that*,' said the little voice close to her ear: 'something about "you *would* if you could, you know".'

'Don't tease so,' said Alice, looking about in vain to see where the voice came from. 'If you're so anxious to have a joke made, why don't you make one yourself?'

The little voice sighed deeply. It was *very* unhappy, evidently, and Alice would have said something pitying to comfort it, 'if it would only sigh like other people!' she thought. But this was such a wonderfully small sigh, that she wouldn't have heard it at all, if it hadn't come *quite* close to her ear. The consequence of this was that it tickled her ear very much, and quite took off her thoughts from the unhappiness of the poor little creature.

'I know you are a friend,' the little voice went on: 'a dear friend, and an old friend. And you wo'n't hurt me, though I *am* an insect.'

'What kind of insect?' Alice inquired, a little anxiously. What she really wanted to know was, whether it could sting or not, but she thought this wouldn't be quite a civil question to ask.

'What, then you don't—' the little voice began, when it was drowned by a shrill scream from the engine, and everybody jumped up in alarm, Alice among the rest.

The Horse, who had put his head out of the window, quietly drew it in and said 'It's only a brook we have to jump over.' Everybody seemed satisfied with this, though Alice felt a little nervous at the idea of trains jumping at all. 'However, it'll take us into the Fourth Square, that's some comfort!' she said to herself. In another moment she felt the carriage rise straight up into the air, and in her fright she caught at the thing nearest to her hand, which happened to be the Goat's beard.*

*   *   *   *   *

*   *   *   *

*   *   *   *

But the beard seemed to melt away as she touched it, and she found herself sitting quietly under a tree*—while the Gnat* (for that was the insect she had been talking to) was balancing itself on a twig just over her head, and fanning her with its wings.

It certainly was a *very* large Gnat: 'about the size of a chicken,' Alice thought. Still, she couldn't feel nervous with it, after they had been talking together so long.

'—then you don't like *all* insects?' the Gnat went on, as quietly as if nothing had happened.

'I like them when they can talk,' Alice said. 'None of them ever talk, where *I* come from.'

'What sort of insects do you rejoice in, where *you* come from?' the Gnat inquired.

'I don't *rejoice* in insects at all,' Alice explained, 'because I'm rather afraid of them—at least the large kinds. But I can tell you the names of some of them.'

'Of course they answer to their names?' the Gnat remarked carelessly.

'I never knew them do it.'

'What's the use of their having names,' the Gnat said, 'if they wo'n't answer to them?'

'No use to *them*,' said Alice; 'but it's useful to the people that name them, I suppose. If not, why do things have names at all?'

'I ca'n't say,' the Gnat replied. 'Further on, in the wood down there, they've got no names—however, go on with your list of insects: you're wasting time.'

'Well, there's the Horse-fly,' Alice began, counting off the names on her fingers.

'All right,' said the Gnat. 'Half way up that bush, you'll see

a Rocking-horse-fly, if you look. It's made entirely of wood, and gets about by swinging itself from branch to branch.'

'What does it live on?' Alice asked, with great curiosity.

'Sap and sawdust,' said the Gnat. 'Go on with the list.'

Alice looked at the Rocking-horse-fly with great interest, and made up her mind that it must have been just repainted, it looked so bright and sticky; and then she went on.

'And there's the Dragon-fly.'

'Look on the branch above your head,' said the Gnat, 'and there you'll find a Snap-dragon-fly. Its body is made of plum-pudding, its wings of holly-leaves, and its head is a raisin burning in brandy.'*

'And what does it live on?' Alice asked, as before.

'Frumenty* and mince-pie,' the Gnat replied; 'and it makes its nest in a Christmas-box.'

'And then there's the Butterfly,' Alice went on, after she had taken a good look at the insect with its head on fire, and had thought to herself, 'I wonder if that's the reason insects are so fond of flying into candles—because they want to turn into Snap-dragon-flies!'

'Crawling at your feet,' said the Gnat (Alice drew her feet back in some alarm), 'you may observe a Bread-and-butter-fly. Its wings are thin slices of bread-and-butter, its body is a crust, and its head is a lump of sugar.'

'And what does *it* live on?'

'Weak tea with cream in it.'

A new difficulty came into Alice's head. 'Supposing it couldn't find any?' she suggested.

'Then it would die, of course.'

'But that must happen very often,' Alice remarked thoughtfully.

'It always happens,' said the Gnat.

After this, Alice was silent for a minute or two, pondering. The Gnat amused itself meanwhile by humming round and round her head: at last it settled again and remarked 'I suppose you don't want to lose your name?'

'No, indeed,' Alice said, a little anxiously.

'And yet I don't know,' the Gnat went on in a careless tone: 'only think how convenient it would be if you could manage to go home without it! For instance, if the governess wanted to call you to your lessons, she would call out "Come here——," and there she would have to leave off, because there wouldn't be any name for her to call, and of course you wouldn't have to go, you know.'

'That would never do, I'm sure,' said Alice: 'the governess would never think of excusing me lessons for that. If she couldn't remember my name, she'd call me "Miss," as the servants do.'

'Well, if she said "Miss," and didn't say anything more,' the Gnat remarked, 'of course you'd miss your lessons. That's a joke. I wish *you* had made it.'

'Why do you wish *I* had made it?' Alice asked. 'It's a very bad one.'

But the Gnat only sighed deeply, while two large tears came rolling down its cheeks.

'You shouldn't make jokes,' Alice said, 'if it makes you so unhappy.'

Then came another of those melancholy little sighs, and this time the poor Gnat really seemed to have sighed itself away, for, when Alice looked up, there was nothing whatever to be seen on the twig, and, as she was getting quite chilly with sitting still so long, she got up and walked on.

She very soon came to an open field, with a wood on the other side of it: it looked much darker than the last wood, and Alice felt a *little* timid about going into it. However, on second thoughts, she made up her mind to go on: 'for I certainly won't go *back*,' she thought to herself, and this was the only way to the Eighth Square.

'This must be the wood,' she said thoughtfully to herself, 'where things have no names. I wonder what'll become of *my* name when I go in? I shouldn't like to lose it at all——because they'd have to give me another, and it would be almost certain to be an ugly one. But then the fun would be, trying to find the

creature that had got my old name! That's just like the advertisements, you know, when people lose dogs——
"*answers to the name of 'Dash': had on a brass collar*"——just fancy calling everything you met "Alice," till one of them answered! Only they wouldn't answer at all, if they were wise.'

She was rambling on in this way when she reached the wood: it looked very cool and shady. 'Well, at any rate it's a great comfort,' she said as she stepped under the trees, 'after being so hot, to get into the—into the—into *what?*' she went on, rather surprised at not being able to think of the word. 'I mean to get under the—under the—under *this*, you know!' putting her hand on the trunk of the tree. 'What *does* it call itself, I wonder? I do believe it's got no name—why, to be sure it hasn't!'

She stood silent for a minute, thinking: then she suddenly began again. 'Then it really *has* happened, after all! And now, who am I? I *will* remember, if I can! I'm determined to do it!' But being determined didn't help her much, and all she could say, after a great deal of puzzling, was 'L, I *know* it begins with L!'*

Just then a Fawn came wandering by: it looked at Alice with its large gentle eyes, but didn't seem at all frightened. 'Here then! Here then!' Alice said, as she held out her hand and tried to stroke it; but it only started back a little, and then stood looking at her again.

'What do you call yourself?' the Fawn said at last. Such a soft sweet voice it had!

'I wish I knew!' thought poor Alice. She answered, rather sadly, 'Nothing, just now.'

'Think again,' it said: 'that wo'n't do.'

Alice thought, but nothing came of it. 'Please, would you tell me what *you* call yourself?' she said timidly. 'I think that might help a little.'

'I'll tell you, if you'll come a little further on,' the Fawn said. 'I ca'n't remember *here*.'

So they walked on together through the wood, Alice with

her arms clasped lovingly round the soft neck of the Fawn,
till they came out into another open field, and here the Fawn
gave a sudden bound into the air, and shook itself free from
Alice's arm. 'I'm a Fawn!' it cried out in a voice of delight.
'And, dear me! you're a human child!' A sudden look of alarm
came into its beautiful brown eyes, and in another moment it
had darted away at full speed.

Alice stood looking after it, almost ready to cry with vexation at having lost her dear little fellow-traveler so suddenly.
'However, I know my name now,' she said: 'that's *some* comfort. Alice—Alice—I wo'n't forget it again. And now, which
of these finger-posts ought I to follow, I wonder?'

It was not a very difficult question to answer, as there was
only one road through the wood, and the two finger-posts both
pointed along it. 'I'll settle it,' Alice said to herself, 'when the
road divides and they point different ways.'

But this did not seem likely to happen. She went on and on,
a long way, but, wherever the road divided, there were sure

to be two finger-posts pointing the same way, one marked 'TO TWEEDLEDUM'S HOUSE,' and the other 'TO THE HOUSE OF TWEEDLEDEE.'

'I do believe,' said Alice at last, 'that they live in the *same* house! I wonder I never thought of that before—But I ca'n't stay there long. I'll just call and say "How d'ye do?" and ask them the way out of the wood. If I could only get to the Eighth Square before it gets dark!' So she wandered on, talking to herself as she went, till, on turning a sharp corner, she came upon two fat little men, so suddenly that she could not help starting back, but in another moment she recovered herself, feeling sure that they must be*

CHAPTER IV

TWEEDLEDUM AND TWEEDLEDEE*

THEY were standing under a tree, each with an arm round the other's neck, and Alice knew which was which in a moment, because one of them had 'DUM' embroidered on his collar, and the other 'DEE.' 'I suppose they've each got "TWEEDLE" round at the back of the collar,' she said to herself.

They stood so still that she quite forgot they were alive, and she was just going round to see if the word 'TWEEDLE' was written at the back of each collar, when she was startled by a voice coming from the one marked 'DUM.'

'If you think we're wax-works,' he said, 'you ought to pay, you know. Wax-works weren't made to be looked at for nothing. Nohow!'

'Contrariwise,' added the one marked 'DEE,' 'if you think we're alive, you ought to speak.'

'I'm sure I'm very sorry,' was all Alice could say; for the words of the old song kept ringing through her head like the ticking of a clock, and she could hardly help saying them out loud:—

'*Tweedledum and Tweedledee*
Agreed to have a battle;
For Tweedledum said Tweedledee
Had spoiled his nice new rattle.

Just then flew down a monstrous crow,
As black as a tar-barrel;
Which frightened both the heroes so,
They quite forgot their quarrel.'

'I know what you're thinking about,' said Tweedledum; 'but it isn't so, nohow.'

'Contrariwise,' continued Tweedledee, 'if it was so, it might be; and if it were so, it would be; but as it isn't, it ain't. That's logic.'*

'I was thinking,' Alice said very politely, 'which is the best way out of this wood: it's getting so dark. Would you tell me, please?'

But the fat little men only looked at each other and grinned.

They looked so exactly like a couple of great schoolboys, that Alice couldn't help pointing her finger at Tweedledum, and saying 'First Boy!'

'Nohow!' Tweedledum cried out briskly, and shut his mouth up again with a snap.

'Next Boy!' said Alice, passing on to Tweedledee, though she felt quite certain he would only shout out 'Contrariwise!' and so he did.

'You've begun wrong!' cried Tweedledum. 'The first thing in a visit is to say "How d'ye do?" and shake hands!' And here the two brothers gave each other a hug, and then they held out the two hands that were free, to shake hands with her.

Alice did not like shaking hands with either of them first, for fear of hurting the other one's feelings; so, as the best way out of the difficulty, she took hold of both hands at once: the next moment they were dancing round in a ring. This seemed quite natural (she remembered afterwards), and she was not even surprised to hear music playing: it seemed to come from the tree under which they were dancing, and it was done (as well as she could make it out) by the branches rubbing one across the other, like fiddles and fiddle-sticks.

'But it certainly *was* funny,' (Alice said afterwards, when she was telling her sister the history of all this,) 'to find myself singing "*Here we go round the mulberry bush.*"* I don't know when I began it, but somehow I felt as if I'd been singing it a long long time!'

The other two dancers were fat, and very soon out of breath. 'Four times round is enough for one dance,' Tweedledum panted out, and they left off dancing as suddenly as they had begun: the music stopped at the same moment.

Then they let go of Alice's hands, and stood looking at her for a minute: there was a rather awkward pause, as Alice didn't know how to begin a conversation with people she had just been dancing with. 'It would never do to say "How d'ye do?" *now*,' she said to herself: 'we seem to have got beyond that, somehow!'

'I hope you're not much tired?' she said at last.

'Nohow. And thank you *very* much for asking,' said Tweedledum.

'So *much* obliged!' added Tweedledee. 'You like poetry?'

'Ye-es, pretty well—*some* poetry,' Alice said doubtfully. 'Would you tell me which road leads out of the wood?'

'What shall I repeat to her?' said Tweedledee, looking round at Tweedledum with great solemn eyes, and not noticing Alice's question.

'"*The Walrus and the Carpenter*"* is the longest,' Tweedledum replied, giving his brother an affectionate hug.

Tweedledee began instantly:

'*The sun was shining*——'

Here Alice ventured to interrupt him. 'If it's *very* long,' she said, as politely as she could, 'would you please tell me first which road——'

Tweedledee smiled gently, and began again:

> 'The sun was shining on the sea,
>   Shining with all his might:
> He did his very best to make
>   The billows smooth and bright—
> And this was odd, because it was
>   The middle of the night.
>
> The moon was shining sulkily,
>   Because she thought the sun
> Had got no business to be there
>   After the day was done—
> "It's very rude of him," she said,
>   "To come and spoil the fun!"
>
> The sea was wet as wet could be,
>   The sands were dry as dry.
> You could not see a cloud, because
>   No cloud was in the sky:
> No birds were flying overhead—
>   There were no birds to fly.
>
> The Walrus and the Carpenter
>   Were walking close at hand:*
> They wept like anything to see
>   Such quantities of sand:
> "If this were only cleared away,"
>   They said, "it would be grand!"
>
> "If seven maids with seven mops
>   Swept it for half a year,
> Do you suppose," the Walrus said,
>   "That they could get it clear?"

"I doubt it," said the Carpenter,
*   And shed a bitter tear.*

"O Oysters, come and walk with us!"
*   The Walrus did beseech.*
"A pleasant walk, a pleasant talk,
*   Along the briny beach:*
We cannot do with more than four,
*   To give a hand to each."*

The eldest Oyster looked at him,
*   But never a word he said:*
The eldest Oyster winked his eye,
*   And shook his heavy head—*
Meaning to say he did not choose
*   To leave the oyster-bed.   .*

But four young Oysters hurried up,
*   All eager for the treat:*
Their coats were brushed, their faces washed,
*   Their shoes were clean and neat—*
And this was odd, because, you know,
*   They hadn't any feet.*

Four other Oysters followed them,
  And yet another four;
And thick and fast they came at last,
  And more, and more, and more—
All hopping through the frothy waves,
  And scrambling to the shore.

The Walrus and the Carpenter
  Walked on a mile or so,
And then they rested on a rock
  Conveniently low:
And all the little Oysters stood
  And waited in a row.

"The time has come," the Walrus said,
  "To talk of many things:
Of shoes—and ships—and sealing-wax—
  Of cabbages—and kings—
And why the sea is boiling hot—
  And whether pigs have wings."

"But wait a bit," the Oysters cried,
  "Before we have our chat;
For some of us are out of breath,
  And all of us are fat!"
"No hurry!" said the Carpenter.
  They thanked him much for that.

"A loaf of bread," the Walrus said,
  "Is what we chiefly need:
Pepper and vinegar besides
  Are very good indeed—
Now, if you're ready, Oysters dear,
  We can begin to feed."

"*But not on us!*" *the Oysters cried,*
   Turning a little blue.
"*After such kindness, that would be*
   A dismal thing to do!"
"*The night is fine,*" *the Walrus said.*
   "*Do you admire the view?*

"*It was so kind of you to come!*
   And you are very nice!"
The Carpenter said nothing but
   "*Cut us another slice.*
I wish you were not quite so deaf—
   I've had to ask you twice!"

"*It seems a shame,*" *the Walrus said,*
   "*To play them such a trick.*
After we've brought them out so far,
   And made them trot so quick!"
The Carpenter said nothing but
   "*The butter's spread too thick!*"

"*I weep for you,*" *the Walrus said:*
    "*I deeply sympathize.*"
With sobs and tears he sorted out
    Those of the largest size,
Holding his pocket-handkerchief
    Before his streaming eyes.

"*O Oysters,*" *said the Carpenter,*
    "*You've had a pleasant run!*
Shall we be trotting home again?"
    But answer came there none—
And this was scarcely odd, because
    They'd eaten every one.'*

'I like the Walrus best,' said Alice: 'because he was a *little*
sorry for the poor oysters.'

'He ate more than the Carpenter, though,' said Tweedledee.
'You see he held his handkerchief in front, so that the Carpenter couldn't count how many he took: contrariwise.'

'That was mean!' Alice said indignantly. 'Then I like the
Carpenter best—if he didn't eat so many as the Walrus.'

'But he ate as many as he could get,' said Tweedledum.

This was a puzzler. After a pause, Alice began, 'Well! They were *both* very unpleasant characters——' Here she checked herself in some alarm, at hearing something that sounded to her like the puffing of a large steam-engine in the wood near them, though she feared it was more likely to be a wild beast. 'Are there any lions or tigers about here?' she asked timidly.

'It's only the Red King snoring,' said Tweedledee.

'Come and look at him!' the brothers cried, and they each took one of Alice's hands, and led her up to where the King was sleeping.

'Isn't he a *lovely* sight?' said Tweedledum.

Alice couldn't say honestly that he was. He had a tall red night-cap on, with a tassel, and he was lying crumpled up into a sort of untidy heap, and snoring loud——'fit to snore his head off!' as Tweedledum remarked.

'I'm afraid he'll catch cold with lying on the damp grass,' said Alice, who was a very thoughtful little girl.

'He's dreaming now,' said Tweedledee: 'and what do you think he's dreaming about?'

Alice said 'Nobody can guess that.'

'Why, about *you!*' Tweedledee exclaimed, clapping his hands triumphantly. 'And if he left off dreaming about you, where do you suppose you'd be?'

'Where I am now, of course,' said Alice.

'Not you!' Tweedledee retorted contemptuously. 'You'd be nowhere. Why, you're only a sort of thing in his dream!'

'If that there King was to wake,' added Tweedledum, 'you'd go out—bang!—just like a candle!'

'I shouldn't!' Alice exclaimed indignantly. 'Besides, if *I'm* only a sort of thing in his dream, what are *you*, I should like to know?'

'Ditto,' said Tweedledum.

'Ditto, ditto!' cried Tweedledee.

He shouted this so loud that Alice couldn't help saying 'Hush! You'll be waking him, I'm afraid, if you make so much noise.'

'Well, it's no use *your* talking about waking him,' said Tweedledum, 'when you're only one of the things in his dream. You know very well you're not real.'

'I *am* real!' said Alice, and began to cry.

'You wo'n't make yourself a bit realler by crying,' Tweedledee remarked: 'there's nothing to cry about.'

'If I wasn't real,' Alice said—half-laughing through her tears, it all seemed so ridiculous—'I shouldn't be able to cry.'

'I hope you don't suppose those are *real* tears?' Tweedledum interrupted in a tone of great contempt.

'I know they're talking nonsense,' Alice thought to herself: 'and it's foolish to cry about it.' So she brushed away her tears, and went on, as cheerfully as she could, 'At any rate I'd better be getting out of the wood, for really it's coming on very dark. Do you think it's going to rain?'

Tweedledum spread a large umbrella over himself and his brother, and looked up into it. 'No, I don't think it is,' he said: 'at least—not under *here*. Nohow.'

'But it may rain *outside?*'

'It may—if it chooses,' said Tweedledee: 'we've no objection. Contrariwise.'

'Selfish things!' thought Alice, and she was just going to say 'Good-night' and leave them, when Tweedledum sprang out from under the umbrella, and seized her by the wrist.

'Do you see *that?*' he said, in a voice choking with passion, and his eyes grew large and yellow all in a moment, as he pointed with a trembling finger at a small white thing lying under the tree.

'It's only a rattle,'* Alice said, after a careful examination of the little white thing. 'Not a rattle-*snake*, you know,' she added hastily, thinking that he was frightened: 'only an old rattle— quite old and broken.'

'I knew it was!' cried Tweedledum, beginning to stamp about wildly and tear his hair. 'It's spoilt, of course!' Here he

looked at Tweedledee, who immediately sat down on the ground, and tried to hide himself under the umbrella.

Alice laid her hand upon his arm, and said, in a soothing tone, 'You needn't be so angry about an old rattle.'

'But it *isn't* old!' Tweedledum cried, in a greater fury than ever. 'It's *new*, I tell you—I bought it yesterday—my nice NEW RATTLE!' and his voice rose to a perfect scream.

All this time Tweedledee was trying his best to fold up the umbrella, with himself in it: which was such an extraordinary thing to do, that it quite took off Alice's attention from the angry brother. But he couldn't quite succeed, and it ended in his rolling over, bundled up in the umbrella, with only his head out: and there he lay, opening and shutting his mouth and his large eyes——'looking more like a fish than anything else,' Alice thought.

'Of course you agree to have a battle?' Tweedledum said in a calmer tone.

'I suppose so,' the other sulkily replied, as he crawled out of the umbrella: 'only *she* must help us to dress up, you know.'

So the two brothers went off hand-in-hand into the wood, and returned in a minute with their arms full of things—such as bolsters, blankets, hearth-rugs, table-cloths, dish-covers, and coal-scuttles. 'I hope you're a good hand at pinning and tying strings?' Tweedledum remarked. 'Every one of these things has got to go on, somehow or other.'

Alice said afterwards she had never seen such a fuss made about anything in all her life—the way those two bustled about—and the quantity of things they put on—and the trouble they gave her in tying strings and fastening buttons ——'Really they'll be more like bundles of old clothes than anything else, by the time they're ready!' she said to herself, as she arranged a bolster round the neck of Tweedledee, 'to keep his head from being cut off,' as he said.

'You know,' he added very gravely, 'it's one of the most serious things that can possibly happen to one in a battle— to get one's head cut off.'

Alice laughed loud: but she managed to turn it into a cough, for fear of hurting his feelings.

'Do I look very pale?' said Tweedledum, coming up to have his helmet tied on. (He *called* it a helmet, though it certainly looked much more like a saucepan.)

'Well—yes—a *little*,' Alice replied gently.

'I'm very brave, generally,' he went on in a low voice: 'only to-day I happen to have a headache.'

'And *I've* got a toothache!' said Tweedledee, who had over-heard the remark. 'I'm far worse than you!'

'Then you'd better not fight to-day,' said Alice, thinking it a good opportunity to make peace.

'We *must* have a bit of a fight, but I don't care about going on long,' said Tweedledum. 'What's the time now?'

Tweedledee looked at his watch, and said 'Half-past four.'

'Let's fight till six, and then have dinner,' said Tweedledum.

'Very well,' the other said, rather sadly: 'and *she* can watch us—only you'd better not come *very* close,' he added: 'I generally hit every thing I can see—when I get really excited.'

'And *I* hit every thing within reach,' cried Tweedledum, 'whether I can see it or not!'

Alice laughed. 'You must hit the *trees* pretty often, I should think,' she said.

Tweedledum looked round him with a satisfied smile. 'I don't suppose,' he said, 'there'll be a tree left standing, for ever so far round, by the time we've finished!'

'And all about a rattle!' said Alice, still hoping to make them a *little* ashamed of fighting for such a trifle.

'I shouldn't have minded it so much,' said Tweedledum, 'if it hadn't been a new one.'

'I wish the monstrous crow would come!' thought Alice.

'There's only one sword, you know,' Tweedledum said to his brother: 'but *you* can have the umbrella—it's quite as sharp. Only we must begin quick. It's getting as dark as it can.'

'And darker,' said Tweedledee.

It was getting dark so suddenly that Alice thought there must be a thunderstorm coming on. 'What a thick black cloud that is!' she said. 'And how fast it comes! Why, I do believe it's got wings!'

'It's the crow!' Tweedledum cried out in a shrill voice of alarm; and the two brothers took to their heels and were out of sight in a moment.

Alice ran a little way into the wood, and stopped under a large tree. 'It can never get at me *here*,' she thought: 'it's far too large to squeeze itself in among the trees. But I wish it wouldn't flap its wings so—it makes quite a hurricane in the wood—here's somebody's shawl being blown away!'

CHAPTER V

SHE caught the shawl as she spoke, and looked about for the owner: in another moment the White Queen came running wildly through the wood,* with both arms stretched out wide, as if she were flying, and Alice very civilly went to meet her with the shawl.

'I'm very glad I happened to be in the way,' Alice said, as she helped her to put on her shawl again.

The White Queen only looked at her in a helpless frightened sort of way, and kept repeating something in a whisper to herself that sounded like 'Bread-and-butter, bread-and-butter,' and Alice felt that if there was to be any conversation at all, she must manage it herself. So she began rather timidly: 'Am I addressing the White Queen?'

'Well, yes, if you call that a-dressing,' the Queen said. 'It isn't *my* notion of the thing, at all.'

Alice thought it would never do to have an argument at the very beginning of their conversation, so she smiled and said 'If your Majesty will only tell me the right way to begin, I'll do it as well as I can.'

'But I don't want it done at all!' groaned the poor Queen. 'I've been a-dressing myself for the last two hours.'

It would have been all the better, as it seemed to Alice, if she had got some one else to dress her, she was so dreadfully untidy. 'Every single thing's crooked,' Alice thought to herself, 'and she's all over pins!——May I put your shawl straight for you?' she added aloud.

'I don't know what's the matter with it!' the Queen said, in a melancholy voice. 'It's out of temper, I think. I've pinned it here, and I've pinned it there, but there's no pleasing it!'

'It *ca'n't* go straight, you know, if you pin it all on one side,' Alice said, as she gently put it right for her; 'and, dear me, what a state your hair is in!'

'The brush has got entangled in it!' the Queen said with a sigh. 'And I lost the comb yesterday.'

Alice carefully released the brush, and did her best to get the hair into order. 'Come, you look rather better now!' she said, after altering most of the pins. 'But really you should have a lady's-maid!'

'I'm sure I'll take *you* with pleasure!' the Queen said. 'Twopence a week, and jam every other day.'

Alice couldn't help laughing, as she said 'I don't want you to hire *me*—and I don't care for jam.'

'It's very good jam,' said the Queen.

'Well, I don't want any *to-day*, at any rate.'

'You couldn't have it if you *did* want it,' the Queen said. 'The rule is, jam to-morrow and jam yesterday—but never jam *to-day*.'*

'It *must* come sometimes to "jam to-day,"' Alice objected.

'No, it ca'n't,' said the Queen. 'It's jam every *other* day: to-day isn't any *other* day, you know.'

'I don't understand you,' said Alice. 'It's dreadfully confusing!'

'That's the effect of living backwards,' the Queen said kindly: 'it always makes one a little giddy at first——'

'Living backwards!' Alice repeated in great astonishment. 'I never heard of such a thing!'

'—but there's one great advantage in it, that one's memory works both ways.'

'I'm sure *mine* only works one way,' Alice remarked. 'I ca'n't remember things before they happen.'

'It's a poor sort of memory that only works backwards,' the Queen remarked.

'What sort of things do *you* remember best?' Alice ventured to ask.

'Oh, things that happened the week after next,' the Queen replied in a careless tone. 'For instance, now,' she went on, sticking a large piece of plaster on her finger as she spoke, 'there's the King's Messenger. He's in prison now, being punished: and the trial doesn't even begin till next Wednesday: and of course the crime comes last of all.'

'Suppose he never commits the crime?' said Alice.

'That would be all the better, wouldn't it?' the Queen said, as she bound the plaster round her finger with a bit of ribbon.

Alice felt there was no denying *that*. 'Of course it

would be all the better,' she said: 'but it wouldn't be all the better his being punished.'

'You're wrong *there*, at any rate,' said the Queen. 'Were *you* ever punished?'

'Only for faults,' said Alice.

'And you were all the better for it, I know!' the Queen said triumphantly.

'Yes, but then I *had* done the things I was punished for,' said Alice: 'that makes all the difference.'

'But if you *hadn't* done them,' the Queen said, 'that would have been better still; better, and better, and better!' Her voice went higher with each 'better,' till it got quite to a squeak at last.

Alice was just beginning to say 'There's a mistake somewhere——,' when the Queen began screaming, so loud that she had to leave the sentence unfinished. 'Oh, oh, oh!' shouted the Queen, shaking her hand about as if she wanted to shake it off. 'My finger's bleeding! Oh, oh, oh, oh!'

Her screams were so exactly like the whistle of a steam-engine, that Alice had to hold both her hands over her ears.

'What *is* the matter?' she said, as soon as there was a chance of making herself heard. 'Have you pricked your finger?'

'I haven't pricked it *yet*,' the Queen said, 'but I soon shall—oh, oh, oh!'

'When do you expect to do it?' Alice asked, feeling very much inclined to laugh.

'When I fasten my shawl again,' the poor Queen groaned out: 'the brooch will come undone directly. Oh, oh!' As she said the words the brooch flew open, and the Queen clutched wildly at it, and tried to clasp it again.

'Take care!' cried Alice. 'You're holding it all crooked!' And she caught at the brooch; but it was too late: the pin had slipped, and the Queen had pricked her finger.

'That accounts for the bleeding, you see,' she said to Alice with a smile. 'Now you understand the way things happen here.'

'But why don't you scream *now?*' Alice asked, holding her hands ready to put over her ears again.

'Why, I've done all the screaming already,' said the Queen. 'What would be the good of having it all over again?'

By this time it was getting light. 'The crow must have flown away, I think,' said Alice: 'I'm so glad it's gone. I thought it was the night coming on.'

'I wish *I* could manage to be glad!' the Queen said. 'Only I never can remember the rule. You must be very happy, living in this wood, and being glad whenever you like!'

'Only it is so *very* lonely here!' Alice said in a melancholy voice; and, at the thought of her loneliness, two large tears came rolling down her cheeks.

'Oh, don't go on like that!' cried the poor Queen, wringing her hands in despair. 'Consider what a great girl you are. Consider what a long way you've come to-day. Consider what o'clock it is. Consider anything, only don't cry!'

Alice could not help laughing at this, even in the midst of her tears. 'Can *you* keep from crying by considering things?' she asked.

'That's the way it's done,' the Queen said with great decision: 'nobody can do two things at once, you know. Let's consider your age to begin with——how old are you?'

'I'm seven and a half, exactly.'

'You needn't say "exactually,"' the Queen remarked. 'I can believe it without that. Now I'll give *you* something to believe. I'm just one hundred and one, five months and a day.'

'I ca'n't believe *that!*' said Alice.

'Ca'n't you?' the Queen said in a pitying tone. 'Try again: draw a long breath, and shut your eyes.'

Alice laughed. 'There's no use trying,' she said: 'one *ca'n't* believe impossible things.'

'I daresay you haven't had much practice,' said the Queen. 'When I was your age, I always did it for half-an-hour a day. Why, sometimes I've believed as many as six impossible things before breakfast. There goes the shawl again!'

The brooch had come undone as she spoke, and a sudden

gust of wind blew the Queen's shawl across a little brook. The Queen spread out her arms again, and went flying after it, and this time she succeeded in catching it for herself. 'I've got it!' she cried in a triumphant tone. 'Now you shall see me pin it on again, all by myself!'

'Then I hope your finger is better now?' Alice said very politely, as she crossed the little brook* after the Queen.

*   *   *   *   *   *

*   *   *   *   *   *

*   *   *   *   *   *

'Oh, much better!' cried the Queen, her voice rising into a squeak as she went on. 'Much be-etter! Be-etter! Be-e-e-etter! Be-e-ehh!' The last word ended in a long bleat, so like a sheep that Alice quite started.

She looked at the Queen, who seemed to have suddenly wrapped herself up in wool.* Alice rubbed her eyes, and looked again. She couldn't make out what had happened at all. Was she in a shop?* And was that really—was it really a *sheep* that was sitting on the other side of the counter? Rub as she would, she could make nothing more of it: she was in a little dark shop, leaning with her elbows on the counter, and opposite to her was an old Sheep, sitting in an arm-chair, knitting, and every now and then leaving off to look at her through a great pair of spectacles.

'What is it you want to buy?' the Sheep said at last, looking up for a moment from her knitting.

'I don't *quite* know yet,' Alice said very gently. 'I should like to look all round me first, if I might.'

'You may look in front of you, and on both sides, if you like,' said the Sheep; 'but you ca'n't look *all* round you—unless you've got eyes at the back of your head.'

But these, as it happened, Alice had *not* got: so she contented herself with turning round, looking at the shelves as she came to them.

The shop seemed to be full of all manner of curious things —but the oddest part of it all was that, whenever she looked

hard at any shelf, to make out exactly what it had on it, that particular shelf was always quite empty, though the others round it were crowded as full as they could hold.

'Things flow about so here!' she said at last in a plaintive tone, after she had spent a minute or so in vainly pursuing a large bright thing, that looked sometimes like a doll and sometimes like a work-box, and was always in the shelf next above the one she was looking at. 'And this one is the most provoking of all—but I'll tell you what——' she added, as a sudden thought struck her. 'I'll follow it up to the very top shelf of all. It'll puzzle it to go through the ceiling, I expect!'

But even this plan failed: the 'thing' went through the ceiling as quietly as possible, as if it were quite used to it.*

'Are you a child or a teetotum?'* the Sheep said, as she took up another pair of needles. 'You'll make me giddy soon, if you go on turning round like that.' She was now working with fourteen pairs at once, and Alice couldn't help looking at her in great astonishment.

'How *can* she knit with so many?' the puzzled child thought to herself. 'She gets more and more like a porcupine every minute!'

'Can you row?' the Sheep asked, handing her a pair of knitting-needles as she spoke.

'Yes, a little—but not on land—and not with needles——' Alice was beginning to say, when suddenly the needles turned into oars in her hands, and she found they were in a little boat, gliding along between banks: so there was nothing for it but to do her best.

'Feather!'* cried the Sheep, as she took up another pair of needles.

This didn't sound like a remark that needed any answer: so Alice said nothing, but pulled away. There was something very queer about the water, she thought, as every now and then the oars got fast in it, and would hardly come out again.

'Feather! Feather!' the Sheep cried again, taking more needles. 'You'll be catching a crab* directly.'

'A dear little crab!' thought Alice. 'I should like that.'

'Didn't you hear me say "Feather"?' the Sheep cried angrily, taking up quite a bunch of needles.

'Indeed I did,' said Alice: 'you've said it very often—and very loud. Please where *are* the crabs?'

'In the water, of course!' said the Sheep, sticking some of the needles into her hair, as her hands were full. 'Feather, I say!'

'*Why* do you say "Feather" so often?' Alice asked at last, rather vexed. 'I'm not a bird!'

'You are,' said the Sheep: 'you're a little goose.'

This offended Alice a little, so there was no more conversation for a minute or two, while the boat glided gently on, sometimes among beds of weeds (which made the oars stick fast in the water, worse than ever), and sometimes under trees, but always with the same tall river-banks frowning over their heads.

'Oh, please! There are some scented rushes!' Alice cried in a sudden transport of delight. 'There really are—and *such* beauties!'*

'You needn't say "please" to *me* about 'em,' the Sheep said, without looking up from her knitting: 'I didn't put 'em there, and I'm not going to take 'em away.'

'No, but I meant—please, may we wait and pick some?' Alice pleaded. 'If you don't mind stopping the boat for a minute.'

'How am *I* to stop it?' said the Sheep. 'If you leave off rowing, it'll stop of itself.'

So the boat was left to drift down the stream as it would, till it glided gently in among the waving rushes. And then the little sleeves were carefully rolled up, and the little arms were plunged in elbow-deep, to get hold of the rushes a good long way down before breaking them off—and for a while Alice forgot all about the Sheep and the knitting, as she bent over the side of the boat, with just the ends of her tangled hair dipping into the water—while with bright eager eyes she caught at one bunch after another of the darling scented rushes.

'I only hope the boat won't tipple over!' she said to herself. 'Oh, *what* a lovely one! Only I couldn't quite reach it.' And it certainly *did* seem a little provoking ('almost as if it happened on purpose,' she thought) that, though she managed to pick plenty of beautiful rushes as the boat glided by, there was always a more lovely one that she couldn't reach.

'The prettiest are always further!' she said at last, with a sigh at the obstinacy of the rushes in growing so far off, as, with flushed cheeks and dripping hair and hands, she scrambled back into her place, and began to arrange her new-found treasures.

What mattered it to her just then that the rushes had begun to fade, and to lose all their scent and beauty, from the very moment that she picked them? Even real scented rushes, you know, last only a very little while—and these, being dream-rushes, melted away almost like snow, as they lay in heaps at her feet—but Alice hardly noticed this, there were so many other curious things to think about.

They hadn't gone much farther before the blade of one of the oars got fast in the water and *wouldn't* come out again (so Alice explained it afterwards), and the consequence was that the handle of it caught her under the chin, and, in spite of a series of little shrieks of 'Oh, oh, oh!' from poor Alice, it swept her straight off the seat, and down among the heap of rushes.

However, she wasn't a bit hurt, and was soon up again: the Sheep went on with her knitting all the while, just as if nothing had happened. 'That was a nice crab you caught!' she remarked, as Alice got back into her place, very much relieved to find herself still in the boat.

'Was it? I didn't see it,' said Alice, peeping cautiously over the side of the boat into the dark water. 'I wish it hadn't let go—I should so like a little crab to take home with me!' But the Sheep only laughed scornfully, and went on with her knitting.

'Are there many crabs here?' said Alice.

'Crabs, and all sorts of things,' said the Sheep: 'plenty of choice, only make up your mind. Now, what *do* you want to buy?'

'To buy!' Alice echoed in a tone that was half astonished and half frightened—for the oars, and the boat, and the river, had vanished all in a moment, and she was back again in the little dark shop.

'I should like to buy an egg, please,' she said timidly. 'How do you sell them?'

'Fivepence farthing for one—twopence for two,' the Sheep replied.

'Then two are cheaper than one?'* Alice said in a surprised tone, taking out her purse.

'Only you *must* eat them both, if you buy two,' said the Sheep.

'Then I'll have *one*, please,' said Alice, as she put the money down on the counter. For she thought to herself, 'They mightn't be at all nice, you know.'

The Sheep took the money, and put it away in a box: then she said 'I never put things into people's hands—that would never do—you must get it for yourself.' And so saying, she went off to the other end of the shop,* and set the egg upright on a shelf.

'I wonder *why* it wouldn't do?' thought Alice, as she groped her way among the tables and chairs, for the shop was very dark towards the end. 'The egg seems to get further away the more I walk towards it. Let me see, is this a chair? Why, it's got branches, I declare! How very odd to find trees growing here! And actually here's a little brook!* Well, this is the very queerest shop I ever saw!'

*   *   *   *   *

*   *   *   *   *

*   *   *   *   *

So she went on, wondering more and more at every step, as everything turned into a tree the moment she came up to it, and she quite expected the egg to do the same.

CHAPTER VI

HUMPTY DUMPTY*

HOWEVER, the egg only got larger and larger, and more and more human: when she had come within a few yards of it, she saw that it had eyes and a nose and mouth; and, when she had come close to it, she saw clearly that it was HUMPTY DUMPTY himself. 'It ca'n't be anybody else!' she said to herself. 'I'm as certain of it, as if his name were written all over his face!'

It might have been written a hundred times, easily, on that enormous face. Humpty Dumpty was sitting, with his legs crossed like a Turk, on the top of a high wall—such a narrow one that Alice quite wondered how he could keep his balance—and, as his eyes were steadily fixed in the opposite direction, and he didn't take the least notice of her, she thought he must be a stuffed figure, after all.

'And how exactly like an egg he is!' she said aloud, standing with her hands ready to catch him, for she was every moment expecting him to fall.

'It's *very* provoking,' Humpty Dumpty said after a long silence, looking away from Alice as he spoke, 'to be called an egg—*very!*'

'I said you *looked* like an egg, Sir,' Alice gently explained. 'And some eggs are very pretty, you know,' she added, hoping to turn her remark into a sort of compliment.

'Some people,' said Humpty Dumpty, looking away from her as usual, 'have no more sense than a baby!'

Alice didn't know what to say to this: it wasn't at all like conversation, she thought, as he never said anything to *her;* in fact, his last remark was evidently addressed to a tree—so she stood and softly repeated to herself:—

> '*Humpty Dumpty sat on a wall:*
> *Humpty Dumpty had a great fall.*
> *All the King's horses and all the King's men*
> *Couldn't put Humpty Dumpty in his place again.*'

'That last line is much too long for the poetry,' she added, almost out loud, forgetting that Humpty Dumpty would hear her.

'Don't stand chattering to yourself like that,' Humpty Dumpty said, looking at her for the first time, 'but tell me your name and your business.'

'My *name* is Alice, but——'

'It's a stupid name enough!' Humpty Dumpty interrupted impatiently. 'What does it mean?'

'*Must* a name mean something?' Alice asked doubtfully.

'Of course it must,' Humpty Dumpty said with a short laugh: '*my* name means the shape I am—and a good handsome shape it is, too. With a name like yours, you might be any shape, almost.'

'Why do you sit out here all alone?' said Alice, not wishing to begin an argument.

'Why, because there's nobody with me!' cried Humpty Dumpty. 'Did you think I didn't know the answer to *that*? Ask another.'

'Don't you think you'd be safer down on the ground?' Alice went on, not with any idea of making another riddle, but simply in her good-natured anxiety for the queer creature. 'That wall is so *very* narrow!'

'What tremendously easy riddles you ask!' Humpty Dumpty growled out. 'Of course I don't think so! Why, if ever I *did* fall off—which there's no chance of—but *if* I did——' Here he pursed up his lips, and looked so solemn and grand that Alice could hardly help laughing. '*If* I *did* fall,' he went on, '*the King has promised me*—ah, you may turn pale, if you like! You didn't think I was going to say that, did you? *The King has promised me—with his very own mouth*—to—to——'

'To send all his horses and all his men,' Alice interrupted, rather unwisely.

'Now I declare that's too bad!' Humpty Dumpty cried, breaking into a sudden passion. 'You've been listening at doors—and behind trees—and down chimneys—or you couldn't have known it!'

'I haven't, indeed!' Alice said very gently. 'It's in a book.'

'Ah, well! They may write such things in a *book*,' Humpty Dumpty said in a calmer tone. 'That's what you call a History of England, that is. Now, take a good look at me! I'm one that has spoken to a King, *I* am: mayhap you'll never see such

another: and, to show you I'm not proud, you may shake hands with me!' And he grinned almost from ear to ear, as he leant forwards (and as nearly as possible fell off the wall in doing so) and offered Alice his hand. She watched him a little anxiously as she took it. 'If he smiled much more the ends of his mouth might meet behind,' she thought: 'and then I don't know *what* would happen to his head! I'm afraid it would come off!'

'Yes, all his horses and all his men,' Humpty Dumpty went on. 'They'd pick me up again in a minute, *they* would! However, this conversation is going on a little too fast: let's go back to the last remark but one.'

'I'm afraid I ca'n't quite remember it,' Alice said, very politely.

'In that case we start afresh,' said Humpty Dumpty, 'and it's my turn to choose a subject——' ('He talks about it just as if it was a game!' thought Alice.) 'So here's a question for you. How old did you say you were?'

Alice made a short calculation, and said 'Seven years and six months.'

'<u>Wrong</u>!' Humpty Dumpty exclaimed triumphantly. '<u>You never said a word like it!</u>'

'I thought you meant "How old *are* you?"' Alice explained.

'If I'd meant that, I'd have said it,' said Humpty Dumpty.

Alice didn't want to begin another argument, so she said nothing.

'Seven years and six months!' Humpty Dumpty repeated thoughtfully. 'An uncomfortable sort of age. Now if you'd asked *my* advice, I'd have said "Leave off at seven"——but it's too late now.'

'I never ask advice about growing,' Alice said indignantly.

'Too proud?' the other enquired.

Alice felt even more indignant at this suggestion. 'I mean,' she said, 'that one ca'n't help growing older.'

'*One* ca'n't, perhaps,' said Humpty Dumpty; 'but *two* can. With proper assistance, you might have left off at seven.'

'What a beautiful belt you've got on!' Alice suddenly remarked. (They had had quite enough of the subject of age, she thought: and, if they really were to take turns in choosing subjects, it was *her* turn now.) 'At least,' she corrected herself on second thoughts, 'a beautiful cravat, I should have said—no, a belt, I mean—I beg your pardon!' she added in dismay, for Humpty Dumpty looked thoroughly offended, and she began to wish she hadn't chosen that subject. 'If only I knew,' she thought to herself, 'which was neck and which was waist!'

Evidently Humpty Dumpty was very angry, though he said nothing for a minute or two. When he *did* speak again, it was in a deep growl.

'It is a—*most*—*provoking*—thing,' he said at last, 'when a person doesn't know a cravat from a belt!'

'I know it's very ignorant of me,' Alice said, in so humble a tone that Humpty Dumpty relented.

'It's a cravat, child, and a beautiful one, as you say. It's a present from the White King and Queen. There now!'

'Is it really?' said Alice, quite pleased to find that she *had* chosen a good subject, after all.

'They gave it me,' Humpty Dumpty continued thoughtfully, as he crossed one knee over the other and clasped his hands round it, 'they gave it me—for an un-birthday present.'*

'I beg your pardon?' Alice said with a puzzled air.

'I'm not offended,' said Humpty Dumpty.

'I mean, what *is* an un-birthday present?'

'A present given when it isn't your birthday, of course.'

Alice considered a little. 'I like birthday presents best,' she said at last.

'You don't know what you're talking about!' cried Humpty Dumpty. 'How many days are there in a year?'

'Three hundred and sixty-five,' said Alice.

'And how many birthdays have you?'

'One.'

'And if you take one from three hundred and sixty-five, what remains?'

'Three hundred and sixty-four, of course.'

Humpty Dumpty looked doubtful. 'I'd rather see that done on paper,' he said.

Alice couldn't help smiling as she took out her memorandum-book, and worked the sum for him:

$$\begin{array}{r} 365 \\ 1 \\ \hline 364 \end{array}$$

Humpty Dumpty took the book, and looked at it carefully. 'That seems to be done right——' he began.

'You're holding it upside down!' Alice interrupted.

'To be sure I was!' Humpty Dumpty said gaily, as she turned it round for him. 'I thought it looked a little queer. As I was saying, that *seems* to be done right—though I haven't time to look it over thoroughly just now—and that shows that there are three hundred and sixty-four days when you might get un-birthday presents——'

'Certainly,' said Alice.

'And only *one* for birthday presents, you know. There's glory for you!'

'I don't know what you mean by "glory,"' Alice said.

Humpty Dumpty smiled contemptuously. 'Of course you don't—till I tell you. I meant "there's a nice knock-down argument for you!"'

'But "glory" doesn't mean "a nice knock-down argument,"' Alice objected.

'When *I* use a word,'* Humpty Dumpty said, in rather a scornful tone, 'it means just what I choose it to mean—neither more nor less.'

'The question is,' said Alice, 'whether you *can* make words mean so many different things.'

'The question is,' said Humpty Dumpty, 'which is to be master——that's all.'

Alice was too much puzzled to say anything; so after a minute Humpty Dumpty began again. 'They've a temper, some of them—particularly verbs: they're the proudest—adjectives you can do anything with, but not verbs—however,

I can manage the whole lot of them! Impenetrability! That's what *I* say!'

'Would you tell me, please,' said Alice, 'what that means?'

'Now you talk like a reasonable child,' said Humpty Dumpty, looking very much pleased. 'I meant by "impenetrability" that we've had enough of that subject, and it would be just as well if you'd mention what you mean to do next, as I suppose you don't mean to stop here all the rest of your life.'

'That's a great deal to make one word mean,' Alice said in a thoughtful tone.

'When I make a word do a lot of work like that,' said Humpty Dumpty, 'I always pay it extra.'

'Oh!' said Alice. She was too much puzzled to make any other remark.

'Ah, you should see 'em come round me of a Saturday night,' Humpty Dumpty went on, wagging his head gravely from side to side, 'for to get their wages, you know.'

(Alice didn't venture to ask what he paid them with; and so you see I ca'n't tell *you*.)

'You seem very clever at explaining words, Sir,' said Alice. 'Would you kindly tell me the meaning of the poem called "Jabberwocky"?'

'Let's hear it,' said Humpty Dumpty. 'I can explain all the poems that ever were invented—and a good many that haven't been invented just yet.'

This sounded very hopeful, so Alice repeated the first verse:—

> '*Twas brillig, and the slithy toves*
> *Did gyre and gimble in the wabe:*
> *All mimsy were the borogoves,*
> *And the mome raths outgrabe.*'

'That's enough to begin with,' Humpty Dumpty interrupted: 'there are plenty of hard words there. "*Brillig*" means four o'clock in the afternoon—the time when you begin *broiling* things for dinner.'

Whoever controls meaning,
controls thought > this mishmash
of rules here

'That'll do very well,' said Alice: 'and "*slithy*"?'

'Well, "*slithy*" means "lithe and slimy." "Lithe" is the same as "active." You see it's like a portmanteau*—there are two meanings packed up into one word.'

'I see it now,' Alice remarked thoughtfully: 'and what are "*toves*"?'

'Well, "*toves*" are something like badgers—they're something like lizards—and they're something like corkscrews.'

'They must be very curious-looking creatures.'

'They are that,' said Humpty Dumpty: 'also they make their nests under sun-dials—also they live on cheese.'

'And what's to "*gyre*" and to "*gimble*"?'

'To "*gyre*" is to go round and round like a gyroscope. To "*gimble*" is to make holes like a gimblet.'

'And "*the wabe*" is the grass-plot round a sun-dial, I suppose?' said Alice, surprised at her own ingenuity.

'Of course it is. It's called "*wabe*," you know, because it goes a long way before it, and a long way behind it——'

'And a long way beyond it on each side,' Alice added.

'Exactly so. Well then, "*mimsy*" is "flimsy and miserable" (there's another portmanteau for you). And a "*borogove*" is a thin shabby-looking bird with its feathers sticking out all round—something like a live mop.'

'And then "*mome raths*"?' said Alice. 'I'm afraid I'm giving you a great deal of trouble.'

'Well, a "*rath*" is a sort of green pig: but "*mome*" I'm not certain about. I think it's short for "from home"—meaning that they'd lost their way, you know.'

'And what does "*outgrabe*" mean?'

'Well, "*outgribing*" is something between bellowing and whistling, with a kind of sneeze in the middle: however, you'll hear it done, maybe—down in the wood yonder—and, when you've once heard it, you'll be *quite* content. Who's been repeating all that hard stuff to you?'

'I read it in a book,' said Alice. 'But I *had* some poetry repeated to me much easier than that, by—Tweedledee, I think it was.'

'As to poetry, you know,' said Humpty Dumpty, stretching out one of his great hands, '*I* can repeat poetry as well as other folk, if it comes to that——'

'Oh, it needn't come to that!' Alice hastily said, hoping to keep him from beginning.

'The piece I'm going to repeat,' he went on without noticing her remark, 'was written entirely for your amusement.'

Alice felt that in that case she really *ought* to listen to it; so she sat down, and said 'Thank you' rather sadly.

> '*In winter, when the fields are white,**
> *I sing this song for your delight——*

only I don't sing it,' he added, as an explanation.

'I see you don't,' said Alice.

'If you can *see* whether I'm singing or not, you've sharper eyes than most,' Humpty Dumpty remarked severely. Alice was silent.

> '*In spring, when woods are getting green,*
> *I'll try and tell you what I mean:*'

'Thank you very much,' said Alice.

> '*In summer, when the days are long,*
> *Perhaps you'll understand the song:*
>
> *In autumn, when the leaves are brown,*
> *Take pen and ink, and write it down.*'

'I will, if I can remember it so long,' said Alice.

'You needn't go on making remarks like that,' Humpty Dumpty said: 'they're not sensible, and they put me out.'

> '*I sent a message to the fish:*
> *I told them "This is what I wish."*
>
> *The little fishes of the sea,*
> *They sent an answer back to me.*
>
> *The little fishes' answer was*
> *"We cannot do it, Sir, because——"*'

'I'm afraid I don't quite understand,' said Alice.

'It gets easier further on,' Humpty Dumpty replied.

> '*I sent to them again to say*
> *"It will be better to obey."*
>
> *The fishes answered, with a grin,*
> *"Why, what a temper you are in!"*'

I told them once, I told them twice:
They would not listen to advice.

I took a kettle large and new,
Fit for the deed I had to do.

My heart went hop, my heart went thump:
I filled the kettle at the pump.

Then some one came to me and said
"The little fishes are in bed."

I said to him, I said it plain,
"Then you must wake them up again."

I said it very loud and clear:
I went and shouted in his ear.'

Humpty Dumpty raised his voice almost to a scream as he repeated this verse, and Alice thought, with a shudder, 'I wouldn't have been the messenger for *anything!*'

> *'But he was very stiff and proud:*
> *He said "You needn't shout so loud!"*
>
> *And he was very proud and stiff:*
> *He said "I'd go and wake them, if——"*
>
> *I took a corkscrew from the shelf:*
> *I went to wake them up myself.*
>
> *And when I found the door was locked,*
> *I pulled and pushed and kicked and knocked.*
>
> *And when I found the door was shut,*
> *I tried to turn the handle, but——'*

There was a long pause.

'Is that all?' Alice timidly asked.

'That's all,' said Humpty Dumpty. 'Good-bye.'

This was rather sudden, Alice thought: but, after such a *very* strong hint that she ought to be going, she felt that it would hardly be civil to stay. So she got up, and held out her hand. 'Good-bye, till we meet again!' she said as cheerfully as she could.

'I shouldn't know you again if we *did* meet,' Humpty Dumpty replied in a discontented tone, giving her one of his fingers to shake:* 'you're so exactly like other people.'

'The face is what one goes by, generally,' Alice remarked in a thoughtful tone.

'That's just what I complain of,' said Humpty Dumpty. 'Your face is the same as everybody has—the two eyes, so——' (marking their places in the air with his thumb) 'nose in the middle, mouth under. It's always the same. Now if you had the two eyes on the same side of the nose, for instance—or the mouth at the top—that would be *some* help.'

'It wouldn't look nice,' Alice objected. But Humpty Dumpty only shut his eyes, and said 'Wait till you've tried.'

Alice waited a minute to see if he would speak again, but, as he never opened his eyes or took any further notice of her, she said 'Good-bye!' once more, and, getting no answer to this, she quietly walked away: but she couldn't help saying to herself, as she went, 'Of all the unsatisfactory——' (she repeated this aloud, as it was a great comfort to have such a long word to say) 'of all the unsatisfactory people I *ever* met——' She never finished the sentence, for at this moment a heavy crash shook the forest from end to end.

CHAPTER VII

THE LION AND THE UNICORN

THE next moment soldiers came running through the wood, at first in twos and threes, then ten or twenty together, and at last in such crowds that they seemed to fill the whole forest. Alice got behind a tree, for fear of being run over, and watched them go by.

She thought that in all her life she had never seen soldiers so uncertain on their feet: they were always tripping over something or other, and whenever one went down, several more always fell over him, so that the ground was soon covered with little heaps of men.

Then came the horses. Having four feet, these managed rather better than the foot-soldiers; but even *they* stumbled now and then; and it seemed to be a regular rule that, whenever a horse stumbled, the rider fell off instantly. The confusion got worse every moment, and Alice was very glad to get out of the wood into an open place, where she found the White King seated on the ground, busily writing in his memorandum-book.

'I've sent them all!' the King cried in a tone of delight, on seeing Alice. 'Did you happen to meet any soldiers, my dear, as you came through the wood?'

'Yes, I did,' said Alice: 'several thousand, I should think.'

'Four thousand two hundred and seven, that's the exact number,' the King said, referring to his book. 'I couldn't send all the horses, you know, because two of them are wanted in the game. And I haven't sent the two Messengers, either. They're both gone to the town. Just look along the road, and tell me if you can see either of them.'

'I see nobody on the road,' said Alice.

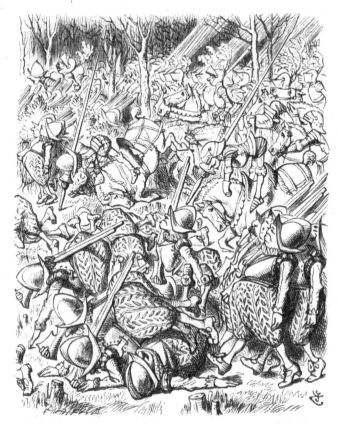

'I only wish *I* had such eyes,' the King remarked in a fret-ful tone. 'To be able to see Nobody! And at that distance too! Why, it's as much as *I* can do to see real people, by this light!'

All this was lost on Alice, who was still looking intently along the road, shading her eyes with one hand. 'I see some-body now!' she exclaimed at last. 'But he's coming very slowly —and what curious attitudes he goes into!' (For the Messenger kept skipping up and down, and wriggling like an eel, as he came along, with his great hands spread out like fans on each side.)

'Not at all,' said the King. 'He's an Anglo-Saxon Messenger —and those are Anglo-Saxon attitudes.* He only does them when he's happy. His name is Haigha.'* (He pronounced it so as to rhyme with 'mayor.')

'I love my love with an H,'* Alice couldn't help beginning, 'because he is Happy. I hate him with an H, because he is Hideous. I fed him with—with—with Ham-sandwiches and Hay. His name is Haigha, and he lives——'

'He lives on the Hill,' the King remarked simply, without the least idea that he was joining in the game, while Alice was still hesitating for the name of a town beginning with H. 'The other Messenger's called Hatta. I must have *two*, you know—to come and go. One to come, and one to go.'

'I beg your pardon?' said Alice.

'It isn't respectable to beg,' said the King.

'I only meant that I didn't understand,' said Alice. 'Why one to come and one to go?'

'Don't I tell you?' the King repeated impatiently. 'I must have *two*—to fetch and carry. One to fetch, and one to carry.'

At this moment the Messenger arrived: he was far too much out of breath to say a word, and could only wave his hands about, and make the most fearful faces at the poor King.

'This young lady loves you with an H,' the King said, introducing Alice in the hope of turning off the Messenger's attention from himself—but it was of no use—the Anglo-Saxon attitudes only got more extraordinary every moment, while the great eyes rolled wildly from side to side.

'You alarm me!' said the King. 'I feel faint——Give me a ham sandwich!'

On which the Messenger, to Alice's great amusement, opened a bag that hung round his neck, and handed a sandwich to the King, who devoured it greedily.

'Another sandwich!' said the King.

'There's nothing but hay left now,' the Messenger said, peeping into the bag.

'Hay, then,' the King murmured in a faint whisper.

Alice was glad to see that it revived him a good deal. 'There's nothing like eating hay when you're faint,' he remarked to her, as he munched away.

'I should think throwing cold water over you would be better,' Alice suggested: '—or some sal-volatile.'*

'I didn't say there was nothing *better*,' the King replied. 'I said there was nothing *like* it.' Which Alice did not venture to deny.

'Who did you pass on the road?' the King went on, holding out his hand to the Messenger for some more hay.

'Nobody,' said the Messenger.

'Quite right,' said the King: 'this young lady saw him too. So of course Nobody walks slower than you.'*

'I do my best,' the Messenger said in a sullen tone. 'I'm sure nobody walks much faster than I do!'

'He ca'n't do that,' said the King, 'or else he'd have been here first. However, now you've got your breath, you may tell us what's happened in the town.'

'I'll whisper it,' said the Messenger, putting his hands to his mouth in the shape of a trumpet and stooping so as to get close to the King's ear. Alice was sorry for this, as she wanted to hear the news too. However, instead of whispering, he simply shouted, at the top of his voice, 'They're at it again!'

'Do you call *that* a whisper?' cried the poor King, jumping up and shaking himself. 'If you do such a thing again, I'll have you buttered! It went through and through my head like an earthquake!'

'It would have to be a very tiny earthquake!' thought Alice. 'Who are at it again?' she ventured to ask.

'Why, the Lion and the Unicorn, of course,' said the King.

'Fighting for the crown?'

'Yes, to be sure,' said the King: 'and the best of the joke is, that it's *my* crown all the while! Let's run and see them.' And they trotted off, Alice repeating to herself, as she ran, the words of the old song:—

'The Lion and the Unicorn were fighting for the crown. *
The Lion beat the Unicorn all round the town.
Some gave them white bread, some gave them brown:
Some gave them plum-cake and drummed them out of town.'

'Does——the one——that wins——get the crown?' she asked, as well as she could, for the run was putting her quite out of breath.

'Dear me, no!' said the King. 'What an idea!'

'Would you—be good enough——' Alice panted out, after running a little further, 'to stop a minute—just to get—one's breath again?'

'I'm *good* enough,' the King said, 'only I'm not *strong* enough. You see, a minute goes by so fearfully quick. You might as well try to stop a Bandersnatch!'

Alice had no more breath for talking; so they trotted on in silence, till they came into sight of a great crowd, in the middle of which the Lion and Unicorn were fighting. They were in such a cloud of dust, that at first Alice could not make out

which was which; but she soon managed to distinguish the
Unicorn by his horn.

They placed themselves close to where Hatta, the other
Messenger, was standing watching the fight, with a cup of
tea in one hand and a piece of bread-and-butter in the
other.

'He's only just out of prison, and he hadn't finished his
tea when he was sent in,' Haigha whispered to Alice: 'and
they only give them oyster-shells* in there—so you see
he's very hungry and thirsty. How are you, dear child?'
he went on, putting his arm affectionately round Hatta's
neck.

Hatta looked round and nodded, and went on with his
bread-and-butter.

'Were you happy in prison, dear child?' said Haigha.

Hatta looked round once more, and this time a tear or two
trickled down his cheek; but not a word would he say.

'Speak, ca'n't you!' Haigha cried impatiently. But Hatta
only munched away, and drank some more tea.

'Speak, wo'n't you!' cried the King. 'How are they getting on with the fight?'

Hatta made a desperate effort, and swallowed a large piece of bread-and-butter. 'They're getting on very well,' he said in a choking voice: 'each of them has been down about eighty-seven times.'*

'Then I suppose they'll soon bring the white bread and the brown?' Alice ventured to remark.

'It's waiting for 'em now,' said Hatta; 'this is a bit of it as I'm eating.'

There was a pause in the fight just then, and the Lion and the Unicorn sat down, panting, while the King called out 'Ten minutes allowed for refreshments!' Haigha and Hatta set to work at once, carrying round trays of white and brown bread. Alice took a piece to taste, but it was *very* dry.

'I don't think they'll fight any more today,' the King said to Hatta: 'go and order the drums to begin.' And Hatta went bounding away like a grasshopper.

For a minute or two Alice stood silent, watching him. Suddenly she brightened up. 'Look, look!' she cried, point-ing eagerly. 'There's the White Queen running across the country! She came flying out of the wood over yonder—— How fast those Queens *can* run!'*

'There's some enemy after her, no doubt,' the King said, without even looking round. 'That wood's full of them.'

'But aren't you going to run and help her?' Alice asked, very much surprised at his taking it so quietly.

'No use, no use!' said the King. 'She runs so fearfully quick. You might as well try to catch a Bandersnatch! But I'll make a memorandum about her, if you like—— She's a dear good creature,' he repeated softly to himself, as he opened his memorandum-book. 'Do you spell "creature" with a double "e"?'

At this moment the Unicorn sauntered by them, with his

hands in his pockets. 'I had the best of it this time?' he said to the King, just glancing at him as he passed.

'A little—a little,' the King replied, rather nervously. 'You shouldn't have run him through with your horn, you know.'

'It didn't hurt him,' the Unicorn said carelessly, and he was going on, when his eye happened to fall upon Alice: he turned round instantly, and stood for some time looking at her with an air of the deepest disgust.

'What—is—this?' he said at last.

'This is a child!' Haigha replied eagerly, coming in front of Alice to introduce her, and spreading out both his hands towards her in an Anglo-Saxon attitude. 'We only found it to-day. It's as large as life, and twice as natural!'*

'I always thought they were fabulous monsters!' said the Unicorn. 'Is it alive?'

'It can talk,' said Haigha solemnly.

The Unicorn looked dreamily at Alice, and said 'Talk, child.'

Alice could not help her lips curling up into a smile as she began: 'Do you know, I always thought Unicorns were fabulous monsters, too? I never saw one alive before!'

'Well, now that we *have* seen each other,' said the Unicorn, 'if you'll believe in me, I'll believe in you. Is that a bargain?'

'Yes, if you like,' said Alice.

'Come, fetch out the plum-cake, old man!' the Unicorn went on, turning from her to the King. 'None of your brown bread for me!'

'Certainly—certainly!' the King muttered, and beckoned to Haigha. 'Open the bag!' he whispered. 'Quick! Not that one—that's full of hay!'

Haigha took a large cake out of the bag, and gave it to Alice to hold, while he got out a dish and carving-knife. How they all came out of it Alice couldn't guess. It was just like a conjuring-trick, she thought.

The Lion had joined them while this was going on: he

looked very tired and sleepy, and his eyes were half shut.
'What's this!' he said, blinking lazily at Alice, and speaking in
a deep hollow tone that sounded like the tolling of a great bell.

'Ah, what *is* it, now?' the Unicorn cried eagerly. 'You'll
never guess! *I* couldn't.'

The Lion looked at Alice wearily. 'Are you animal—or
vegetable—or mineral?'* he said, yawning at every other word.

'It's a fabulous monster!' the Unicorn cried out, before
Alice could reply.

'Then hand round the plum-cake, Monster,' the Lion said,
lying down and putting his chin on his paws. 'And sit down,
both of you,' (to the King and the Unicorn): 'fair play with
the cake, you know!'

The King was evidently very uncomfortable at having to
sit down between the two great creatures; but there was no
other place for him.

'What a fight we might have for the crown, *now!*' the
Unicorn said, looking slyly up at the crown, which the poor
King was nearly shaking off his head, he trembled so much.

'I should win easy,' said the Lion.

'I'm not so sure of that,' said the Unicorn.

'Why, I beat you all round the town, you chicken!' the Lion replied angrily, half getting up as he spoke.

Here the King interrupted, to prevent the quarrel going on: he was very nervous, and his voice quite quivered. 'All round the town?' he said. 'That's a good long way. Did you go by the old bridge, or the market-place? You get the best view by the old bridge.'

'I'm sure I don't know,' the Lion growled out as he lay down again. 'There was too much dust to see anything. What a time the Monster is, cutting up that cake!'

Alice had seated herself on the bank of a little brook, with the great dish on her knees, and was sawing away diligently with the knife. 'It's very provoking!' she said, in reply to the Lion (she was getting quite used to being called 'the Monster'). 'I've cut several slices already, but they always join on again!'

'You don't know how to manage Looking-glass cakes,' the Unicorn remarked. 'Hand it round first, and cut it afterwards.'

This sounded nonsense, but Alice very obediently got up, and carried the dish round, and the cake divided itself into three pieces as she did so. '*Now* cut it up,' said the Lion, as she returned to her place with the empty dish.

'I say, this isn't fair!' cried the Unicorn, as Alice sat with the knife in her hand, very much puzzled how to begin. 'The Monster has given the Lion twice as much as me!'

'She's kept none for herself, anyhow,' said the Lion. 'Do you like plum-cake, Monster?'

But before Alice could answer him, the drums began.

Where the noise came from, she couldn't make out: the air seemed full of it, and it rang through and through her head till she felt quite deafened. She started to her feet and sprang across the little brook* in her terror,

    *   *   *   *   *   *

       *   *   *   *   *

    *   *   *   *   *   *

and had just time to see the Lion and the Unicorn rise to their feet, with angry looks at being interrupted in their feast, before she dropped to her knees, and put her hands over her ears, vainly trying to shut out the dreadful uproar.

'If *that* doesn't "drum them out of town,"' she thought to herself, 'nothing ever will!'

CHAPTER VIII

'IT'S MY OWN INVENTION'

AFTER a while the noise seemed gradually to die away, till all was dead silence, and Alice lifted up her head in some alarm. There was no one to be seen, and her first thought was that she must have been dreaming about the Lion and the Unicorn and those queer Anglo-Saxon Messengers. However, there was the great dish still lying at her feet, on which she had tried to cut the plum-cake, 'So I wasn't dreaming, after all,' she said to herself, 'unless—unless we're all part of the same dream. Only I do hope it's *my* dream, and not the Red King's! I don't like belonging to another person's dream,' she went on in a rather complaining tone: 'I've a great mind to go and wake him, and see what happens!'

At this moment her thoughts were interrupted by a loud shouting of 'Ahoy! Ahoy! Check!' and a Knight, dressed in crimson armour, came galloping down upon her,* brandishing a great club. Just as he reached her, the horse stopped suddenly: 'You're my prisoner!' the Knight cried, as he tumbled off his horse.

Startled as she was, Alice was more frightened for him than for herself at the moment, and watched him with some anxiety as he mounted again. As soon as he was comfortably in the saddle, he began once more 'You're my——' but here another voice broke in 'Ahoy! Ahoy! Check!' and Alice looked round in some surprise for the new enemy.

This time it was a White Knight.* He drew up at Alice's side, and tumbled off his horse just as the Red Knight had done: then he got on again, and the two Knights sat and looked at each other for some time without speaking. Alice looked from one to the other in some bewilderment.

'She's *my* prisoner, you know!' the Red Knight said at last.

'Yes, but then *I* came and rescued her!' the White Knight replied.

'Well, we must fight for her, then,' said the Red Knight, as he took up his helmet (which hung from the saddle, and was something the shape of a horse's head) and put it on.

'You will observe the Rules of Battle, of course?' the White Knight remarked, putting on his helmet too.

'I always do,' said the Red Knight, and they began banging away at each other with such fury that Alice got behind a tree to be out of the way of the blows.

'I wonder, now, what the Rules of Battle are,' she said to herself, as she watched the fight, timidly peeping out from her hiding-place. 'One Rule seems to be, that if one Knight hits the other, he knocks him off his horse; and, if he misses, he tumbles off himself—and another Rule seems to be that they hold their clubs with their arms, as if they were Punch and

Judy——What a noise they make when they tumble! Just like a whole set of fire-irons falling into the fender! And how quiet the horses are! They let them get on and off them just as if they were tables!'

Another Rule of Battle, that Alice had not noticed, seemed to be that they always fell on their heads; and the battle ended with their both falling off in this way, side by side. When they got up again, they shook hands, and then the Red Knight mounted and galloped off.*

'It was a glorious victory,* wasn't it?' said the White Knight, as he came up panting.

'I don't know,' Alice said doubtfully. 'I don't want to be anybody's prisoner. I want to be a Queen.'

'So you will, when you've crossed the next brook,' said the White Knight. 'I'll see you safe to the end of the wood—and then I must go back, you know. That's the end of my move.'*

'Thank you very much,' said Alice. 'May I help you off with your helmet?' It was evidently more than he could manage by himself: however she managed to shake him out of it at last.

'Now one can breathe more easily,' said the Knight, putting back his shaggy hair with both hands, and turning his gentle face and large mild eyes to Alice. She thought she had never seen such a strange-looking soldier in all her life.

He was dressed in tin armour, which seemed to fit him very badly, and he had a queer-shaped little deal box fastened across his shoulders, upside-down, and with the lid hanging open. Alice looked at it with great curiosity.

'I see you're admiring my little box,' the Knight said in a friendly tone. 'It's my own invention—to keep clothes and sandwiches in. You see I carry it upside-down, so that the rain ca'n't get in.'

'But the things can get *out*,' Alice gently remarked. 'Do you know the lid's open?'

'I didn't know it,' the Knight said, a shade of vexation passing over his face. 'Then all the things must have fallen out! And the box is no use without them.' He unfastened it as he spoke, and was just going to throw it into the bushes, when a sudden thought seemed to strike him, and he hung it carefully on a tree. 'Can you guess why I did that?' he said to Alice.

Alice shook her head.

'In hopes some bees may make a nest in it—then I should get the honey.'

'But you've got a bee-hive—or something like one—fastened to the saddle,' said Alice.

'Yes, it's a very good bee-hive,' the Knight said in a discontented tone, 'one of the best kind. But not a single bee has come near it yet. And the other thing is a mouse-trap. I suppose the mice keep the bees out—or the bees keep the mice out, I don't know which.'

'I was wondering what the mouse-trap was for,' said Alice. 'It isn't very likely there would be any mice on the horse's back.'

'Not very likely, perhaps,' said the Knight; 'but, if they *do* come, I don't choose to have them running all about.'

'You see,' he went on after a pause, 'it's as well to be provided for *everything*. That's the reason the horse has all those anklets round his feet.'

'But what are they for?' Alice asked in a tone of great curiosity.

'To guard against the bites of sharks,' the Knight replied. 'It's an invention of my own. And now help me on. I'll go with you to the end of the wood——What's that dish for?'

'It's meant for plum-cake,' said Alice.

'We'd better take it with us,' the Knight said. 'It'll come in handy if we find any plum-cake. Help me to get it into this bag.'

This took a long time to manage, though Alice held the bag open very carefully, because the Knight was so *very* awkward in putting in the dish: the first two or three times that he tried he fell in himself instead. 'It's rather a tight fit, you see,' he said, as they got it in at last; 'there are so many candlesticks in the bag.' And he hung it to the saddle, which was already loaded with bunches of carrots, and fire-irons, and many other things.

'I hope you've got your hair well fastened on?' he continued, as they set off.

'Only in the usual way,' Alice said, smiling.

'That's hardly enough,' he said, anxiously. 'You see the wind is so *very* strong here. It's as strong as soup.'

'Have you invented a plan for keeping the hair from being blown off?' Alice enquired.

'Not yet,' said the Knight. 'But I've got a plan for keeping it from *falling* off.'

'I should like to hear it, very much.'

'First you take an upright stick,' said the Knight. 'Then you make your hair creep up it, like a fruit-tree. Now the reason hair falls off is because it hangs *down*—things never fall *upwards*, you know. It's a plan of my own invention. You may try it if you like.'

It didn't sound a comfortable plan, Alice thought, and for a few minutes she walked on in silence, puzzling over the idea, and every now and then stopping to help the poor Knight, who certainly was *not* a good rider.

Whenever the horse stopped (which it did very often), he fell

off in front; and, whenever it went on again (which it generally did rather suddenly), he fell off behind. Otherwise he kept on pretty well, except that he had a habit of now and then falling off sideways; and, as he generally did this on the side on which Alice was walking, she soon found that it was the best plan not to walk *quite* close to the horse.

'I'm afraid you've not had much practice in riding,' she ventured to say, as she was helping him up from his fifth tumble.

The Knight looked very much surprised, and a little offended at the remark. 'What makes you say that?' he asked, as he scrambled back into the saddle, keeping hold of Alice's hair with one hand, to save himself from falling over on the other side.

'Because people don't fall off quite so often, when they've had much practice.'

'I've had plenty of practice,' the Knight said very gravely: 'plenty of practice!'

Alice could think of nothing better to say than 'Indeed?' but she said it as heartily as she could. They went on a little way in silence after this, the Knight with his eyes shut, muttering to himself, and Alice watching anxiously for the next tumble.

'The great art of riding,' the Knight suddenly began in a loud voice, waving his right arm as he spoke, 'is to keep——' Here the sentence ended as suddenly as it had begun, as the Knight fell heavily on the top of his head exactly in the path where Alice was walking. She was quite frightened this time, and said in an anxious tone, as she picked him up, 'I hope no bones are broken?'

'None to speak of,' the Knight said, as if he didn't mind breaking two or three of them. 'The great art of riding, as I was saying, is—to keep your balance properly. Like this, you know——'

He let go the bridle, and stretched out both his arms to show Alice what he meant, and this time he fell flat on his back, right under the horse's feet.

'Plenty of practice!' he went on repeating, all the time that Alice was getting him on his feet again. 'Plenty of practice!'

'It's too ridiculous!' cried Alice, losing all her patience this time. 'You ought to have a wooden horse on wheels, that you ought!'

'Does that kind go smoothly?' the Knight asked in a tone of great interest, clasping his arms round the horse's neck as he spoke, just in time to save himself from tumbling off again.

'Much more smoothly than a live horse,' Alice said, with a little scream of laughter, in spite of all she could do to prevent it.

'I'll get one,' the Knight said thoughtfully to himself. 'One or two—several.'

There was a short silence after this, and then the Knight went on again. 'I'm a great hand at inventing things. Now, I daresay you noticed, the last time you picked me up, that I was looking rather thoughtful?'

'You *were* a little grave,' said Alice.

'Well, just then I was inventing a new way of getting over a gate—would you like to hear it?'

'Very much indeed,' Alice said politely.

'I'll tell you how I came to think of it,' said the Knight. 'You see, I said to myself "The only difficulty is with the feet: the *head* is high enough already." Now, first I put my head on the top of the gate—then the head's high enough—then I stand on my head—then the feet are high enough, you see— then I'm over, you see.'

'Yes, I suppose you'd be over when that was done,' Alice said thoughtfully: 'but don't you think it would be rather hard?'

'I haven't tried it yet,' the Knight said, gravely; 'so I ca'n't tell for certain—but I'm afraid it *would* be a little hard.'

He looked so vexed at the idea, that Alice changed the subject hastily. 'What a curious helmet you've got!' she said cheerfully. 'Is that your invention too?'

The Knight looked down proudly at his helmet, which hung from the saddle. 'Yes,' he said; 'but I've invented a better one than that—like a sugar-loaf.* When I used to wear it, if I fell off the horse, it always touched the ground directly. So I had a *very* little way to fall, you see—But there *was* the danger of falling *into* it, to be sure. That happened to me once —and the worst of it was, before I could get out again, the other White Knight came and put it on. He thought it was his own helmet.'

The Knight looked so solemn about it that Alice did not dare to laugh. 'I'm afraid you must have hurt him,' she said in a trembling voice, 'being on the top of his head.'

'I had to kick him, of course,' the Knight said, very seriously. 'And then he took the helmet off again—but it took hours and hours to get me out. I was as fast as—as lightning, you know.'

'But that's a different kind of fastness,' Alice objected.

The Knight shook his head. 'It was all kinds of fastness with me, I can assure you!' he said. He raised his hands in some excitement as he said this, and instantly rolled out of the saddle, and fell headlong into a deep ditch.

Alice ran to the side of the ditch to look for him. She was rather startled by the fall, as for some time he had kept on very well, and she was afraid that he really *was* hurt this time. However, though she could see nothing but the soles of his feet, she was much relieved to hear that he was talking on in his usual tone. 'All kinds of fastness,' he repeated: 'but it was careless of him to put another man's helmet on—with the man in it, too.'

'How *can* you go on talking so quietly, head downwards?' Alice asked, as she dragged him out by the feet, and laid him in a heap on the bank.

The Knight looked surprised at the question. 'What does it matter where my body happens to be?' he said. 'My mind goes on working all the same. In fact, the more head-downwards I am, the more I keep inventing new things.'

'Now the cleverest thing of the sort that I ever did,' he went

on after a pause, 'was inventing a new pudding during the
meat-course.'

'In time to have it cooked for the next course?' said Alice.
'Well, that *was* quick work, certainly!'

'Well, not the *next* course,' the Knight said in a slow
thoughtful tone: 'no, certainly not the next *course*.'

'Then it would have to be the next day. I suppose you
wouldn't have two pudding-courses in one dinner?'

'Well, not the *next* day,' the Knight repeated as before:
'not the next *day*. In fact,' he went on, holding his head down,
and his voice getting lower and lower, 'I don't believe that
pudding ever *was* cooked! In fact, I don't believe that pudding ever *will* be cooked! And yet it was a very clever pudding
to invent.'

'What did you mean it to be made of?' Alice asked, hoping
to cheer him up, for the poor Knight seemed quite low-
spirited about it.

'It began with blotting-paper,' the Knight answered with
a groan.

'That wouldn't be very nice, I'm afraid——'

'Not very nice *alone*,' he interrupted, quite eagerly: 'but
you've no idea what a difference it makes, mixing it with other

things—such as gunpowder and sealing-wax. And here I must leave you.' They had just come to the end of the wood.

Alice could only look puzzled: she was thinking of the pudding.

'You are sad,' the Knight said in an anxious tone: 'let me sing you a song to comfort you.'

'Is it very long?' Alice asked, for she had heard a good deal of poetry that day.

'It's long,' said the Knight, 'but it's very, *very* beautiful. Everybody that hears me sing it—either it brings the *tears* into their eyes, or else——'

'Or else what?' said Alice, for the Knight had made a sudden pause.

'Or else it doesn't, you know. The name of the song is called* "*Haddocks' Eyes*."'

'Oh, that's the name of the song, is it?' Alice said, trying to feel interested.

'No, you don't understand,' the Knight said, looking a little vexed. 'That's what the name is *called*. The name really *is* "*The Aged Aged Man*."'

'Then I ought to have said "That's what the *song* is called"?' Alice corrected herself.

'No, you oughtn't: that's quite another thing! The *song* is called "*Ways And Means*": but that's only what it's *called*, you know!'

'Well, what *is* the song, then?' said Alice, who was by this time completely bewildered.

'I was coming to that,' the Knight said. 'The song really *is* "*A-sitting On A Gate*": and the tune's my own invention.'

So saying, he stopped his horse and let the reins fall on its neck: then, slowly beating time with one hand, and with a faint smile lighting up his gentle foolish face, as if he enjoyed the music of his song, he began.

Of all the strange things that Alice saw in her journey Through The Looking-Glass, this was the one that she always remembered most clearly. Years afterwards she could bring the whole scene back again, as if it had been only yesterday—the mild blue eyes* and kindly smile of the Knight —the setting sun gleaming through his hair, and shining on his armour in a blaze of light that quite dazzled her—the horse quietly moving about, with the reins hanging loose on his neck, cropping the grass at her feet—and the black shadows of the forest behind—all this she took in like a picture, as, with one hand shading her eyes, she leant against a tree, watching the strange pair, and listening, in a half-dream, to the melancholy music of the song.

'But the tune *isn't* his own invention,' she said to herself: 'it's "*I give thee all, I can no more.*"'* She stood and listened very attentively, but no tears came into her eyes.

> '*I'll tell thee everything I can:**
> *There's little to relate.*
> *I saw an aged aged man,*
> *A-sitting on a gate.*
> "*Who are you, aged man?*" *I said.*
> "*And how is it you live?*"
> *And his answer trickled through my head,*
> *Like water through a sieve.*
>
> *He said* "*I look for butterflies*
> *That sleep among the wheat:*
> *I make them into mutton-pies,*
> *And sell them in the street.*
> *I sell them unto men,*" *he said,*
> "*Who sail on stormy seas;*
> *And that's the way I get my bread—*
> *A trifle, if you please.*"
>
> *But I was thinking of a plan*
> *To dye one's whiskers green,*
> *And always use so large a fan*
> *That they could not be seen.*

So, having no reply to give
To what the old man said,
I cried "Come, tell me how you live!"
And thumped him on the head.

His accents mild took up the tale:
He said "I go my ways,
And when I find a mountain-rill,
I set it in a blaze;
And thence they make a stuff they call
Rowland's Macassar-Oil*—
Yet twopence-halfpenny is all
They give me for my toil."

But I was thinking of a way
To feed oneself on batter,
And so go on from day to day
Getting a little fatter.
I shook him well from side to side,
Until his face was blue:
"Come, tell me how you live," I cried,
"And what it is you do!"

He said "I hunt for haddocks' eyes
   Among the heather bright,
And work them into waistcoat-buttons
   In the silent night.
And these I do not sell for gold
   Or coin of silvery shine,
But for a copper halfpenny,
   And that will purchase nine.

"I sometimes dig for buttered rolls,
   Or set limed twigs* for crabs:
I sometimes search the grassy knolls
   For wheels of Hansom-cabs.*
And that's the way" (he gave a wink)
   "By which I get my wealth—
And very gladly will I drink
   Your Honour's noble health."

I heard him then, for I had just
   Completed my design
To keep the Menai bridge* from rust
   By boiling it in wine.
I thanked him much for telling me
   The way he got his wealth,
But chiefly for his wish that he
   Might drink my noble health.

And now, if e'er by chance I put
   My fingers into glue,
Or madly squeeze a right-hand foot
   Into a left-hand shoe,
Or if I drop upon my toe
   A very heavy weight,
I weep, for it reminds me so
Of that old man I used to know—
Whose look was mild, whose speech was slow,
Whose hair was whiter than the snow,

> *Whose face was very like a crow,*
> *With eyes, like cinders, all aglow,*
> *Who seemed distracted with his woe,*
> *Who rocked his body to and fro,*
> *And muttered mumblingly and low,*
> *As if his mouth were full of dough,*
> *Who snorted like a buffalo——*
> *That summer evening long ago,*
>   *A-sitting on a gate.'*

As the Knight sang the last words of the ballad, he gathered up the reins, and turned his horse's head along the road by which they had come. 'You've only a few yards to go,' he said, 'down the hill and over that little brook, and then you'll be a Queen*——But you'll stay and see me off first?' he added as Alice turned with an eager look in the direction to which he pointed. 'I sha'n't be long. You'll wait and wave your handkerchief when I get to that turn in the road! I think it'll encourage me, you see.'

'Of course I'll wait,' said Alice: 'and thank you very much for coming so far—and for the song—I liked it very much.'

'I hope so,' the Knight said doubtfully: 'but you didn't cry so much as I thought you would.'

So they shook hands, and then the Knight rode slowly away into the forest. 'It wo'n't take long to see him *off*, I expect,' Alice said to herself, as she stood watching him. 'There he goes! Right on his head as usual! However, he gets on again pretty easily—that comes of having so many things hung round the horse——' So she went on talking to herself, as she watched the horse walking leisurely along the road, and the Knight tumbling off, first on one side and then on the other. After the fourth or fifth tumble he reached the turn,* and then she waved her handkerchief to him, and waited till he was out of sight.

'I hope it encouraged him,' she said, as she turned to run down the hill: 'and now for the last brook, and to be a Queen! How grand it sounds!' A very few steps brought her to the edge of the brook.* 'The Eighth Square at last!' she cried as she bounded across,*

*   *   *   *   *   *

  *   *   *   *   *

*   *   *   *   *   *

and threw herself down to rest on a lawn as soft as moss, with little flower-beds dotted about it here and there. 'Oh, how glad I am to get here! And what *is* this on my head?' she exclaimed in a tone of dismay, as she put her hands up to something very heavy, that fitted tight all round her head.

'But how *can* it have got there without my knowing it?' she said to herself, as she lifted it off, and set it on her lap to make out what it could possibly be.

It was a golden crown.

CHAPTER IX

QUEEN ALICE

'WELL, this *is* grand!' said Alice. 'I never expected I should be a Queen so soon—and I'll tell you what it is, your Majesty,' she went on, in a severe tone (she was always rather fond of scolding herself), 'it'll never do for you to be lolling about on the grass like that! Queens have to be dignified, you know!'

So she got up and walked about—rather stiffly just at first, as she was afraid that the crown might come off: but she comforted herself with the thought that there was nobody to see her, 'and if I really am a Queen,' she said as she sat down again, 'I shall be able to manage it quite well in time.'

Everything was happening so oddly that she didn't feel a bit surprised at finding the Red Queen and the White Queen sitting close to her, one on each side:* she would have liked very much to ask them how they came there, but she feared it would not be quite civil. However, there would be no harm, she thought, in asking if the game was over. 'Please, would you tell me——' she began, looking timidly at the Red Queen.

'Speak when you're spoken to!' the Queen sharply interrupted her.

'But if everybody obeyed that rule,' said Alice, who was always ready for a little argument, 'and if you only spoke when you were spoken to, and the other person always waited for *you* to begin, you see nobody would ever say anything, so that——'

'Ridiculous!' cried the Queen. 'Why, don't you see, child——' here she broke off with a frown, and, after thinking for a minute, suddenly changed the subject of the conversation. 'What do you mean by "If you really are a Queen"? What right have you to call yourself so? You ca'n't be a

Queen, you know, till you've passed the proper examination. And the sooner we begin it, the better.'

'I only said "if"!' poor Alice pleaded in a piteous tone.

The two Queens looked at each other, and the Red Queen remarked, with a little shudder, 'She *says* she only said "if"——'

'But she said a great deal more than that!' the White Queen moaned, wringing her hands. 'Oh, ever so much more than that!'

'So you did, you know,' the Red Queen said to Alice. 'Always speak the truth—think before you speak—and write it down afterwards.'

'I'm sure I didn't mean——' Alice was beginning, but the Red Queen interrupted her impatiently.

'That's just what I complain of! You *should* have meant! What do you suppose is the use of a child without any meaning? Even a joke should have some meaning—and a child's more important than a joke, I hope. You couldn't deny that, even if you tried with both hands.'

'I don't deny things with my *hands*,' Alice objected.

'Nobody said you did,' said the Red Queen. 'I said you couldn't if you tried.'

'She's in that state of mind,' said the White Queen, 'that she wants to deny *something*—only she doesn't know what to deny!'

'A nasty, vicious temper,' the Red Queen remarked; and then there was an uncomfortable silence for a minute or two.

The Red Queen broke the silence by saying, to the White Queen, 'I invite you to Alice's dinner-party this afternoon.'

The White Queen smiled feebly, and said 'And I invite *you*.'

'I didn't know I was to have a party at all,' said Alice; 'but, if there *is* to be one, I think *I* ought to invite the guests.'

'We gave you the opportunity of doing it,' the Red Queen remarked: 'but I daresay you've not had many lessons in manners yet?'

'Manners are not taught in lessons,' said Alice. 'Lessons teach you to do sums, and things of that sort.'

'Can you do Addition?' the White Queen asked. 'What's one and one and one and one and one and one and one and one and one and one?'

'I don't know,' said Alice. 'I lost count.'

'She ca'n't do Addition,' the Red Queen interrupted. 'Can you do Subtraction? Take nine from eight.'

'Nine from eight I ca'n't, you know,' Alice replied very readily: 'but——'

'She ca'n't do Substraction,' said the White Queen. 'Can you do Division? Divide a loaf by a knife—what's the answer to *that?*'

'I suppose——' Alice was beginning, but the Red Queen answered for her. 'Bread-and-butter, of course. Try another Subtraction sum. Take a bone from a dog: what remains?'

Alice considered. 'The bone wouldn't remain, of course, if I took it—and the dog wouldn't remain: it would come to bite me—and I'm sure *I* shouldn't remain!'

'Then you think nothing would remain?' said the Red Queen.

'I think that's the answer.'

'Wrong, as usual,' said the Red Queen: 'the dog's temper would remain.'

'But I don't see how——'

'Why, look here!' the Red Queen cried. 'The dog would lose its temper, wouldn't it?'

'Perhaps it would,' Alice replied cautiously.

'Then if the dog went away, its temper would remain!' the Queen exclaimed triumphantly.

Alice said, as gravely as she could, 'They might go different ways.' But she couldn't help thinking to herself 'What dreadful nonsense we *are* talking!'

'She ca'n't do sums a *bit!*' the Queens said together, with great emphasis.

'Can *you* do sums?' Alice said, turning suddenly on the White Queen, for she didn't like being found fault with so much.

The Queen gasped and shut her eyes. 'I can do Addition,' she said, 'if you give me time—but I ca'n't do Substraction under *any* circumstances!'

'Of course you know your ABC?' said the Red Queen.

'To be sure I do,' said Alice.

'So do I,' the White Queen whispered: 'we'll often say it over together, dear. And I'll tell you a secret—I can read words of one letter! Isn't *that* grand? However, don't be discouraged. You'll come to it in time.'

Here the Red Queen began again. 'Can you answer useful questions?'* she said. 'How is bread made?'

'I know *that!*' Alice cried eagerly. 'You take some flour——'

'Where do you pick the flower?' the White Queen asked. 'In a garden or in the hedges?'

'Well, it isn't *picked* at all,' Alice explained: 'it's *ground*——'

'How many acres of ground?' said the White Queen. 'You mustn't leave out so many things.'

'Fan her head!' the Red Queen anxiously interrupted. 'She'll be feverish after so much thinking.' So they set to work and fanned her with bunches of leaves, till she had to beg them to leave off, it blew her hair about so.

'She's all right again now,' said the Red Queen. 'Do you know Languages? What's the French for fiddle-de-dee?'*

'Fiddle-de-dee's not English,' Alice replied gravely.

'Who ever said it was?' said the Red Queen.

Alice thought she saw a way out of the difficulty, this time. 'If you'll tell me what language "fiddle-de-dee" is, I'll tell you the French for it!' she exclaimed triumphantly.

But the Red Queen drew herself up rather stiffly, and said 'Queens never make bargains.'

'I wish Queens never asked questions,' Alice thought to herself.

'Don't let us quarrel,' the White Queen said in an anxious tone. 'What is the cause of lightning?'

'The cause of lightning,' Alice said very decidedly, for she felt quite certain about this, 'is the thunder—no, no!' she hastily corrected herself. 'I meant the other way.'

'It's too late to correct it,' said the Red Queen: 'when you've once said a thing, that fixes it, and you must take the consequences.'

'Which reminds me——' the White Queen said, looking down and nervously clasping and unclasping her hands, 'we had *such* a thunderstorm last Tuesday—I mean one of the last set of Tuesdays, you know.'

Alice was puzzled. 'In *our* country,' she remarked, 'there's only one day at a time.'

The Red Queen said 'That's a poor thin way of doing things. Now *here*, we mostly have days and nights two or three at a time, and sometimes in the winter we take as many as five nights together—for warmth, you know.'

'Are five nights warmer than one night, then?' Alice ventured to ask.

'Five times as warm, of course.'

'But they should be five times as *cold*, by the same rule——'

'Just so!' cried the Red Queen. 'Five times as warm, *and*

five times as cold—just as I'm five times as rich as you are, *and* five times as clever!'

Alice sighed and gave it up. 'It's exactly like a riddle with no answer!' she thought.

'Humpty Dumpty saw it too,' the White Queen went on in a low voice, more as if she were talking to herself. 'He came to the door with a corkscrew in his hand——'

'What did he want?' said the Red Queen.

'He said he *would* come in,' the White Queen went on, 'because he was looking for a hippopotamus. Now, as it happened, there wasn't such a thing in the house, that morning.'

'Is there generally?' Alice asked in an astonished tone.

'Well, only on Thursdays,' said the Queen.

'I know what he came for,' said Alice: 'he wanted to punish the fish, because——'

Here the White Queen began again. 'It was *such* a thunder-storm, you ca'n't think!' ('She *never* could, you know,' said the Red Queen.) 'And part of the roof came off, and ever so much thunder got in—and it went rolling round the room in great lumps—and knocking over the tables and things —till I was so frightened, I couldn't remember my own name!'

Alice thought to herself 'I never should *try* to remember my name in the middle of an accident! Where would be the use of it?' but she did not say this aloud, for fear of hurting the poor Queen's feelings.

'Your Majesty must excuse her,' the Red Queen said to Alice, taking one of the White Queen's hands in her own, and gently stroking it: 'she means well, but she ca'n't help saying foolish things, as a general rule.'

The White Queen looked timidly at Alice, who felt she *ought* to say something kind, but really couldn't think of any-thing at the moment.

'She never was really well brought up,' the Red Queen went on: 'but it's amazing how good-tempered she is! Pat her on the head, and see how pleased she'll be!' But this was more than Alice had courage to do.

'A little kindness—and putting her hair in papers*—would do wonders with her——'

The White Queen gave a deep sigh, and laid her head on Alice's shoulder. 'I *am* so sleepy!' she moaned.

'She's tired, poor thing!' said the Red Queen. 'Smoothe her hair—lend her your nightcap—and sing her a soothing lullaby.'

'I haven't got a nightcap with me,' said Alice, as she tried to obey the first direction: 'and I don't know any soothing lullabies.'

'I must do it myself, then,' said the Red Queen, and she began:—

> *'Hush-a-by lady,* in Alice's lap!*
> *Till the feast's ready, we've time for a nap.*
> *When the feast's over, we'll go to the ball—*
> *Red Queen, and White Queen, and Alice, and all!'*

'And now you know the words,' she added, as she put her head down on Alice's other shoulder, 'just sing it through to *me*. I'm getting sleepy, too.' In another moment both Queens were fast asleep, and snoring loud.

'What *am* I to do?' exclaimed Alice, looking about in great perplexity, as first one round head, and then the other, rolled down from her shoulder, and lay like a heavy lump in her lap. 'I don't think it *ever* happened before, that any one had to take care of two Queens asleep at once! No, not in all the History of England—it couldn't, you know, because there never was more than one Queen at a time. Do wake up, you heavy things!' she went on in an impatient tone; but there was no answer but a gentle snoring.

The snoring got more distinct every minute, and sounded more like a tune: at last she could even make out words, and she listened so eagerly that, when the two great heads suddenly vanished* from her lap, she hardly missed them.

She was standing before an arched doorway, over which were the words 'QUEEN ALICE' in large letters, and on each side of the arch there was a bell-handle; one was marked 'Visitors' Bell,' and the other 'Servants' Bell.'

'I'll wait till the song's over,' thought Alice, 'and then I'll ring the—the—*which* bell must I ring?' she went on, very much puzzled by the names. 'I'm not a visitor, and I'm not a servant. There *ought* to be one marked "Queen," you know——'

Just then the door opened a little way, and a creature with a long beak put its head out for a moment and said 'No admittance till the week after next!' and shut the door again with a bang.

Alice knocked and rang in vain for a long time; but at last a very old Frog, who was sitting under a tree, got up and hobbled slowly towards her: he was dressed in bright yellow, and had enormous boots on.

'What is it, now?' the Frog said in a deep hoarse whisper.

Alice turned round, ready to find fault with anybody. 'Where's the servant whose business it is to answer the door?' she began angrily.

'Which door?' said the Frog.

Alice almost stamped with irritation at the slow drawl in which he spoke. '*This* door, of course!'

The Frog looked at the door with his large dull eyes for a minute: then he went nearer and rubbed it with his thumb, as if he were trying whether the paint would come off: then he looked at Alice.

'To answer the door?' he said. 'What's it been asking of?' He was so hoarse that Alice could scarcely hear him.

'I don't know what you mean,' she said.

'I speaks English, doesn't I?' the Frog went on. 'Or are you deaf? What did it ask you?'

'Nothing!' Alice said impatiently. 'I've been knocking at it!'

'Shouldn't do that—shouldn't do that——' the Frog muttered. 'Wexes it, you know.' Then he went up and gave the door a kick with one of his great feet. 'You let *it* alone,' he panted out, as he hobbled back to his tree, 'and it'll let *you* alone, you know.'

At this moment the door was flung open, and a shrill voice was heard singing:—

> '*To the Looking-Glass world* it was Alice that said*
> *"I've a sceptre in hand, I've a crown on my head.*
> *Let the Looking-Glass creatures, whatever they be*
> *Come and dine with the Red Queen, the White Queen,*
>   *and me!"* '

And hundreds of voices joined in the chorus:—

> '*Then fill up the glasses as quick as you can,*
> *And sprinkle the table with buttons and bran:*
> *Put cats in the coffee, and mice in the tea—*
> *And welcome Queen Alice with thirty-times-three!*'*

Then followed a confused noise of cheering, and Alice thought to herself 'Thirty times three makes ninety. I wonder if any one's counting?' In a minute there was silence again, and the same shrill voice sang another verse:—

> '*"O Looking-Glass creatures," quoth Alice, "draw near!*
> *'Tis an honour to see me, a favour to hear:*
> *'Tis a privilege high to have dinner and tea*
> *Along with the Red Queen, the White Queen, and me!"* '

Then came the chorus again:—

> '*Then fill up the glasses with treacle and ink,*
> *Or anything else that is pleasant to drink:*
> *Mix sand with the cider, and wool with the wine—*
> *And welcome Queen Alice with ninety-times-nine!*'

'Ninety times nine!' Alice repeated in despair. 'Oh, that'll never be done! I'd better go in at once——' and in she went, and there was a dead silence the moment she appeared.

Alice glanced nervously along the table, as she walked up the large hall,* and noticed that there were about fifty guests, of all kinds: some were animals, some birds, and there were even a few flowers among them. 'I'm glad they've come without waiting to be asked,' she thought: 'I should never have known who were the right people to invite!'

There were three chairs at the head of the table: the Red and White Queens had already taken two of them, but the middle one was empty. Alice sat down in it, rather uncomfortable at the silence, and longing for some one to speak.

At last the Red Queen began. 'You've missed the soup and fish,' she said. 'Put on the joint!' And the waiters set a leg of mutton before Alice, who looked at it rather anxiously, as she had never had to carve a joint before.

'You look a little shy: let me introduce you to that leg of mutton,' said the Red Queen. 'Alice ——Mutton: Mutton—— Alice.'* The leg of mutton got up in the dish and made a little bow to Alice; and Alice returned the bow, not knowing whether to be frightened or amused.

'May I give you a slice?' she said, taking up the knife and fork, and looking from one Queen to the other.

'Certainly not,' the Red Queen said, very decidedly: 'it isn't etiquette to cut any one you've been introduced to. Remove the joint!' And the waiters carried it off, and brought a large plum-pudding in its place.

'I wo'n't be introduced to the pudding, please,' Alice said rather hastily, 'or we shall get no dinner at all. May I give you some?'

But the Red Queen looked sulky, and growled 'Pudding ——Alice: Alice——Pudding. Remove the pudding!', and the waiters took it away so quickly that Alice couldn't return its bow.

However, she didn't see why the Red Queen should be the only one to give orders; so, as an experiment, she called out 'Waiter! Bring back the pudding!', and there it was again in a moment, like a conjuring-trick. It was so large that she couldn't help feeling a *little* shy with it, as she had been with the mutton: however, she conquered her shyness by a great effort, and cut a slice and handed it to the Red Queen.

'What impertinence!' said the Pudding. 'I wonder how you'd like it, if I were to cut a slice out of *you*, you creature!'

It spoke in a thick, suety sort of voice, and Alice hadn't a word to say in reply: she could only sit and look at it and gasp.

'Make a remark,' said the Red Queen: 'it's ridiculous to leave all the conversation to the pudding!'

'Do you know, I've had such a quantity of poetry repeated to me to-day,' Alice began, a little frightened at finding that, the moment she opened her lips, there was dead silence, and all eyes were fixed upon her; 'and it's a very curious thing, I think—every poem was about fishes in some way. Do you know why they're so fond of fishes, all about here?'

She spoke to the Red Queen, whose answer was a little wide of the mark. 'As to fishes,' she said, very slowly and solemnly, putting her mouth close to Alice's ear, 'her White Majesty knows a lovely riddle—all in poetry—all about fishes. Shall she repeat it?'

'Her Red Majesty's very kind to mention it,' the White Queen murmured into Alice's other ear, in a voice like the cooing of a pigeon. 'It would be *such* a treat! May I?'

'Please do,' Alice said very politely.

The White Queen laughed with delight, and stroked Alice's cheek. Then she began:

> ' "First, the fish must be caught."
> That is easy: a baby, I think, could have caught it.
> "Next, the fish must be bought."
> That is easy: a penny, I think, would have bought it.
>
> "Now cook me the fish!"
> That is easy, and will not take more than a minute.
> "Let it lie in a dish!"
> That is easy, because it already is in it.
>
> "Bring it here! Let me sup!"
> It is easy to set such a dish on the table.
> "Take the dish-cover up!"
> Ah, that is so hard that I fear I'm unable!
>
> For it holds it like glue—
> Holds the lid to the dish, while it lies in the middle:
> Which is easiest to do,
> Un-dish-cover the fish, or dishcover the riddle?'

'Take a minute to think about it, and then guess,'* said the Red Queen. 'Meanwhile, we'll drink your health—Queen Alice's health!' she screamed at the top of her voice, and all the guests began drinking it directly, and very queerly they managed it: some of them put their glasses upon their heads like extinguishers,* and drank all that trickled down their faces—others upset the decanters, and drank the wine as it ran off the edges of the table—and three of them (who looked like kangaroos) scrambled into the dish of roast mutton, and began eagerly lapping up the gravy, 'just like pigs in a trough!' thought Alice.

'You ought to return thanks in a neat speech,' the Red Queen said, frowning at Alice as she spoke.

'We must support you, you know,' the White Queen

whispered, as Alice got up to do it, very obediently, but a little frightened.

'Thank you very much,' she whispered in reply, 'but I can do quite well without.'

'That wouldn't be at all the thing,' the Red Queen said very decidedly: so Alice tried to submit to it with a good grace.

('And they *did* push so!' she said afterwards, when she was telling her sister the history of the feast. 'You would have thought they wanted to squeeze me flat!')

In fact it was rather difficult for her to keep in her place while she made her speech: the two Queens pushed her so, one on each side, that they nearly lifted her up into the air. 'I rise to return thanks——' Alice began: and she really *did* rise as she spoke, several inches; but she got hold of the edge of the table, and managed to pull herself down again.

'Take care of yourself!' screamed the White Queen, seizing Alice's hair with both her hands. 'Something's going to happen!'

And then (as Alice afterwards described it) all sorts of things happened in a moment. The candles all grew up to the ceiling, looking something like a bed of rushes with fireworks at the top. As to the bottles, they each took a pair of plates, which they hastily fitted on as wings, and so, with forks for legs, went fluttering about in all directions: 'and very like birds they look,' Alice thought to herself, as well as she could in the dreadful confusion that was beginning.

At this moment she heard a hoarse laugh at her side, and turned to see what was the matter with the White Queen; but, instead of the Queen, there was the leg of mutton sitting in the chair. 'Here I am!' cried a voice from the soup-tureen,* and Alice turned again, just in time to see the Queen's broad good-natured face grinning at her for a moment over the edge of the tureen, before she disappeared into the soup.

There was not a moment to be lost. Already several of the guests were lying down in the dishes, and the soup-ladle was walking up the table towards Alice's chair, and beckoning to her impatiently to get out of its way.

'I ca'n't stand this any longer!' she cried, as she jumped up and seized the tablecloth with both hands: one good pull, and plates, dishes, guests, and candles came crashing down together in a heap on the floor.

'And as for *you*,' she went on, turning fiercely upon the Red Queen, whom she considered as the cause of all the mischief—but the Queen was no longer at her side—she had suddenly dwindled down to the size of a little doll, and was now on the table, merrily running round and round after her own shawl, which was trailing behind her.

At any other time, Alice would have felt surprised at this, but she was far too much excited to be surprised at anything *now*. 'As for *you*,' she repeated, catching hold of the little creature in the very act of jumping over a bottle which had just lighted upon the table, 'I'll shake you into a kitten,* that I will!'

CHAPTER X

SHAKING

S<small>HE</small> took her off the table as she spoke, and shook her backwards and forwards with all her might.*

The Red Queen made no resistance whatever: only her face grew very small, and her eyes got large and green: and still, as Alice went on shaking her, she kept on growing shorter—and fatter—and softer—and rounder—and——

CHAPTER XI

WAKING

——and it really *was* a kitten, after all.

CHAPTER XII

WHICH DREAMED IT?

'YOUR Red Majesty shouldn't purr so loud,' Alice said, rubbing her eyes, and addressing the kitten, respectfully, yet with some severity. 'You woke me out of oh! such a nice dream! And you've been along with me, Kitty—all through the Looking-Glass world. Did you know it, dear?'

It is a very inconvenient habit of kittens (Alice had once made the remark) that, whatever you say to them, they *always* purr. 'If they would only purr for "yes," and mew for "no," or any rule of that sort,' she had said, 'so that one could keep up a conversation! But how *can* you talk with a person if they *always* say the same thing?'

On this occasion the kitten only purred: and it was impossible to guess whether it meant 'yes' or 'no.'

So Alice hunted among the chessmen on the table till she had found the Red Queen: then she went down on her knees on the hearth-rug, and put the kitten and the Queen to look at each other. 'Now, Kitty!' she cried, clapping her hands triumphantly. 'Confess that was what you turned into!'

('But it wouldn't look at it,' she said, when she was explaining the thing afterwards to her sister: 'it turned away its head, and pretended not to see it: but it looked a *little* ashamed of itself, so I think it *must* have been the Red Queen.')

'Sit up a little more stiffly, dear!' Alice cried with a merry laugh. 'And curtsey while you're thinking what to—what to purr. It saves time, remember!' And she caught it up and gave it one little kiss, 'just in honour of its having been a Red Queen.'

'Snowdrop, my pet!' she went on, looking over her shoulder at the White Kitten, which was still patiently undergoing its

toilet, 'when *will* Dinah have finished with your White Majesty, I wonder? That must be the reason you were so untidy in my dream.——Dinah! Do you know that you're scrubbing a White Queen? Really, it's most disrespectful of you!

'And what did *Dinah* turn to, I wonder?' she prattled on, as she settled comfortably down, with one elbow on the rug, and her chin in her hand, to watch the kittens. 'Tell me, Dinah, did you turn to Humpty Dumpty? I *think* you did—however, you'd better not mention it to your friends just yet, for I'm not sure.

'By the way, Kitty, if only you'd been really with me in my dream, there was one thing you *would* have enjoyed——I had such a quantity of poetry said to me, all about fishes! To-morrow morning you shall have a real treat. All the time you're eating your breakfast, I'll repeat "The Walrus and the Carpenter" to you; and then you can make believe it's oysters, dear!

'Now, Kitty, let's consider who it was that dreamed it all. This is a serious question, my dear, and you should *not* go on licking your paw like that—as if Dinah hadn't washed you this morning! You see, Kitty, it *must* have been either me or the Red King. He was part of my dream, of course—but then I was part of his dream, too! *Was* it the Red King, Kitty? You were his wife, my dear, so you ought to know—— Oh, Kitty, *do* help to settle it! I'm sure your paw can wait!' But the provoking kitten only began on the other paw, and pretended it hadn't heard the question.

Which do *you* think it was?

A BOAT, beneath a sunny sky*
Lingering onward dreamily
In an evening of July—

Children three that nestle near,
Eager eye and willing ear,
Pleased a simple tale to hear—

Long has paled that sunny sky:
Echoes fade and memories die:
Autumn frosts have slain July.

Still she haunts me, phantomwise,
Alice moving under skies
Never seen by waking eyes.

Children yet, the tale to hear,
Eager eye and willing ear,
Lovingly shall nestle near.

In a Wonderland they lie,
Dreaming as the days go by,
Dreaming as the summers die:

Ever drifting down the stream—
Lingering in the golden gleam—
Life, what is it but a dream?*

THE END

CHRISTMAS-GREETINGS

[FROM A FAIRY TO A CHILD]

LADY dear, if Fairies may
    For a moment lay aside
Cunning tricks and elfish play,
    'Tis at happy Christmas-tide.

We have heard the children say—
    Gentle children, whom we love—
Long ago, on Christmas Day,
    Came a message from above.

Still, as Christmas-tide comes round,
    They remember it again—
Echo still the joyful sound
    'Peace on earth, good-will to men!'

Yet the hearts must childlike be
    Where such heavenly guests abide;
Unto children, in their glee,
    All the year is Christmas-tide!

Thus, forgetting tricks and play
    For a moment, Lady dear,
We would wish you, if we may,
    Merry Christmas, glad New Year!

Christmas, 1867.

TO ALL CHILD-READERS OF 'ALICE'S ADVENTURES IN WONDERLAND'

DEAR CHILDREN,

At Christmas-time a few grave words are not quite out of place, I hope, even at the end of a book of nonsense—and I want to take this opportunity of thanking the thousands of children who have read 'Alice's Adventures in Wonderland,' for the kindly interest they have taken in my little dream-child.

The thought of the many English firesides where happy faces have smiled her a welcome, and of the many English children to whom she has brought an hour of (I trust) innocent amusement, is one of the brightest and pleasantest thoughts of my life. I have a host of young friends already, whose names and faces I know—but I cannot help feeling as if, through 'Alice's Adventures' I had made friends with many many other dear children, whose faces I shall never see.

To all my little friends, known and unknown, I wish with all my heart, 'A Merry Christmas and a Happy New Year.' May God bless you, dear children, and make each Christmas-tide, as it comes round to you, more bright and beautiful than the last—bright with the presence of that unseen Friend, who once on earth blessed little children—and beautiful with memories of a loving life, which has sought and found that truest kind of happiness, the only kind that is really worth the having, the happiness of making others happy too!

Your affectionate Friend,

LEWIS CARROLL

Christmas, 1871

AN EASTER GREETING
TO EVERY CHILD WHO LOVES
'*ALICE*'

DEAR CHILD,

Please to fancy, if you can, that you are reading a real letter, from a real friend whom you have seen, and whose voice you can seem to yourself to hear wishing you, as I do now with all my heart, a happy Easter.

Do you know that delicious dreamy feeling when one first wakes on a summer morning, with the twitter of birds in the air, and the fresh breeze coming in at the open window——when, lying lazily with eyes half shut, one sees as in a dream green boughs waving, or waters rippling in a golden light? It is a pleasure very near to sadness, bringing tears to one's eyes like a beautiful picture or poem. And is not that a Mother's gentle hand that undraws your curtains, and a Mother's sweet voice that summons you to rise? To rise and forget, in the bright sunlight, the ugly dreams that frightened you so when all was dark——to rise and enjoy another happy day, first kneeling to thank that unseen Friend, who sends you the beautiful sun?

Are these strange words from a writer of such tales as 'Alice'? And is this a strange letter to find in a book of nonsense? It may be so. Some perhaps may blame me for thus mixing together things grave and gay; others may smile and think it odd that any one should speak of solemn things at all, except in church and on a Sunday: but I think—nay, I am sure—that some children will read this gently and lovingly, and in the spirit in which I have written it.

For I do not believe God means us thus to divide life into two halves——to wear a grave face on Sunday, and to think it out-of-place to even so much as mention Him on a week-day. Do you think He cares to see only kneeling figures, and to hear only tones of prayer——and that He does not also love to see the lambs leaping in the sunlight, and to hear the merry voices of the children, as they roll among the hay? Surely their innocent laughter is as sweet in His ears as the grandest anthem that ever rolled up from the 'dim religious light' of some solemn cathedral?

And if I have written anything to add to those stores of innocent and healthy amusement that are laid up in books for the children I love so well, it is surely something I may hope to look back upon without shame and sorrow (as how much of life must then be recalled!) when my turn comes to walk through the valley of shadows.

This Easter sun will rise on you, dear child, feeling your 'life in every limb,' and eager to rush out into the fresh morning air ——and many an Easter-day will come and go, before it finds you feeble and gray-headed, creeping wearily out to bask once more in the sunlight——but it is good, even now, to think sometimes of that great morning when the 'Sun of Righteousness shall arise with healing in his wings.'

Surely your gladness need not be the less for the thought that you will one day see a brighter dawn than this——when lovelier sights will meet your eyes than any waving trees or rippling waters—— when angel-hands shall undraw your curtains, and sweeter tones than ever loving Mother breathed shall wake you to a new and glorious day——and when all the sadness, and the sin, that darkened life on this little earth, shall be forgotten like the dreams of a night that is past!

Your affectionate friend,

LEWIS CARROLL

Easter, 1876

APPENDIX

THE WASP IN A WIG

This episode was cut from the galley-proofs of *Through the Looking-Glass*. It would have appeared on p. 223 of this edition, following the line 'A very few steps brought her to the edge of the brook'. See the Introduction, p. xxix, and note to p. 223.

. . . and she was just going to spring over, when she heard a deep sigh, which seemed to come from the wood behind her.

'There's somebody *very* unhappy there,' she thought, looking anxiously back to see what was the matter. Something like a very old man (only that his face was more like a wasp) was sitting on the ground, leaning against a tree, all huddled up together, and shivering as if he were very cold.

'I don't *think* I can be of any use to him,' was Alice's first thought, as she turned to spring over the brook:—'but I'll just ask him what's the matter,' she added, checking herself on the very edge. 'If I once jump over, everything will change, and then I can't help him.'

So she went back to the Wasp—rather unwillingly, for she was *very* anxious to be a Queen.

'Oh, my old bones, my old bones!' he was grumbling as Alice came up to him.

'It's rheumatism, I should think,' Alice said to herself, and she stooped over him, and said very kindly, 'I hope you're not in much pain?'

The Wasp only shook his shoulders, and turned his head away. 'Ah, dreary me!' he said to himself.

'Can I do anything for you?' Alice went on. 'Aren't you rather cold here?'

'How you go on!' the Wasp said in a peevish tone. 'Worrity, worrity! There never was such a child!'

Alice felt rather offended at this answer, and was very nearly walking on and leaving him, but she thought to herself 'Perhaps it's only pain that makes him so cross.' So she tried once more.

'Won't you let me help you round to the other side? You'll be out of the cold wind there.'

The Wasp took her arm, and let her help him round the tree, but when he got settled down again he only said, as before, 'Worrity, worrity! Can't you leave a body alone?'

'Would you like me to read you a bit of this?' Alice went on, as she picked up a newspaper which had been lying at his feet.

'You may read it if you've a mind to,' the Wasp said, rather sulkily. 'Nobody's hindering you, that *I* know of.'

So Alice sat down by him, and spread out the paper on her knees, and began. '*Latest News. The Exploring Party have made another tour in the Pantry, and have found five new lumps of white sugar, large and in fine condition. In coming back—*'

'Any brown sugar?' the Wasp interrupted.

Alice hastily ran her eye down the paper and said 'No. It says nothing about brown.'

'No brown sugar!' grumbled the Wasp. 'A nice exploring party!'

'*In coming back,*' Alice went on reading, '*they found a lake of treacle. The banks of the lake were blue and white, and looked like china. While tasting the treacle, they had a sad accident: two of their party were engulphed—*'

'Were *what*?' the Wasp asked in a very cross voice.

'En-gulph-ed,' Alice repeated, dividing the word into syllables.

'There's no such word in the language!' said the Wasp.

'It's in this newspaper, though,' Alice said a little timidly.

'Let it stop there!' said the Wasp, fretfully turning away his head.

Alice put down the newspaper. 'I'm afraid you're not well,' she said in a soothing tone. 'Can't I do anything for you?'

'It's all along of the wig,' the Wasp said in a much gentler voice.

'Along of the wig?' Alice repeated, quite pleased to find that he was recovering his temper.

'You'd be cross too, if you'd a wig like mine,' the Wasp went on. 'They jokes at one. And they worrits one. And then I gets cross. And I gets cold. And I gets under a tree. And I gets a yellow handkerchief. And I ties up my face—as at the present.'

Alice looked pityingly at him. 'Tying up the face is very good for the toothache,' she said.

'And it's very good for the conceit,' added the Wasp.

Alice didn't catch the word exactly. 'Is that a kind of tooth-ache?' she asked.

The Wasp considered a little. 'Well, no,' he said: 'it's when you hold up your head—*so*—without bending your neck.'

'Oh, you mean stiff-neck,' said Alice.

The Wasp said 'That's a new-fangled name. They called it conceit in my time.'

'Conceit isn't a disease at all,' Alice remarked.

'It is, though,' said the Wasp: 'wait till you have it, and then you'll know. And when you catches it, just try tying a yellow handkerchief round your face. It'll cure you in no time!'

He untied the handkerchief as he spoke, and Alice looked at his wig in great surprise. It was bright yellow like the hand-kerchief, and all tangled and tumbled about like a heap of seaweed. 'You could make your wig much neater,' she said, 'if only you had a comb.'

'What, you're a Bee, are you?' the Wasp said, looking at her with more interest. 'And you've got a comb. Much honey?'

'It isn't that kind,' Alice hastily explained. 'It's to comb hair with—your wig's so *very* rough, you know.'

'I'll tell you how I came to wear it,' the Wasp said. 'When I was young, you know, my ringlets used to wave—'

A curious idea came into Alice's head. Almost every one she had met had repeated poetry to her, and she thought she would try if the Wasp couldn't do it too. 'Would you mind saying it in rhyme?' she asked very politely.

'It ain't what I'm used to,' said the Wasp: 'however I'll try; wait a bit.' He was silent for a few moments, and then began again—

'When I was young, my ringlets waved
  And curled and crinkled on my head:
And then they said "You should be shaved,
  And wear a yellow wig instead."

But when I followed their advice,
  And they had noticed the effect,
They said I did not look so nice
  As they had ventured to expect.

They said it did not fit, and so
  It made me look extremely plain:
But what was I to do, you know?
  My ringlets would not grow again.

So now that I am old and gray,
  And all my hair is nearly gone,
They take my wig from me and say
  "How can you put such rubbish on?"

And still, whenever I appear,
  They hoot at me and call me "Pig!"
And that is why they do it, dear,
  Because I wear a yellow wig.'

'I'm very sorry for you,' Alice said heartily: 'and I think if your wig fitted a little better, they wouldn't tease you quite so much.'

'*Your* wig fits very well,' the Wasp murmured, looking at her with an expression of admiration: 'it's the shape of your head as does it. Your jaws ain't well shaped, though—I should think you couldn't bite well?'

Alice began with a little scream of laughter, which she turned into a cough as well as she could. At last she managed to say gravely, 'I can bite anything I want.'

'Not with a mouth as small as that,' the Wasp persisted. 'If you was a-fighting, now—could you get hold of the other one by the back of the neck?'

'I'm afraid not,' said Alice.

'Well, that's because your jaws are too short,' the Wasp went on: 'but the top of your head is nice and round.' He took off his own wig as he spoke, and stretched out one claw towards Alice, as if he wished to do the same for her, but she kept out of reach, and would not take the hint. So he went on with his criticisms.

'Then your eyes—they're too much in front, no doubt. One would have done as well as two, if you *must* have them so close—'

Alice did not like having so many personal remarks made on her, and as the Wasp had quite recovered his spirits, and was getting very talkative, she thought she might safely leave him. 'I think I must be going on now,' she said. 'Good-bye.'

'Good-bye, and thank-ye,' said the Wasp, and Alice tripped down the hill again, quite pleased that she had gone back and given a few minutes to making the poor old creature comfortable.

EXPLANATORY NOTES

ABBREVIATIONS

AAU	*Alice's Adventures under Ground* (1886)
AAW	*Alice's Adventures in Wonderland*
Batey	Mavis Batey, *The World of Alice* (Norwich: Pitkin, 1998)
Goldthwaite	John Goldthwaite, *The Natural History of Make-Believe* (New York: Oxford University Press, 1996)
Guiliano	Edward Guiliano (ed.), *Lewis Carroll: A Celebration* (New York: Clarkson N. Potter, 1981)
LCPB	Stuart Dodgson Collingwood, *The Lewis Carroll Picture Book* (London: T. Fisher Unwin, 1899)
LLLC	Stuart Dodgson Collingwood *The Life and Letters of Lewis Carroll (Rev. C. L. Dodgson)* (London: T. Fisher Unwin, 1899)
LG	*Through the Looking-Glass*
MG	Martin Gardner, *The Annotated Alice: The Definitive Edition* (New York: Norton, 2000)
ODNB	*Oxford Dictionary of National Biography*
Opies	Iona and Peter Opie, *The Oxford Dictionary of Nursery Rhymes* (Oxford: Clarendon Press, 1973)
RLG	notes from, or adapted from, Roger Lancelyn Green's World's Classics edition of the 'Alice' books (Oxford: Oxford University Press, 1982)
RP	Robert Phillips (ed.), *Aspects of Alice* (Harmondsworth: Penguin, 1974)
SOED	*Shorter Oxford English Dictionary*

1 [*Title*: *Alice's Adventures in Wonderland*]: in a postscript to a letter to Tom Taylor (later editor of *Punch*) (10 June 1864), Dodgson debated the title:

> I first thought of 'Alice's Adventures under Ground,' but that was pronounced too like a lesson-book, in which instructions about mines would be administered in the form of a grill; then I took 'Alice's Golden Hour' but that I gave up, having a dark suspicion that there is already a book called 'Lily's Golden Hours'.
>
> Here are the other names I have thought of

$$\text{Alice among the} \begin{cases} \text{elves} \\ \text{goblins} \end{cases} \quad \text{Alice's} \begin{cases} \text{hour} \\ \text{doings} \\ \text{adventures} \end{cases} \quad \text{in} \begin{cases} \text{elf-land} \\ \text{wonderland} \end{cases}$$

Of these I at present prefer 'Alice's Adventures in Wonderland'. In spite of your 'morality', I want something sensational.

By 'grill' Dodgson presumably means the litanies that composed many nineteenth-century children's books (and see note to p. 227). (The *SOED* does not give 'grill' as 'to subject to severe questioning, US' until 1928.)

He was almost right about his 'dark suspicions': there was a book called *Lilian's Golden Hours* by Eliza Meteyard (1816–79), illustrated by Absolon, 1857. Meteyard was an advocate of women's rights. *Golden Hours—A Magazine for Sunday Reading*, edited by W. M. Whittemore, ran monthly from January 1864 to December 1884.

3 *Prima . . . Secunda . . . Tertia*: Alice and her sisters: Prima is Lorina Charlotte Liddell (11 May 1849–29 October 1930); Secunda, Alice Pleasance Liddell (4 May 1852–15 November 1934); Tertia, Edith Mary Liddell (23 January 1854–26 June 1876).

5 *on the Stage*: *Alice in Wonderland. A Musical Dream Play, in Two Acts, for Children and Others* by Henry Savile Clarke, with music by Walter Slaughter, opened at the Prince of Wales theatre in London on 23 December 1886. It ran for fifty performances and toured the provinces. Dodgson provided some extra materials, and wrote an article, ' "Alice" on the Stage', in *The Theatre* (April 1887), which partly restates the story of the first telling, and is in part an effusive review. (In 1877 a proposed collaboration with Arthur Sullivan was unsuccessful.)

6 *the Nursery 'Alice'*: *The Nursery 'Alice' . . . with Text Adapted to Nursery Readers* was written by Dodgson between 28 December 1888 and 20 February 1889. It was published, with 'twenty coloured enlargements from Tenniel's Illustrations', in 1890; experts think that these were not coloured by Tenniel, although a Diary entry of 29 March 1885 refers to 'twenty pictures [that] are now being coloured by Mr Tenniel'. Roger Lancelyn Green, in *The Diaries of Lewis Carroll* (London: Cassell, 1955; New York: Oxford University Press, 1954), describes it as 'this charming book . . . As a book for children under five it is only surpassed by the best of Beatrix Potter' (ii. 469). Critics more usually regard it as the antithesis of the acerbic Potter style.

9 *a White Rabbit*: variously identified as Dr Spooner, by William Empson (RP, 415), as Dr Henry Wentworth Acland, 'who was involved in the building of the Oxford Natural History Museum', by Jo Elwyn Jones and J. Francis Gladstone (*The* Alice *Companion*

(Basingstoke: Macmillan, 1998), 5–6, 185–7), and as Lord Newry, an undergraduate at Christ Church, by John Goldthwaite (pp. 146–53). A rabbit is mentioned in one line of the third chapter of George MacDonald's *Phantastes, a Faerie Romance* (1858), the first of many motifs in that book that also occur in the 'Alice' books.

10 *'ORANGE MARMALADE'*: according to her grandson, Lorinda Liddell, Alice's mother and wife of the Dean of Christ Church, gave the original recipe for the most famous Oxford Marmalade ('Frank Cooper's') to Mrs Cooper. She may have obtained it from the Dean's mother, who belonged to the Lyon family (later Bowes-Lyon). Elizabeth Bowes-Lyon was the mother of Queen Elizabeth II (RLG).

even if I fell off the top of the house: Dodgson was not alone in his black humour: Beatrix Potter's *The Tale of Peter Rabbit* (1902) contains a death joke on the second page.

11 *right through the earth*: MG points out (p. 13) that, 'ignoring air resistance and the coriolis force', it would take an object just over 42 minutes to fall through the earth. Compare Dodgson's use of the number 42 elsewhere (see note to p. 105).

Dinah: a tabby cat owned by the Liddell children; she and her kittens appear in the first chapter of *Through the Looking-Glass*. She was named from a popular folk song, later a music-hall song, 'Villikins [or, in various versions, Villikens or Vilikins or Young Vilikins or Wilkins or Willikins] and his Dinah'. The tune was 'Toorali oorali oorali ay'.

12 *all made of . . . golden key*: the Grimms' *Fairy Tales* feature a final fragment, 'The Golden Key', and Perrault's 'Bluebeard' is centred on a key: Maria Tatar points out that nineteenth-century dramatizations of that story 'bore subtitles such as . . . "The Hazards of Female Curiosity" ' (*The Annotated Classic Fairy Tales* (New York: Norton, 2002), 151). Alice's key was possibly suggested by George Mac-Donald's poem 'The Golden Key', published in *Victoria Regis* (1861). MacDonald also wrote a story, 'The Golden Key', which was published in *Dealings with the Fairies* (1867), which Dodgson may have seen in manuscript. It begins: 'There was a boy who used to sit in the twilight and listen to his great-aunt's stories. She told him that if he could reach the place where the end of the rainbow stands he would find there a golden key. "And what is the key for?" the boy would ask. "What is it the key of? What will it open?" "That nobody knows," his aunt would reply.'

13 *How she longed . . . through the doorway*: there have been suggestions that this is an image of birth, or a metaphor for Dodgson's exclusion from the Deanery garden, or from the Garden of Eden. The garden had long been used in literature—and in children's books—as a symbol of a place of security and growth. A notable expression of

this is in Frances Hodgson Burnett's *The Secret Garden* (1911), which also involves a key.

Echoes of this scene occur in T. S. Eliot's 'Burnt Norton' (1935) (*Four Quartets*, 1943): '. . . Down the passage which we did not take | Towards the door we never opened | Into the rose-garden.' One of similar echoes in *The Family Reunion* (1939) also alludes, perhaps, to the crow that frightens Tweedledee and Tweedledum in *LG* (p. 172):

> I only looked through the little door
> When the sun was shining on the rose-garden:
> And heard in the distance tiny voices
> And then the black raven flew over.
>
> (Act 2, Scene 2)

15 *'EAT ME'*: Humphrey Carpenter interprets 'EAT ME' and 'DRINK ME' as 'Alice's anti-Communion', a parody of the Eucharist which is 'a negation of the Christian concept of the nature of human beings. Alice is the victim of a mindless, Godless universe' (*Secret Gardens* (1985; London: Unwin, 1987), 66, 67).

16 [*Illustration*]: Batey (p. 9) notes the resemblance between the long-necked Alice and the brass firedogs in the fireplaces in the Hall in Christ Church.

17 *a large fan*: in *AAU*, the rabbit is carrying a nosegay.

18 *Ada . . . Mabel*: in *AAU* these were Gertrude and Florence, cousins of the Liddell children. Dodgson described Gertrude as 'the youngest Liddell . . . she has quite the most lovely face I ever saw in a child' (MG, 157).

19 *at that rate*: Gardner cites Alexander L. Taylor's suggestion that Alice will never get to 20 because '4 times 5 actually *is* 12 in a number system using a base of 18. Four times 6 is 13 in a system with a base of 21. If we continue this progression, always increasing the base by 3, our products keep increasing by one until we reach 20, where for the first time the scheme breaks down. Four times 13 is not 20 (in a number-system with a base of 42), but "1" followed by whatever symbol is adopted for "10"' (MG, 23, and see Taylor, *The White Knight: A Study of C. L. Dodgson* (Edinburgh: Oliver and Boyd, 1952), 47).

How doth the little crocodile: a parody of the first two stanzas of Song XX 'Against Idleness and Mischief' by Isaac Watts (1674–1748) from his *Divine Songs Attempted in Easy Language for the Use of Children* (1715), 29. The book remained popular well into the nineteenth century. The original reads:

> How doth the little busy Bee
> Improve each shining Hour,

> And gather Honey all the day
> From ev'ry opening Flower!
>
> How skilfully she builds her Cell!
> How neat she spreads the Wax!
> And labours hard to store it well
> With the sweet Food she makes.

20 *the cause of this was the fan*: in *AAU*, it is the Rabbit's nosegay that causes her to shrink.

and in that case . . . to p. 21, a railway-station: not in *AAU*.

Alice had been to the seaside once in her life: Alice Liddell visited Llandudno in 1861, and Dean Liddell built a house there in 1865. Dodgson, despite Llandudno's protestations, did *not* visit.

bathing-machines: small changing-huts on wheels, common in Victorian seaside towns. They were drawn by horses into the sea so that bathers could change and enter the water unobserved. In *The Hunting of the Snark* the Bellman explains ways of identifying 'the warranted genuine Snark':

> The fourth is its fondness for bathing machines,
>   Which it constantly carries about,
> And believes that they add to the beauty of scenes—
>   A sentiment open to doubt.

> (2. 19)

21 *it was only a mouse*: the mouse may well caricature Miss Prickett, the Liddells' governess. Mary Prickett (1833–1913) married Charles Foster, a wine merchant, and became landlady of the Mitre Hotel (now a listed building dating from *c.*1630, 18 High Street, Oxford). On 17 May 1857, Dodgson wrote in his Diary that his interest in the children was being 'construed by some men into attentions to the governess, Miss Prickett', and decided to avoid the children to save embarrassment. Karoline Leach (*In the Shadow of the Dreamchild: A New Understanding of Lewis Carroll* (London: Peter Owen 1999)) argues that this is part of the evidence that Dodgson was not, in fact, interested in young girls at all, but older women (including Mrs Liddell).

her brother: Alice Liddell's elder brother was Harry—Edward Henry (1847–1911). Dodgson tutored him briefly in 1856.

Latin Grammar: probably that by Benjamin Hall Kennedy, first published 1843 (RLG).

(Alice thought . . . O mouse!): not in *AAU*.

the first sentence in her French lesson-book: this is the first sentence of the first lesson in *La Bagatelle: Intended to introduce children of three or four years old to some knowledge of the French language* (1804) (RLG).

22 *show you our cat Dinah*: Shane Leslie (1933), in an article now widely regarded as satirical, suggested that *AAW* was a 'secret history' of the Oxford Movement—Dinah is the 'Catholic enemy' of the church mouse . . . 'the Duchess is Bishop Wilberforce, the Cheshire Cat, who sits aloft and grins, is a likely skit on Cardinal Wiseman' (RP, 259, 260) and so on.

23 *there was a Duck . . . other curious creatures*: the Duck was the Revd Robinson Duckworth (1834–1911), fellow of Trinity College, Oxford; later canon of Westminster. Dodgson inscribed a copy of the facsimile *AAU* (1886): 'The Duck from the Dodo'. Dodgson, like most of his siblings, had a lifelong speech impediment or stammer (hence 'Do-do-Dodgson'), which may have restricted his work in the Church and affected his lecturing. There appears to be no truth in the suggestion that his stammer was less troublesome when he was with children. The Lory was Alice's sister, Lorinda (a Lory is an Australasian parrot), and the Eaglet probably Alice's sister Edith.

25 *"William the Conqueror . . . insolence of his Normans"*: a quotation from Havilland Chepmell's *A Short Course of History* (1862) which Miss Prickett was using with the Liddell children.

26 *Caucus-race*: a sardonic commentary on committee work, probably aimed at Oxford disputes. A caucus is a meeting designed to pull political strings. In 1866, Dodgson published a satirical pamphlet on *The Elections to the Hebdominal Council*, which contained in a footnote 'I never go to a *caucus* without reluctance: I never write a canvassing letter without a feeling of repugnance to my task' (*LCPB*, 82).

What I was going to say . . . quite dry again: this story exists in three versions. The first is a diary entry for Tuesday, 17 June 1862, describing an expedition downriver to Nuneham:

> Duckworth (of Trinity) and Ina, Alice, and Edith came with us . . . About a mile above Nuneham heavy rain came on, and after bearing it a short time I settled that we had better leave the boat and walk; three miles of this drenched us pretty well. I went on first with the children, as they could walk much faster than Elizabeth, and took them to the only house I knew in Sandford, Mrs Broughton's, where Ranken lodges. I left them with her to get their clothes dried, and went off to find a vehicle, but none was to be had there, so on the others arriving, Duckworth and I walked on to Iffley, whence we sent them a fly. We all had tea in my rooms about 8½ after which I took the children home, and we adjourned to Bayne's rooms for music and singing, 'Adelaida,' etc.

In *Alice's Adventures under Ground*, this becomes:

> 'I only meant to say,' said the Dodo in a rather offended tone, 'that I know of a house near here, where we could get the young lady and the rest of the party dried, and then we could listen comfortably to the story which I think you were good enough to promise to tell us,' bowing gravely to the mouse.
>
> The mouse made no objection to this, and the whole party moved along the river bank, (for the pool had by this time begun to flow out of the hall, and the edge of it was fringed with rushes and forget-me-nots,) in a slow procession, the Dodo leading the way. After a time the Dodo became impatient, and, leaving the Duck to bring up the rest of the party, moved on at a quicker pace with Alice, the Lory, and the Eaglet, and soon brought them to a little cottage, and there they sat snugly by the fire, wrapped up in blankets, until the rest of the party had arrived, and they were all dry again. (pp. 26–7)

26 *in the pictures of him*: a minor mystery: no commentators have been able to trace such images.

comfits: seeds, nuts, spices or (dried) fruit covered with layers of sugar, including sugar-plums. Lynne Vallone (*Disciplines of Virtue* (New Haven: Yale University Press, 1995), 107) detects a pun—Alice is dis-comfited.

27 [*Illustration*]: the ape in the background has caused speculation that it may refer to the Darwinian Thomas Huxley's encounter with the Bishop of Oxford, Samuel Wilberforce, in 1860, when he said that he would rather be descended from a monkey than a bishop. As Batey (p. 16) points out, Dodgson took a photograph of Huxley afterwards. Tenniel used a very similar image in a *Punch* cartoon in 1856, satirizing 'King Bomba' (King Ferdinand II of the Two Sicilies) (see Michael Hancher, '*Punch* and *Alice*: Through Tenniel's Looking-Glass', in Guiliano, 46).

28 *something like this*: in *AAU*, this poem was completely different, and began,

> We lived beneath the mat
> Warm and snug and fat
> But one woe, & that
> Was the cat!

29 *'Oh, do let me help to undo it!'*: Dodgson used this phrase at the head of the appendix to *A Tangled Tale*, which appeared in *The Monthly Packet* 'as a serial' from April 1880, and in book form in 1885. The introductory verses to the book are addressed to his 'beloved pupil' and certainly seem to refer to Alice Liddell:

> Then onward! Let the voice of Fame
> From Age to Age repeat thy story,
> Till thou hast won thyself a name
> Exceeding even Euclid's glory.

30 *'I wish I hadn't mentioned . . . finish his story*: the equivalent paragraph in *AAU* reads:

> She sat for some while sorrowful and silent, but she was not long before she recovered her spirits, and began talking to herself again as usual: 'I do wish some of them had stayed a little longer! and I was getting to be such friends with them—really the Lory and I were almost like sisters! and so was that dear little Eaglet! And then the Duck and the Dodo! How nicely the Duck sang to us as we came along through the water: and if the Dodo hadn't known the way to that nice little cottage, I don't know when we should have got dry again—' and there is no knowing how long she might have prattled on in this way, if she had not suddenly caught the sound of pattering feet.

31 *The Duchess*: in *AAU* she is 'the Marchioness'.

Mary Ann: Anne Clark suggests that she may be the parlour maid of the photographer Julia Margaret Cameron (who, with her hands stained with chemicals, would have worn gloves) (Ann Clark, *Lewis Carroll: A Biography* (London: Dent, 1979), 134).

33 *there's no room to grow up any more here*: James R. Kincaid suggests that this shows (the real) Alice's unproblematic acceptance of growing up and growing away from Dodgson, and compares this with the problematic non-growth of 'Peter Pan' (*Child-Loving: The Erotic Child and Victorian Culture* (New York and London: Routledge, 1992), 290).

34 *Digging for apples*: 'Irish apples' was, and occasionally is, a slang term for potatoes. This may also be a play on *pommes de terre*.

37 *The poor little Lizard, Bill*: Kenneth Grahame, in 'The Headswoman', *The Yellow Book* (October 1894), refers to him: ' "Beg pardon, your worship," put in Master Robinet, the tanner, who had been sitting with a petrified, Bill-the-Lizard sort of expression during the speechifying: "but are we to understand as how this here young lady is going to be the public executioner of this here town?" '

40 *[Illustration]*: in *The Nursery 'Alice'*, Alice encounters the large Blue Caterpillar: 'And do you see its long nose and chin? At least, they *look* exactly like a nose and chin, don't they? But they really *are* two of its legs. You know a Caterpillar has got *quantities* of legs: you can see more of them, further down.' Tenniel also provided the Caterpillar with academic sleeves.

42 *"You are old, Father William"*: a parody of Robert Southey's 'The Old Man's Comforts and How He Gained Them', first published in *The Annual Anthology*, 1 (1799).

> You are old, Father William, the young man cried,
>   The few locks which are left you are grey;
> You are hale, Father William, a hearty old man,
>   Now tell me the reason, I pray.
>
> In the days of my youth, Father William replied,
>   I remember'd that youth would fly fast,
> And abused not my health and my vigour at first,
>   That I never might need them at last.

In deference to the Kaiser, the first German translation read: 'Ihr seid alt, Vater Martin' (Derek Hudson, *Lewis Carroll: An Illustrated Biography* (1954; rev. edn., London: Constable, 1976), 130).

Dodgson used the poem again in 1876 as the basis for an acrostic poem addressed to Adelaide Paine, which begins:

> 'Are you deaf? Father William!' the young man said,
> 'Did you hear what I told you just now?
> 'Excuse me for shouting! Don't waggle your head
> 'Like a blundering, sleepy old cow! . . .'

43 *one shilling the box*: in *AAU* it cost 5 shillings (RLG).

45 *[Illustration]*: the structure in the right background is an eel-weir—wicker baskets to trap eels (Hancher in Guiliano, 41–3). Batey (pp. 16–17) points out that there were such traps in the backwater at Godstow, where Dodgson and the Liddell girls had their picnics.

46 *will make you grow shorter*: in *AAU*, the Caterpillar remarks: 'the top will make you grow taller, and the stalk will make you grow shorter', and Alice then picks the mushroom and 'carefully broke it in two, taking the stalk in one hand, and the top in the other' and nibbling appropriately. It is perhaps not surprising that in the 1960s (especially) the hookah and the magic mushroom suggested a connection between Alice's psychedelic experiences and the drug culture.

47 *'Serpent!'*: William Empson noted in '*Alice in Wonderland*: The Child as Swain': 'Alice knows several reasons why she should object to growing up, and does not at all like being an obvious angel, a head out of contact with its body that has to come down from the sky and gets mistaken for a Paradisal serpent of the knowledge of good and evil, and by the pigeon of the Annunciation, too' (RP, 414). Rose Lovell-Smith, in 'Eggs and Serpents: Natural History Reference in Lewis Carroll's Scene of Alice and the Pigeon', *Children's Literature*, 35 (2007), 27–53, thinks it is better read 'in the context of Victorian

depictions of the struggle for survival in nature' and a common 'egg-thief' topos (p. 36).

49 *As she said this*: in *AAU* this sentence continues at the end of the *AAW*'s Chapter VII when Alice notices the tree with the door in it (p. 68). Chapters VI and VII are additions.

50 [*Illustration*]: Tenniel's illustration may have been influenced by the work of the French caricaturist 'J. J. Grandville' (Jean-Ignace-Isadore Gérard, 1803–47) who portrayed human bodies with animal heads, often for the French satirical magazine *Charivari* (for many years *Punch* bore the subtitle *The London Charivari*).

52 *a large kitchen*: in children's literature, kitchens are very often symbols of warmth, food, and security—as, for example, in Kenneth Grahame's *The Wind in the Willows* (1908, ch. 4); the empty kitchen is particularly desolating, as in E. Nesbit's *The Railway Children* (1906, ch. 4). In Dodgson's version, everything is violent, unstable, and unsettling; for another dysfunctional kitchen, compare Emily Brontë's *Wuthering Heights* (1847, ch. 1).

the Duchess: Tenniel's drawing resembles—at least in the headdress—the Flemish Quinten Massy's *A Grotesque Old Woman* (*c.*1525–30) (National Gallery, London). Michael Hancher (*The Tenniel Illustrations to the 'Alice' Books* (Columbus, Ohio: Ohio State University Press, 1985)) [available on line, Ohio State University Press Open Access Initiative] discusses, exhaustively, other candidates (pp. 40–7).

53 *too much pepper*: Marina Warner (*No Go the Bogeyman* (London: Chatto and Windus, 1998), 153) suggests that Harry Graham had this scene in mind in his *Ruthless Rhymes for Heartless Homes* (1899):

> Nurse, who peppered baby's face
> (She mistook it for a muffin) . . .
> Mother, seeing baby blinded,
> Said 'Oh nurse, how absent-minded!'

'It's a Cheshire-Cat': 'to grin like a Cheshire-cat' is an old English saying, of obscure origin. Dodgson may well have followed a discussion in *Notes and Queries* (1850–2—at his death his library included over a hundred volumes of this journal) which suggested, among other theories, that it was because Cheshire cheese was made in the shape of a cat. The Liddell coat of arms featured three snarling leopards, and, as Cohen notes, 'the leopards from Cardinal Wolsey's coat of arms that graces the fabric of Christ Church . . . are known as "Ch Ch cats"' (Morton N. Cohen, *Lewis Carroll: A Biography* (London and Basingstoke: Macmillan, 1995), 136).

Also, Dodgson was born in Cheshire, and in St Peter's church, Croft-on-Tees, where his father was rector, 'on the south side of the

chancel you will see a fourteenth-century triple sedilia—three stone
arches with seats for the priest, deacon, and sub-deacon. On the right
side of the sedilia is the carved face of a cat which appears to be
smiling' (Charlie Lovett, *Lewis Carroll's England: An Illustrated Guide
for the Literary Tourist* (London: White Stone Publishing/The Lewis
Carroll Society, 1998), 9–10).

Karen McGavock, 'Lewis Carroll and the Deconstruction of
Childhood', feels that Dodgson 'parodies the role of the omniscient
narrator through the Cheshire Cat' (Rosie Finlay and Sébastien
Salbayre (eds.), *Histoires d'Enfant, Histoires d'Enfance* (Tours: Presses
Universitaires François Rabelais, 2007), 44). Goldthwaite (pp. 84–5)
regards the cat as Dodgson: sympathetic to Alice, helpful, and
omniscient. Alderson suggests that Dodgson's use of it 'may stem
from his reading of *The Water Babies* since the evanescent beast was
not present in his first draft of the story' (Charles Kingsley, *The Water
Babies*, ed. Brian Alderson (Oxford: Oxford University Press, 1995),
213).

54 *Speak roughly to your little boy*: a parody of 'Speak Gently' by David
Bates, published in the *Philadelphia Inquirer* in 1845, and in *Sharpe's
London Magazine* in 1845 which was edited by Frank Smedley, a
minor novelist, and a collaborator of Edmund Yates, of the magazine
The Train. He was the cousin of Dodgson's cousin, Menella Bute
Smedley (*ODNB*). The third stanza reads:

> Speak gently to the little child!
> Its love be sure to gain;
> Teach it in accents soft and mild—
> It may not long remain.

Dodgson added extra dialogue for Savile Clarke's stage production,
and an extra verse for the cook:

> Boil it so easily,
> Mix it so greasily,
> Stir it so sneezily,
> One! Two!! Three!!!

56 *neither more nor less than a pig*: in an example of historical speculation,
RLG cites C. W. Scott-Giles, Fitzalan Pursuivant of Arms Extraordinary, who suggests that this might be a reference to Richard III,
son of Richard Duke of York, who was called 'the hog' in political
lampoons. The Duke in *AAW* does not appear: Richard Duke of York
was living in retirement at the time of his son's birth. At the end of
AAW the Queen has the gardeners paint the white roses (of York) red
(the Lancastrian colour).

57 *they're both mad*: 'mad as a Hatter' is first recorded in *Blackwood's*

Magazine in 1829, and in Canada in *The Clockmaker* by Thomas
Chandler Haliburton in 1836, and is thought to come from the fact
that mercurous nitrate, used in hat-making, produced chorea (St
Vitus's Dance) and other neurological effects. Dodgson may have
based his Hatter on an Oxford eccentric, Theophilus Carter, who
resembled the prime minister, Gladstone, and who invented 'the
Alarm Clock Bed', which tipped its occupant out (it was exhibited at
the Great Exhibition at London's Crystal Palace in 1851). He was a
cabinetmaker with a shop at 48 High Street, Oxford. Tenniel may
have sketched him from life. However, Bishop T. B. Strong wrote:
'I do not think Dodgson observed people enough to construct his
characters in that way [from life]' ('Mr Dodgson: Lewis Carroll at
Oxford', *The Times*, 27 January 1932).

The philosopher Bertrand Russell bore some resemblance to the
Hatter, and he and his contemporaries, the philosophers J. M. E.
McTaggart and G. E. Moore, were known in Cambridge as the Mad
Tea Party of Trinity.

'As mad as a March Hare' is an old English saying, first recorded
*c.*1500, referring to the belief that hares behave oddly in the mating
season.

58 *as this is May*: Alice Liddell's birthday was 4 May; talking to the
Mad Hatter, Alice gives the date as the fourth (p. 62), and when she
is talking to Humpty Dumpty (p. 188) in *LG*—which is set on
4 November (p. 125)—she says that she is 'seven years and six
months'.

60 *'Why is a raven like a writing-desk?'*: Dodgson supplied an answer in
the Preface dated December 1896 (see p. 6). 'Because it can produce a
few notes, though they are *very* flat; and it is never put with the wrong
end in front!' MG (p. 72) cites a claim that Dodgson originally spelled
'never' as 'nevar'—'raven' (almost) spelled backwards: thus 'it is
nevar put with the wrong end in front!' (Denis Crutch, 'A Note on
the Hatter's riddle', *Jabberwocky*, 25 (5/1) (winter 1976), 32). The
Pennyroyal Edition, text edited by Selwyn Goodacre (West Hadfield,
Mass.: Pennyroyal Press, 1982), prints 'nevar'. The *American
Cyclopedia of Puzzles* (1914) suggested a different answer to the
riddle: 'because Poe wrote on both'.

62 *'Two days wrong!'*: Alexander L. Taylor (in *The White Knight*, 57)
points out that if the Hatter's watch measures time by the phases of
the moon, on '4 May 1862, there was exactly two days' difference
between the two ways of reckoning the date ... There can be no
doubt that Dodgson consulted an almanac.'

63 *Twinkle, twinkle, little bat!*: a parody of Jane Taylor's (1783–1824)
'The Star' from *Rhymes for the Nursery* (1806), which begins

> Twinkle, twinkle, little star,
> How I wonder what you are!
> Up above the world so high,
> Like a diamond in the sky.

The daughter of Professor Bartholomew Price, Dodgson's tutor and friend, claimed that 'bat' was Price's nickname, and that this reference was included as a compliment.

65 *Elsie, Lacie, and Tillie*: the three little/Liddell sisters: Elsie is a pun on Lorinda Charlotte's initials, 'Lacie' is an anagram of Alice, and Tillie is an abbreviation of Matilda, Edith's nickname.

66 *treacle-well*: medicinal springs in Oxfordshire were known as 'treacle wells'—treacle meaning 'balm' (and see Introduction, p. xxxvi).

67 *into the teapot*: a 'favourite artificial nest' for pet dormice is said to have been an old teapot filled with moss or dried grass (Marghanita Laski, *Times Literary Supplement*, 6 May 1965). Charlotte M. Yonge (*John Keble's Parish*, 1898) remarks that 'the smooth round dormouse (or sleep-mouse, as the children call it) is a favourite gift imprisoned in an old tea-pot' (RLG).

70 *Alice was rather doubtful . . . to p. 71, and waited*: not in *AAU*.

71 [*Illustration*]: the dome in the background is the Oxford Botanic Garden's water lily house.

the Knave of Hearts: Goldthwaite (p. 144) detects another self-portrait of Dodgson: 'not only is the Knave the nicest person in the book; he is the *only* nice person in the book'.

72 *only a pack of cards*: Dodgson had invented a card game, 'Court Circular', for the Liddell children, which he had printed in January 1860 (revised April 1862).

crimson with fury: in his article ' "Alice" on the Stage' (1881) Dodgson wrote: 'I pictured to myself the Queen of Hearts as a sort of embodiment of ungovernable passion—a blind and aimless Fury' (*LCPB*, 171).

73 *'Can you play croquet?'*: Dodgson often played croquet with the Liddell sisters in the Deanery garden, and had invented a new version of the game, *Castle Croquet* (privately printed 4 May 1863) (*LCPB*, 271–4) (RLG).

flamingoes: ostriches in *AAU*.

74 *about once in a minute . . . to p. 82, cost them their lives*: not in *AAU*.

75 *I should have croqueted the Queen's hedgehog*: to croquet is to drive away a ball, after hitting it with one's own, by placing the two in contact and striking one's own with the mallet (*SOED*).

76 *'A cat may look at a king'*: proverb first recorded in J. Heywood, *Dialogue of Proverbs* (1546).

79 *camomile*: an oil extracted from camomile flowers, administered as a cure for stomach and other complaints and as a sleep aid; often as an ingredient in herbal tea. At the end of Beatrix Potter's *The Tale of Peter Rabbit* (1902): 'I am sorry to say that Peter was not very well during the evening. His mother put him to bed, and made some camomile tea; and she gave a dose of it to Peter! "One table-spoonful to be taken at bed-time." '

moral, if only you can find it: Dodgson used much the same expression in his pamphlet on *The New Belfry of Christ Church, Oxford* (1872): 'Everything has a moral if you choose to look for it' (*LCPB*, 117). 'There's a moral in everything, if we would only avail ourselves of it,' is a saying of the less than estimable Louisa Chick, sister of Paul Dombey senior in Dickens's *Dombey and Son* (ch. 2) (1846–8).

80 *'tis love, that makes the world go round!*: originally the refrain of a French folk song, which is quoted by Charles Kingsley in *The Water-Babies* (ch. 2): 'C'est l'amour . . . Qui fait la monde à la ronde'. The Duchess is quoting from a popular translation, 'The Dawn of Love', Birmingham, *c.*1820. Goldthwaite (pp. 113–14) sees this as Dodgson satirizing Kingsley.

sounds will take care of themselves: from the English proverb: 'Take care of the pence and the pounds will take care of themselves', attributed to William Lowndes (1652–1724), Secretary to the Treasury. Suzanne Holthuis, 'Alice in Wonderland: Aspects of Inter-textuality' in Rachel Fordyce (ed.), *Semiotics and Linguistics in Alice's Worlds* (Berlin: de Gruyter, 1994), 134, describes this sentence as 'a prototype of lexical substitutions and play on words preserving the phonological structure'.

81 *'It's a mineral, I think'*: the first reference in the 'Alice' books to a Victorian parlour game, 'Animal, Vegetable, or Mineral?' or 'Twenty Questions'. It is referred to in Gilbert and Sullivan's *The Pirates of Penzance* (1879), in the Major-General's song: 'I've information vegetable, animal and mineral'. The Lion refers to it in *LG* (206).

as pigs have to fly: traditional Scots proverb, recorded by John Withal, 1586.

82 *Mock Turtle Soup*: an eighteenth-century substitute for green turtle soup, based on a calf's head and Madeira wine, although there are many modern variants—in the USA, oxtail is used. The Mock Turtle's calf's head and feet in the illustration on p. 85 were suggested to Tenniel by Canon Duckworth.

83 *a Gryphon*: or griffin—a classical (Greek) monster—the crest of

Trinity College, Oxford. On 1 August 1862, Dodgson went to the Deanery 'and remained a short time, for me to write the names in the books for crests etc. which I have given to Alice and Edith'. Donald Thomas points out that 'When *The Oxford Companion to Classical Literature* was published in 1937, it directed the reader in search of an image of the monster to "Tenniel's illustrations of the Gryphon in 'Alice in Wonderland'"' (*Lewis Carroll: A Portrait with Background* (London: John Murray, 1996), 158).

84 *'Hjckrrh!'*: Jo Elwyn Jones and Francis Gladstone detect a reference to Ruskin in the Gryphon's exclamation, deriving it from John (Jh) Ruskin (Rk), and the remaining letters 'Chr' from 'Ruskin's pet-name to his child-friends . . . St Chrysostom'. 'Our critics', they observe, 'find this argument strained' (*The Alice Companion*, 13).

   'Yes, we went to school in the sea . . .' to p. 88 *he went on again*: not in *AAU*.

86 *Drawling-master*: RLG detects a private joke: John Ruskin, who had been a 'gentleman-commoner' studying at Christ Church (graduated 1836), taught the Liddell sisters drawing, once a week. Some of the caricatures of Ruskin (for example, in *Punch*, 18 December 1880)— and some photographs—give him conger-eel-like characteristics. In a letter to E. Gertrude Thompson (24 January 1869) Dodgson described him as 'numbering among my friends'. Ruskin (like Dodgson) has been suspected or accused of (latent) paedophilia by his biographers.

   Reeling and Writhing . . . Laughing and Grief: puns on usual educational subjects, Reading, Writing, Addition, Subtraction, Multiplication, Division, History, Geography, Drawing, Sketching, Painting in Oils, Latin, and Greek (RLG).

88 *a Lobster-Quadrille*: a parody of the quadrille, an early form of square-dance, which was fashionable. On 3 July 1862, Dodgson lunched at the Deanery, and noted that 'the three sang "Sally Come Up" with great spirit'. 'Sally Come Up' was a song 'in the blackface minstrel tradition', which, as Norman Cazden, Herbert Haufrecht, and Norman Studer note in *Folk Songs of the Catskills* (Albany: SUNY Press, 1982), was designed to ridicule the ugly, and negroes in particular. The sheet music was published in England in 1859, and the least offensive of the verses reads:

> Sally come up, Oh, Sally come down,
> Oh Sally, come twist your heels around.
> De old man, he's gone down to town,
> Oh, Sally, come down de middle.

Dodgson parodied this in *AAU*:

> Salmon come up! Salmon go down!
> Salmon come twist your tail around!
> Of all the fishes in the sea
>   There's none so good as Salmon!

90 *very slowly and sadly* . . . p. 94, *will you, old fellow?*: not in *AAU*.

'*Will you walk a little faster?*': this poem replaces *AAU*'s 'Salmon come up!'. It is a parody of Mary Howitt's 'The Spider and the Fly', first published in *The New Year's Gift, and Juvenile Souvenir* (1829):

> 'Will you walk into my parlour?' said the Spider to the Fly,
> ''Tis the prettiest little parlour that ever you did spy;
> The way into my parlour is up a winding stair,
> And I have many curious things to show when you are there.'
> 'Oh no, no,' said the little Fly, 'to ask me is in vain,
> For who goes up your winding stair can ne'er come down again.'

91 *They have their tails in their mouths*: whiting, a white fish of the cod family, stocks of which have declined in recent years. Collingwood (*LLLC*, 402) prints an account of Dodgson's visit to a children's writer, Miss M. E. Manners, in 1889, where he said: 'When I wrote that, I believed that whiting really did have their tails in their mouths, but I have since been told that fishmongers put the tail through the eye, not in the mouth at all.' Thus prepared, the whiting were then fried in breadcrumbs.

blacking: shoe polish.

92 '*Don't you mean "purpose"?*': Goldthwaite (p. 91) thinks that the purpose | porpoise pun is an attack on Charles Kingsley's didacticism.

93 *'Tis the voice of the Lobster*: a parody of Isaac Watts, 'The Sluggard' from 'A Slight Specimen of Moral Songs' in *Divine Songs*, 46–7:

> 'Tis the Voice of the *Sluggard*. I hear him complain
> *You have wak'd me too soon, I must slumber again.*
> As the Door on its Hinges, so he on his Bed,
> Turns his Sides and his Shoulders, and his heavy Head.

As noted in the 'Preface to the Seventy-ninth Thousand' (p. 5) the second four lines of the first stanza (*When the sands* . . .) and the last six lines of the second (*The Panther took pie crust* . . .) of Dodgson's parody were added for Savile Clarke's play and then added to the book (RLG).

94 '*It's the first position in dancing*': in which the heels are together and the toes turned out (as in the illustration on p. 93).

I passed by his garden: the third stanza of 'The Sluggard' (see note to p. 93) begins:

> I past by his Garden, and saw the wild Bryar
> The Thorn and the Thistle grow broader and higher:
>
> (p. 47)

For William Boyd's *Songs from Alice's Adventures in Wonderland* (1870) Dodgson added two lines:

> While the duck and the Dodo, the lizard and cat,
> Were swimming in milk round the brim of a hat.

95 *Beautiful Soup, so rich and green*: a parody of 'Beautiful Star', which Dodgson heard Alice and Edith Liddell sing on 1 August 1862. The song was written in 1855 by James M. Sayles (harmonized and arranged by Henry Tucker, Albany [NY], J. Hidley). One British edition, published by Chas. Sheard and Co, London, attributed it to S. M. Sayles, in a series 'Favourite American Melodies Sung by the Christy Minstrels'. It begins:

> Beautiful star in heav'n so bright
> Softly falls thy silv'ry light,
> As thou movest from earth so far,
> Star of the evening, beautiful star,
> Beau—ti-ful star,
> Beau—ti-ful star,
> Star-r of the eve-ning,
> Beautiful, beautiful star.

Batey (p. 25) points out that when turtle soup was on the menu, 'Christ Church children were allowed to ride on the live turtles around the kitchen'.

96 *WHO STOLE THE TARTS?*: Kimberley Reynolds and Nicola Humble, in *Victorian Heroines* (Hemel Hempstead: Harvester Wheatsheaf, 1993), 129, point out that the trial scene 'with its innuendoes about sexual intrigue in the palace, revealed in the Knave's verse-letter . . . and its atmosphere of amoral chaos lurking beneath the familiar furniture of Victorian bourgeois life . . . owes a clear debt to the sensation novel'. Goldthwaite (pp. 146–53) decodes the whole trial as an allegory of 'the Lord Newry affair' (casting the White Rabbit as Newry), suggesting that Newry, a rowing companion of Dodgson, and a friend of the Liddell family, impugned Dodgson's character, leading to Mrs Liddell's estrangement from Dodgson in 1863. Dodgson is the innocent Knave of Hearts.

when they arrived . . . to p. 109 '*You're nothing but a pack of cards!*': not in *AAU*.

98 *she made some tarts*: the first six lines of four twelve-line stanzas from *The European Magazine* (April 1782): the others deal with the court cards of the other suits (see Opies, 359–60).

103 *ALICE'S EVIDENCE*: David Rudd (*Enid Blyton and the Mystery of Children's Literature* (Basingstoke: Macmillan, 2000), 70–1) notes that the final scene of the first Noddy book, *Noddy Goes to Toyland* (1949), is an echo of this scene. He also notes that in the 'Noddy' books there is 'much sub-Carrollian word-play . . . [as when] . . . Noddy says, "I can't add up. I can't add down either." '

with the edge of her skirt: this has been seen as part of the symbolic empowerment of Alice (and females).

105 *Rule Forty-two*: a favourite number of Dodgson's. There are 42 illustrations in *AAW* and *LG* was originally planned to have 42, rather than 50; 42 is the age of the narrator in *Phantasmagoria* (1869)—the narrator finds a ghost in his house:

> 'No doubt,' said I, 'they settled who
> Was fittest to be sent:
> Yet still to choose a brat like you,
> To haunt a man of forty-two
> Was no great compliment!'

In *LG* (198) the White King sends 4207 horses (7 is a factor of 42) (MG, 120), Alice's age in *Looking-Glass* is 7 years and 6 months (7 × 6 = 42), it would take 42 minutes to fall through the earth (see note to p. 11)—and many other connections have been noted.

In *The Hunting of the Snark*, the preface mentions Rule 42 of the Naval Code: '*No one shall speak to the Man at the Helm.*' In Fit the First (stanza 7), the Beaver

> . . . had forty-two boxes, all carefully packed,
> With his name painted clearly on each:
> But since he omitted to mention the fact,
> They were all left behind on the beach.

Douglas Adams, in his *Hitch Hiker's Guide to the Galaxy* series, chose 42 as the answer to the secret of the universe, claiming it to be purely arbitrary.

106 *They told me you had been to her*: a version of a poem Dodgson published in *Comic Times*, 8 September 1855. Although that poem was titled 'She's All My Fancy Painted Him', after the first line of William Mee's sentimental and tragic 'Alice Gray' (music by Mrs P. Millard), it is not a parody of that poem, and no source has been traced. The coincidence of the name 'Alice' has not been overlooked.

110 *such a curious dream!*: casting the story as a dream indicates the limits of the freedom and power that Alice has been given and is widely thought by critics to undercut the effect of the book. It is a common device in children's literature: for example, Mrs Molesworth's *The Cuckoo Clock* (1877) or John Masefield's *The Box of Delights* (1935).

and this was her dream: the sentimentalizing of Alice, and the adult rationalization of her dream, has produced a lot of critical speculation as to Dodgson's relationship to fantasy. In *AAU*, the sister's dream is far more personal:

> She saw an ancient city, and a quiet river winding near it along the plain, and up the stream went slowly gliding a boat with a merry party of children on board—she could hear their voices and laughter like music over the water—and among them was another little Alice, who sat listening with bright eager eyes to a tale that was being told, and she listened for the words of the tale, and lo! it was the dream of her own little sister. So the boat wound slowly along, beneath the bright summer-day, with its merry crew and its music of voices and laughter, till it passed round one of the many turnings of the stream, and she saw it no more. (pp. 89–90)

THROUGH THE LOOKING-GLASS

112 [*Frontispiece*]: the picture of the White Knight and Alice has a slight resemblance to Sir John Everett Millais's painting, *A Dream of the Past: Sir Isumbras at the Ford* (1857: Lady Lever Art Gallery, Port Sunlight).

113 [*Title: Through the Looking-Glass and What Alice Found There*]: the title was apparently suggested by Dodgson's friend Henry Parry Liddon. On 12 January 1869, Dodgson noted in his Diary: 'Finished and sent off to Macmillan the first chapter of *Behind the Looking-Glass, and what Alice Saw There*'; at proof stage it was *Looking-Glass House and what Alice saw there*. The device was apparently suggested to Dodgson through a meeting with a cousin, Alice Raikes, probably while he was staying at his Uncle Skeffington's house in August 1868.

John Ringo has written a science fiction series beginning with *Into the Looking-Glass* (Riverdale, NY: Baen, 2005): other volumes include *Vorpal Blade* (2007) and *Manxome Foe* (2008).

114 [*The Chess Board*]: on 30 August 1878, Dodgson complained to Macmillan that in a copy of the 42nd thousand of *Through the Looking-Glass*, the Kings had been omitted. The reply (10 September 1878) suggested that this may have happened when the preliminary matter was transferred to electrotype in the 22nd thousand (Morton N. Cohen and Anita Gandolfo, *Lewis Carroll and the House of Macmillan* (Cambridge: Cambridge University Press, 1987)). (Scholarly opinions differ on this.)

115 *DRAMATIS PERSONÆ*: MG (p. 136) notes that the Bishops (who are not mentioned in the book, probably because of Dodgson's religious scruples) are identified with Sheep, Aged Man, Walrus and Crow, 'though for no discernable reason'.

116 *pleasance*: Dodgson altered this from 'pleasures' in the proofs.

117 *not worth buying*: on 21 November 1893, Dodgson wrote to Macmillan: 'Having promised to give a copy of *Through the Looking-Glass* to a lady-friend, and having no copies on hand, I wrote to you for 6. They arrived this morning . . . Of the 50 pictures, 26 are over-printed, 8 of them being so much as to be quite spoiled . . . On no consideration whatsoever must any more of this impression [the 60th thousand] be sold [60 had been] . . . the 940 copies must be at once destroyed, and the book must be "out of print" for the present . . . Evidently there has been gross carelessness' (Cohen and Gandolfo, *Lewis Carroll and the House of Macmillan*, 292–3). The 'Preface to the Sixty-First Thousand' points out that 'fresh electrotypes have been taken from the wood-blocks'.

118 *the chess-problem*: opinion varies as to whether the game is correct, eccentric, or impossible, technically. In literary terms, its oddity may be explained by Alice's limited perspective as pawn (she only speaks to pieces that are in squares adjacent to hers), or to the eccentric rules of the looking-glass world. Moves are noted on the following pages. In her old age, Alice Liddell Hargreaves recalled that 'Much of *Through the Looking-Glass* is made up of [Dodgson's stories] particularly the ones to do with chessmen, which are dated by the period when we were excitedly learning chess' ('Alice's Recollections of Carrollian Days, as Told to her Son', *Cornhill Magazine*, 73 (July 1932), in Morton N. Cohen (ed.), *Lewis Carroll: Interviews and Recollections* (London: Palgrave Macmillan, 1989), 84).

In May 1910, *The British Chess Magazine*, 30 (181) published a game by Donald M. Liddell which 'reproduces the whole story' in 68 moves.

123 *had nothing to do with it*: Kathleen Tillotson ('Lewis Carroll and the Kitten on the Hearth', *English*, 8/45 (1950), 136–8) argues that Dodgson was recollecting a parody of Dickens's *The Cricket on the Hearth* in 'Advice to an Intending Serialist' by William Edmondstoune Aytoun, *Blackwood's Magazine*, 60 (November 1845), 590–605 (RLG).

worsted: 'a fine and soft yarn spun of long-staple wool combed to lay the fibres parallel' (*SOED*).

125 *what to-morrow is*: Guy Fawkes' Day was celebrated with a big bonfire in Peckwater Quadrangle at Christ Church on 5 November. *AAW* takes place exactly six months before. Critics have noted the balance between the summery atmosphere of the beginning and end of *AAW* and the snow of *LG*. Alice's account of the boys collecting sticks demonstrates her cloistered life.

Snowdrop: said to be a cat belonging to Mary, second daughter of George MacDonald (William Raeper, *George MacDonald* (Tring: Lion, 1987), 172).

127 *the Red Queen*: in his article ' "Alice" on the Stage' (1881) Dodgson wrote that he pictured her as a Fury of a different type from the Queen of Hearts: '*her* passion must be cold and calm; she must be formal and strict, yet not unkindly; pedantic to the tenth degree, the concentrated essence of all governesses!' (*LCPB*, 171).

130 *the White Queen*: Dodgson wrote that the White Queen seemed 'to my dreaming fancy, gentle, stupid, fat and pale; helpless as an infant; and with a slow, maundering, bewildered air about her just *suggesting* imbecility, but never quite passing into it; that would be, I think, fatal to any comic effect she might otherwise produce' (*LCPB*, 171). He also compares her to a character in Wilkie Collins's novel *No Name* (1862): 'Mrs. Wragg [*sic*] and the White Queen might have been twin-sisters'—although Mrs Wragge is 6 feet 3 inches tall:

> The figure terminated at its upper extremity in a large, smooth, white round face like a moon, encircled by a cap and green ribbons, and dimly irradiated by eyes of mild and faded blue, which looked straight-forward into vacancy, and took not the smallest notice . . . 'Mrs Wragge is not deaf,' explained the Captain. 'She's only a little slow. Constitutionally torpid—if I may use the expression.'

Kimberley Reynolds and Nicola Humble (in *Victorian Heroines*, 129) parallel Alice's ministrations to the Queen with Magdalen's ministrations to Mrs Wragge in *No Name*: 'the kindness and sympathy shown by the intelligent, active young woman to the less capable old woman has precisely the same emotional tone in each case'.

131 *My imperial kitten!*: who is later 'too young to play'—this may be an in-joke reference to George MacDonald's eldest daughter, Lilia (Raeper, *George Macdonald*, 171).

134 *Jabberwocky*: on 24 January 1868, Dodgson enquired of Macmillan about the cost of preparing 'reverse' woodblocks, and by 31 January 1869 he had decided that 'it will be too troublesome for the reader to have 2 pages of "reverse" type to make out, and that we had better limit it to one or 2 stanzas' (Cohen and Gandolfo, *Lewis Carroll and the House of Macmillan*, 59, 77).

The first four lines appeared in the last of the Rectory MS magazines, *Mischmasch* in 1855, with 'learned' footnotes. According to Collingwood (*LLLC*, 143) Dodgson 'composed this poem while staying with his cousins, the Misses Wilcox, at Whitburn, near Sunderland. To while away an evening the whole party sat down to a game of verse-making, and "Jabberwocky" was his contribution'—

although it is not clear whether this visit was in 1855, 1867, or some other date. It may be based on a poem translated by Dodgson's cousin, Menella Bute Smedley, 'The Shepherd of the Giant Mountains' (*Sharpe's London Magazine*, 7 and 20 March, 1846), which has the line 'Come to my heart, my true and gallant son' and is described in Kipling's bitter autobiographical story 'Baa Baa Black Sheep', in *Wee Willie Winkie* (1888):

> He put the brown book in the cupboard where his school-books lived and accidentally tumbled out a venerable volume, without covers, labelled *Sharpe's Magazine*. There was the most portentous picture of a Griffin on the first page, with verses below. The Griffin carried off one sheep a day from a German village, till a man came with a 'falchion' and split the Griffin open. Goodness only knew what a falchion was, but there was the Griffin and his history was an improvement upon the eternal Cat.
>
> 'This,' said Punch, 'means things, and now I will know all about everything in all the world.' He read till the light failed, not understanding a tithe of the meaning, but tantalised by glimpses of new worlds hereafter to be revealed.
>
> 'What is a "falchion"? What is a "e-wee lamb"? What is a "base *uss*urper"? What is a "verdant mead"?' he demanded, with flushed cheeks, at bedtime, of the astonished Aunty Rosa.
>
> 'Say your prayers and go to sleep,' she replied, and that was all the help Punch then or afterwards found at her hands in the new and delightful exercise of reading.

'Jabberwocky' also became something of an in-joke at Oxford. In February 1872, Dr Robert Scott, Dean of Rochester (and the collaborator on the Greek Lexicon with Dean Liddell), published an article in *Macmillan's Magazine*, 'The Jabberwock Traced to its True Source'—which was said to be from the German, 'Der Jammerwoch': this begins

> Es brillig war. Die schlichte Toven
> Wirrten und wimmelten in Waben

Scott also wrote to Dodgson:

> Are we to suppose, after all, that the Saga of Jabberwocky is one of the universal heirlooms which the Aryan race at its dispersion carried with it from the great cradle of the family? You must really consult Max Müller about this. [Müller was a founder of the discipline of Comparative Religion, and Taylorian Professor of Modern European Languages and Professor of Comparative Philology at Oxford. And honorary member of Christ Church.

Dodgson had photographed him and his family (see MG, 390).] It begins to be probable that the *origo originalissima* may be discovered in Sanscrit, and that we shall by and by have a *Iabrivokaveda*. The hero will turn out to be the Sun-god in one of his *Avatars*; and the TumTum tree the great as *Ygdrasil* of the Scandinavian mythology. (*LLLC*, 143)

Collingwood quotes a Latin translation, made by A. A. Vansittart of Trinity College, Cambridge, in 1872, which begins thus:

> Cœsper erat: tunc lubriciles utravia circum
> Urgebant gyros gimbiculosque tophi

and is complete with a glossary of Latin portmanteau words (*LLLC*, 143).

Dodgson's uncle, Hassard Dodgson, produced a version 'Rendered into Latin Elegiacs' which begins:

> Hora aderat briligi. Nuc et Slythæia Tova
> Plurima gyrabant gymbilitare vabo;
>   (*LCPB*, 364)

Translations have appeared in many other languages, including Esperanto and Klingon, parodies, and several spell-checked versions ('Twas billing and the slithery toes . . .').

James Reaney (*Lewis Carroll's Alice Through the Looking-Glass Adapted for the Stage* (Erin, Ont.: The Porcupine's Quill, 1994), 127) points out that these lines are reminiscent of *genuine* Anglo-Saxon poetry. In *Beowulf*, the monster Grendel 'came stalking in the dusky night': 'cóm on wanre niht' (l. 702). Not only that, he was satiated: 'wælfylle' (l. 125)—and 'him of éagum stód | ligge gelícost léohht unfaéger': 'from his eyes came a horrible light, most like a flame' (l. 726).

Given that Dodgson devotes some time to lampooning textual scholars in the person of Humpty-Dumpty and his interpretation of 'Jabberwocky' in Chapter VI (pp. 191–3), it is (perhaps) surprising that so much scholarly ink has been spilt on interpreting genuine nonsense (one gloss on 'Tumtum', for example, cites the three meanings given by the *Oxford English Dictionary*, and concludes that 'none seems to have any connection'). Words are glossed here only where some explanation is provided by Dodgson. Humpty-Dumpty's definition of 'portmanteau word' (p. 192)—'two meanings packed into one word'—has entered the language.

brillig: spelt *'bryllyg'* in *Mischmasch*: the meaning given is '(derived from the verb to *BRYL* or *BROIL*). "the time of broiling dinner, i.e. the close of the afternoon." ' Humpty-Dumpty agrees.

slithy toves: in the preface to *The Hunting of the Snark* (1876), Dodgson wrote: 'As this poem is to some extent connected with the lay of the Jabberwock, let me take this opportunity of answering a question that has often been asked me, how to pronounce "slithy toves". The "i" in "slithy" is long, as in "writhe"; and "toves" is pronounced so as to rhyme with "groves".' *Mischmasch* glosses 'Slithy' as '(compounded of *SLIMY* and *LITHE*.) "Smooth and active" ', and 'Tove' as 'A species of Badger. They had smooth white hair, long hind legs, and short horns like a stag; lived chiefly on cheese.' (Humpty-Dumpty adds that they nest under sundials.)

gyre and gymble: *Mischmasch*: '<u>GYRE</u> verb (derived from GYAOUR or GIAOUR, "a dog") to scratch like a dog'; '<u>GYMBLE</u> (whence GIMBLET). To screw out holes in anything.'

wabe: *Mischmasch*: '(derived from the verb to *SWAB* or *SOAK*) "the side of a hill" (from its being *soaked* by the rain)'.

mimsy: *Mischmasch*: '(whence *MIMSERABLE* and *MISERABLE*) "unhappy" '. Dodgson uses it again in *The Hunting of the Snark* (7. 9) when a Bandersnatch, with frumious jaws, attacks the Banker:

> Down he sat in his chair—ran his hands through his hair—
>   And chanted in mimsiest tones
> Words whose utter inanity proved his insanity,
>   While he rattled a couple of bones.

borogoves: *Mischmasch*: 'An extinct kind of Parrot. The [*sic*] have no wings, beaks turned up, and made their nests under sun-dials. Lived on veal.' In the preface to *The Hunting of the Snark*, Dodgson added: 'Again, the first "o" in "Borogoves" is pronounced like the "o" in "borrow". I have heard people try to give it the sound of the "o" in "worry". Such is Human Perversity.' The borogove in Tenniel's picture is said to have originated in a stuffed bird sent from South America to Dodgson's friend, the Revd W. D. Parish, vicar of Selmeston, Sussex. The bird disintegrated considerably on the journey but 'the late Vicar had its head and long legs mounted on a stand. It was shown to Lewis Carroll who became infatuated with it and a picture of this curious looking "make-up" was printed in his book *Through the Looking-Glass*' (obituary of W. D. Parish, *Sussex Daily News*, 24 September 1904) (RLG).

mome: *mischmasch*: '(hence *SOLEMOME, SOLEMONE* and *SOLEMN*). "Grave" '.

raths: *Mischmasch*: 'A species of land turtle. Head erect; mouth like a shark; fore legs curved out so that the animal walked on it's [*sic*] knees; smooth green body: lived on swallows and oysters.' Or, says Humpty-Dumpty, a green pig.

outgrabe: *Mischmasch*: 'past tense of the verb to *OUTGRIBE* (it is

connected with the old verb to *GRIKE* or *SHRIKE*, from which are
derived "shriek" and "creak"). "Squeaked." ' Dodgson used the word
again in *The Hunting of the Snark* (5. 10):

> The Beaver had counted with scrupulous care,
>   Attending to every word:
> But it fairly lost heart, and outgrabe in despair
>   When the third repetition occurred.

Hence, Dodgson wrote: 'the literal English of the passage is "It was
evening and the smooth active badgers were scratching and boring
holes in the hill side; all unhappy were the parrots; and the grave
turtles squeaked out." There were probably sundials on top of the
hill, and the "borogoves" were afraid that their nests would be
undermined. The hill was probably full of the nests of "raths", which
ran out squeaking with fear on hearing the "toves" scratching outside.
This is an obscure, but yet deeply affecting, relic of ancient poetry'
(*LCPB*, 37–8).

Jabberwock: Collingwood (*LLLC*, 274) reports that around 1884
Dodgson was asked by 'the Fourth class of the Girl's [*sic*] Latin
School at Boston, U. S.' if they might call their magazine *The
Jabberwock*. He gave them permission, and wrote: 'He finds that the
Anglo-Saxon word "wocer" or "wocor" signifies "offspring" or
"fruit." Taking "jabber" in its ordinary acceptation of "excited and
voluble discussion," that would give the meaning of "the result of
much excited discussion". Whether this phrase will have any application to the projected periodical, it will be for the future historian of
American literature to determine.' Michael Bakewell (*Lewis Carroll:
A Biography* (London: Heinemann, 1996), 285) reports that in one
of the issues that the girls sent him there was a limerick: 'There was
an old deacon of Lynn | Who confessed he was given to sin . . .'
'Dodgson was not amused . . . and he forbade them to send any more
copies.' *Night of the Jabberwock* by Fredric Brown (1950) is a comedy
thriller narrated by a small-town newspaper man who is a Carroll
enthusiast. The book is suffused by Carrollian references, but they are
only incidental to the ingenious plot. In contrast, in 'Mimsy Were the
Borogoves', a science-fiction story by Lewis Padgett (Henry Kuttner
and C. L. Moore) first published in *Astounding Science-Fiction*
(1943), 'Jabberwocky' is mathematical code that allows travel to other
dimensions. It was filmed as *The Last Mimzy* in 2007 (dir. Robert
Shaye). In Graham Masterton's horror novel, *Mirror* (London:
Sphere, 1988), which uses several elements of *Through the Looking-
Glass*, the Jabberwock is the mirror image of Satan. The narrator
buys a mirror which is part of Satan's plan to destroy the world, and
this is explained by reference to 'an unpublished commentary on

Unusual Properties of Looking-Glasses' by Dodgson, in which he claims
to have had a near-death experience that showed that in the looking-
glass world 'not just writing, and pictures, but Christian mortality
itself had been turned from left to right. Inside the mirror was . . . the
ante-room of Hell itself' (pp. 232–3).

Jubjub: this bird also appears in *The Hunting of the Snark* as ('that
desperate bird' (4. 18)), and in Fit the Fifth:

> Then a scream, shrill and high, rent the shuddering sky,
>   And they knew that some danger was near:
> The Beaver turned pale to the tip of its tail,
>   And even the Butcher felt queer.
>
> (5.6)

> ' 'Tis the voice of the Jubjub!' he suddenly cried
>
> (5.8)

> 'Its flavour when cooked is more exquisite far
>   Than mutton, or oysters, or eggs:
> (Some think it keeps best in an Ivory jar,
>   And some, in mahogany kegs:)'
>
> (5.23)

frumious: in the preface to *The Hunting of the Snark*, Dodgson
wrote: 'take the two words "fuming" and "furious". Make up your
mind that you will say both words, but leave it unsettled which you
will say first. Now, open your mouth and speak. If your thoughts
incline ever so little towards "fuming", you will say "fuming-
furious"; if they turn, by even a hair's breadth, towards "furious",
you will say "furious-fuming"; but if you have that rarest of gifts, a
perfectly balanced mind, you will say "frumious." '

Bandersnatch: Mollie Hardwick's mystery novel, *The Bandersnatch*
(1989), about a kidnapping, uses a good deal of Carrollian reference,
although this is not instrumental to the plot. In Ed McBain's
'87th Precinct' novel, *The Frumious Bandersnatch* (2004), also about a
kidnapping, *Bandersnatch* is a new music album: one of the characters,
who has never heard of Lewis Carroll, observes that 'it sounds some-
what pornographic'. RLG notes that 'bandar' means 'monkey' in
Hindi, and that 'Bandarsnatch' would 'so well describe Kaa or
Bagheera' in Kipling's *The Jungle Book*.

vorpal: Graham Masterton in *Mirror* (1988), 234 suggests that it has
a quasi-biblical origin: that Satan can only be destroyed with a sword
engraved with the words '*V*ictory *O*ver *R*uin, *P*estilence, *A*nd *L*ust'.

uffish: Dodgson wrote to his 'child friend' Maud Standen, on 18
December 1877: 'I *did* make an explanation once for "uffish thought."
It seems to suggest a state of mind when the voice is gruffish, the

manner roughish, and the temper huffish.' In *The Hunting of the Snark* (4. 1) 'The Bellman looked uffish'.

burbled: in the same letter, Dodgson wrote 'if you take the three verbs "bleat", "murmur" and "warble", and select the bits I have underlined, it certainly *makes* "burble": though I am afraid I can't distinctly remember having made it that way'.

snicker-snack: probably from 'snickersnee', a large knife or, in *The Mikado*, Act 2, a cutlass, with which Ko-ko decapitates a criminal (1885), and possibly from Thackeray's ballad, 'Little Billee' ('There were three sailors in Bristol City, | Who took a boat and went to sea'); when gorging Jack and guzzling Jimmy decide to eat little Billee:

> When Bill he heard this information,
> He used his pocket-handkerchie.
> 'First let me say my catechism
> Which my poor mother taught to me.'
> 'Make haste! make haste!' says guzzling Jimmy,
> While Jack pulled out his snickersnee.

galumphing: now part of the language; Dodgson used it in *The Hunting of the Snark* (4. 17): 'The Beaver went simply galumphing about'; it was certainly part of Arthur Ransome's child characters' vocabulary. Two examples from *Swallowdale* (1931): 'Titty came galumphing down' (p. 285); 'a thought . . . that would have made the able-seaman galumph' (p. 355).

beamish: variant of 'beaming' (*OED*: from 1530), and see *The Hunting of the Snark*, 3. 10: 'But oh, beamish nephew'. If Kipling's *Stalky and Co* (1899) is any indication, 'burble' and 'frabjous' passed into the argot of the public schools. When Stalky suggests putting a dead cat under the floorboards of a rival dormitory: ' "Come to my arms, my beamish boy," carolled M'Turk, and they fell into each other's arms dancing. "Oh, frabjous day! Calloo, callay!" ' ('An Unsavoury Interlude'). However, this is virtually the only point in the book at which specific Carrollian language is used.

135 [*Illustration*]: Tenniel may have been influenced by Paolo Uccello's *St George and the Dragon* (*c.* 1470).

137 *THE GARDEN OF LIVE FLOWERS*: the idea of the garden of live flowers may have been taken from, or have been a parody of, Tennyson's 'Maud' (1855):

> There has fallen a splendid tear
>   From the passion-flower at the gate.
> She is coming, my dove, my dear;
>   She is coming, my life, my fate;

> The red rose cries, 'She is near, she is near;'
> And the white rose weeps, 'She is late;'
> The larkspur listens, 'I hear, I hear;'
> And the lily whispers, 'I wait.'

138 *'O Tiger-lily!'*: Collingwood (*LLLC*, 150–1) noted: 'In his original manuscript the bad-tempered flower . . . was the passion-flower; the sacred origin of the name never struck him, until it was pointed out to him by a friend, when he at once changed it into the tiger-lily. Another friend asked him if the final scene was based upon the triumphal conclusion of "Pilgrim's Progress." He repudiated the idea, saying that he would consider such trespassing on holy ground as highly irreverent.'

139 *the Rose*: probably Alice's younger sister, Rhoda Caroline Anne Liddell (1858–1947).

140 *a Violet*: probably Alice's youngest sister, Violet Constance Liddell (1864–1927).

141 *one of the kind that has nine spikes*: in 1897, Dodgson changed this from the original 'She's one of the thorny kind', which may identify the Red Queen with the governess Miss Prickett, whose nickname was 'Pricks', and instead refers to the chess-queen's crown.

along the gravel-walk: a parody of the first two lines of a stanza from 'Maud':

> She is coming, my own, my sweet;
> Were it ever so airy a tread

142 *face to face with the Red Queen*: Alice is on square Q2.

143 *little hill*: biographers have suggested that this chapter is based on a visit (4–7 April 1863) by Dodgson to the Liddell children who were on holiday at Charlton Kings, near Cheltenham, during which they walked on Leckhampton Hill, and looked down at the chequered landscape. (This is the only point in the book where Alice, the pawn, can see more than is in her immediate vicinity.)

[*Illustration*]: Alice was in the foreground of Tenniel's original illustration; he removed her at Dodgson's request (Bakewell, *Lewis Carroll: A Biography*, 193).

147 *she was gone*: Red Queen to KR4.

149 *the first of the six little brooks*: Alice to Q4 (this is her first move, which is two squares).

a thousand pounds a minute!: possibly a reference to contemporary advertisements for Beecham's Pills (a laxative): 'worth a guinea a box'.

150 *the gentleman sitting opposite to her*: a caricature of Benjamin Disraeli—as William Empson (RP, 402) described him: 'dressed in news-

papers—the new man who gets on by self-advertisement, the newspaper-fed man who believes in progress', while the goat is possibly Gladstone. Alice's hat and muff are very similar to those in John Everett Millais's (1829–96) painting *My First Sermon* (1863); the general layout of the picture resembles Augustus Leopold Egg's (1816–63) *The Travelling Companions* (1862).

151 *as she's got a head on her*: a reference to the Queen's head on postage stamps (Victorian slang).

152 *the Goat's beard*: Collingwood (*LLLC*, 147–9), reproduces a letter from Tenniel to Dodgson (1 June 1870): 'My dear Dodgson. I think that when the jump occurs in the Railway scene you might very well make Alice lay hold of the Goat's beard as being the object nearest to her hand—instead of the old lady's hair. The jerk would naturally throw them together.'

she found herself sitting quietly under a tree: Alice to Q4.

the Gnat: Kincaid (*Child-Loving*, 297) thinks that the Gnat, like the Dodo in *AAW*, and the White Knight in *LG*, represents Dodgson himself. The Gnat's 'soft and persistent attempts to woo Alice to come join us and be a child again . . . finally dwindles to conversation about death'. Empson concurs: 'at first it sounds tiny because it means so little to her' (*RP*, 417).

153 *raisin burning in brandy*: snapdragon (or flapdragon) was an old game, usually played at Christmas, when players tried to snatch raisins out of a dish of burning brandy, and eat them while still alight. There is a reference to it in *Love's Labour's Lost* (v. i): '*Costard*: Oh they have lived long on the alms-basket of words. I marvel thy master hast not eaten thee for a word; for thou art not so long by the head as honorificabilitudinitatibus; thou art easier swallowed than a flap-dragon.' It is defined in Johnson's *Dictionary*, and appears in Dickens's *The Pickwick Papers* (1836), and Trollope's *Orley Farm* (1861).

154 *Frumenty*: medieval dish of cracked or hulled wheat boiled in milk, with sugar, and cinnamon and other spices.

156 *begins with L!*: either Lily, the pawn whose part Alice has taken, or a quiet in-joke—rather nostalgic, as Dodgson had lost touch with the Liddells as a family friend.

158 *they must be*: Dodgson clearly intended 'they must be | TWEEDLEDUM AND TWEEDLEDEE' as a couplet. A full stop was introduced, in error, in the 1897 edition.

159 *TWEEDLEDUM AND TWEEDLEDEE*: the Opies (p. 418) trace the nursery rhyme to 1805, and attribute the names to John Byrom in a verse about a feud between Bononcini and Handel:

> Some say, compar'd to Bononcini,
> That Mynheer Handel's but a Ninny;
> Others aver, that he to Handel
> Is scarcely fit to hold a Candle:
> Strange all this difference should be
> 'Twixt Tweedle-dum and Tweedle-dee!

(There are other candidates!)

160 *That's logic*: Dodgson's first reference to writing about logic appears in his Diary, 6 September 1855, and in February 1896 he published *Symbolic Logic, Part 1: Elementary*, 'a fascinating mental recreation for the young'. See Robin Wilson, *Lewis Carroll in Numberland: His Fantastical Mathematical Logical Life* (London: Allen Lane, 2008), 171–98.

161 *"Here we go round the mulberry bush"*: traditional game rhyme for a 'ring dance'.

161 *"The Walrus and the Carpenter"*: the Walrus was probably suggested by a stuffed walrus in the Sunderland Museum, which Dodgson had known since childhood (RLG). For the other character, Tenniel at first objected to drawing a Carpenter, 'but finally preferred him to either of the two dactylic replacements that Dodgson had obligingly offered, "Baronet", or "Butterfly" ' (Guiliano, 40). The poem follows the metre and style of Thomas Hood's 'The Dream of Eugene Aram' (*The Gem*, 1829) which begins:

> 'Twas in the prime of summer time,
>   An evening calm and cool,
> And four and twenty happy boys
>   Came bounding out of school:
> There were some that ran and some that leapt
>   Like troutlets in a pool.

(RLG)

However, in a letter to his uncle, Hassard Dodgson, on 14 May 1872, Dodgson says 'I had no particular poem in my mind.'

Michael Hancher notes (Guiliano, 38–40) that Tenniel was illustrating a satire in *Punch* called 'Reversing the Proverb' (4 June 1864) while he was working on *AAW*, in which 'the reform-minded Lord Chancellor, Lord Bethel, discusses the proverb "A shell for him, a shell for thee | The oyster is the lawyer's fee." '. The verse ends:

> Again he smiled, so says the fable,
> And drew his chair up near the table,
> When all the Oysters, seen and hid,
> Cried 'Eat, and welcome.' And he did.

'Lewis Carroll' was John Lennon's favourite author; the song 'I am the Walrus' was recorded 5–29 September 1967. 'Lennon later regretted picking the Walrus after re-reading Carroll's poem and realising that he was "the bad guy" ' (Ian MacDonald, *Revolution in the Head: The Beatles' Records and the Sixties* (London: Pimlico, 2005), 268).

162 *close at hand*: originally 'hand in hand'. Tenniel suggested the change.

165 [*Illustration*]: Hancher (Guiliano, 34, 36) points out that this picture is 'a recasting of Tenniel's cartoon of the English beef admonishing the German sausages under the gaze of the French wine' (9 January 1864).

166 [*Illustration*]: Hancher (Guiliano, 37–9) notes the close resemblance between the Carpenter and an oyster-eating lawyer in a Tenniel cartoon 'Law and Lunacy, Or A Glorious Oyster Season for the Lawyers' (25 January 1862).

They'd eaten every one: for Savile Clarke's stage version of the 'Alice' books, Dodgson wrote extra verses with a moral touch:

> The Carpenter he ceased to sob;
> The Walrus ceased to weep;
> They'd finished all the oysters;
> And they laid them down to sleep—
> And of their craft and cruelty
> The punishment to reap.

The punishment consists of one ghost-oyster sitting on the chest of the Carpenter, a second stamping on the Walrus; a third dances a hornpipe.

169 *only a rattle*: the illustration contains a visual pun (supplied by Tenniel) of the wrong sort of rattle (a watchman's rattle rather than a child's rattle). Dodgson complained to Henry Savile Clarke (29 November 1886) that 'Mr Tenniel has introduced a false "reading" in his picture'.

173 *WOOL AND WATER*: the Beatles' 'Lucy in the Sky with Diamonds' (from *Sgt Pepper's Lonely Hearts Club Band*, 1967) 'took its atmosphere from [this] hallucinatory chapter ... The *Alice* books were canonised by the [1960s] counterculture for their surreal wit and drug-dream undertones' (MacDonald, *Revolution in the Head*, 240). Dodgson's picture is included on the cover of the album.

came running wildly through the wood: White Queen to QB4.

174 *never jam to-day*: MG (p. 196) points out that this may be a play on the Latin *iam/jam*—*iam* meaning 'now', but only in the past and future tenses. The present tense is *nunc*. The phrase has become proverbial.

178 *crossed the little brook*: Alice to Q5.

178 *wrapped herself up in wool*: White Queen to QB5.

in a shop: Tenniel's illustration is of a grocer's shop, 83 St Aldate's, Oxford, now 'Alice's Shop: the Old Sheep Shop' (with a clone branch in Craven Terrace, London).

179 *Things flow about … quite used to it*: MG (p. 201) quotes a suggestion that Dodgson may have been inspired by a passage from Blaise Pascal's *Pensées* (Jeffrey Stern, 'Lewis Carroll and Blaise Pascal (1623–62)', *Jabberwocky*, 54 (12/2) (spring 1983), 35–8). Equally, the American surrealist artist Edward Gorey may have had this episode in mind in his *The Sinking Spell* (1964).

teetotum: a cube-shaped spinning-top with letters on four sides. *SOED*: 'the letters were orig. the initials of Latin words, viz. T *totum* [all], A *aufer* [carry off], D *depone* [deposit], N *nihil* [nothing]'.

180 *'Feather!'*: turning the blades of the oars horizontally while drawing them back for the next stroke.

catching a crab: catching the oar in the water unintentionally.

181 *and such beauties!*: Elizabeth Sewell (*The Field of Nonsense* (London: Chatto and Windus, 1952), 107) felt that one of the dangers that beauty has for nonsense is that 'the beholder's detachment and indifference are no longer intact, and the dream side of the mind comes into play'. This is the first instance in the Alice books (the second is Alice's farewell to the White Knight (p. 222)) when 'at once the atmosphere of the work is impaired and the passages threaten to break the fabric of the Nonsense universe … In each passage the dream almost wins, but the writer recovers himself just in time to save his world from disruption by the forces admitted by beauty.'

183 *two are cheaper than one*: a reference to the practice at Christ Church that if an undergraduate 'ordered one boiled egg he was served with two, but one was invariably bad' (Elma K. Paget, *Henry Luke Paget* (London: Longmans Green, 1939), 62) (RLG).

to the other end of the shop: White Queen to KB8.

184 *here's a little brook!*: Alice to Q6.

185 *HUMPTY DUMPTY*: 'a short, dumpy, hump-shouldered person; short and fat' (*SOED*, 1785). The Opies (pp. 213–16) trace the first manuscript of this riddle to *c.*1803, and it may derive from a game much earlier than this. Forms of this riddle exist all over Europe. Bryan Talbot suggests (in *Alice in Sunderland* (London: Cape, 2007), 167) that Dodgson may have been satirizing George Hudson, the 'railway king … who mirrors his prodigious girth, pompous attitude, royal toadying and refusal to acknowledge his inevitable fall into bankruptcy'. J. B. Priestley, on the other hand, sees him as 'a prophetic figure, and Lewis Carroll, in drawing him, was satirizing a race of

critics that did not then exist' (*I, For* One (London: John Lane The Bodley Head, 1923), 193).

189　*un-birthday present*: in the Disney film, the song 'A Very Merry Un-Birthday' is sung by the Mad Hatter and the March Hare (Ed Wynn and Jerry Colonna).

190　*'When I use a word'*: Humpty-Dumpty's view of language at this point is a rather solipsistic version of the views of modern linguisticians—words only 'mean' what the language community decides, rather than having intrinsic meanings or intrinsic power (as opposed to his view of what Alice's name means). In an appendix to his *Symbolic Logic* (1896), 'Addressed to Teachers', Dodgson tackled the ' "Existential Import" of Propositions':

> The logicians 'speak of the Copula of a Proposition "with bated breath" almost as if it were a living, conscious, Entity, capable of declaring for itself what it chose to mean, and that we, poor human creatures, had nothing to do but to ascertain *what* was it's sovereign will and pleasure and submit to it.
>
> In opposition to this view, I maintain that any writer of a book is fully authorised in attaching any meaning he likes to any word or phrase he intends to use. If I find an author saying, at the beginning of his book, "Let it be understood that by the word '*black*' I shall always mean '*white*', and that by the word '*white*' I shall always mean '*black*'," I meekly accept his ruling, however injudicious I may think it.'

192　*like a portmanteau*: 'portmanteau word' has entered the language, and portmanteau words were essential to James Joyce's *Finnegans Wake*. Examples are: 'Hear we here her first poseproem of suora unto suora? Alicious, twinstreams, twinewstraines, through alluring glass or alas in jumboland?' (London: Faber and Faber, 1939, 528).

　　　[illustration]: Dodgson objected to the original version of this picture. Tenniel wrote to the engravers, the Dalziel brothers: 'Will you please clear away the ear of the central animal . . . Mr Dodgson sees a second face, the ears forming the snout' (Michael Bakewell, *Lewis Carroll: A Biography* (London: Heinemann, 1996), 193).

194　*In winter, when the fields are white*: MG (p. 216) suggests that the inspiration for this poem (it does not seem to be a parody) might be 'Summer Days' by Wathen Mark Wilks Call, a freethinker (1817–90), which begins:

> In summer, when the days were long,
> We walked, two friends, in field and wood

196　*one of his fingers to shake*: it was the custom of the aristocracy to offer only two fingers for a 'handshake' with the 'lower orders'; Humpty-Dumpty takes this to an extreme.

199 [*illustration*]: Tenniel's battle scene mimics many such in contemporary popular history books, and bears some resemblance to panels in St Fridewide's window in Christ Church, by Edward Burne-Jones.

200 *Anglo-Saxon attitudes*: a pun on attitudes physical and social, said to be based on an exaggerated style of English drawing (ninth–eleventh centuries). Its immediate inspiration may have been theatricals in Christ Church noted in Dodgson's Diary (5 December 1863), at which the Liddells were present and 'a particular point was made of Anglo-Saxon costumes, settings, etc' (RLG). The expression is now idiomatic, and was the title of a novel by Angus Wilson (1956). Batey (p. 27) suggests that Tenniel's illustration was based on the Caedmon Genesis (*c.* AD 1000) in the Bodleian Library, displayed in 1863.

Haigha: apart from the pun, Dodgson may have been alluding to an expert on the Saxons, Revd Daniel Henry Haigh, who contributed to *Memorials of King Alfred* (1863), and founded the church of SS Thomas and Edmund of Canterbury, in Birmingham (1848).

'*I love my love with an H*': a popular Victorian extempore word-game.

201 *sal-volatile*: smelling salts: a mixture of ammonium carbonate in alcohol and ammonium in water, with aromatics such as lemon oil and lavender oil.

Nobody walks slower than you: some commentators detect an echo of Ulysses' stratagem when he and his men were captured by Polyphemus, the Cyclops (*Odyssey*, 9): Ulysses tells him that his name is Noman, and when he is asleep, they put out his eye with a stake: the other Cyclops respond to his cries: ' "Surely no man is carrying off your sheep? Surely no man is trying to kill you either by fraud or by force?" But Polyphemus shouted to them from inside the cave: "No man is killing me by fraud. No man is killing me by force." "Then" said they, "if no man is attacking you, you must be ill . . ." ' (Samuel Butler's translation, 1900).

202 *fighting for the crown*: Alice quotes the first two verses of an old nursery rhyme first recorded 1709. An alternative second verse appeared in a chapbook *c.*1806 (Opies, 269):

> And when he had beat him out,
>   He beat him in again;
> He beat him three times over,
>   His power to maintain.

The verses are thought to refer to the Union of England and Scotland under King James I and VI, and possibly to hostilities after the Hanoverian succession (1714). On the Royal Coat of Arms of the United Kingdom, the shield is supported by two creatures, the Lion representing England on the left, and the Unicorn (chained) Scotland

on the right. On the Royal Coat of Arms of Scotland, the positions
are reversed. The Unicorn was adopted in the fourteenth century by
Robert III as part of the Royal Seal. Dodgson noted in his Diary that
the Liddell children were collecting crests and sticking them in books
(1 August 1862).

203 *only give them oyster-shells*: another reference to what remains after the
lawyers have taken their fee (see note to p. 161).

204 *about eighty-seven times*: the choice of number may well be arbitrary,
but it happens to be the number of a particularly apposite
Shakespearean sonnet, which begins

>   Farewell, thou art too dear for my possessing

and ends

>   Thus have I had thee, as a dream doth flatter,
>   In sleep a king, but waking no such matter.

How fast those Queens can run!: a reference to Queens in chess, who
can move in any direction for any number of (unimpeded) squares.
White Queen to QB8.

205 *twice as natural!*: Dodgson substituted 'twice' for the 'quite' of
the traditional saying, and this has become common usage (MG,
228).

206 *[illustration]*: critics have taken the Lion and the Unicorn to represent
Gladstone and Disraeli; Michael Hancher regards them as representing England and Scotland (Guiliano, 45–7).

animal—or vegetable—or mineral?: a second reference to the Victorian
parlour game.

207 *across the little brook*: Alice to Q7.

209 *came galloping down upon her*: Red Knight to K2. Goldthwaite (p. 122)
sees the Red Knight as Charles Kingsley 'met as an equal on the
jousting-ground of comedy'.

White Knight: commonly identified as a self-portrait of Dodgson,
other candidates include Don Quixote and Tenniel. Judith Bloom-
ingdale ('Alice as *Anima*: the image of Woman in Carroll's Classic')
goes further: 'As absurd hero of his age, the White Knight sums up
the history of western civilisation: he is at once Christ, St George, the
Knight of the Grail, Lancelot, Don Quixote, and finally modern man
. . . [Alice] *sees* in her Knight's "gentle foolish face" . . . the face of the
Lord of Life' (RP, 449). In 1892, Dodgson wrote on a game he
had made for a child-friend: 'Olive Butler, from the White Knight,
Nov. 21, 1892'.

211 *mounted and galloped off*: White Knight takes Red Knight.

211 *a glorious victory*: Janis Lull points out (Guiliano, 102) that we should
     recall Humpty Dumpty's definition of 'glory' as a 'nice knock-down
     argument'.

     That's the end of my move: the beginning of a complex piece of self-
     portraiture. Elizabeth Sewell (*Field of Nonsense*, 149) points out that
     this scene breaks another rule about nonsense—that there should be
     no relationships. 'When the Nonsense writer is detached and in con-
     trol of his material, our play goes along beautifully; but the minute he
     loses his detachment we also become implicated, and the atmosphere
     changes at once, generating emotion or a sense of the reality and
     earnestness of what is going on instead of that state of security, free-
     dom and purely mental delight which is proper to the game. We are
     acted upon instead of acting.' The White Knight stands out because
     'not one individual is kind to the child the whole way through both
     stories, with the possible exception of the White Knight, who at least
     is not unkind' (ibid. 113).

216 *sugar-loaf*: in the late nineteenth century sugar was usually sold in
     solid cones called sugar-loaves.

218 *The name of the song is called*: commentators have made this sequence
     of establishing linguistic precision rather more difficult than it is. It
     can be reduced to:

                         The name is called . . .
                         The name really is . . .
                         The song is called . . .
                         The song really is . . .

     Surprisingly for Dodgson, there is, however, a logical mistake here or,
     as Roger W. Holmes ('The Philosopher's *Alice in Wonderland*', *Antioch
     Review* (Summer 1959)) has it, 'Carroll was definitely pulling our leg'
     (RP, 206). The Knight says, ' "The song really *is* . . ." ' and then gives
     another name for it. The song *really is* what he *sings* (see also Robert
     D. Sutherland, *Language and Lewis Carroll* (The Hague: Mouton,
     1970), 118–20).

219 *mild blue eyes*: Isa Bowman, in *The Story of Lewis Carroll: Told for
     Young People by the Real Alice in Wonderland Miss Isa Bowman*
     (London: Dent, 1899; reprinted as *Lewis Carroll as I Knew Him*
     (New York: Dover, 1972)), wrote: 'When I knew him his hair was
     silvery-grey, rather longer than it was the fashion to wear, and his
     eyes were a deep blue' (Cohen (ed.), *Lewis Carroll: Interviews and
     Recollections*, 90).

     "I give thee all, I can no more": Alice refers to Thomas Moore's (1779–
     1852) 'My Heart and Lute', music by Sir Henry Rowley Bishop

(1786–1855) (who was Professor of Music at Oxford (1848) and also wrote 'There's No Place Like Home').

> I give thee all—I can no more—
> Though poor the off'ring be;
> My heart and lute are all the store
> That I can bring to thee . . .

219 *I'll tell thee everything I can*: this poem (rather unkindly) parodies the garrulous narrators in Wordsworth's poems concerned with country people. The prime target is 'Resolution and Independence' (*Poems in Two Volumes*, 1807), in which the narrator asks the old leech gatherer what he does *twice*, while musing on life:

> 'What kind of work is that which you pursue?
> This is a lonesome place for one like you.'
> He answered me with pleasure and surprise,
> And there was, while he spake, a fire about his eyes . . .
>
> (95–8)

> The old man still stood talking by my side,
> But now his voice to me was like a stream
> Scarce heard . . .
>
> (113–15)

> And now, not knowing what the old man had said,
> My question eagerly did I renew,
> 'How is it that you live, and what is it you do?'
>
> He with a smile did then his words repeat . . .
>
> (124–7)

The verse form, however, is the same as another bucolic poem, 'The Thorn' (*Lyrical Ballads*, 1798), which has been much ridiculed for lines such as

> And to the left, three yards beyond,
> You see a little muddy pond
> Of water, never dry.
> I've measured it from side to side;
> 'Tis three feet long and two feet wide.
>
> (29–33)

It also contains the lines 'I'll tell you everything I know' (105), 'I'll give you the best help I can' (111), 'I'll tell you all I know' (114), 'No more I know—I wish I did | And I would tell it all to you' (155–6), 'There's no-one knows, as I have said' (162), 'I cannot tell, but some will say' (214).

Dodgson's original version began:

> I met an aged, aged man
> > Upon the lonely moor:
> I knew I was a gentleman,
> > And he was but a boor.
> So I stopped and roughly questioned him,
> > 'Come, tell me how you live!'
> But his words impressed my ear no more
> > Than if it were a sieve.

Dodgson also used this version as part of a playful verse-writing contest with Lionel, Tennyson's second son, Easter 1862 (*LLLC*, 92).

220 *Rowland's Macassar-Oil*: the most famous brand of hair oil in the nineteenth century, made from oil supposedly imported from what is now Indonesia. Lord Byron (who used it) wrote, in his sardonic (alleged) description of his wife in *Don Juan* (1819),

> In virtues nothing earthly could surpass her,
> Save thine 'incomparable oil', Macassar!
> > (II. xvii. 135–6)

From this oil is derived 'antimacassar', a piece of fabric draped over the back of a seat to keep heads from marking it.

221 *limed twigs*: birdlime, a sticky substance made from holly or other plants, was used to catch small birds.

Hansom-cabs: a two-wheel cab, patented by Joseph A. Hansom in 1836.

Menai bridge: either the bridge built by Thomas Telford between the North Wales mainland and Anglesey, which opened in 1826 (Dodgson had crossed it on a family holiday to Beaumaris when he was about 10 years old), or Robert Stephenson's tubular railway bridge, the 'Britannia' bridge, completed in 1850.

222 *then you'll be a Queen*: when pawns in a game of chess reach the final rank on the board, they become queens.

reached the turn: White Knight to KB5.

223 *edge of the brook*: at which point, in the galley-proofs there was an extra episode, 'The Wasp in a Wig' (reprinted in the Appendix to this edition). In June 1974 the proof sheets appeared in a catalogue issued by the London auctioneers Sotheby's, with the note that they had been 'bought at the sale of the author's furniture, personal effects, and library, Oxford, 1898'. A limited edition was published in 1977 by the Lewis Carroll Society of North America, edited by Martin Gardner. Dodgson's acquiescence to the cut may also have been because he realized that the 'Wasp' episode repeats the idea of Alice

leaving an old man, which he had explored in the previous scene, with the White Knight—and also sours the idyllic and nostalgic atmosphere that he had created (and see Robert Dupree, 'The White Knight's Whiskers and the Wasp's Wig in *Through the Looking-Glass*', in Guiliano, 112–22).

as she bounded across: Alice reaches Q8.

224 *one on each side*: Red Queen to K1.

226 [*illustration*]: note the frame under the crinoline skirts: Michael Hancher (Guiliano, 33) notes that '*Punch* waged a relentless war against the vanity and vulgarity of crinoline, then the current fashion'.

227 '*Can you answer useful questions?*': this episode is a parody of the 'instructive' question-and-answer sessions often introduced into nineteenth-century children's novels. Alicia Catherine Mant's *The Cottage in the Chalk Pit* (1822) is typical:

> 'What can it be?' Exclaimed all the children at once.
> 'Crystals, of some sort,' replied Mrs Gardiner; 'but I cannot define it nearer . . .'
> 'What did you mean by *geological* just now, mamma' said Edward, who had been thinking it over, ever since his mother had made use of the word some little time before.
> 'It is an adjective from Geology,' replied Mrs Gardiner; 'and Geology means that science which "embraces the study of the earth in general . . ." '

228 *fiddle-de-dee*: since 1784 synonymous with 'Nonsense!' (RLG).

230 *putting her hair in papers*: curl-papers, round which the hair was wrapped overnight to produce 'corkscrew curls' (RLG).

Hush-a-by lady: parody of what the Opies (p. 61) call 'the best-known lullaby both in England and America'. It is first recorded in *Mother Goose's Melody* (*c.*1765) and the tune is a variant of 'Lillibulero' (or 'Lilliburlero').

231 *suddenly vanished*: the Queens 'castle'.

232 [*Illustration*]: Batey suggests (p. 9) that this is the door of Christ Church Chapter House. The original illustration showed Alice in a crinoline, rather resembling a chess piece; Dodgson objected. Tenniel also used this Romanesque arch in drawings for *Punch* (Guiliano, 43).

233 *To the Looking-Glass world . . .*: parody of Sir Walter Scott's song 'Bonnie Dundee', from his play *The Doom of Devorgoil* (1830), ii. ii. The first stanza and chorus:

To the Lords of Convention 'twas Claver'se [Claverhouse] who spoke,
'Ere the King's crown shall fall there are crowns to be broke;
So let each Cavalier who loves honour and me,
Come follow the bonnet of Bonny Dundee.
> Come fill up my cup, come fill up my can.
> Come saddle your horses and call up your men;
> Come open the West Port, and let me gang free,
> And it's room for the bonnets of Bonny Dundee!'

(RLG)

233 *thirty-times-three*: Bryan Talbot suggests (*Alice in Sunderland*, 166) that Dodgson, who often visited Sunderland, may be recalling a verse on a Sunderland souvenir bowl (*c.*1835) depicting Thomas Paine's iron bridge (1796) over the River Wear:

> Then fill up the bumper, Britannia appears . . .
> King William we hail with three times three cheers.

234 *walked up the large hall*: Alice castles.

Mutton——Alice: one of Dodgson's distant relatives was Sir Richard Houghton, at whose table 'King James I is supposed to have solemnly "knighted" the loin of beef'. Derek Hudson (*Lewis Carroll: An Illustrated Biography*, 34) suggests that this legendary incident may have inspired Alice's introduction to the leg of mutton.

236 *and then guess*: the answer to the riddle is 'an oyster'.

extinguishers: candle extinguishers, cups made of metal or porcelain, often conical. The Royal Worcester company started making extinguishers in the 1850s.

237 *from the soup-tureen*: White Queen to QR6.

239 *shake you into a kitten*: MG (p. 266) suggests that 'this is Alice's capture of the Red Queen. It results in a legitimate checkmate of the Red King, who has slept throughout the entire chess problem without moving.'

240 *with all her might*: Alice takes Red Queen and wins.

245 *A BOAT, beneath a sunny sky*: an acrostic poem, the first letters of each line spelling Alice Pleasance Liddell. It has echoes of Wordsworth's 'Lines written near Richmond, upon the Thames, at Evening' (*Lyrical Ballads*, 1798):

> How rich the wave in front, impressed
> With evening twilight's summer hues,
> While, facing this the crimson west,
> The boat her silent path pursues!

(1–4)

245 *Life, what is it but a dream?*: many critics have noted an echo of the English nursery rhyme. However, the most commonly quoted version of the lyrics ('Row, row, row your boat | Gently down the stream. | Merrily, merrily, merrily, merrily | Life is but a dream) are attributed to Eliphalet Oram Lyte (1842–1913) who set them to music (*The Franklin Square Song Collection*, New York, 1881). The epigraph to chapter XXV of MacDonald's *Phantastes* is from Novalis: 'Our life is no dream, but it ought to become one, and perhaps will.'